THE HIDDEN WORLD

Also by Melinda Snodgrass and coming soon from Titan Books

THE HIGH GROUND
IN EVIL TIMES
A TRIUMVIRATE OF HATE (July 2019)
BREAKING THE YOKE (July 2020)

THE HIDDEN WORLD

THE IMPERIALS SAGA

MELINDA SNODGRASS

TITAN BOOKS

The Hidden World
Print edition ISBN: 9781783295869
E-book edition ISBN: 9781783295876

Published by Titan Books
A division of Titan Publishing Group Ltd
144 Southwark Street, London
SE1 0UP

First edition: July 2018
10 9 8 7 6 5 4 3 2 1

A CIP catalogue record for this title is available from the British Library.

Printed and bound in the USA.

This book is for Sage Walker, writer, physician, advisor, and dear friend, and someone who writes the best sex scenes in the business. I hope mine are half as good as yours, Sage, even though I was blushing the entire time I wrote them.

1

WE WERE GOING TO BE RICH

"Of course it would be you looting the dead. You always were a jackal."

And the day had started out so well, thought Oliver Xavier Randall, who hadn't begun life with that appellation.

"You know this person, Admiral?" asked one of the suited figures standing at the side of Beauregard Honorius Sinclair Cullen, the Duque de Argento y Pepco, royal consort to the Infanta, Mercedes Adalina Saturnina Inez de Arango, heir to the Solar League.

Oliver felt the eyes of his crew upon him, and he was pretty sure that Jax and Dalea were goggling at the radio aboard the ship. It was going to be an unpleasant conversation when they demanded an explanation about why he had lied to them for all these years. Oliver wondered why the universe hated him? Because clearly it did. Thus far the only positive out of this shit sandwich was the fact his crew had not recognized the suited figure as the imperial consort.

Squaring his shoulders, Oliver forced himself to look up and defiantly meet the gaze of the man behind the helmet's faceplate. The fact that Cullen topped him by four inches *and* was Vidstream-star handsome *and* didn't seem to have aged a day since the last time they'd met, *and* was now a vice *admiral* just added to Oliver's sense of ill-usage.

"Believe it or not, Lieutenant, this *intitulado* was once an officer in the *Orden de la Estrella,*" Cullen said. "I attended the High Ground with him." Cullen gave a theatrical sigh. "Further proof that the academy and the officers' corp is no place for commoners."

Behind Oliver loomed a massive abandoned spaceship resting on the rock and ice surface of a medium-sized asteroid in a worthless solar system that lacked any viable planets and was so far off the beaten path that the arrival of an imperial ship much less a squadron was so improbable as to be impossible. Which proved Oliver's point about the universe hating him.

The members of Oliver's crew who had been busily removing the cargo from the derelict ship and onto a loader from their own, far smaller ship were gathered protectively around the machine and the looted—*appropriated,* Oliver amended—goods.

"We'll be taking custody of that," Cullen said with a wave at the loader.

Oliver inclined his head. He was damned if he'd bow. Over the radio came a murmur of objection from his crew. Oliver gestured with just the fingers of his gloved left hand—*shut up!* He swallowed his rage. It went down like glass shards.

"Of course, your grace."

Cullen gestured to one of his *fusileros*. The man climbed

up into the cab and jerked a thumb at Luis Baca, who had been driving. The man climbed slowly down. Oliver and his crew watched as the loader rolled away toward the open doors of a waiting military shuttle.

"We were going to be rich…" Luis said mournfully.

Hours earlier Luis Baca had caroled, "We're going to be rich!" as they stood staring up at the massive abandoned spaceship.

Oliver could understand his crew member's excitement. The previous owners of this ship, the Cara'ot, had been master traders carrying only the most expensive and unusual items for trade—unique jewels, Sidone spider-silk weavings, *objets d'art*, rare books, antiques… and medicines manufactured in the shipboard labs.

It was the medicines that were most precious, but also problematic. In addition to being traders the enigmatic Cara'ot had been masters of genetic engineering, and the major thing they wanted in trade was DNA from every creature, sentient or not, that they came across.

When humans had finally figured out how to transcend light speed they discovered to their horror they were not the ultimate creation in the universe. True to form, Oliver's species had attacked and conquered every other known race, founded the Solar League and wanted no part of the Cara'ot's genetic shenanigans. There was no way the perfection that was humanity was going to be contaminated with alien cooties. Especially when the aliens in question had no standard body type or gender. The Cara'ot could continue to distort their own corrupted bodies, but they were outlawed from doing so to any other race now under the sway of the human League, and the punishment for appropriating human DNA was death. The paranoia was so great that it ended up extending even to the Cara'ot mastery of medicine. Once Oliver had shared the disgust and fear of the Cara'ot, but ultimately he'd decided the ban was absurd. And it wasn't just because he and his crew made a lot of money smuggling black-market medicines.

Fortunately, there were places unknown to the League and beyond the reach of imperial law enforcement that didn't share the League's obsession with the now vanished Cara'ot. The crew of the *Selkie* could sell the drugs they would loot from the abandoned vessel to Hidden Worlds and on the black market. Yep, they were going to be rich.

Oliver's gaze raked the length of the massive ship as it lay against the wall of an ice-rimmed crater. The Cara'ot ship made his own ship, the *Selkie,* look like a child's toy. Oliver couldn't decide if the derelict was more reminiscent of a fallen skyscraper or a beached whale. He decided skyscraper for it seemed to be studded with lights and ports—all dark now—and there were strange superstructures, which looked like balconies, whose function he couldn't even begin to guess.

"Still, you'd think the damn aliens would have been a bit more considerate and abandoned their ships in more pleasant places," Luis added. "Why not a tropical paradise?"

"Perhaps we aliens enjoy making life miserable for humans," Graarack said. The words were punctuated with clicks from her beak.

It was odd for the spider-like alien to make a sassy remark, and it amused Oliver. He tried to stifle his chuckle but it carried over the helmet radio and Luis gave an exasperated sigh and turned to look at him. Even through the faceplate Oliver could see the *et tu* expression on his comm officer's face.

"Really, *hombre,* I get no support from a fellow human?" Luis asked. "You might notice we're, like, really outnumbered."

"And one of those aliens... who outnumber you... thinks you humans could maybe stop chattering so we can crack open this treasure box," Dalea, their ship doctor, radioed from the ship. Oliver figured the gentle, sweet-faced Hajin would be eager to get her hands on the medicines.

"I would second that request," came the fluting tones of Jax over their suit radios. The Tiponi Flute wasn't much use when it came to hauling heavy objects, given that he looked like an attenuated stalk of bamboo with agile but fragile fronds for appendages. He had remained on the ship with Dalea.

Oliver glanced back to where his ship rested on a flat, methane-ice-coated plain. Despite the name his ship wasn't a graceful beauty. It was squat, and broad, the outer hull pitted in places and patched in others. She was a truck designed to carry goods while keeping air inside so the inhabitants could survive as they made their way between worlds with those trade goods. Still, she was his—or at least three quarters of it was his.

A blown Fold converter six years ago had necessitated that he sell shares to cover the repair costs. Jax had been the only buyer of the shares, and it had worked out. The Tiponi Flute had integrated smoothly with the rest of the crew and Oliver was grateful not to have to manage the books any longer. Math had always been his best subject in school but he hated double-entry accounting and Jax lived for it. The Tiponi had also improved profit margins with his wise and detailed choices of cargo. Oliver could have bought the alien out a few years back, but the Flute was one of them now, sharing in the profits and the losses. But today was going to be a giant payday.

A dark figure raced across the hull of the abandoned ship. Jahan's tail was held stiffly upright—a sure sign of excitement—and she had dropped to all fours for better purchase on the ice-rimed hull. She launched herself off the ship and almost too late Oliver realized she was heading straight for him. He braced and she hit his chest. He clutched at his second-in-command, and her suited arms clasped around his neck. The force of her landing sent him sliding backward across the ice. He managed to keep upright, but just barely.

Their faceplates were only inches apart. Large neotenous dark eyes, golden fur-covered face with a darker fur on her head that formed a widow's peak. Her lips parted in a smile, revealing the sharp canines of her species.

"*Madre de Dios,* Jahan," Oliver exploded. "What if I hadn't caught you? You could have damaged your suit." A new thought intruded. "For that matter you could have damaged *my* suit if you'd knocked me down," he added aggrievedly. "These aren't military grade."

"I had faith in your elite military training."

He set her on her feet. She wasn't quite four feet tall and he felt like an indulgent parent as he looked down at her. "Over a decade ago."

"So you're saying you're fat and flabby now?"

"Oh, for God's sake! There's a fortune waiting. Can we get to it?" Baca exploded.

"What did you find?" Oliver asked the executive officer.

"Airlocks are on the side facing the crater wall. Outer doors are locked open, no indication anybody's been inside before us."

"Did I mention we're going to be rich!" Baca said.

"Several times," Oliver said dryly.

Jahan continued. "It's tight on that other side. They must have been really skinny or just left with the suits on their backs. It would be easier to offload the cargo on this side and it's closer to the *Selkie*."

"So we cut," Graarack hissed.

By now they had reached the side of the ship. Oliver craned his head to look up the towering metal. "Well, that's going to be a bitch. It took three missiles hitting pretty much at the same point to breach the hull on Cara'ot ships during the Expansion Wars."

"And there's that military background again," Jahan whispered to Graarack, who giggled. It should have been disconcerting for Oliver, emerging as it did from a five-and-a-half-foot tall spider, but the fact that it wasn't indicated how comfortable he had become serving with aliens.

"Be easier to cut at the ports," Oliver said, trying to ignore the two aliens. "Go get the loader," he ordered.

Baca went loping away in long, floating jumps in the low gravity.

"And don't forget the torch," Jahan yelled after him. He waved to indicate he wouldn't.

While they waited Oliver took a sip of water from the nipple in his helmet. He was trying to tamp down his excitement, but wasn't having a lot of success.

It took a long time to cut a sufficiently large opening in the ship's side. Long enough that they'd had to replace oxygen canisters in their suits. "So, what are you going to do with your share, Captain?" Luis asked as he braced the torch against his thigh. Blobs of molten metal fell like steel tears onto the platform of the loader.

I'm going to pay off the bogus debt that I owe the Orden de la Estrella *so I can go home and see my father.* But Oliver said none of that. "Not sure. Maybe replace the starboard engine on the *Selkie*."

"If this is as good as we expect, you can buy a new ship," Jahan said.

Graarack gasped. "Sell the *Selkie*? I hope she didn't hear you say that." Jahan and Oliver exchanged glances. The Sidone navigator's habit of anthropomorphizing the freighter was a source of fond amusement to her crew mates.

"Hey, *hombre*, I'm flagging here." Oliver took over the torch from Luis and checked the fuel.

"Getting low here."

Graarack swarmed up the struts to the platform carrying a fuel canister in one of her eight claws. As she snapped it into place she asked, "Why did they do it?"

"Who?"

"The Cara'ot," the spider replied.

"Do what? Disappear?"

She nodded. "Yeah, that. Abandon everything. Vanish."

"To make us crazy," Baca said. "Shit, I got called up because the Emperor and O-Trell got their panties in a wad. They were sure the war was starting again. And then they extended my tour. Had to spend an extra three years humping a rifle."

"That must have been uncomfortable," Jahan said blandly.

"Not humping like humping humping… you know, sex humping."

"One never knows with you creatures," the Isanjo smirked.

"Seriously, do you know, Captain?" Graarack pressed.

"I have a theory," Oliver said slowly. Memory fled back fifteen years. Standing in a warehouse while a half-human/half-Cara'ot child had clung to his leg. He snapped off the torch and set it aside. "The Cara'ot broke the genetic laws. They convinced some humans to mix DNA and they produced alien-human hybrids. When a human governor arrived to take over the planet the children were discovered and he ordered them killed."

"Killed?" It was Dalea. She had obviously been listening in on their conversation from the ship. Horror laced the single word.

"I never heard about this," Luis said skeptically.

Oliver struggled to keep his tone neutral as he said, "The crown covered it up."

"Then how do you know?" Jahan asked. She was perched on the top of the ship, and she peered over the curving edge at him. In her spacesuit she looked like a robot gargoyle.

"Because I was there." He cleared his throat, and grabbed up the torch again. "Let's get this thing open."

Jax's voice came fluting over the radio. "Did you kill children?"

"No!" A single explosive word. Oliver snapped on the cutter. *I killed human soldiers to save them and ruined my life.*

A few minutes later he was able to deliver a hard kick to the metal and it fell into the ship. He felt the concussion as it hit through the soles of his boots. There wasn't enough atmosphere on this rock to carry any sound. Interior atmosphere puffed out, occluded his faceplate for an instant, then turned to snow and drifted toward the stony ground.

After that they split up and began looting—*salvaging,* Oliver amended—the alien ship.

And now he stood watching their gigantic payday vanish into an O-Trell shuttle. Cullen smiled as he correctly interpreted Oliver's expression.

"Be glad I'm not arresting you all and seizing your ship," Cullen said.

Which begged the question, why wasn't Cullen arresting them? The answer arrived with blinding force. *Because he intends to keep it for himself! Son of a bitch!*

Oliver's gloved hands balled into fists. The words *you fucking asshole* battered at the back of his teeth, and he pictured his fist driving into the faceplate, cracks appearing, Cullen choking and dying. Mercifully his thinking head decided to take over from his desire to measure dicks. Oliver briefly closed his eyes and heard his father's voice urging him to show civility and courtesy at all times to his "betters." He bowed and managed to grit out, "Thank you, sir."

"Still too proud. Whine, Belmanor. Grovel for me."

Twenty-six fucking years and nothing had changed. Cullen had said almost the exact same thing back in the tailor shop when they had both been eighteen. And this time there was no imperial cousin to intervene or father to punish his own son for impudence. Oliver knew what he should do. He also knew he couldn't.

"It's our fault, your grace," a new voice intruded. Graarack's eight legs had dropped to approximate a human curtsy. Even with the sibilation the abjection was obvious as she bowed and scraped. "Captain Randall—" She broke off abruptly as she realized that she no longer knew if that was his name. "Our captain wanted to inform League authorities, but we—" she gestured with her four appendage limbs indicating the rest of the crew "—outvoted him." She bowed her head almost to her knees. "We're a bad influence." She then looked up and gave him a limpid look from those enormous, faceted eyes.

Her intentions were good, but humans had an instinctive recoil reaction to big spiders. Also, like Oliver, Cullen had been trained at the academy to think of aliens in terms of their potential threat. Add to that it was rare to see a Sidone off their harsh and rocky world, and a bad outcome was inevitable. Oliver could see the anger and disgust rising in Cullen's green eyes. He quickly stepped between them. For Graarack, for the rest of the crew, he would eat shit. It was the least he could do after lying to them for all these years.

He gave a perfectly executed court bow. "Your grace, I most humbly beg your pardon. My crew should not be punished for my lack of judgment." He risked a quick glance at Cullen's face. *Not enough.* He swallowed bile. "Once again you have schooled me in proper behavior and I deeply appreciate it."

A smile curved those perfect lips. Lips that touched—Oliver recoiled from where that thought would lead him. Cullen slowly clapped. "Bravo, Belmanor. I enjoyed that." He turned and walked to his shuttle trailed by his officers and guards.

The crew of the *Selkie* and her captain stood in the icy darkness and watched the fire of the shuttle's engines melt the ice. It dwindled to a star and vanished into the bay of the frigate in orbit above them.

"Old friend of yours?" Baca asked, irony dripping off every word.

"And he took our loader," Graarack said mournfully.

The crew began heading toward the *Selkie,* dejection etched in every line of their tired bodies. The chances of them ever stumbling across another Cara'ot ship were astronomical.

"What did he do to you that you hate him so?" Jahan asked quietly. She had used a private channel so the others wouldn't hear.

"I don't want to discuss it."

She shrugged, a suit-yourself gesture, and headed for the ship. Oliver stood by the derelict feeling as empty and abandoned as the ship.

He married the woman I loved. The woman who broke my heart.

2

IS ANYTHING ABOUT YOU TRUE?

Oliver sat in the galley of the *Selkie* staring into his coffee cup. Through the soles of his boots he could feel the soft rumble of the engines as they made their way toward the edge of the solar system. There they could safely make the translation into Fold. The tension on the bridge as he'd given orders had been displayed as a silence so deep it seemed a weight pressing on his skull. His normally garrulous crew had been voiceless automatons. He had left Baca and Jahan switching out the transponder so if Cullen did report them they couldn't be traced. Oliver had retreated to the galley.

The coffee had long since gone cold. He took another sip. The liquid hit his acid-filled stomach and bile rose into the back of his throat. He stood and put the cup into the *cocinar* to reheat. He probably wouldn't drink it, but he needed something to occupy his hands during the upcoming confrontation.

One by one they entered. Baca's footfalls firm and loud. Dalea's two hooves clip-clopping delicately on the floor, Graarack's eight claws clicking. Jax was a soft rustling as he undulated into the room and took up a position in his pool of nutrient-fortified water. Jahan's furred and padded feet made no sound as she darted in and took the chair at the other end of the table. There were awkward, inconsequential conversational exchanges as coffee, tea, and the thick red bilge that Graarack liked to drink, and snacks were obtained.

Once everyone had settled Jahan gave him a cold stare out of her huge eyes. "Okay, Captain. So who are you? Really?"

An excellent question, Jahan. Wish I had an answer beyond the obvious.

He sighed, spun the coffee mug and finally said, "My name is Thracius—Tracy—Ransom Belmanor, formerly Captain Lieutenant Belmanor of His Imperial Majesty's star command."

"I thought you were just an *hombre,* a grunt like me," Luis yelped. "You were a fucking officer?"

"'Fraid so."

"Only aristos, fucking Fortune Five Hundred pukes, get to go to the High Ground," Baca raged.

"That officer called the captain an *intitulado,*" Jax fluted. "That means untitled so he's not FFH."

"I was a scholarship student," Tracy said.

"Best tell us everything, sir," Graarack hissed softly.

Tracy sighed, began. "I was born on Ouranos. My father is a tailor in the capital. I grew up for the most part in the capital city, Hissilek. I was given a full ride to the High Ground. I graduated, served about six years and then I got court-martialed. That's the story." He shrugged and took a sip of the coffee.

"Why did they court-martial you?" Dalea asked. Her

large eyes were fixed unblinking on him and she was absently running her hand back and forth along the length of her black and red mane.

"Did it have to do with that story you told us? About those half-Cara'ot children?" Graarack asked shrewdly.

"Indirectly, yes. They trumped up charges. Said that I stole from O-Trell."

"So, you did kill kids," Luis said. His tone was stony.

"No!" Again too loud and too sharp. He moderated his tone. "That part was true. I protected them until cooler heads prevailed. The crown wanted to bury the story. They might have been half-breeds, but the citizens wouldn't have reacted well to stories of children being butchered. I tried to get it out, go public. They found a way to stop me." He shrugged again. "As they say—*never bet against the house*."

"And this man… this man who confronted us," Jahan said.

"And stole from us," Luis added aggrievedly. Jahan's tail twitched in irritation. "Sorry," the comm officer muttered.

Jahan looked back to Tracy. "What is he to you and is he likely to become a problem for *us*?"

Of its own volition his hand went to the scar on his left temple. The scar that pulled his eyebrow up, giving him a constantly sardonic look. The scar that Boho had bestowed on him. It was a great relief that none of his crew had twigged to the identity of their nemesis. How many more awkward and unanswerable questions would have been raised if the crew figured out that Cullen was the imperial consort? If they had Tracy would have had to lie to them again, and he really wanted to avoid that outcome.

"Oh, shit," Luis breathed. "You didn't get that in a sodding engineering accident. That's a fucking dueling scar." There was no point denying it. Tracy nodded. "*Dios mío!* Is there anything about you that's true?"

There didn't seem to be a good answer so Tracy stayed silent. Into that accusatory quiet Jahan spoke:

"What is true is that he's a very good captain. That he has dealt fairly with all of us." She turned her large eyes on Luis. "Gave you an extra share when your mother needed surgery." A glance to Dalea. "Let you have seven months at home when your sister's pregnancy wasn't going well, and you still shared in the profits from those runs."

"Let me buy an interest in the ship even though I'm an alien," Jax offered.

Tracy couldn't bear the fact they were forgiving him. He unlocked his chair, pushed it back, and stood. "Look, I'm sorry. I shouldn't have lied to you, but I didn't want to burden you with keeping my secret, and there's a lien against Thracius Belmanor. O-Trell can garnish my income and any holdings until my debt is repaid. If you want me off the ship I'll understand. There's no reason for the rest of you to be in danger because of me."

"Oh, don't be ridiculous!" Jahan snapped.

"I would like to know how you came by the money to make the down payment on this ship," Jax said. There were nods of agreement from the rest of the crew.

Tracy gripped the back of the chair. "I'd gone looking for my batBEM. He was a Cara'ot. I didn't realize that was the day they had all disappeared. I ended up in a Cara'ot warehouse down at the Cristóbal Colón Spaceport. Fortunately nobody else had twigged that they were gone either. I… uh… appropriated some goods."

"Goods like these?" Jahan asked as she reached into the pocket of her coveralls and pulled out a handful of vials. There was a gasp of reaction from the assembled crew.

"You are goddamn lucky that officer didn't order all of us searched," Tracy exploded at his XO.

She shrugged in that boneless way of the Isanjo. "I figured they wouldn't want to risk alien cooties. And you're welcome. There's enough medicine here to get us at least a modest payday. But back to you. What did you steal?" His wince made her grin, exposing her long canines. "Oh, excuse me, *appropriate,* Ollie… Thracius…" She gave her head an irritated shake. "My God that's a mouthful."

"Use Tracy. That's what most people called me."

"That's gonna take some getting used to," Luis muttered.

"Not medicine. I was on Ouranos, in the capital. The Cara'ot weren't going to risk having contraband drugs around, but there were a lot of luxury items. I took a pouch full of Phantasm gems."

Jax gave a glissando whistle. "Yes, that would explain why you have so much equity in this spaceship."

Tracy gestured at the vials. "Do we know what those are?"

"Not a clue," Jahan said cheerfully. "I figure Dr. Engelberg will tell us."

"And find us buyers," Jax added.

"He'll want a cut," Luis said.

"He's entitled. He's taking most of the risk and he uses the money to keep his clinic afloat," Tracy said.

"Sorry. Didn't mean to be a dick. I'm just still really upset about watching a fortune get stolen right out from under us. The damn League will just sell it and take the money to build a new gold-plated bidet to wash the Emperor's royal ass."

"I don't think Cu— that officer has any intention of turning over the contents," Tracy said.

"Shit, that makes it even worse! Can we report him? Come on, Captain. You know the guy. Let's snitch on him."

"And draw attention to us?" Jahan yipped. "Don't be an idiot."

An alarm sounded. Tracy pushed back from the table and used the surface to lever himself to his feet. He was numb with exhaustion. "We're at the Fold point. Let's get to the bridge."

New Hope was an unprepossessing rock that didn't spin on its axis, which meant that the thin strip between the sun side and the night side was the only livable area. It was the first planet settled by humans after the Folddrive had been invented. The fact they had stopped and put down roots on such a marginal world was a mystery to Tracy. Perhaps they were sick of being in a tin can or they feared the next few systems they explored would be worse. The harsh conditions on many of the first settled worlds were one reason that women had become precious commodities, the act of childbearing critical to the survival of the early colonies.

New Hope had survived because the conditions had led to a highly developed medical community. Over the centuries the colony realized that this was their best hope to build a viable economy so the five biggest cities all boasted major hospitals with various specialties. The wealthy and elite came to New Hope to be treated, and doctors trained at the medical schools left for League worlds where they catered to the nobility and the well-connected and became very rich.

The *Selkie*'s crew came to see Dr. Michael Engelberg, a brilliant physician with a no-nonsense attitude, strong opinions, and a clinic that treated the less elevated members of society, with a particular focus on children. In addition to handing out medical care Dr. Michael set aside funds to cover the cost of tickets to the planet for poorer families. The doctor was also one of their fences for contraband medicines the *Selkie* picked up on the various Hidden Worlds where they clandestinely traded.

Their best seller was hormonal contraceptives. With the Cara'ot gone it had become more difficult for women to obtain the banned substance and a vigorous black market had arisen. Tracy preferred to stay away from the criminal cartels that manufactured the illegal drugs. Apart from unsympathetic men with large guns, the drugs the cartels made had varying degrees of effectiveness and some had proved to be deadly when corners were cut. On Hidden Worlds with less draconian laws the *Selkie* crew were able to buy drugs directly from actual pharmaceutical companies. Tracy supposed it was a distinction without a difference since League laws required citizens to report any Hidden Worlds to the government, so Tracy and his crew were still breaking the law. They were just breaking a different one and not dealing with violent people. Dr. Michael never asked where they came by the banned medicines and Tracy never offered an explanation. The fewer people that knew the safer those Hidden Worlds would remain.

Engelberg's clinic was in the fifth city on the planet, Caduceus. Given the paucity of livable land all ships docked at the orbiting *cosmódromo* and visitors were ferried down via shuttle. They explained their frequent stops at New Hope with the claim that Tracy was a patient of Dr. Engelberg's suffering from a chronic heart condition. To explain how he could afford this level of care Tracy had cultivated the idea that Oliver Randall was the ne'er-do-well fourth son of a knightly family. His years at the High Ground and those spent serving among highborn officers had enabled him to ape the rounded vowels and clipped consonants of the FFH. Tracy's false papers were first rate, and each time they passed through a planet with stricter entry control Tracy inserted saliva packets into his cheeks in case he was pulled out for a saliva swab. There was a reason false identities cost so much to obtain. At birth every human child's DNA was checked to make sure there were no alien additions to the human genome. Those results were then placed in a database. The criminals who sold false identities had to supply not only IDs, vehicle licenses, and Medicare cards, but also place the fake identity's DNA in the database and provide you with a sample of the saliva, which they would be happy to refill for you at a cost. Fortunately, Tracy had a doctor who could handle that for him. Thus far he had never been pulled aside for the swab, but he always wore the cheek implants just in case.

Since this time they were carrying Cara'ot vials, they wanted to be damn sure he wasn't searched so Dalea had, in addition to the other treatments, dosed Tracy with a tincture that had turned his eyes red and blotched his pale skin into an unattractive piebald. He affected a hacking cough, and a stage blood packet secreted under his tongue left his handkerchief alarmingly gory. Given his state the officer at the entry checkpoint seemed reluctant to touch his ID, much less subject him to a search. They did, however, do a thorough search of Jahan and the agent knew enough to check her marsupial pouch. They found nothing beyond the normal objects. Tracy was carrying a holdall that contained a bewildering array of prescription bottles, an elegant straight razor, and underwear. The Cara'ot vials were in among that welter of medicines. Tracy had placed the underwear on the top. When the agent started to remove the briefs to get to the bottles he noticed a blood smear on one of them, some crap on another, and snatched back his hand. They were waved through and were soon headed to the planet.

Dr. Michael and his much younger wife, Kathy (who was called a lab technician but was actually a very fine researcher in her own right), met them at the terminal. They were hustled into a waiting flitter. Once the security damper was up Engelberg turned his pale, blue-eyed gaze on Tracy. It was always disconcerting to Tracy; the eye color was so unusual among humans, and against his dark skin his eyes seemed to glow.

"Always with the flair for the dramatic. What, you were enacting the last act of *La Traviata*? A case of tuberculosis hasn't been seen in three hundred years," the doctor complained.

"What, you didn't like the blood? I thought it was a nice touch," Tracy said as he spit out the blood packet.

"Someday you'll be so clever you'll hang yourself," Engelberg said sourly.

Kathy punched her husband on the upper arm. "You don't have to sound like you're looking forward to that, Michael."

"So, what have you got for us, Oliver?"

Jahan gave him a glance pregnant with questions. Tracy gave a minute shake of his head. She acquiesced. Tracy fished out the vials and handed them over to Engelberg. "Not sure. We came across a Cara'ot ship. Unfortunately, this was all we managed to get."

"What happened?" Engelberg asked as he turned the vials between long, narrow fingers, held them up to the dome light, and squinted at the contents.

"The League happened," Jahan said.

The physicians exchanged alarmed looks. "Did you lead them to us?" Engelberg asked.

"And why aren't you in jail?" Kathy added.

"We think the commander wanted a payday," Jahan answered when it became clear that Tracy wouldn't.

"Ah, well then," Kathy said and she snatched a vial away from her husband, and began subjecting it to the same assessment.

"Good to know venality extends even to our noble troops," Engelberg grunted. "Have you got my contraceptives?"

"Yeah, Dalea mixed them in with a bunch of legal drugs. They would have had to check every pill in every bottle to locate them."

"Still a risk."

"Yeah, well, being a..." Tracy paused, searching for a less pejorative term.

Jahan had no such scruples. "Crook," she said. Tracy winced.

"Anyway, whatever we call it, what we do is risky."

Off to the east there was the distant glow of the sun side. In the other direction a curtain of darkness. Here in the temperate zone the light was that of a cloudy day and of course it was constant. There was never a night on New Hope.

At the clinic Kathy rushed away with the Cara'ot vials and the holdall. In her lab she would separate out the birth control from the other pills, and analyze what might be in the faceted vials. Engelberg brought out a bottle of wine. He was a known connoisseur so Tracy eagerly awaited the first sip. This particular red didn't disappoint. It was like an explosion of roses in the mouth. A sampling of cheese and crackers provided a counterpoint to the lush flavor of the wine.

The doctor leaned across the coffee table and handed Tracy a bottle of pills. "Here's the prescription for Jackson. We'll figure out the monetary part of your payment once Kathy gets back to me."

"Great." Tracy slipped the bottle into his pocket. "So, what's the word? We've been in Fold for the past ten days so we've missed any news."

"Not a lot. There was much dark grumbling from the more

conservative outlets because New Dublin on Dullahan elected its first woman mayor. She's a vet, retired from star command a few years ago. Interestingly the first lady of Dullahan, Lady Maribel Brangaza, spoke out in support of the woman."

Memory returned of the gardens at the palace the day of Tracy's graduation. The graceful older woman hugging Mercedes. The similarity in their eyes and the height of their cheekbones. Mercedes' rather aggressive blade of a nose she had from her father, but her mother was etched in her features.

"Well, she'd sort of have to," Tracy said. "She is the Infanta's actual mother."

Engelberg looked surprised. "I should have remembered that, but we only see Empress Constanza. One rather forgets about the other four wives." He paused for a sip of wine and to smear some of the cranberry-infused cheese onto a cracker. "I do find myself worrying about the succession and what's going to happen. The Infanta has to be in her mid-forties now and still no legitimate heir."

This shouldn't have the power to bother me. Not any longer. I haven't seen her in fourteen years and it's been over twenty since she broke my heart by marrying Boho, but for God's sake, Michael, shut the fuck up. Tracy hoped none of it showed on his face.

"Oh, there is one interesting bit of trivia. O-Trell increased their standard order of battlefield medicines."

Tracy rubbed his chin, feeling the rasp of stubble. He and Jahan exchanged a quick glance. He knew she was thinking the same thing as him—that the League had discovered another Hidden World and was preparing an annexation. He hoped it wasn't one of their trading partners.

"Might indicate a training operation," Tracy said. "Now that the panic over the Cara'ot vanishing has faded it's been a peacetime footing for all the branches." Kathy returned and her dark eyes were bright, and there was added color in her chocolate-brown cheeks. "High command might be trying to hone the blade a bit."

"Just so long as they don't actually use it," Kathy said. "War is not healthy for children and other living things."

"That sounded like a quote," Jahan said. "I like it."

She smiled at the alien. "It is and I do too. It was coined by a woman six centuries ago, Lorraine Schneider, an anti-war activist."

"That stance didn't seem to get much traction among you humans," Jahan said dryly.

"Because we're a bunch of truculent, murderous monkeys," Engelberg said.

"Doesn't mean we stop trying," Kathy countered. "My darling, you are such a pessimist."

"I've seen little to make me an optimist," the doctor replied. He picked up her left hand and pressed a kiss onto her palm. "Apart from you."

Kathy ran her free hand down her husband's cheek. "You say the sweetest things." Tracy glanced over at Jahan. She looked dotingly on the couple. Tracy sighed.

"So what did they bring us?" Engelberg asked as he poured a glass of wine for his wife.

She raised her glass to Tracy. "Congratulations, you hit a jackpot. It's ten vials of dementia treatment."

"Can you synthesize a generic?" Engelberg asked his wife.

"I'm going to try, but even if I fail we've got enough to treat at least eighty people."

"How about the contraceptives?"

"Enough to fill five hundred prescriptions for a year."

The older man rose, went to his desk, and pulled out his credit spike. Tracy didn't ask how much they were getting. He didn't haggle with Engelberg. The man had always dealt with them fairly.

3

PULLING STRINGS

The Foldstream video was shaky, indicating nerves or excitement on the part of the person handling the camera. It was also filled with brief flickers and freezes indicating it had been transferred through multiple relays to try and hide its point of origin. What was absolutely clear were the sulky / devastated / frightened faces of the *Orden de la Estrella* officers who were seated in front of the *corsario* spokesman. His pleasure was evident as he walked back and forth behind the line of forty-three shackled men and two women. The officers from the three captured O-Trell ships.

"So, we look forward to seeing those Reals get deposited in the account." He paused and added, attempting to ape his betters, "*Tout suite.* He had dark auburn hair, latte skin, and a rogue's grin. He was an attractive man who carried himself with the air of someone who knew it. "Once that happens you'll be able to pick up your people. Oh, one last thing. The ships are ours. To the victors go the spoils." There was a snort of laughter and a belated, "Highness."

The screen went dark. The two people in the elegant

office stood silent. The only sounds were the ticking of the antique grandfather clock, the rain pounding against the windows, and the banshee cry of the wind as it swirled around the cornices that graced the imperial palace.

The hands of Mercedes Adalina Saturnina Inez de Arango, the Infanta, had balled into fists. "I'm going to slap that smirk right off his damn face."

"While I can't disagree with the impulse, Majesty, I'm not sure how you're going to pull that off," Admiral Lord Davin Pulkkinen said. "The League has been trying to find Edward Cornell for years."

Davin had begun life as a mere caballero, the lowest rank of nobility in the Solar League, but after his promotion to admiral, and being designated as the "Admiral of the Blue," which gave him command over half the fleet, it was decided that a more grandiose title was in order. And if there was a touch of insubordination and a bubble of laughter in the words, Davin could get away with it. They had been classmates all those years ago at the High Ground.

Mercedes' fingers relaxed. She glanced down. Her nails had left indentations in her palms. She gave her hands a shake and found her eyes drawn to Davin's right hand. The lights flashed and left trails of luminescence through the clear plastic. They were a visual manifestation of the brain impulses shooting down the filaments into the prosthesis, causing the fingers to waggle like those of a cartoon pianist preparing to play. Davin could have covered the missing arm and hand with artificial skin, but never had. Mercedes had always lacked the courage to ask him why. *Or the*

Cara'ot could have regrown it if we'd permitted them to, she thought. *Too late now.*

She searched the man's face for some trace of the class clown, and found it only in the twinkle in his amber-colored eyes. When they'd been young Davin had been one of her husband's wingmen—if she was being generous, capering court jester if she wasn't. The years had etched crow's feet around his eyes and he showed gray at the temples. These signs of life's toll brought her to her own age. Forty-four. No children. An errant husband whose affairs were the talk of the tabloid press. An increasingly querulous father. Squabbling siblings and their broods—another constant reminder of her own barrenness. And the cherry on top—the five known bastards Boho had sired. And now this. A military and financial disaster and a PR nightmare for the crown once the news got out.

Some of it must have shown on her face for Davin reached out and brushed her cheek with the back of his real hand. "Hey, Mer. We'll handle this."

She grabbed his hand and gave it a squeeze. "I'm *so* glad you didn't quit the service after..." she gestured at his prosthetic.

"It is my honor to serve."

"Oh, please, no formality between us." She gestured at one of the armchairs on the far side of her desk. She took its companion rather than remain behind her elegant and cluttered workspace. "So how the hell did this happen, Davi? The *corsarios* have never taken military vessels before. What do you know about..." She checked her ScoopRing. "This

Captain Esteban Singh? How did he manage to get three ships captured?" She continued reading the dossier on the man. "*Dios!* He's only twenty-seven! How the hell did he make captain, much less be given command of a small squadron?"

Davin cast his eyes up toward the elaborate molding and painting of nymphs and fawns that graced the ceiling. "The promotion board has become rather... generous of late. New members."

"Boho's been in charge of appointments to the board." Their eyes met and Davin jumped to his feet.

"Let's take a walk. I could use some fresh air after months in a tin can."

She glanced out the window at the gardens beyond. The late autumn rain was lashing the plants and the trees and bushes bent under the unrelenting wind. "Yes, the weather is *lovely*," she said.

He gave her another grin and she sighed.

Her secretary and general factotum Jaakon gave her a surprised look as they left the inner office. "Is there something you need, ma'am?"

"An umbrella. A big one," Mercedes answered. Jaakon hurried away and returned a few minutes later with the requested umbrella.

Davin took her arm as they strolled down the halls filled with hurrying servants and bureaucrats. The western wing of the sprawling palace housed administrative offices. The eastern wing was the family quarters. In the center was the state dining room, the throne room, and the gigantic ballroom. The ballroom didn't get as much use now that the other eight imperial daughters had left home. Only the heir remained, sharing the space with her father and her resentful stepmother.

They exited through large French doors onto a marble veranda. Davin opened the umbrella and got it over their heads before the rain soaked them both. An expanse of manicured lawn with crushed stone paths fell away before them. At intervals elaborate fountains threw water high into the air like exclamation points. Mercedes watched the raindrops dance frenziedly on the top of the balustrade. The umbrella wasn't just large, it also hung down past their shoulders, effectively shielding their features from the security bots that circled overhead.

"Oh, your assistant is *good*," Davin breathed.

"He knew we couldn't be walking in this weather for pleasure," Mercedes said sourly. "Let's go down by the centaur fountain. Even more splash to defeat any listening ears."

Davin offered his arm. She took it and they strolled down the path while water bubbled past. She could feel the wet invading her shoes, and his artificial limb was hard beneath her hand. They reached the fountain where four massive centaurs reared and stamped around the central spray. They held aloft spears and horns. Water streamed over their faces and their fierce expressions seemed more like grimaces of discomfort. Mercedes sympathized. She and Davin sat down on the rim of the fountain. Davin lowered the umbrella so much she could feel her hair brushing against the ribs and cloth. To make sure any listening ears were foiled she keyed the privacy setting on her ScoopRing.

Over the sounds of rain, fountain and the hum from the ring she said, "So what's the terrible thing that you wanted to tell me that you didn't want overheard even by my loyal security?"

"The promotion board has been bought. I began investigating after I started getting all these puppies masquerading as captains. A few questions, and the scam was revealed. Give the board members money, get promoted. It started out with the board members just pushing their own family members, but then someone realized there was money to be made."

Mercedes saw where he was going and what he didn't want overheard. "Is Boho a party to this?"

"I don't know. If he is it's hidden deep, but they've been getting sloppy since they've been able to operate for so long without anyone reacting."

"How long?"

"Started six years ago."

"When Boho took over." Her voice sounded hollow.

Davin gave her a sympathetic glance. "It's really ramped up in the past two years." He cleared his throat. "Has anything… changed that might account for it?"

"We put Boho on an allowance."

"Ah… oh."

She started to stand. A new thought intruded and she sat back down. "Have you taken a look at the academy?"

He looked surprised at the statement. "No," Davin said slowly. "I normally only pay attention to the puppies once they're graduated. And truthfully assignments are handled farther down the food chain. Would you like me to?"

Mercedes pressed a hand against her forehead. "No, I'll do it. I wish Father and Rohan hadn't gotten cross ways. Rohan was a wonderful patron for the High Ground."

"I take it Rohan as prime minister isn't as amendable to imperial desires?" Davin asked shrewdly.

"Quite so. And Father's become…well, let's just say less sharp." She sighed.

Davin gave her a regretful look. "I'm sorry to have laid all this on you, but losing three ships to the corsairs is a blow."

"I'd call that an understatement. It's a disaster. With actual warships under their control they'll be an even greater danger to other military vessels and commercial ships," Mercedes said.

Davin considered. "They don't usually have enough trained crew to fully man one ship, more so now since the redesign of the *exploradors* has increased the crew complement. Perhaps we'll be lucky and they'll just go for the quick and easy money. Sell them for parts."

"That assumes we'll meet their demands," Mercedes said.

"You're proposing to mount a rescue?"

"That or deliver an object lesson."

"That could endanger the hostages." He hesitated and spent a moment watching the lights play through his hand.

"You have someone… special among the captives?"

"My wife's nephew. Bright kid. Bit of a protégé of mine."

"Noted," Mercedes said and she ducked from beneath the umbrella, stood and felt water squish between her toes. Her shoes were probably ruined. "Thank you for bringing this matter to my attention, my lord."

Davin knew they had transitioned from Mer and Davi back into the Infanta and Admiral Lord Pulkkinen. He stood arranged the umbrella over her head and then bowed deeply. "My pleasure, Your Highness."

They started back to the palace. The damp cold permeated her bones and put a chill on her heart. The frightened faces of the O-Trell officers hung before her. That had to be the first priority. After that she would begin an investigation, pull the threads, and she very much feared where they would lead—

Straight back to her husband. Beauregard Honorius Sinclair Cullen, the Duque de Argento y Pepco.

The massive space station that housed the League's premier military academy swam in the front viewport of the shuttle. Mercedes was piloting, agitating the nerves of her security detail. It both amused and irritated her. The past few years hadn't given her a lot of opportunity to use her skills, and she wanted to stay current. While at the academy she posted the highest scores in the League's *Infierno* fighters. The imperial shuttle, while large and bulky, wasn't that different and she loved the feel of the couch that read her muscle movements, and the headset that registered every shift of her eyes.

The *cosmódromo* was not a thing of loveliness. Only at the top where the massive solar panels were arrayed did it have any hint of gracefulness. It had been described as a donut with a sausage stuck through the hole, and three squat extrusions on the bottom like fat round legs on an extremely tall three-legged stool. One leg was substantially shorter than the other two, which made the station seem on the verge of tipping. The primary classrooms, dorms, dining room, and gym of the High Ground were housed in one leg. The newer, smaller one held quarters for the daughters of the nobility, who were now required to join their brothers in military training. The third leg held the hydroponic gardens that grew some food for the inhabitants, and manufacturing centers for making water and oxygen for the station.

The exterior of the massive ring contained docking bays for the great space liners bringing visitors from around the League eager to enjoy the wonders of the imperial capital of Hissilek. Inside were found restaurants, hotels, shops, parks, and brothels for the traveling public's pleasure. Mercedes flipped to a rear camera view of the planet, enjoying the spectacle of its massive single continent and the blue of its ocean. There was a sense of relief to no longer be on the surface, in the palace, in her office, in the midst of bureaucratic tasks. There was a certain simplicity to the military, a hierarchy upon which one could rely. Not like politics, where smiles and warm handshakes were often masks for duplicity.

For the first few years after noble daughters were also required to serve, Mercedes had been trotted up to the High Ground to give the commencement address, using her as a sock puppet to say—*see, girls can serve too*. But the fact she was the heir to the throne and whoever held that throne was required to be a military leader sort of undercut the message. As long as her royal rump was destined for that seat she was going to be an officer in the *Orden de la Estrella* whether qualified or not. *She* knew she was qualified. She wondered how many of her subjects actually believed that?

After the fifth time she had delegated that task, first to her sister Beatrisa, who was still in active service as a commander aboard a flagship, but as the years slipped past it had fallen back into the more normal pattern of paunchy politicians extolling the virtues of the military. Mercedes realized with shock that it had been six years since she had last visited.

She keyed the radio and contacted High Ground docking control. "Shuttle N751923Alpha requesting permission to dock." She left off the "imperial" to see if the *estrella hombre* would actually bother to check the call number. He didn't.

"We had no word of your arrival, N751923Alpha." The flight controller sounded bored and more than a bit dismissive. "Regulation 27a—"

"This is Rear Admiral Princess Mercedes Adalina Saturnina Inez de Arango, the Infanta. You really want to quote regs to me, *hombre*?"

"Um yes, ma'am. I mean… no, ma'am! Sending docking instructions now. Bay three."

"Thank you," she said sweetly and cut the connection.

The bay door yawned open and she piloted them in, dropping the shuttle lightly onto the landing pad. Once the doors closed and the bay re-pressurized, the inner airlock opened and Vice Admiral Duque Maximilian Vertrant, the commandant of the High Ground, rushed in. He was still buttoning the final button on the coat of his dress uniform while his ceremonial saber flailed around his knees, almost tripping him.

Mercedes unplugged the helmet from the couch and set it aside. She rose, stretched, and moved slowly to the airlock. Once it opened and the ramp lowered, she strolled out. Vertrant's eyes flicked across her attire. Not the gown of an FFH lady or the elegant lines of the dress blues. Instead she wore a working officer's day fatigues. His pursed mouth became even smaller as his lips tightened. When she reached him, she found herself looking down into his thin face because Vertrant was a small man and Mercedes was nearly six feet tall in her stocking feet. His dark skin imperfectly hid the rising flush that Mercedes suspected had more to do with irritation and resentment rather than shyness over being confronted, without warning, by the Infanta.

Vertrant gave a court bow. "Your Highness, your arrival is an unexpected pleasure. How may we serve?"

Commander Marquis Chand Ganguly, standing behind and just to the left of his superior officer's left shoulder, looked as if he'd been stuffed. Over the years he had become more rotund as Vertrant had become even more lean. Ganguly's raven-wing black hair was now touched with gray while Vertrant's had pretty much vanished, giving him an even more skull-like appearance. As she watched, a fat bead of sweat slithered out of Ganguly's right sideburn and rolled across one round dark-bronze cheek.

My, my, Mercedes thought. *I seem to have thrown the cat among the pigeons with my arrival.*

"Just thought it was time I took a look at how things were going at the old alma mater," she said breezily.

"Tea, Your Highness?" Vertrant suggested.

"That would be delightful." Ganguly whispered an order to his ScoopRing.

On her previous visits she had gone directly from the shuttle bay to the cloakroom behind the parade ground and from there onto the raised dais like the prow of a mighty ship of stone sailing toward a sea of blue. Now as she walked the interior halls with Vertrant and Ganguly, and trailed by two members of her security detail, she was transported back in time. Eighteen, frightened, forced to take this mad step to satisfy her father's desperate need to have one of his children succeed him, even though he had to change the law to place a woman on the throne. He had given her two commands—graduate, and find a consort. She had done both. Only one had turned out reasonably well.

They passed a door and another memory rushed back. Standing outside that door desperate for Tracy's help to tailor men's uniforms to fit female bodies. He had touched her at the point where inner thigh met crotch as he measured. She had been a virgin. Now she knew what that surge of sensation meant. *I should have slept with him,* she thought. Too late. He had vanished from her life years ago.

Her reveries and regrets were interrupted by Ganguly choking out, "Anything in particular you wanted to see, ma'am?"

"Pretty much everything," she said cheerfully. More sweat popped out on Ganguly's forehead.

When they reached Vertrant's office Mercedes immediately circled behind the desk and took the commandant's chair. The action knocked him even more off balance. For a few minutes they made small talk about families. From childhood it had been drilled into Mercedes to remember details about noble families. That didn't mean she was above reviewing those details before she met with individuals. She had done that for both Vertrant and Ganguly. At least this time she only had to memorize the names, sexes, and ages of the spawn and spouses for two men, she thought, as Vertrant droned on about each of his three children. When it was a ball or a state dinner she had to remember tedious details for hundreds of people. Then it was Ganguly's turn to tell her about his eleven children. She noted the glances that were exchanged between the two men. Clearly Ganguly despised Vertrant. Clearly Vertrant hated having his pointed nose rubbed in this evidence of Ganguly's superior virility.

In due course an Isanjo, eyes carefully lowered and his supple body bent almost double, slipped into the office carrying a loaded tea tray clutched in his furred hands. The cups, teapot, creamer, and sugar bowl filled the tray so the alien carried the plate of cookies and sliced cake with his prehensile tail.

Vertrant's mouth tightened and his eyes narrowed. "Disgusting, Trem! It never occurred to you to make two trips? Return to the kitchen and throw away those sweets."

The alien lowered his long lashes to conceal his eyes, placed the tray on the desk, bowed, and retreated. Mercedes suspected the alien batBEMs would enjoy the rejected desserts. Though to be fair Mercedes wasn't excited to eat cookies that had been that close to an Isanjo's ass. Tea was poured, milk, lemon, or sugar added depending upon the tastes of the three people. Trem returned with a new selection of treats. Mercedes noticed that the batBEM's claws were partially extended. After the alien left she set aside the fragile bone-china cup and abruptly changed the subject away from the upcoming soccer game between the High Ground and the University of Caledonia.

"So now that the niceties have been observed… I'd like to inspect the books, review the résumés of the teaching staff, the number of scholarship students admitted, *prueba* pass rates, and graduation rates."

"Is there any particular reason for this snap inspection?" Vertrant asked.

"It's been a number of years since I've been to the academy. I feel a great deal of affection for the school and since Rohan stepped down as patron I haven't heard as much."

Glances were exchanged and Ganguly spoke up. "With the expansion it seemed unnecessary to have a patron. It seemed a quaint holdover from a time when only men attended."

"Perhaps the solution would be to have a male and a female patron," Mercedes suggested.

"An interesting notion, Highness, but so few women make a career out of the military," Vertrant said smoothly.

"Rohan wasn't a career military man," Mercedes gently reminded.

"True, but after the scare and military build-up after the Cara'ot vanished, it seemed wiser to have oversight in the hands of career military."

There was something to what Vertrant was saying, but still the sensation niggled that murky currents were at work here. "Well, perhaps my sister, Commander Princess

Beatrisa, can fill that role," Mercedes said. "Every indication is that she intends to die with her boots on."

"An interesting suggestion," Vertrant said.

Tea was sipped, cookies and cake consumed. Mercedes, very aware of the seventeen pounds she had gained over the past decade, confined herself to a single cookie. Once the social chatter had been satisfied, Vertrant authorized her to access the High Ground's files. As files floated over the desk Mercedes wished she had one of the computer wizards from her class to see if anything had been hidden or removed. Commander Marqués Ernesto Chapman-Owiti came to mind, as did Tracy. She put him firmly aside.

"You can leave us, Commandant," she ordered. "I'm sure you have duties to attend to."

"Hard to do when I don't have access to my office, Highness," he said, just barely avoiding insolence.

"I have faith in you, Vertrant. I'm sure you'll manage."

There was nothing more he could say. She stood. He bowed. She saluted. He hesitated then saluted. Ganguly's eyes met hers. He got the message. In this moment she was not a princess. She was a flag captain and the future commander-in-chief of the armed forces of the Solar League.

4

SENDING MESSAGES

Hours later Mercedes stretched. Vertebrae in her back popped and shifted. She reached for her now cold cup of tea and thought better of it. Her stomach had become a tight ball and she feared what might happen if she swallowed anything. Anything beyond the disgust and rage she had been eating for the past hours.

Her instinct was to call Vertrant onto the carpet and rip him in his own office and remove him instantly. But years at her father's side had taught her caution. Vertrant had allies in the parliament and he was well liked by the conservative old guard, who were still furious over the inclusion of women in the Rule of Service. Now noble daughters in the FFH also attended the High Ground and promised five years of service to the League if they passed the *prueba* at the end of the first year and graduated.

What the records had revealed was that a surprisingly large number of women were making it to graduation but were then being placed in safe, groundside postings, and from there being mustered out due to a variety of questionable medical issues. Virtually every male was passing and entering active duty. Mercedes' class had started with over eight hundred students. Only three hundred and three of them had actually graduated. Now close to eighteen hundred were graduating in each class. She also noticed a steady drop in the number of scholarship students over the years. That was another troubling statistic. Selecting the brightest *intitulados* from high schools all across the League worlds meant they always had bright minds joining the officers' corp.

She swept a hand through the computer files where they hung in the air before her, banishing them. Leaning back, she placed her forefingers against her lips and considered. The inflated graduation rates when wedded to what she had learned about the promotions board suggested an institution in crisis. Her fury and disgust with her husband drove her to her feet. Mercedes paced the office.

Like her, Boho knew about the dangers in Sector 470. A place where ships vanished without trace. Add to that the mystery of the Cara'ot. The last thing the League needed was an armed force in decline with an incompetent officer class at the helm. She considered Ganguly's behavior and decided he was the weak link. She would start there.

She left the office and wasn't surprised to find Ganguly conveniently passing by the door where her two SPI agents stood watch. She gave him a smile. "Walk with me, Commander. I've a mind to see the gym again." In that large space and at this time of day, filled with the snarl of gunfire and the shouts of students practicing hand-to-hand skills, it would make surveillance far less likely.

"Is Chief Deal still active?" she asked as they walked down the corridors.

"No, Your Highness. He retired some years ago."

"Pity. He was quite hard on me, but in retrospect it was deserved and it certainly came in handy during my years of active service." Ganguly made a non-committal noise.

They entered the enormous room. A running track circled the space. There was the crash of weights being returned to their cradles. Sharp, controlled bursts of gunfire, and the grunts, smack of flesh on flesh, and shouts of "*kiai*" echoed off the clear dome of the roof. Beyond the glass dome the nebula hung, its twisting colors like the trailing scarves of an exotic dancer. Mercedes led them onto the track, waved off her security, and began to jog. Ganguly had to join her in order to keep up. Their boots scritched on the sand underfoot. Mercedes was annoyed to discover how quickly her breathing increased. She clearly needed to stop riding a desk for so many hours each day. Ganguly was soon gasping. If he wasn't as dark as herself Mercedes suspected he would be red-faced.

As they ran side by side Mercedes said quietly, "So, are you going to go down with him?"

Ganguly's head snapped to the side to look at her and he stumbled. Mercedes grabbed his arm to keep him upright. "Not for the seventeen and half percent he shares with me," he forced past stiff lips. "What are you offering?"

"A tragic but necessary retirement."

"What about my pension?"

"Haven't you saved any of that seventeen and half percent? Pity if you haven't."

His lips tightened. Large beads of sweat oozed from his hairline and rolled across his plump cheeks. Some of it was exertion. Mercedes suspected a lot of it was fear.

"What do you want?"

"You must know where the bodies are buried. Testify against him. You'll be shocked… shocked to discover there was corruption at the High Ground and you brought it to the crown's attention."

"I suppose I don't have any other option."

"No. You don't. Are there any other parties involved in this?" She dreaded the answer.

"I… I think so, but I don't know who they are." She felt a surge of relief that Ganguly didn't know about Boho. If he had he would have had to share Vertrant's fate.

"You have to get me away from him," he wheezed. "If he suspects…"

"I'll handle it." Mercedes slowed to a jog, then a walk. She left the track heading to the doors. She keyed her ScoopRing and called Vertrant. "Commandant, thank you so much. Do meet me at the shuttle so I can say farewell."

"Of course, Highness." There was a long pause. "The computer has no record of your searches. Was there a problem? I could help if there—"

"Not necessary." She cut the link. Glanced over at Ganguly. "Best get the door keyed to your palm and eye."

"You're… you're putting me in charge? Vertrant won't stand—"

"Unless he's going to eat a bullet, and he's never struck me as the type, he'll be leaving with me. Therefore someone has to be in charge. That would be you. At least for now." They were out in the corridor. "Now go and handle the necessary arrangements."

"I should accompany you—"

"I know the way to the shuttle bay. And just as I doubt he'll suicide, I doubt he'll attack me."

Ganguly walked away with a rolling waddle. Mercedes headed for her shuttle. Vertrant was waiting in the docking bay. He did have a pair of *fusileros* with him. Mercedes sized them up. They seemed to be more of a security blanket for Vertrant than an actual threat. And realistically what starman would lift a weapon against the Infanta? She also knew that Captain Lord Ian Rogers, the head of her security detail, was aboard the royal shuttle with seven *fusileros* who had seen actual combat to augment her SPI agents.

She held out her hand to the commandant. Vertrant bowed over it, his lips brushing the air. She leaned in and whispered in his ear, "I'm going to offer you an invitation to return with me back to Hissilek, and you're going to be delighted to accept. Aren't you?" His gaze jerked up to meet her implacable one. She watched him dither then leaned in even closer. "Or you can be subject to the humiliation of having me arrest you on the spot." She glanced around the docking bay where *hombres* were at work on the engine of a shuttle, others cleaning the deck. "The gossip will be all over the academy before the bay doors finish closing. I'm sure you want to spare your wife and children that mortification."

The narrow shoulders slumped. Mercedes stepped back. "My father was just mentioning how much he would like to see you. Do allow me to offer you a lift down to the planet."

"Your Majesty is too gracious," Vertrant murmured.

She gestured toward the ramp and allowed him to precede her onto the shuttle. Ian was waiting inside with a pair of security cuffs.

Once she had played hide and seek behind the long drapes and under the massive, elegant desk. Mercedes would have loved to have been that six-year-old girl again who knew that her father was the greatest man in the universe. That life was hugs and the scratch of stubble on her cheek, the smell of aftershave and pipe tobacco. A deep basso voice telling her she was his little *querida*. Now he was frowning at the images that flickered in the air over his desk. The years had added another chin, and heavy jowls. He was still a handsome man with his skin a deep mahogany color, the black hair lightly tinged with gray, which only added to his aura of distinguished authority. The nose was still an aggressive blade, but the dark eyes were not as bright as once they had been, and he often became confused. Everyone knew what that portended. No one wanted to say the word—dementia.

The message from Edward Cornell ended. Lord Kemel Dorian DeLonge, the head of SEGU, the Imperial Intelligence Agency, stood and closed the file. One of DeLonge's soft-footed aides brought up the lights. The Emperor's jaw was working as if he had the *corsario* leader between his teeth and was grinding him to pulp. There were six people in the room. Kemel and his two aides, Davin, her father, and Mercedes. Over the years she had become accustomed to being the only estrogen in a room full of testosterone, but she wished that one of her sisters could have shared in these meetings where fates were decided and dominance exercised.

"So how much is this going to cost me?" her father asked. It emerged as a growl. Glances flew between Davin, Mercedes, and DeLonge. "What? You're conniving. Don't think I don't see it."

A discreet gesture from the old security chief had Davin and Mercedes stepping back. DeLonge stepped to the desk and leaned in close. "Fernán, this is a unique and disquieting situation. While it has been our practice to ransom the crews and passengers of civilian ships, we think this is a new and alarming escalation and we wanted your guidance."

The furrows on her father's forehead were smoothing. Mercedes slumped a bit with relief. She was reminded again that being an intelligence officer went beyond merely snooping. A strong grounding in psychology played a part as well. There was also the advantage that the two men had known each other since the Emperor had been a teenager and Kemel a wet-behind-the-ears young agent. She just found it sad that her father, younger by seven years, was far less sharp than the SEGU head.

"Yes, yes, I understand why you'd be concerned. Good you came to me." The Emperor looked at Davin. "What do you have, Admiral?"

"Nothing yet, sir, but we're working closely with SEGU

to pinpoint the location of our troops."

"Good. Good." Her father paused. "And then?"

It was Mercedes' cue. She sat on a corner of the desk closest to her father. "We go in and get them."

"Send a message, eh?" He gazed at her fondly.

"Yes, sir."

"Davin going to lead this?" Fernán asked. "Or Boho?"

Davin stepped in on the other side of the Emperor. Mercedes reflected that this had all the hallmarks of an intricate dance. "I think it would send a more powerful message if the Infanta herself were to be in command of the strike force."

"Show the people the importance you place on our brave soldiers," Kemel added.

Her father straightened in his chair and unconsciously tried to suck in his gut. "Perhaps I should dust off the uniform and handle this myself."

She and Davin exchanged panicked glances. Before she could speak Kemel stepped in. "An excellent suggestion, Highness." He motioned for them to start heading for the door. Every fiber in her body strained against that, but Mercedes obeyed, deferring to the intelligence chief's reading of the situation and the forty-year friendship between the two men.

Just before they reached the door, Kemel paused, looked back. "Sir, what about the press?"

"Eh, what?"

"They're such jackals. How do you think they'll interpret you leaving the capital rather than trusting to your heir?" Her father's frown was back. "I'm also concerned because you and the Empress are due to take your annual skiing holiday. If you cancel it elevates these corsairs in the minds of the public. Instead of criminals they become a threat worthy of the attention of the Emperor himself. I hate to see them dignified in that way."

"Hmm, I see your point." He smiled at Mercedes. "So, are you ready to bloody a few noses and send some men to Hell?"

"Absolutely, sir, if it will get back our people." She saluted her father then added, "I'll make you proud, sir."

"You always do." He looked back to some papers on his desk, glanced back at her with a rather melancholy smile. "Just wish you'd make me a grandpa."

And in one statement her victory turned to ash.

5

CONVENIENT COUPLES

The world beneath them was a jewel. Green and blue, white banded clouds like the veils on an exotic dancer, but it was a cruel cheat, and an ironic, cosmic lie. When the planet had first been discovered the early settlers had named it Paradise and the first settlement Eden. Human expansion to the stars had been a story of a truculent and aggressive species meeting and conquering the unsuspecting members of the five great alien races in this particular spiral arm of the galaxy. The conquest even extended to Terran plant life. Local flora wilted and died in the face of this new invading challenger.

We're the kudzu of the galaxy, Tracy reflected as he gazed at the beautiful globe. *But not here.*

On this world the local flora carried a plant virus that was fatal to humans and their animals and it managed to infect the Earth plants with the same virus. No food could be grown on the planet. No Earth animals could graze the lush meadows. No human could enjoy the magnificent vistas of snowcapped mountains, sapphire lakes, majestic forests, and warm oceans without wearing a hazmat suit. Not because the air would kill them, but because they would inhale the spores, and inevitably sneeze or cough and bring the deadly pathogen inside the sealed and filtered domes where the population had to live. Inside the domes they grew what food they could and imported the majority. There was virtually no livestock, just house pets. The descendants of those first hopeful settlers had petitioned to change it in the planetary registry—it was now known as Paradise Lost. Few people immigrated to the planet; mostly the elderly, looking for a place to retire in an astoundingly sterile environment with low housing costs, people with auto-immune deficiencies, terrible asthma or allergies. Yet somehow the planet had managed to create a robust economy. Not on the planet, but in orbit above it at the San Pedro *cosmódromo* where used ships and ship parts were bought and sold.

Tracy used the sensors to plot a course through the maze of metal dancing in complex orbits over the world below. There were older model racing pinnaces, battered shuttles, freighters, even one ancient space liner. Rarely were there military craft, but occasionally something small would slip through. It was here that Tracy had acquired the decommissioned Talon to use as a shuttle for the *Selkie*. An actual shuttle craft was too large for the cargo bay on the freighter. The Talon was a good compromise, and it had the added bonus of looking very cool with its swept-back wings and needle nose. Naturally the one they had bought had had the guns and missiles removed.

He couldn't resist occasionally glancing through the viewport. Only at the massive shipyard at Cuandru and at fleet headquarters at Hellfire could one see more ships or pieces of ships. It was a kaleidoscope of metal and engineering that glittered in the unfiltered light from the star. Some men's hearts soared at the sight of natural beauty or a beautiful woman. Tracy loved ships. Loved everything they represented. The chance to break free of constraints, of gravity, of economics, of society, of class, and of birth. Not that there wasn't a woman waiting for him on the *cosmódromo*. He had sent Lisbet a message as soon as they translated out of Fold at the edge of the solar system.

"Docking instructions coming through, Ollie... Trac... Captain." Baca's stutter lamely ended up on the title.

Tracy nodded and plotted their final approach. The halo of metal was left behind and the station was in view. It was a traditional torus. Ships nuzzled against the rim like nursing piglets. They were almost all freighters, but he did spot one elegant private yacht. Someone clearly had something essential break. This wasn't a place that normally catered to the FFH, being far too rough, and with none of the amenities that the nobility demanded. Tracy left his chair and went to stand at Luis' shoulder as he feathered the engines to bring them in to dock.

"You trying to make me nervous?" Baca asked.

"Giving you moral support."

"He did fine at New Hope," Jahan said. "Put your ass back in the chair and stop micro-managing. You're the one who said there needs to be more than one person who can fly this crate," the Isanjo concluded.

"Don't call her a crate," Graarack said and she stroked

her console with a claw. "She doesn't like it."

Tracy and his XO exchanged a glance. The Sidone did tend to be deeply into the mystical. "Woo woo" as Jax put it, and right on cue the Tiponi rustled his fronds. His version of a derisive chuckle. Graarack clicked her beak in mock annoyance. It had taken Tracy years to learn to read the meanings and nuances of his alien crew mates' behaviors, and he sensed he had only scratched the surface. Perhaps there was a reason, apart from sheer xenophobia, that humans had just conquered the alien races they had met rather than try to negotiate. Understanding a different person wasn't easy. When it was an alien race... well, humans weren't known for their patience.

"Damn it, stop using my own words against me," Tracy complained, but he returned to his chair. He tried to keep his hands from either gripping the arms or his fingers from moving as if handling the controls. He wasn't sure he succeeded, but Luis was focused on his task and didn't notice. Jahan did and she gave him a fang-revealing grin. He glared at her.

Luis did a good job. The actual touch on the docking clamps was a bit harder than Tracy liked, but overall it was handled well. Graarack powered down the engines. Jax readied the docking documents. Dalea entered the bridge carrying a tap-pad.

"Who's going onto the station?" she asked.

"All of us if we're smart," Luis caroled.

"Thank you," the gentle Hajin said. "I was actually planning to stay aboard."

"Sorry," the younger human muttered. Tracy hid a grin.

The seventeen years that separated him from Luis felt like a lifetime sometimes.

"Point is we need to replenish our groceries and I have a list." Luis looked miserable.

"I'll handle it," Tracy said. He keyed his ring and Dalea sent over the list. "I expect Luis wants to get his rockets… er… lubed."

"Like you're not going to the Sweet Retreat. And I'm not planning on paying for it, *el viejo*."

Tracy let the *old man* crack and the reminder he was going to be spending his time in a whore house pass, and not just because he had to deliver the contraceptives. Once he had been twenty-seven and stupid. "Go on then, *el muchacho*." He enjoyed sliding in the diminutive, but Luis was too excited to notice.

He went clattering off the bridge. "I gotta change!"

"God alone knows what ridiculous getup he'll put on," Jahan said with a huffing laugh.

"I will handle the fees and paperwork on my way to the misting," Jax said. "Then I'll go check out loaders. We need to replace the one that was stolen." Tracy sighed. That was going to put them back a grand.

"Graarack, what about you?" Tracy asked.

"A nice dinner," the spider replied.

Tracy shot an inquiring glance at his XO. "I have family working on ships here. A nephew and his wife. We'll have dinner together at their apartment."

Tracy nodded. He knew that Jahan had three sisters and two brothers and this was the seventh nephew he had heard about. He wondered what it would have been like to grow up in a large extended family. There was only Tracy's father. His mother had died when he was six and Alexander had never remarried, which was a very uncommon thing in the League. The government had promoted policies that encouraged large families in an effort to outbreed the conquered aliens. The League took it so seriously that one-child families and unmarried citizens paid a penalty to the government. Only a medical diagnosis could get you out of the fine. Since Oliver Randall was a fabrication, Tracy had procured just such a document to go along with all his other fake papers so he could avoid paying. Better to be thought sterile than try and create a phantom family. First rule of living under an assumed identity—keep it simple. Too much complexity could raise flags and give the authorities an investigative hook.

He gathered up his holdall with the contraband birth control carefully repacked in candy wrappers. Inspections were lax at San Pedro, and no bored customs agent wanted to tear open packaging. In case they ran across an agent with a sweet tooth there were a few actual candies that could be offered. "Well, I'm off. See you all tomorrow."

"Captain," Jahan called. "Do you have something for Lisbet?"

Tracy glanced back at the Isanjo. "We're not kids on a first date."

"Is she a woman?" the alien asked.

"Yeah." His tone screamed *obviously.*

"Then you should have a little something for her. Especially after all these months. My hubby knows I would hand him his ears if he didn't have something for me."

"We're just friends—"

"Who fuck. You really don't know much about women, do you, Captain? At least take her a bouquet of flowers. It might deepen your understanding of our sex."

"We are not afflicted by all this romance nonsense," Jax said with a superior sniff.

"Yeah, because you don't actually have sexes and you're a *tree*," Jahan said.

"It might also be an example of how you are aping human culture," the Flute said.

"No, it's an example of how I'm warm-blooded and passionate and I love my husband."

"Despite spending so much time apart from him."

Tracy fled before the argument between his shipmates became even more heated.

His ScoopRing was pricking his index finger. Boho tried to ignore it since his prick was busily plowing the deepest recesses of Señora Daphne's warm cunt. It was a sunny afternoon in Kronos's capital city and being that it was an afternoon on a weekday Señora Daphne's banker husband was off at the aforementioned bank busily toting up the value of the goods from the Cara'ot ship. Even after the bloodsucker took his cut, Boho was going to come out with a tidy sum. Enough to pay off his debt to the casino, buy a bauble for Marquis Lacey's greedy but lovely youngest daughter, and buy the silence of the captain who actually ran his ship while

Boho served as the commodore of the squadron.

The pricking didn't stop and in fact it went to emergency signal, sending a jolt of electricity into his finger that left his right hand cramping from the pain.

"Fuck!" he bellowed and felt his penis deflate.

Daphne's eyes snapped open. "What? What's wrong?"

He kissed her pouting lips, swollen from his kisses and bites. "Sorry, love, duty calls. I have to take this."

He pulled out and rolled off of her. Padded naked across the room toward the window. As he passed the elegant full-length framed mirror he paused to study his reflection. Forty-four but he believed he could pass for early thirties. A few crow's feet spiked around his eyes, but for the most part his caramel skin was smooth. His hair was still thick and glossy black, and the few gray hairs had been expertly removed by his valet. Three years before he had grown a mustache and he liked the rakish look it gave him. He also knew that Mercedes didn't, which made him like it all the more. It was a small and probably unworthy form of rebellion, but it still gave him comfort. Life as the consort had proved to be more chafing than he had expected. Perhaps if they'd ever managed to have children… But the role of royal stud had eluded him. At least he knew it wasn't his fault. His hand went unconsciously to his cock and he cupped it for a moment. Five healthy kids. Three girls and two boys. And a couple of them had inherited his green eyes.

Boho disabled the visual function before he accepted the call and controlled his desire to snarl a greeting. It might be his wife. But it wasn't Mercedes. It was Captain Lord Eugene

Montgomery, head of the promotions board. A hologram of the man's face sprang up from the ring. There was an ashen hue to his dark skin.

"Why the hell are you dark?" Montgomery demanded. "Where are you? Who's with you?"

"I was in the can," Boho snapped. "And it's none of your business."

"I need to know who's listening."

Boho threw a smile back toward his mistress where she lay in a welter of silk sheets. Against the blazing white of the material she was like a delectable chocolate. She was idly flicking through the fashion sites on her ring. Since the sheet was at her waist her heavy breasts were very much in evidence. Boho was a breast man. Unlike Daphne, Mercedes was tall and, despite middle age adding a few bulges, still quite muscular, and she had a great rack. Daphne was a plump little armful. He went into the bathroom and closed the door. It was a gold and porcelain temple and, as far as Boho was concerned, in terrible taste, but what could one expect from the nouveau riche?

"Some cunt I'm fucking. I'll turn on security, but I doubt she's an interstellar spy."

"I don't need your contempt, Cullen. This is serious. I've been summoned to the palace. Wherever the fuck you are, and whoever the hell you're fucking, you need to get back to Ouranos and back me up. The order came from SEGU under the seal of the Infanta and it was signed by old DeLonge himself. They asked for all my records, but in particular those of Esteban Singh. Something must have happened. What do you know about Singh?"

"Why should I know anything about him? You're the one with the records. You tell me."

Montgomery *ummed* and *aaahed* and finally produced words. "Sort of an *intitulado*. Father is a wealthy industrialist. They allowed the wife's childless sister to adopt the boy. She had married into a knight's family, which allowed Singh to attend the High Ground. The actual father paid the… ah… fee for his son. I tried to pull up information from fleet headquarters, but any information about Singh is interdicted. What the hell did he do?"

"Look, calm down. I'll head back to Ouranos, but it's going to take me a few days. I can't pull my squadron off its normal rotation. I'll have to buy a ticket on a commercial vessel or hitch a ride on a military ship heading back to the capital. Don't say anything until I get there."

"They want to see me in two days!"

"Then hire a damn lawyer and stall them."

"That will make me look guilty," Montgomery almost wailed.

His rather slender reserves of patience having been exhausted, Boho snapped, "Probably because you are."

"Fuck you, Cullen! You better fix this. I'm not hanging alone!"

The connection ended. Boho stared at his now darkened ring then picked up the elaborate gilt toilet-paper holder and smashed the mirror over the sinks. His features reflected back to him in a kaleidoscope of falling glass.

"*Cariño*, are you all right? Are you hurt?" He heard

Daphne's bare feet slapping on the polished wood floor.

"Fine, fine, but I fear I must leave." He opened the door and stepped out. "I'm afraid I did break your mirror, however."

"Oh, *Dios*! How am I going to explain that to Donald?" She didn't look as pretty when she was glaring at him.

It was probably time to end the relationship. Which would sadly necessitate ending his relationship with her banker husband, but Boho was certain he could find another compliant but venal and seemingly respectable stooge to work on his behalf.

He threw on his uniform and left. By the time he was partway down the hall she had gone from pleading to yelling imprecations at him. As the shrill cries pursued him Boho decided that the wealthy bourgeoisie probably weren't the best place to find playmates. They didn't seem to understand the rules. By and large the ladies of his own class knew how to stray without causing scenes, and the lower classes could always be cowed.

Outside the forty-story residential tower the streets were filled with people returning from lunch. Boho signaled to his security detail, who waited nearby, that he was heading back to the port. A passing taxi caught his eye. Rather than wait for his detail to reach their flitter and return for him, he flagged it down. They could bloody well get their butts in gear and follow. It sank down and the door raised. He climbed in and was startled to see his driver was a human woman. She correctly read his expression and grinned at him. "If you want a different cab, sir, I'll understand, but I was in O-Trell, and learned to fly shuttles. I won't crash you."

"No, no, it's quite a charming change. The spaceport, please."

"Aye, sir."

After Boho alerted the shuttle he was returning he decided to pass the time by engaging with the woman. "So, your husband doesn't mind that you're—"

"My man got killed. Mining accident on Nephilim. Wasn't much work for a woman to do there so I dumped the kids with my mama and enlisted. After five years I had my muster out money, the insurance settlement for my man, so I gathered up the kids and relocated to Kronos. Bought a cab." She shrugged. "Sometimes men get out, but a lot of ladies like to travel with me. I do all right."

"How old were your children?" He found the story startling.

She shrugged. "Young. But you do what you have to, right? Mama did good by them. I sent home my pay, and we've gotten to know each other again. Kids are tough. They'll do okay."

Boho leaned back trying to digest what he'd just heard. He wondered if his and Mercedes' kids would do "okay" if they ever had any. A mother destined to rule an empire. A father who was… what? Royal drone? Military figurehead? What exactly was his role?

They reached the spaceport. Boho inserted his credit spike and gave her a tip as large as the fee. The woman gave him a startled look when she saw the amount. "Thank you, sir, thank you most kindly. "She then noticed his name. Her expression was balm to Boho's wounded and worried soul.

"Oh, *Dios*! My lord... Excellency! Forgive me for my foolish chatter." She was trying to salute, trying to curtsy while seated. "If I had realized—"

Boho held up a restraining hand. "Please, no need to apologize. The Infanta and I are grateful for your service."

Her gabbling thanks were cut off by the closing of the flitter door. His SPI detail were tumbling out of their flitter and running to catch up as Boho walked to the waiting shuttle and the honor guard of *fusileros* who saluted as he walked between them. The stamp of booted feet and clash as rifle butts hit the concrete was a hollow echo of his non-existent power.

The air scrubbers on the San Pedro station weren't top of the line, so Tracy got a clashing mélange of all the restaurants and food stands in this area of the torus, seasoned with a whiff of the septic tanks. Unlike the stations orbiting more upscale planets and catering to upscale travelers, San Pedro lacked the central park running through the torus to help sweeten the air. Instead there were a few sickly-looking trees in pots, and planters of flowers. There were a lot of Tiponi Flutes around. Maybe the station administrators were hoping the ambulatory plants could help with the oxygenation issues. While the humans still outnumbered them, the San Pedro station had a lot of aliens. Isanjo and Flutes primarily, but there were a few Hajin. Tracy had just finished purchasing a bouquet of flowers from a Hajin florist. There weren't a lot of choices. The creature mostly carried the herbs that went into the Flutes' aromatic and slightly hallucinatory stim sticks. There were various fresh chilis for Isanjo cuisine, and a Hajin plant that provided leaves that the Hajin enjoyed chewing but made humans violently ill. Bottom line, the flowers weren't all that pretty, but the Hajin had tied them together with a shiny ribbon and wrapped the bouquet in a cone of glitter-covered blue paper.

Deciding that maybe the daisies weren't enough, Tracy made a dinner reservation at one of the better restaurants on San Pedro. Meaning it had tablecloths, china plates, and real silverware. He then hopped on a tram heading around the torus. The Sweet Retreat was a nondescript building in a row of nondescript buildings. The church didn't approve of prostitution, but was wise enough to know it couldn't be proscribed in a culture that put such a premium on the celebration of machismo. Since the government paid subsidies to people with children, the brothels also had an alternate source of income that allowed the women to start families. Some of the children were put up for adoption to childless couples, but most women ultimately ended up marrying one of their clients and leaving the profession.

Such was not the case with Lisbet Montego. She had stayed in the sex trade and eventually became a madam with her own establishment here on San Pedro. It had been a pure accident that she and Tracy had reconnected. The *Selkie* had stopped at San Pedro for routine ship maintenance, and Tracy had decided that three years of celibacy was too much and maybe *he* needed a bit of maintenance too. He had gone in search of a joy house. He had walked through the door and met the eyes of the proprietress, and had a dislocating moment of being sixteen years old and faced with his first nearly naked woman. His father had taken him to the Candy Box, the brothel in their neighborhood in Hissilek, for that rite of manhood that was so much a part of League culture. Girls had their *quinceañera,* boys got taken by their fathers to whore houses for their first sexual encounter.

Lisbet had been nineteen, experienced but close enough to him in age that she wasn't too intimidating. He had visited her a few more times before he had gone off to school at the High Ground, but by the time he returned to the capital after his court martial she had been gone. Now, all these years later, here she was again.

He hadn't been certain she would remember him, but in case she did he'd rushed to her, hand outstretched, and introduced himself, *"Oliver Randall,"* he had said with emphasis, and watched the quick understanding as recognition become calculation in those dark eyes.

"So pleased to meet you, Oliver. Welcome."

They then had a lovely and private reunion. She hadn't asked him why he was using an alias. He never offered to explain. Their relationship was one of a shared present, never looking forward or back. All very convenient.

That had him check his long strides toward the back door. *Convenient.* He had never asked if the arrangement was equally convenient for Lisbet. Not that Lisbet had ever indicated that she wanted something more and she was a strong enough woman that he figured she would have spoken up. He shook off the discomfort and touched the door panel.

It had been keyed to his palm, another indication of just how convenient the rut had become. The back hallway took him past the kitchen where a young woman was spooning apple sauce into the rosebud mouth of an infant in a high chair. The baby kept making spit and apple sauce bubbles that then burst to cover her mouth and chin with goo. Tracy thought it was disgusting. The young mother kept laughing, clearly delighted. The baby spotted him and let out a sound like a chuckling loon. The girl looked around.

"Oh, Oliver, welcome. Lisbet is in the office doing payroll." She nodded toward the flowers. "How pretty. Are those for her? Let me get a vase for you." She stood. The baby's face folded into a shape of misery and let out a wail at this abandonment. "Shush, Stacy, I'll be right back."

"Yeah, Stacy, don't be such a baby," Tracy said. The girl laughed. Tracy wanted to kick himself for the ponderous attempt at humor. What the hell was wrong with him?

Armed with a vase and the bouquet Tracy continued down the hall to the office. Lisbet looked up with a warm smile. She had dyed her hair again, this time to resemble the multi-colors of a Hajin's mane. She had chosen streaks of gold, silver, and red to weave through the elaborate braids, and it looked amazing against her smooth coffee-colored skin. She came around from behind the desk and gave him a kiss. He tried to hug her and ended up tipping a bit of water down her back.

"Damn, I'm sorry."

She was laughing. "It's all right. Why you sweet thing, you brought me flowers." She took the bouquet and buried her nose in the petals. She looked delighted and Tracy gave a mental sigh about how much crow he was going to have to eat when he next saw Jahan, because the Isanjo was sure to bring it up. He set the vase on the desk, and pulled Lisbet into a proper embrace. She tasted of coffee and the caramel candies she liked.

"I made us a reservation at Graze. That okay?"

She pushed him back and studied his face. There was mischief dancing in her eyes. "All right. Either you've done something that you think is going to make me really angry. Or… you've hired a relationship coach. Which is it?"

He felt himself blushing. "Neither… well, maybe sort of… My XO, she said… well, she just said some… things… got me thinking…"

"Tell her thank you for me." She returned to her desk, and arranged the flowers in the vase.

Tracy trailed after her, and removed the disguised contraceptives. Lisbet swept them into a drawer, pulled out her credit spike. "Any price increase?"

"Not this time."

"Wish whoever is supplying these to you would move to the patches. Those Cara'ot patches were so great. Remembering to take a pill is a pain." As the money transferred to the *Selkie*'s account Tracy again felt that sense that the relationship between himself and Lisbet was very one-way. She paid him for the birth control, plus a markup, and he paid her nothing for the time he spent with her apart from delivering the medicine.

Unaware of his roiling thought she smiled up at him.

"Let me finish up here and I'll be right with you. What time is the reservation? Is there time for us to... relax?"

"Yes."

"I'll meet you in the bedroom."

When Lisbet entered she was carrying the vase of flowers. Tracy, propped up in bed, keyed off his ScoopRing and watched as she placed them on the dresser and gave them a final careful adjustment. She then catwalked toward the bed. Her fingers found the zipper on her dress. The sound was a rasping purr and the dress dropped to puddle around her feet. She stepped out of it. The lacy lilac bra and panties were lovely against her dark skin. She crawled up the bed snagging the covers away until she rested against his naked body. Despite his mental turmoil his body had no doubts. It responded with enthusiasm.

6

WHAT HAPPENED TO US?

When Boho's shuttle landed at the Cristóbal Colón Spaceport there was no imperial flitter waiting to take him to the Palacio Colina. The shuttle pilot had radioed ahead informing the palace of his arrival. This wasn't an oversight. It was a calculated slight. Being forced to take public transport, Boho would be required to stop at the gates and prove his bona fides before being allowed into his own home. Clearly Montgomery had not exaggerated the direness of the situation. A small cold knot formed in the pit of his stomach. Boho grabbed up the jewelry box. The bauble he'd intended for the youngest Lacey daughter had become a gift for Mercedes. He had a feeling he should have gotten bigger emeralds.

He was recognized by the young *fusilero* at the gates. The boy had stayed magnificently expressionless at the arrival of the imperial consort in a common cab with his security squeezed inside with him. The cabbie was paid, and Boho walked through the gates.

"Would you like transport home, your grace?" the guard asked.

"No, it's lovely. I'll walk and enjoy the sunset." Now that he was within the confines of the palace his shadows peeled away to give him the privacy he desperately needed.

The indigenous flora that had managed to survive the onslaught of the Earth-evolved plants filled the late afternoon air with perfume. All the vegetation, both terrestrial and that native to Ouranos, were taking advantage of the cooler temperatures and the autumn rains to blossom and pollinate. The nasal passages accustomed to the filtered air aboard ship reacted to the onslaught and Boho gave a mighty sneeze. With a clap of wings birds just settling down to roost for the night erupted from the trees, and a *lapin*, serenely grazing on the lawn, bolted for the clipped hedges, its long tail and equally long ears flapping in alarm.

At the pinnacle of the hill sat the royal palace. Private quarters and public rooms, it was like white fondant icing on the top of a cake. Boho took the walkway that led around the hill. On the far side, facing the chaparral, was the palace that had been given to Mercedes and himself on their wedding day. The Phantasiestück Palace had been built by a previous emperor to house his lover. In the years since Boho had carried Mercedes across that threshold love had faded into boredom. Mercedes still lived in the palace. It had been seven years since Boho had spent any significant time in the tiny, jewel-like house.

The old Hajin butler was gone. A new, younger alien now stood at the open door. Apparently the guards at the gate had alerted the household of the master's return and the staff was at the ready. "Your grace, welcome. A fire has been laid in the drawing room. Have you any particular requests for dinner?"

"No, I'll take pot luck. Where is the Infanta?" Boho asked.

"Her Imperial Highness is not presently at home."

Boho checked the watch set in the sleeve of his uniform. "Does she usually work this late?"

"Her Majesty often works until eight or even nine each night."

"I see. Has my wife been informed of my return?"

"Yes, sir." Like the gate guard the Hajin's long face remained expressionless.

"I believe I'll retire to our suite and clean up. I'll dine when Mercedes returns."

"Very good, sir."

Boho headed for their bedroom. As he went he glanced into various rooms, noting that they had the look of a place that was lived in. In the vid room there were pillows scattered on the floor in front of the entertainment center. Clearly Mercedes preferred lounging on the floor to watch shows or play games. In the drawing room a small table had been set up and another Hajin was laying out a second set of silverware. It made sense that Mercedes didn't eat in the large dining room, and it also implied that she dined alone. There was a flash of relief and pleasure at that realization. Boho had seen how her long-time aide Jaakon gazed at Mercedes. It seemed they had not become lovers. A good thing, or he might have to insist she find a new factotum.

Entering the bedroom Boho was startled to find a pair of intense blue eyes staring daggers at him from the bed. The lilac point Siamese cat slowly blinked, turned its head away, and washed a paw with all the disdain that only a feline could bring to bear.

"So she *does* have someone in her bed," Boho said. The cat yawned.

An apricot-colored peignoir had been tossed across the back of a settee. Boho picked it up and held it to his face. It was redolent with the scent of Mercedes and her favorite perfume. He felt a stirring in his groin. He rang for a servant and ordered that a tub be run. Life aboard ship didn't leave many opportunities for a good long soak.

After a bath and a cigar Boho strolled naked into the bedroom to find that his batBEM had arrived with his luggage and laid out an outfit appropriate for a late supper with one's spouse—pale gray slacks, soft shoes, silk shirt, and a smoking jacket. Boho found the nervous nature of the herbivorous Hajin irritating, so he had settled on an Isanjo. The neotenous eyes set in the piquant fur-covered faces were pleasing and he liked the quick intelligence and fast reflexes of the creatures. Ivoga also had a rogue's nature and had proved very useful to Boho. The alien did everything from keeping watch for returning husbands, to rifling through the private documents of officers and nobles—and most importantly rival gamblers.

The deft fingers, claws retracted, buttoned his shirt and held the jacket for him to slip into. Boho gave Ivoga a careless pat between the pricked ears and strolled back to the drawing room. It was eight-thirty. A footman entered with a tray of assorted cheeses, grapes, and crackers. He uncorked a bottle of red wine. Boho tested it, swirling the liquid through his mouth, and nodded his approval. Apparently the wine cellar hadn't suffered during his absence.

It was almost nine before he heard the click of heels on the marble floor of the entryway. Her voice, husky and musical, inquired how Fingell's day had been. There was an inaudible answer from the Hajin butler. The footsteps approached and Mercedes paused in the doorway and surveyed him.

"My dear." Boho gestured a greeting with his wine glass.

He studied her. It had been ten months since they'd last been together. He saw the weariness in the bags beneath her eyes, the set of her shoulders, the frown between her brows. He also didn't miss the way her expression hardened as she gazed at him. It was going to be one of *those* sessions. The fact he didn't stand forced her to cross to him. Her eyes flicked to the various servants who had appeared and were pulling out her chair, holding her napkin, entering with plates. She leaned down and gave him a kiss on the cheek. He turned so his lips were against her ear and whispered, "I see the niceties still must be observed before the staff."

"Don't make me rethink that," she whispered back. She took the chair that was being held for her by the new butler. Once she was seated, wine poured and plates delivered she motioned for them to be left alone.

He waited, but she didn't speak, just began to eat. With each bite and passing moment of silence Boho's irritation increased. He finally set aside his fork, mentally flipped through his possible conversational gambits. *You summoned me* was considered and rejected. He finally reached into the pocket of his jacket and pulled out the jeweler's case. With most women it would work. But this one?

He slid it across the table. Mercedes set aside her fork, dabbed at her lips with her napkin, and stared at the box. She finally pulled the silver ribbon and removed the top. The emeralds set in platinum glittered against the midnight velvet. "Very nice, but really not my color." Her tone was colorless.

Boho leaned back, dug his hands into his pockets. "You're going to bust my balls, aren't you?"

No answer. Instead a slim hand stretched out, took the wine bottle. Mercedes refilled her glass, took several slow deliberate sips, the long lashes lifted, and her eyes met his. He thought he saw a shadow of sadness in their brown depths.

"Captain Lord Eugene Montgomery has a wife. Seven children."

Boho grunted. "He's to be commended. Didn't know he had it in him."

A flash of anger crossed Mercedes' face. "The other four men on the promotions board all have families and children as well." Her fingers tightened on the stem of the wine glass. "I've ordered them back on active duty aboard an *explorador* along with the most egregiously unqualified of the officers that bought a promotion. They are being sent to Sector 470."

It was as if ice had replaced his spine. *Sector 470*. There was something in that distant sector that made ships and crews disappear. Worry over what lurked beyond had led to allowing and even encouraging women to join the military, despite the upheaval it was causing in society. Now the sector was carefully off limits until the crown needed to remove an… inconvenience. Assignment to 470 was a way for an emperor… or an infanta… to deal with a problem and leave no fingerprints. Boho shoved back his chair, stood, and walked to the fireplace. He studied the flames, tried to quiet his jumping pulse. Anxiety knotted his gut.

"And will I be aboard that ship of death?"

"Don't be absurd. You're my husband." He sagged with relief. *Saved, saved, saved!* Mercedes continued, "Your father is too highly placed, I need you to reassure the conservatives, and the press loves you."

And what about you? Boho thought, but he didn't allow the words to pass his lips. He feared the answer. He cleared his throat. His initial relief had passed, leaving behind the oily taste of guilt. Men were going to die because of his scheme. The thought of living with that knowledge, and how he had escaped the noose, was not something he contemplated with any pleasure. He searched for another angle. Another scheme. Another way. He turned back to face her and was shocked at the contempt he saw in her eyes.

He recovered and said, "This seems extreme, Mercedes. You couldn't just court-martial them?"

"The danger is too great that they would implicate *you*."

"So make it a soft landing. Suggest they retire. Losing a ship, even one of the older *exploradors*, is an expensive proposition. You could buy them off for far less."

"And allow them to blackmail the crown?" She shook her head in disgust. "You caused this, Boho. These deaths are on you."

"Oh, no, I'm not going to eat that sin, my dear. *You* gave the order. Or did you pass the buck to Daddy? And how far will this purge extend? A lot of families paid bribes," Boho said.

"They didn't realize *you* were one of the beneficiaries of their largesse. At least you were that careful. And I've kept this from Father. You can thank me for that too." She threw down her napkin. "I've lost my appetite. You can sleep in the blue room tonight." She left.

She had dismissed Tako, the Hajin batBEM who had been with her since her days at the academy, telling the alien she would handle her own evening ablutions, but she hadn't. Mercedes was still dressed, gazing out the window at the darkness of a rare moonless night on a planet with three of them. The expanse of the canopied bed yawned behind her but she was too agitated to sleep. Even the sybaritic Mist had abandoned the comfort of pillows and comforters. He had joined her, sitting on the windowsill, dilated blue eyes also staring out at the darkness. His purrs were a quiet rumble in the silent room, his fur soft and warm beneath her fingers as she slowly stroked him. Occasionally his head butted against her stomach. She wished there was someone to rub her shoulders, some shoulder where she could rest her head.

The guilt she had seen in Boho's eyes matched the gnawing sickness she had felt ever since the order had been given. Unlike her father she had put only the guilty aboard that ship. He had always been willing to sacrifice innocent crew to kill one man. It didn't help much to salve her guilt.

But the problem of Boho remained. Placing him on an

allowance had clearly backfired and led to this disaster. At least he hadn't used that whining excuse to try and justify what he'd done. Maybe if she'd explained that the recession had reduced tax revenue and that there was a new upstart political faction arguing that the royals were a parasitical institution he would have understood, but process and detail had always bored him. So she had kept silent and now the *republicanos* held two seats in parliament. It was negligible support but they were the first, and it might signal a shift in public attitude toward the crown and the FFH.

And lurking in the background was the ever-present and smoldering resentment of her father's first cousin and once his heir. As the years had passed and none of the Emperor's wives had borne sons, Musa del Campo, Duque Agua de Negra, became convinced the throne would be his. Then just before Mercedes' eighteenth birthday the Emperor had forced through parliament a change that would allow a woman to take the throne, assuming she attended and graduated from the High Ground and served her five years. Mercedes and two of her half-sisters had done that, which meant that three bodies now stood between Musa and the throne. Unfortunately, none of those three had children to secure the succession. If the Arango line was going to hold power one of the three qualified daughters had to get busy. God knew Mercedes had been trying to no avail. Beatrisa was a lost cause. She was still in the service and loving it. She was also a lesbian who had no desire to "whelp" as she put it. Carisa, the youngest of the Emperor's daughters, had wanted to stay in O-Trell. Mercedes suspected it was a way for her to get away from her smothering mother, the current empress, but the Emperor had refused and Carisa had been returned to the palace. Since Carisa was the only unmarried and acceptable daughter left, their father had been holding her as a trump card. Carisa would not be marrying for love. Their father would see that she married for advantage—his advantage. And as much as Mercedes loved Carisa she wasn't sure the girl had the right temperament for rule, the ability to make the hard calls. *Like sending men to die for a cover-up—*

Mercedes jerked away from that line of thought. Musa wasn't pleasant to contemplate, but he was better than that. Musa had become a bitter old man, which left the question—did the three sons share their father's ambition? The youngest del Campo son, Arturo, had been a classmate of Mercedes'. Arturo had done his five years, left O-Trell and entered government service. He had been a secretary to ambassadors, been posted on numerous League worlds, and had recently taken a seat in parliament, but in the Commons rather than the House of Lords. Arturo knew how to move the levers of political power. Mercedes could only conclude Arturo was being positioned by his father to further their ambitions.

Next up was the middle son, Bishop Jose del Campo. In Mercedes' opinion the true viper in the del Campo family. He had bedeviled her during her years of service, managing to be the chaplain on several ships where she had served. After her return to the capital, he had been assigned to serve at the cathedral in Hissilek. She had begun to dread Sundays since Jose's sermons had increasingly focused on the role of women, and how children glorified and blessed a woman, allowing her to find her true role and potential. The sermons dovetailed nicely with the disgusting "Baby Watch" that a tabloid news outlet had begun keeping after Mercedes concluded her five years of mandatory military service. At first they kept count by days, then weeks. Now they kept a running tally of all the years that Mercedes and Boho remained childless. And they never missed an opportunity to report the bastards.

Finally, there was the eldest son, Mihalis, who would presumably take the throne if his father died from an overdose of spleen, and if Mercedes, and her half-sisters, should fail to ascend to the throne. Mihalis had stayed in O-Trell, and for the past three years his father and his conservative allies had been agitating for Mihalis to be made admiral of the Gold fleet. Given Mihalis's status that could probably not be avoided, but it would also give the del Campos command over half the fleet, a worrisome prospect. Thus far that decision had been postponed by the expedient of keeping old Admiral Mustafa Kartirci in command, but reports indicated that it would come sooner than Mercedes or her father might have liked as Kartirci's health and mental acuity were declining. Bottom line, Musa had his tentacles in the church, the state, and the military. The only silver lining was that one of Mercedes' allies controlled one half of the fleet.

Of course that promotion carried its own problems and had probably added to Boho's sense of ill usage. He had wanted the promotion to admiral and command of the Blue fleet, but instead it had gone to Davin. Boho still thought of the other man as his wingman and court jester, not recognizing that Davin had changed, grown, matured. It wasn't that her father hadn't trusted Boho to command the Blue, it was his position as royal consort during those early years of their marriage that had denied him the position. Both she and Boho had traveled almost constantly, their schedules packed with official events—ribbon cuttings, hospital tours, ship christenings. The palace had thought to capitalize on Boho's charm and popularity. None of them had grasped the level of resentment and boredom it would engender. That miscalculation had led Boho to casinos, brothels, and mistresses, resulting in scandals, bastards, and debts. In an effort to get him off the front pages of every news site her father and the high command had given Boho a seven-ship squadron, and made him a vice admiral. What Mercedes now understood was that it hadn't been enough. Nor was he going to meekly accept the allowance. He had found a way to thumb his nose at both crown and wife, an act of rebellion that had now sent men to their deaths.

On her command. To save the honor and reputation of one man—

There was a knock on the door.

The blue room didn't have a canopy bed. Instead Boho, arms folded behind his head, gazed up at a ceiling that held an elaborate painting of Kalliope, her son Orpheus and her sister Terpsichore. As he studied the figures set against the blue vault he figured this room must have belonged to the Emperor's lover Gerhardt who had been a professional musician.

What would he have done if Mercedes had ordered him aboard that ship? Dropped to his knees and begged, threatened, run? Boho didn't think he would have had the nerve to salute and obey. Montgomery and the others would. Because they had no idea what was coming. Not that Boho did. No one did. All he knew was that they would not return.

He threw back the covers and got out of bed. The Sidone silk of his pajama bottoms was soft against his skin, so fine it caught a bit in the hair on his legs. Was it only politics and the avoidance of scandal that had saved him? Or was there still something left between them?

Sorrow and regret were not emotions with which he was very familiar. Boho shrugged into a dressing gown and padded down the halls to the master bedroom. He had a sudden memory of that wonderful first coupling they'd enjoyed on their wedding night. Back then he had been so sure of the path that lay before them. She would get pregnant, he would serve with distinction, the old man would die, and they would jointly rule, content and adored. But here they were.

He tapped on the door. She opened it. He took in her haunted eyes, the lines between her brows. "Mercedes, I'm sorry."

Later as she lay in his arms she said quietly, "What happened to us?"

There were a host of reasons and a multitude of answers. Any of them would shatter the moment and he shied away from the discussion. "I don't know, love."

"Is it fixable?"

He didn't know the answer to that either.

7

ONCE A SOLDIER, ALWAYS A SOLDIER

A few hours later, Tracy, arms folded behind his head, laid in bed staring at the ceiling and listening to Lisbet's gentle snoring. It was adorable. Her butt, warm and soft, was pressed against his hip. He rolled onto his side and spooned her, let his hand snake around to caress her breasts, lightly pinching her nipples. She woke, stretched, and shimmied around to face him. Gave him a kiss.

"Greedy."

"You have to admit it's much better than an alarm," Tracy said. "Lizzie, I've been thinking—"

"Uh oh." She pulled free, sat up, and twisted her braids into a bun. "Sounds like we're going to have a serious conversation."

"Don't joke. I am serious."

"All right."

"I've been thinking I haven't been fair to you. I never asked if you wanted something more. More permanent, I mean. This was convenient for me so I just kept things as they are. Maybe we should change that. It would be nice to have someone to… come home to."

She gazed at him for a long moment then leaned in and kissed him softly on the lips. "You're a lovely person, you know that? But no, I don't want anything more permanent." An odd mélange of emotions went through him. Relief, a bit of pique, and confusion. She read his face and smiled. "You want to know why."

"Yeah. I do."

"I've been with a lot of men. Not telling you anything you don't know, but you learn to read them. The young ones are easy. Raging hormones, bravado, and anxiety. It's the older men where you start to read their… souls, I guess. Some are lonely even if they're married. Others need a place where they don't have to be competent and in charge. Others are the widowers looking for a place where they can just talk to someone, get their temples rubbed, someone to squeeze hot water down their back."

"So where do I fit into this?"

"Getting to it. Finally there are the men who are just satisfying a normal physical drive, but while they're getting their nuts off they aren't seeing you and they aren't truly in the moment. There is something just beyond their reach that still consumes them. Sometimes it's another woman they're picturing in their arms, another face superimposed over yours. Sometimes it's more elusive than that. It's like they're always hearing a distant call, clutching for a dream that is just out of reach."

Tracy felt ashamed. "I'm sorry if I made you feel that way."

She pushed back his hair where it had flopped onto his forehead. "It's all right." Her voice was gentle.

"So which category do I fall into?"

"Both. So what is that dream? And who was the woman?"

He stared down at the sheet, began to pleat it between his fingers. "The dream was a chimera… no, worse than that, it was a fucking delusion. And the woman…" He gave a cough to clear the sudden obstruction in his throat. "She was someone I could never have." He fell silent, stunned at how badly the wound had been reopened just from seeing Cullen again. Tracy hated his grief so he reached for anger. "And she betrayed me, and in a way that cost me everything. I haven't seen my dad in twelve years. Once I changed my identity and bought the ship I couldn't go home. I occasionally get a letter to him—old school, written on dead tree—but only if someone I trust is heading to Hissilek. If the League found out they'd take everything I've got. I can't do that to my crew."

"You have the alias. Make a few alterations to your looks and go."

He shook his head. "I can't take the risk. They may still be watching."

"You know that sounds deeply paranoid," she said.

The hint of laughter in her voice helped to break the grip of anger and regret. He gave a chuckle. "Not to mention arrogant," Tracy said. He put an arm around her shoulder and pulled her close. Her hair tickled his chin. The smell of her shampoo and conditioner warred with the smell of sex. It was a pleasant mix.

"You didn't tell me about the dream."

He slapped her gently on one rounded buttock. "To spend an afternoon in bed with a sexy, beautiful woman and then take her to dinner. And speaking of... we should shower and get dressed if we want to keep our reservation."

"Nice dodge. Okay, I'll let you get away with it."

An hour later, showered and dressed, they arrived at Graze. The tables were filled, conversations bounced off the steel and concrete surfaces. Graze was one of those restaurants that equated noisy with chic. Tracy pulled out the chair for Lisbet and noted there weren't a lot of women present. The San Pedro *cosmódromo* wasn't a place to settle. It was a place to work, to pass through. He wondered how many of the women were wives and how many fell into Lisbet's category. Apart from her exotically colored hair Lisbet looked like a well-to-do middle-class woman of middle years. Dress, shawl arranged gracefully at her shoulders, sensible heels. He donned one of the suits he wore when he dealt with banks or officials. It looked handmade because it was. He had tailored it himself and it matched any bespoke suit from any upscale tailor. Alexander had taught his son well.

Their table was against the back wall. Next to them was a couple with whom Tracy was peripherally acquainted. Jibran Boudin and his partner Abe Guttermann worked for a large natural resource company. They scouted systems for Goldilocks planets or mining potential, focusing only on the rarer elements like lithium and helium. When they found something, they staked a claim in the name of Interstellar Energy & Assets. They were older than Tracy, bluff and cheerful, and seemed to hear every rumor before anyone else.

"Randall, have you heard? There are goodies on the way." Guttermann tapped a fat forefinger against the side of his nose. A fringe of silver hair circled his skull just above his ears, a bright contrast to his dark skin, giving him the look of a jolly monk with a tipsy halo.

"Give him a little context, Abe," Jibran chided. Jibran was as fat as Abe. A cautious man in his business dealings, less so in his personal life, whether it ran to food or sex. Tracy knew of three wives in disparate parts of the League. Or at least they thought they were wives. Tracy had a feeling the cagey Jibran wouldn't have put anything in writing that could indict him.

"Oh, sorry. Word is that Edward Cornell captured three O-Trell ships. Two frigates and a scout." Guttermann breathed the corsair leader's name with the awe one usually reserved for the Holy Trinity.

The news was shocking enough that it yanked an overloud reaction out of Tracy. "What?"

"Exactly. Our little ship isn't likely to be of much interest, but anybody who carries expensive cargo, well…" Jibran gave an expressive shrug. "Just wanted to give you a heads-up. If Cornell puts those babies in his fleet… commercial shipping better look the hell out."

"Those ships are complex and require a lot of crew," Tracy said. "I doubt they could run even one of the frigates, and even the *explorador* would be difficult since they upped the crew complement to five hundred. Assuming it's one of the newer ships. Is it a new ship?"

"Don't know," Jibran said.

"Which is why they're going to chop them," Abe said pointedly to his partner. It had the feeling of an ongoing argument. "We get one of those O-Trell scanners for the *Bonaventure* and we're going to *clean up*."

Jibran shook his head. "Why do you keep saying that when there is no evidence? It's been weeks. We would have started to see components hit the market by now if they were going to chop them."

Abe's chin thrust out. "They always chop."

"When they capture liners and freighters. This is the first time they've grabbed military ships. Cornell might have *plans*."

"You're an idiot."

The couple descended into squabbling. Tracy lost the thread as he contemplated state-of-the-art military ships in the hands of pirates. It was a terrifying prospect. But if the corsairs couldn't run them and weren't chopping them, what the hell *were* they doing with them? He looked up to find Lisbet staring at him. There was a hollow feeling in the pit of his stomach. Tracy picked up his fork and began walking it between his fingers.

Lisbet reached out and pressed her index finger between his brows. "Hello. You've gone far away."

"Sorry. This is... disquieting news."

She gathered his hands in hers. "I think you won't be spending a few days with me," she said softly.

He pressed a kiss onto her palm. "Forgive me?"

"Of course. You can take the man out of the military, but you can't take the military out of the man."

* * *

"So let me see if I understand this." Baca was speaking very slowly. After three years of having the young man aboard Tracy knew what would happen. The words would come faster and faster and he would get louder and louder. "You want us to go *looking* for the most successful and ruthless *corsario* in League space, instead of avoiding him like the fucking plague!" Luis added a new quirk to his usual rant: After he finished speaking he leaped to his feet and waved his arms over his head.

Jahan imitated the flailing arms. "And what is this? Are you invoking the Holy Spirit? About to speak in tongues?"

"I'm upset," the young human huffed.

"We got that," Graarack said dryly.

Baca gave the aliens an exasperated look, and turned back to Tracy. His outthrust jaw and knotted brows told the tale. "Answer the damn question, Captain."

"Yes."

"That's it?"

"Yes."

"I am going to fucking *explode*!" Luis stormed over to the coffee maker and drew himself a mug.

They were all gathered in the galley. The *Selkie* was in Fold so there wasn't a reason to have anyone stationed on the bridge. There was the faint odor of red curry from last night's dinner, the astringent scent of Jax's wading pool, the faint smell of sweet rot from the meat that fed Graarack. It should have been nauseating. The fact that it wasn't was the clearest indication that they were crew, family.

"To amplify on Luis' concerns, what exactly do you think we can do? You're not proposing we rescue the O-Trell soldiers all by our little selves?" Jahan asked.

"Especially since the fucking O-Trell stole our shit," Baca called. He blew loudly across the surface of his coffee.

Tracy answered Jahan first. "No, of course not." He looked at Luis. "And that wasn't all of O-Trell, it was one guy."

"So if we're not staging a rescue what are we doing?" Dalea asked.

"We get a lead on the *corsarios'* whereabouts and we tell O-Trell or SEGU or whoever will listen to us," Tracy said.

"This is foolishness," Jahan said. "We often carry contraband. We trade with Hidden Worlds, which can earn us a prison sentence—"

"Not to mention the terrible effects on the Hidden Worlds if the League should learn of their location from us," Dalea said. Her tone was disapproving.

"We can't risk this. And you can't ask it of us," Jahan concluded. Her long tail was weaving an agitated pattern in the air behind her head.

Tracy stared down at the tabletop. Drew his finger through a drop of spilled beer. He took a pull from his lager glass, wiped foam off his lip, and reflected that this was the trouble with crew as co-owners. He couldn't just order them.

Jax let out a long trill that segued into words. "The crown and the families of the officers ransom captured soldiers. There is no reason for us to be involved."

Tracy made one last attempt. "Normally I'd agree with you, but this situation isn't normal. Never before have they captured military vessels. And nothing is hitting the markets so the *corsarios* aren't chopping the ships. So what are they doing with them?"

"You're not suggesting they're selling them," Jax said. "No one could afford to buy a frigate, much less two."

"Which might mean they intend to use them," Graarack said.

"Which is why we need to stay the hell away from them," Luis said, thus bringing them full circle.

They began to break up, moving out of the galley. Jahan jumped onto the table and peered into Tracy's face. The tip of her tail brushed his cheek. "Thank God we learned your full background before you tried to sell us on this plan. If you hadn't we'd have all decided you had lost your ever-loving mind. I guess once an O-Trell officer always an O-Trell officer."

"Everybody keeps saying that, but it's not true. They fucked me over. I'm done with them."

"You keep telling yourself that."

Tracy retreated to his cabin. He sat on the edge of the narrow bunk, hands clasped between his knees, and tried to analyze why he felt this need to get involved? Why did he still have such conflicted feelings about the *Orden de la Estrella*? He had fought bitterly to avoid going to the High Ground. He was damned if he'd be a soldier. It had taken an act of cruelty on the part of his father to get him to go. An act that had almost shattered their relationship, until Tracy realized how much his father had actually sacrificed to give his son the opportunity to rise above a life of drudgery in a tailor shop in a rundown neighborhood.

Once he reached the academy, Tracy discovered he was good at it and despite the insults he'd endured from his FFH crew mates he had loved ships and the grandeur of the cosmos. And always lingering at the back of his mind were the stories of *intitulados* who had won acclaim and noble titles through acts of military genius. Tracy himself had won one of the highest honors O-Trell offered and done it in his first year at the High Ground. Now all those years later he felt the perfect fool. If he'd won a title he *might* have been accepted by the FFH, but Mercedes was always going to be beyond his reach.

He forced his thoughts away from pointless memories. When the corsairs captured passengers and crew, ransoms were paid. He imagined that Cornell and his merry band were confidently expecting the same outcome, but this was military personnel and warships and they didn't know the lengths to which the Emperor and his daughter would go. From personal and very painful experience Tracy knew exactly how far they would go. He could see an outcome where both captured crew and *corsarios* found themselves dead. Was that the end result he was trying to avoid, or was it just that, deep inside, the kernel of the O-Trell officer remained? A disgraced officer who wanted to prove he wasn't a disgrace?

He gave his head an angry shake. No, while he was concerned for the fate of the captured crews, the truth was he had been fantasizing about coming before Mercedes with information that would make him the hero.

"Let it go," he whispered to the room. "For God's sake let it go."

8

WE MAY BE CALLED UPON TO SACRIFICE

The throne room was her least favorite place to hold meetings, but in this case it had seemed prudent. She needed to overawe and possibly intimidate. It was a cavernous space, the high glass barrel roof supported by massive carved pillars, and all the glass and marble made sounds harsh and bright. Seven broad steps led up to the imperial throne with its sunburst design on the top. One step down and off to the right was Mercedes' throne. The back formed a five-pointed star. One step below her and to the Emperor's left was the smaller throne for the Empress. Its back was formed to look like a bouquet of lilies. The wall behind the steps and thrones was covered with an enormous and elaborate Sidone tapestry of stars, comets, and galaxies surrounding the imperial crown.

Mercedes waited in the small antechamber behind the tapestry and used the surveillance cameras to study the people assembled at the foot of the dais. Salted among the pacing nobility were *intitulados* who stayed very still at the fringes of the crowd. Mercedes had to admire whichever member of the FFH had thought to include parents whose children were the ordinary *hombres,* who carried no titles and lacked both the money and the status to aid them. They would provide sad stories for the press, and put more pressure on the crown.

She glanced over at her chief security officer. "Well, Ian, do you think they'll riot?"

He sucked at his teeth, scratched his chin. "I expect the *intitulados* to behave, but I put no bets on the rest."

"You have such a low opinion of our class," she murmured. She forced herself to chuckle.

"Long experience. We're an entitled bunch of gits," he said.

"Well, best get this over with. Waiting isn't going to make it go any better," Mercedes said.

Rogers walked away to where Robrecht, the imperial seneschal, waited and tapped him on the shoulder. Nods were exchanged and Robrecht stepped out from behind the tapestry. Mercedes found herself mouthing the words as he called in sonorous tones, "Her Serene Highness Rear Admiral Princess Mercedes Adalina Saturnina Inez de Arango, the Infanta."

If the inclusion of her military rank into her title hadn't been enough of a hint, the message was clearly received when she emerged wearing her dress uniform. That caused some mutters among the waiting members of the FFH. The less well-born citizens remained mute, scarcely daring to raise their eyes. She wanted to stand, but knew that might display her nerves. Instead she forced herself to sink down onto the embroidered pillow that cushioned the hard metal and stone of her throne.

"I understand you have a petition for us," she said.
A man stepped forward. Mercedes had studied the dossiers on everyone who had been cleared by palace security. This was not Commander Singh's adopted father. Instead it was Conde Gustaf Yuen. His son, Cristobal, had been in command of the second frigate. SEGU investigations had indicated that Cristobal hadn't needed a boost from the promotions board to attain the rank of captain. It had just been his misfortune to have to serve under the inexperienced Singh.

Yuen bowed. "Your Majesty, I have been asked to speak on behalf of the families." Mercedes hated these statements of the obvious. She fought back the desire to respond and merely nodded. "Highness, an alarmingly long time has passed since the first demand arrived from the *corsarios*. Recently the demands have become more frequent and..." He gave a delicate cough. "Threatening. We—" he gestured at the waiting parents "—fear that the next messages we receive will carry more tangible evidence of the *corsarios'* waning patience. We sought this meeting so we might, respectfully, inquire as to when the requested monies will be sent."

Mercedes had to admire the word choice *requested monies* rather than ransom. This was a man who understood that words had power. "We share these concerns, Conde, but this situation requires a different solution. These are not innocent civilians—these are officers and *hombres* in the *Orden de la Estrella*. This is, bluntly, an act of war and must be treated as such. Therefore it is the decision of the crown that no ransom will be paid."

There was a moan of despair from several of the women.

A growing rumble from the men. "So our sons suffer because they serve?" one of the noblemen yelled.

"All of us who wear the uniform understand we may be called upon to sacrifice."

"As you sit safe and secure in the imperial palace," another man drawled.

Mercedes stood. "In two days I will be boarding the dreadnaught *San Medel y Celedon*, taking command of a strike force and leading an expedition against the *corsarios*." She waited for the reactions to die down then held up her hand. "Believe me when I say the crown understands the gravity of this situation, and shares your worry. Which is why we are going to get them back."

"You are running a grave risk with the lives of our children," Yuen said. "Once the brigands know you are coming what is to stop them from killing the hostages?"

A new voice intruded, a woman's. Her words were insouciant. "Do credit them with *some* intelligence. Live hostages are leverage. Dead hostages… well, bodies are so messy to clean up."

Equal parts amusement, joy, and irritation washed through Mercedes as she met the quizzical gaze of Commander Lady Cipriana Delacroix whose married name was… Mercedes came up blank. The wedding had taken place off Ouranos. She had sent a gift. She also hadn't seen Cipri in almost five years. Not since Cipriana had been given command of an *Estrella Avanzada* that was far out on the edges of League space and a solid three weeks' journey even in Fold.

Mercedes recovered herself. "Not to mention it earns them only death," Mercedes added. "Commander, your arrival is welcomed if unexpected. To what do we owe—?"

"One of my people back at the star port has a son aboard one of the captured ships. They petitioned for my help."

What wasn't said spoke volumes. Mercedes and Cipriana exchanged a long glance. If this person was FFH they would have been present. Which meant it was someone vital to the running of the station. Another noble pulled Mercedes' attention away from Cipriana.

"Assuming you find the bastards, isn't there a chance the prisoners will be hurt during the attack?"

"I refer you back to my earlier comment regarding risk and the assumption thereof by military personnel. I assume you all have the good sense not to mention our plans beyond the confines of these walls. If word of this reaches the press then the odds of success will diminish. Now if you will excuse me, I have a rescue to arrange." As she walked past Rogers she whispered, "Bring Lady Cipriana to my office."

They fell into each other's arms once the office door closed behind Jaakon.

"Oh God, it's so good to see you!"

"You look frightful."

Mercedes laughed. "I'm so glad to see you haven't changed."

Cipriana lifted a strand of Mercedes' hair that contained

a large streak of gray. "Was there a tragedy on Ouranos that killed all the hairdressers?"

"Nobody cares how I look," Mercedes said.

"Evidently that goes for you too."

Mercedes gestured to the chairs that were arranged by the fireplace. Servants had laid down a fire and it was snapping happily, throwing shadows on the walls. "So who is this person who has the power to send an O-Trell star base commander back to the capital?"

"The head of the machinists and dock workers union. He's demanding an answer about his kid. Repairs and refueling have slowed to a crawl. Next up on the agenda—a complete work stoppage. He knew we were school chums so he's got my tits in a wringer."

"Unpleasant."

"To put it mildly, and I'd like not to have the high command thinking that a woman in charge of a star base is a mistake, even if it's just a safe and dull assignment in which to bury a problem." Mercedes' questioning look made Cipriana chuckle. "You're adorable. Surely you don't think I got this posting as a hat tip to my incredible skills. I just hung on long enough to get promoted into irrelevance."

"Then why did you stay in after…" Mercedes couldn't bring herself to say the word. Cipriana wasn't as squeamish.

"After I got raped? Because I was damaged goods. How could I come home and have Daddy find me an appropriate husband and make babies for him?"

"That doesn't make any sense. You were having sex from sixteen on."

"*My* choice. What Wessen did to me made me realize that we women have no power, no agency. I wanted to be sure I was never that vulnerable again. So I stayed in and just kept getting promoted until I plateaued."

"But you did marry."

"Had to. I didn't need the whispers that I was unnatural." She noted Mercedes wince. "I see you're getting the treatment all powerful women get, from Joan of Arc to Elizabeth the first, to Hillary Clinton. But back on me: I married James, my dreamy professor who is happy to have an extended sabbatical while he writes his book on the philosophical underpinnings of fantasy from Malory, T.H. White, Tolkien, and Martin to Haditha and some Sidone whose name I can't pronounce. Between my salary and the trust Daddy settled on us we have a comfortable life and I'll retire a captain with a decent pension. Would have been nice to get that bump to rear admiral, but that will never happen."

"I could make sure it does," Mercedes said.

Cipriana reared back in her chair. "And be accused of taking advantage of our relationship?" She grinned. Her teeth were bright white against her ebony skin. "I would be delighted."

"I'll handle it as soon as I'm back. Which fleet's in charge of your sector?"

"The Gold, so you shouldn't have any trouble winding old Kartirci around your finger."

"It's so good to see you."

"And you." They leaned forward and embraced again.

"When are you heading back?" Mercedes asked.

"Day after tomorrow. I'll make the obligatory call on the paterfamilias and let mama cry over me." She stood. "You be careful, Mer."

"The problem is going to be finding them. I'm not worried about killing them once we do. That's the easy part."

"The consort, ma'am." Jaakon smooth and elegant as always. Managing to convey with three words both deference and admiration when Mercedes suspected he felt neither. Boho strode past her secretary as if he were part of the furniture.

She ignored him and instead addressed her secretary. "Thank you, Jaakon. Do you have those manifests for me?"

"Momentarily, Highness."

She waved him out and looked up into Boho's face. He was leaning across the desk, using his height to loom over her. "So imagine my surprise when I went looking for my wife this morning only to discover her batBEM packing for her. I thought perhaps a dedication or a funeral, but then I noticed no dresses, no jewelry, no make-up—just uniforms. When were you planning on telling me?"

"Tonight." Mercedes pinched the bridge of her nose.

"That damn Hajin wouldn't tell me a goddamn thing. What are you doing? What is this mission?"

"I'm going after the *corsarios*."

The slap of his palms on the desktop was like a pistol shot. "And it never occurred to you that perhaps *I* ought to lead that effort."

Anger blazed through her; she leaped to her feet, rested

her hands on the desk, and leaned in on him. "Since we're in this situation because of *you,* no, I did not consider it. Not for one moment. You want to take a *bow* after this? Be the big hero? You caused this. You will stay here and do my job, which is tedious and boring and necessary because the work of actually governing isn't glamorous or exciting, but it has to be done and maybe for once you could help me instead of just making my life harder!"

She was panting as if the violence of her feelings had stopped her lungs. There was a flash of hurt in those green eyes, but it was momentary. "Well, I see our detente didn't last long," he said.

"And why would you think what happens in the bedroom has any bearing?"

"Because that's how a normal woman would react," he shot back.

It hurt. Twenty-three years of marriage and she had never known that passion that poets celebrated. Her experience between the sheets had never matched what was described in the romance novels she had read as a girl. Truth was she sometimes dreaded her and Boho's coupling. It had been duty interspersed with the occasional flash of pleasure. Given Beatrisa's sexual preference Mercedes sometimes worried that perhaps she too had those tendencies. While homosexuality was accepted in League society so long as the males donated sperm and women had babies, it would not do for the heir to the throne. Even her great-great-grandfather had married and sired six children while keeping his male lover in the small palace she now inhabited.

"I'm not like your little chippies—"

"Well that's clearly evident—"

"—who can be lulled by your gifts and caresses."

He took a turn around the office. The clenching and unclenching of his hands betrayed the internal struggle, but when he returned to her the anger had been smoothed from his face and he had his ingratiating expression that made him seem younger than his forty-four years.

"You're right, *cariño*, I made some bad decisions. I couldn't have foreseen the outcome, but now that it's happened let me clean up the mess that I may have inadvertently caused. Let me go. Make it up to you."

For an instant she wavered. He was popular, not only with the citizens of the League but with the military. *Which is why you shouldn't.* She had been the workhorse, the drudge toiling in an office. He had been the dashing consort, duque and flag captain paying calls on planetary governors when his squadron stopped for supplies. Being in the news and the public eye.

"No." She walked to the door and opened it. "Rely on Jaakon, he knows everything and is more organized than any computer."

The anger was back. He paused in the doorway. Looked from her to the secretary and back again. "I would prefer to bring in my own person. Someone loyal to me who isn't lusting after my wife."

The blood drained from Jaakon's face leaving him almost gray. Boho had an uncanny ability to stab at an opponent's weakest point. She and Jaakon had carefully ignored what Boho had laid bare.

"Given the behavior of your previous confederates forgive me if I declare that to be a non-starter. I want somebody in this job whom I can trust."

"*Gracias,* Mercedes. I guess that tells me what you think of *me.*"

"You know that isn't how I meant it!" she said and they both knew it was a lie.

"Fine, keep your little spy in place. I'm sure he'll dutifully report any transgression I might commit."

Boho stormed from the office. *So much for fixing the situation,* Mercedes thought. Jaakon carefully straightened every object on his desk while never lifting his eyes.

"I'm sorry," they both said at the same time.

"Please, Highness, you first."

"I apologize for my husband. That accusation was uncalled for."

Jaakon ducked his head. "I'm sorry if my behavior has ever given cause for you or anyone to think—"

"No one does," she said quickly. She returned to her office, shut the door, and leaned against it. *And now I know* everyone *does. It really is best if I go away. Give them all something else to think and gossip about.*

When Mercedes was a child only one front pew was reserved for the royal family. Now they had two to accommodate the spouses of the various daughters and their numerous offspring. When they were all assembled, generally at Christmas, they could damn near mount a platoon. Not that they were all present all the time. With most of the sisters now married they visited the capital rarely, instead residing on various planets with their noble husbands. Only Estella, Carisa, and Tanis still lived in Hissilek.

The thought of Tanis had Mercedes glancing across the nave to where her half-sister sat among her fellow nuns in the *Celestial Novias de Cristo*. The order was dedicated to the bearing of children sired by priests. It was all in furtherance of the goal of the church's dedication to the expansion of humankind to all of God's manifold worlds. Tanis had proved to be a veritable bunny. In the past fourteen years she had borne eight children. Six of them had been fathered by Jose del Campo. Mercedes had a feeling Tanis's loyalty no longer aligned with the Arangos. The coif and wimple suited Tanis. There was a purity to the way they framed her face. At thirty-eight and after multiple pregnancies her body had thickened, but her face held a look of exultation and adoration as she gazed at the altar where Jose was conducting the consecration of the Host. Mercedes didn't think that passion was focused on the Christ figure. As if sensing her scrutiny Tanis turned to look at Mercedes and her expression of exultation morphed into one that seemed perilously close to gloating. Tanis had always been one of those children who snooped and pried, ferreting out secrets about her sisters, servants, etc. She then hoarded them to use later as weapons. Apparently, she hadn't outgrown the habit. Mercedes wondered what Tanis thought she knew? Or was it just enjoyment that she could measure her fecundity against Mercedes' barrenness?

Embarrassed by her wandering thoughts, Mercedes forced her attention back to the altar, the suffering bronze figure on the cross. The light through the stained glass of the rose window threw rainbow shards across the white marble, dappled the altar cloth and the robes of Jose and the young acolytes assisting him. The perfect acoustics of the soaring vaults in the ceiling caught every sonorous intonation as Latin rolled from Jose's lips. The piping responses from the young boys were a sweet counterpoint to his mellifluous baritone.

After the consecration the family moved to the altar to receive communion. The del Campos seated directly behind them didn't wait. Musa unlimbered his cane and pushed through the throng of Arangos. Arturo was at his father's side, offering support. Musa was a few years older than Mercedes' father, and a stroke had affected the left side of his body so he now moved with a lurching gait. Her father and Constanza were off world on vacation, which meant Mercedes should have taken precedence, but she worried that demanding her primacy over a crippled man would do little for her consequence or her reputation, so she allowed Musa and Arturo to go ahead. She enjoyed the momentary flash of pleasure at the thought that no matter how much his children might plot, it was unlikely Musa would live long enough to take the throne. She immediately felt contrite at having such an unworthy thought in God's house. At the altar rail she dropped to her knees and gave a quick prayer for forgiveness. Jose with his attendant acolytes reached her and laid the Host on her tongue. It began to dissolve, as fleeting as this show of family unity that had her kneeling at Musa's side.

Communion continued, worshippers filing past the royal pew while security kept careful watch. Mercedes mentally ran through the reports Kemel had sent. There seemed to be numbers of false trails to the *corsarios*. She juggled personnel numbers, trying to weigh how many *fusileros* versus pilots. If the *corsarios* had a stronghold then marines would be the most use. But if they were using their ships as a flotilla and living like gypsies, then pilots and *Infiernos* would be the better choice. After exhausting analysis of the recording that had been sent, the bright boys at SEGU thought it was a planet-based location, but they weren't one hundred percent certain.

She glanced over at Boho. His eyes were open, but she knew he was actually dozing. Everyone who had made it to graduation from the High Ground soon learned how to sleep standing up and sleep when you looked awake. She envied him. She would love to have turned off her brain, but so much was riding on this mission. The lives of the men and few women in the hands of criminals. The lives of her own troops she would spend if the corsairs decided to fight. Her reputation if she failed.

Jose ascended to the pulpit for his sermon. He arranged his tap-pad, looked across the congregation. He was easily the most handsome of the del Campo sons. Nearly fifty, he had perfectly frosted temples and just enough gray threaded through the dark hair to give him that silver fox look. He had also kept a trim figure. He raised his right hand, the large amethyst in his ring setting a beautiful counterpoint to his coffee-colored skin.

"Before I begin today's lesson I would like to take a moment to offer a prayer for the safe return of our men and, unfortunately, the eight women currently in the hands of criminals."

A reaction ran through the congregation for, of course, the information about the captured crews had been strictly interdicted. Now a prince of the church and a member of the royal family had exposed classified information and, Mercedes reflected, not a damn thing could be done about it. It got worse.

"Heavenly Father, we pray that you stretch out your protective hand over the brave men who preserve our League and our fragile human presence among the stars. Protect the women who have fallen into the hands of barbarians. Guide their rescuers as they seek to free them from bondage, and may you grant to our noble consort the support to prevail in this urgent mission."

The murmurs from the crowd had brought Boho out of his doze. Mercedes watched emotions cascade across his face. Delight, bitter satisfaction, forced concern when he turned to look at her.

"Oh, dear," he said.

Mercedes fought back the urge to slap him. Good manners dictated that she remain quiet and allow the palace press office to correct the record, but as someone had once said, *A lie can travel halfway across the galaxy before the truth can get its boots on*. She was tired. She was angry. She was nervous about the coming mission. She stood and stepped into the aisle.

"Bishop del Campo, I fear someone has misled you. I will be leading the mission. And your prayers would be most welcome." *Since you just told the bastards that we're coming, you son-of-a-bitch, and put in jeopardy the lives of our people.*

She nodded to him, turned, and walked toward the massive bronze doors. Her security detail fell in with her, and Rogers, walking at her side, muttered from the side of his mouth. "Well, that's torn it."

"Get Kemel. I want to know who leaked this."

"And then?"

"We deal with them."

"And what if it's the consort?"

"You are out of line, Captain."

"Apologies, Majesty."

How dare you voice what I fear?

9

SUGAR AND SHAME

"That was foolish, Mercedes." It was rare for Kemel to ever use her given name. He was scrupulous in observing the niceties. It indicated the level of his alarm. "The citizens won't understand the significance of your little public spat, but the FFH reads it clearly. It is now even more imperative that you succeed."

The privacy shutters were down. Both rings were set to dampen any eavesdropping and Jaakon had enabled the office security measures as well. Mercedes sank down into one of the high-backed armchairs that faced her desk. Her stomach felt wobbly and a headache threatened.

"Has Papa been told?"

"Not by me, but you may be sure that the word has reached him… from both your supporters and—"

"Do I have any?" she interrupted. The moment the words left her lips she regretted them. She hoped the old intelligence chief would take them as gallows humor. He didn't.

"No whining, Highness. Yes, though they are outnumbered by your detractors, but I would like to think that while they might have the numbers we hold the advantage in brains and cunning." The barest smile touched his withered lips.

"Putting aside my lack of control, how did he find out? Musa hasn't gotten security briefings since I completed my first shipboard tour."

The security chief shrugged. "Obviously one of the parents talked."

"I don't know how I could have made it any clearer. They had been told this in confidence. This was classified. I wonder which one it was?"

"I could find out who, but I would advise against it. Being seen as going after a worried and grieving parent would be a terrible look for the crown. Solving the situation is a better solution."

"On that front... do you have anything for me?"

"Nothing that I would call firm."

"I can't just flit around the League with this massive strike force. We'll look like a ponderous dinosaur bedeviled by gnats. And the gnats are winning."

"Sometimes a show of force can jar things loose."

The idea of being a jackboot didn't particularly appeal. She jumped up. "Drink?"

"Please. By the way, we've offered a staggering amount of money for any information. No takers."

"I presume that's not all you're doing," she said as she crossed to the bar and poured them both a brandy.

"By no means. We are combing through meta-data to see if we can locate the base using energy signatures, purchasing habits, et cetera." She offered the glass. "Thank you." He took a sip. "But it's like looking for a needle among thousands of stars. Any person can stake a claim on an asteroid and try to eke out a living."

"And in some cases not bother to register the claim at all," Mercedes said. "Just move onto some rock because they don't like the League, want to get away from a nagging wife—"

"Or are in general just a misanthrope," Kemel said with a chuckle.

"So, do I go or wait until you have something solid?" she asked.

Kemel took another sip. "Go. You can react more quickly if you're already in command of the force and on patrol."

Mercedes drank some of her brandy, taking comfort in the warmth it brought. "Their demands are becoming very threatening. What if they actually follow through? Start killing hostages?"

"They probably will. The only comfort is they are probably smart enough not to kill any of the women."

"There are other threats to a woman short of death that can be almost as devastating," Mercedes said.

"True that." His mouth worked for a moment.

"Go ahead, you can say it."

"Forgive me, Highness. I'm an old man. Change doesn't come easy for us. I'm not... fond of the idea that my granddaughters will have to serve. It represents such a change in societal norms, and for an intelligence officer profound change is rarely a good thing."

"I understand." She returned to the bar and refilled her

glass, gestured at Kemel. He nodded. "Selfishly I embraced the idea when Rohan proposed it all those years ago. I needed other women around me as a buffer." She walked back to him and tipped more brandy into his glass. "So I wasn't a unicorn." The old man looked confused. "Meaning one of a kind. If I was the only woman in the service then my father's opponents could rightly say that I wasn't really qualified."

"There are very few noble ladies," Kemel said. "Mostly *intitulados* serve."

"Which actually helps me because like *hombres* they really are doing the hard tasks, the scut work. If they can hold their own in those jobs then it's harder to say women aren't qualified and competent."

"Yes, and they can also die just like a man and that will not go over well." He drained the last of his brandy and stood. "Is there anything you wish me to do while you are off world?"

"Yes." She took a breath. Made herself say it. "Keep an eye on Boho."

10

THE TASTE OF SHAME

Tracy shifted, trying to find a more comfortable position in the taxi. He felt like a prisoner inside his own skin: Kronos was a large world, so Tracy felt like he was carrying an additional forty pounds. He supposed the residents got used to the extra weight but it made him feel lethargic. The saliva packets had also begun to chafe the inside of his cheeks. He was glad this was the last major world they would be visiting for an extended period of time.

Outside the windows of the taxi skyscrapers reached like glass and steel talons looking to scratch the sky. Above and below them various flight lanes were filled with hundreds of flitters. Olympus, the capital city of the planet, was the League's economic hub. Brokerage firms, large banks, and major corporations were located here. This time Tracy was on his own. There was too much security at a bank and the more people you added the more chance there was that someone would make a mistake.

The driver took them down rather too quickly and Tracy's stomach seemed to climb into his throat. The door irised open. He paid the driver, unlimbered his cane, and climbed out. The steel and glass doors loomed over him. "First Stellar Bank & Trust" was etched into the metal. Inside, a wall of dark glass threw back his reflection. The discreet pinstripe blue suit he wore was as good as anything draping the bodies of the bankers who moved through the space.

His heels and the cane rapped out a syncopated rhythm on the marble floors and echoed back from the soaring vaults of the ceiling. There was a heavy human guard presence, which Tracy thought was probably more of a display of wealth and power than out of any real necessity. Tracy took the lift to the third-floor offices. A perfectly groomed male receptionist looked up, evaluated Tracy's clothing, and assumed an obsequious expression. Tracy keyed his ScoopRing, sending over his card and the appointment time to the receptionist. The young man's unctuous attitude faded to be replaced with a smug and supercilious look. He was clearly some younger son of an FFH asshole and the lack of a title in front of Oliver Randall's name and who he was meeting meant Tracy wasn't worth his time, despite the nice suit and elegant overcoat.

The receptionist gestured idly at the chairs and a sofa. "You can wait over there."

Tracy shrugged out of the rich caramel-colored cashmere and Sidone-silk coat. He had found it at a flea market on one of their stops and couldn't resist. Despite being years away from the tailor shop he was still a sucker for fine fabric. He sat down on one of the high-backed chairs to wait.

Twenty minutes later a harried Jackson Wellborn rushed

across the reception. He was puffing for he was quite a heavy man. He ran a handkerchief across his face.

"Sorry, sorry, boss had me in a meeting. You need in your box, right?" Wellborn asked. The delivery sounded forced.

Tracy knew some of the sweat was due to nerves. Each time they made a delivery Wellborn was even more jumpy. It was a worry. If the man cracked, it could betray them all. Tracy hurried to his feet, gave Jackson's hand a vigorous shake, and dropped an arm over his shoulders. "Yes, and it's so good to see you, Jackson. How's the wife?" Tracy didn't mention their daughter and only child. She was the reason they had this arrangement with Wellborn.

"Fine, fine. Thanks for asking."

They went down to a basement floor where the safety deposit boxes were housed. Wellborn pulled out the key to open the heavy door to the vault. His hands were trembling and he almost lost his grip on the key. Tracy tensed. Then they were inside. He handed over his key and Wellborn unlocked the door behind which his box resided. Wellborn pulled the box out, sagging a bit under the weight. Truth was it only held some heavy metal engine parts, but that was necessary for the cover to work. Wellborn forgot his next line. Tracy took the lead.

"I need a room, please."

"Oh, right, of course."

"Would you carry the box for me?" Tracy gestured toward the cane. "Bit awkward to handle with my briefcase and this."

"Certainly."

They went to one of the privacy booths. Tracy allowed the door to fall almost completely closed as Jackson set the box on the desk. No surveillance was allowed in a booth. Tracy quickly pulled the vial of medicine out of his pocket.

Wellborn grabbed it with both hands and pressed it to his chest. "Thank you," he whispered. "Thank you, but I don't think I can keep doing this."

"Okay. Your choice."

A look of agony crossed his face. "But I can't. She's my baby. What else can I do?" He slipped the vial into his pocket and covered his face with his hands.

Tracy felt a flash of pity for a man in such a ghastly situation and shame that he had placed Jackson in it. A desperately ill seven-year-old daughter. Only one medicine that could control her seizures and keep her alive and stable. A medicine that only the very wealthy could afford. Wellborn made enough to provide a solidly middle-class lifestyle for his wife, but not enough money to care for this fragile little girl. If he bankrupted himself and he and the family ended up on Basic, it still wouldn't help because the public heath option was brutally practical about just how far they would go to save a single individual. Right now the cost of caring for Serena precluded Wellborn and his wife having any other children. The medical board probably believed that allowing Serena Wellborn to die would free up the family to have more and healthier children. Clearly not an outcome Wellborn could accept, so he had turned to crime.

Tracy pushed aside his sense that he was taking advantage of a man's desperation. "So, do you have our spikes?"

"Yes, yes."

He removed a box from his breast pocket and handed it over. Tracy flipped it open. As promised it held thirty blank credit spikes like thin crystal icicles nestled in a bed of black velvet. Jackson was in charge of the manufacture and ordering of spikes to be supplied to new customers. In exchange for the medication Wellborn falsified records and skimmed off a few spikes out of the occasional shipment. Tracy put them in his briefcase.

"Thank you. I'll call you when I'm done," Tracy said. Jackson left and Tracy closed the door. He waited ten minutes then opened the door and called, "All done."

Jackson carried the box back into the vault and returned it to its slot. Keys were turned and a key returned to Tracy. They left. They stood in silence in the elevator. The tension was palpable.

Tracy stepped off at the lobby floor. Held the door for a moment. "Hopefully my leg will improve and I won't require so much help from you," Tracy said.

Wellborn was no fool. He understood. "Does this mean you'll be using a different bank?" His face seemed to be melting, the lips and jowls pulling down. The man's hand went into his pocket as if to reassure himself the vial of salvation was still there.

"No. I won't change anything. But like I said you won't have to help so much. Take care, Jackson."

Jackson slumped. His eyes brimmed with gratitude. Tracy allowed the doors to close. His other client was just going to have to work with the spikes they already possessed.

* * *

And she was gone. Boho had hoped for a press event at the spaceport. A place for him to show his support and affection, send the message that she was trusting him with the harder task—to remain, and hold the reins of government. Instead she had ordered the shuttle to land on the dusty chaparral east of the palace but still on palace grounds. The smell of burned chamisa and sage filled his nostrils. His ears still rang with the roar of the shuttle's rockets firing. In the distance a single aria gave a tentative and nervous chirp, testing to see if it was safe to sing again.

The only people present were their security details, Davin, Jaakon, and Kemel. The presence of his erstwhile wingman added to Boho's sense of misuse. Davin had always been the one most ready for high jinks and mischief, but he had become so staid, distant, and, Boho suspected, disapproving. As if they hadn't chased pussy together back in their salad days.

Jaakon had gone forward to talk with Ian Rogers, the captain of Mercedes' guard. Kemel was on his ScoopRing in conference with someone. Boho fell into step with Davin. "Are you hungry? I didn't get breakfast this morning."

Boho watched the hesitation, then Davin nodded. "Bit late for me, but sure. Then I have to get back to headquarters."

"Work, work, work. Don't you delegate?" Boho said lightly.

"No," was the humorless response. "See you at the palace."

"Let's go into the city. Puts you closer to fleet headquarters and frankly I'm sick of the place. I could use some new faces," Boho said.

That did get a quick smile. "You always were restive."

"Gotta stay ahead of angry husbands and *delante del diablo, hombre.*" Boho knew it was a provocative statement and the inclusion of the Devil at the end wasn't going to make it any better. He wasn't quite sure why he had said it. Then Davin's expression stiffened and the surge of satisfaction was balm to Boho's bruised ego. *Ah,* that's *why I said it.*

Boho selected the café with the usual blanching from his security detail. It was a busy place between the two major universities that catered to a young, noisy, and exuberant crowd and stayed open all night serving not only full meals but teeth-achingly strong coffee and hot beignets fresh out of the oven every thirty minutes or so. His fingers were already dusted with powdered sugar as he munched the pastries and waited for Davin to arrive.

Mercedes wasn't wrong that he was popular and one reason for that was his refusal to accept the royal cage. He made a point to go out in public and connect with people… and have people connect with him, he added to himself, as he watched one particularly curvaceous girl walk past. His presence was noted and a few of the youngsters gave him shy hellos, but these were people of his own class and they were too polite to interrupt. His security tried to blend in; some of the younger SPI agents were also eyeing the girls and a few were exchanging information. The older agents were focused more on the coffee and pastries.

And it wasn't like he was in any danger in this part of the city. The patrons were a mix of upper middle-class children who weren't subject to the Rule of Service, and members of the FFH who had washed out of the High Ground at the end of the first year. Young men with cock-of-the-walk struts passing back and forth in front of giggling girls, jackets thrown casually over their right shoulders. Most of the girls had alien chaperones and shopping bags at their feet. The boys' jackets bore the patches of their universities sewn over breast pockets.

Boho blew across the surface of his coffee and watched the flirting language. Once he had been among the young men who flicked their jackets like a matador's cape while girls expressed their interest by shifting one of the small demitasse cups either left or right. At a ball it was harder, for a gentleman couldn't remove his coat. There one had to communicate with looks. The ladies had the advantage: they had their fans and an elaborate code to go along with each open, close, snap, and flutter.

Davin arrived, but his head was down and he was studying his ScoopRing. There was a frown between his brows accentuating the furrows and the wrinkles around his eyes. *We're getting old,* Boho realized and pushed it away, hating the very idea. Davin muted his ring and slid into the chair across from Boho. He ordered a Turkish coffee from the Isanjo waiter. Boho pushed the plate of beignets toward Davin. He waved them off, the lights in his artificial hand flaring at the movement, and patted his gut.

"No thanks, gotta watch the waistline." Again the reminder. Boho's irritation increased.

An awkward silence followed. "Remember when we used to go for late-night coffee in the Plaza del Oro," Boho began. "What was that place called? We picked up those two girls from the Sacred Heart High School. One of them could suck the—"

Davin leaned across the table. His elbow ended up in some spilled sugar. "Look, Boho, let's cut the crap here. We're not sixteen any longer, and this walk down memory lane is tedious, and a waste of my time. So why are we here?"

If Mercedes' Siamese cat had picked up a gun and assaulted him Boho couldn't have been more startled. Davin and Clark had been his closest friends. His thoughts ground ashore on that final word. Had they been? Really? His entourage had been there to direct the prettiest girls in his direction, set him up as the smartest guy in the room. Had they merely been foils? Mirrors to reflect back his own magnificence? That conclusion burned and he shied away, taking refuge in anger.

"We were friends. Since I'm stuck here I thought—"

"I'm going to give you some advice, Boho. Put your nose to the fucking grindstone and do the work. It's not glamorous, no one applauds and no one salutes. The hours are shitty. I know because sometimes I've had to report to Mercedes at nine, ten at night and she's still in the office doing the business of government, but the work has to get done."

Boho leaned in close. "I should have been in charge of the strike force. While she's been pushing files I've been commanding ships, leading men—"

"Degrading star command. Who do you think brought

the information about the promotions board corruption to the Infanta?"

"You dare to make these accusations against me? I'll challenge—"

"Oh, please. We're not at the academy and play acting at dueling. And once Mercedes and I discussed the situation it was pretty damn clear that you were involved. So, no, we're not friends. You've dishonored the corps, and humiliated your wife." Davin stood. "You can't charm your way out of this, Boho. You'll have to work to regain my respect. Until that happens friendship is way off the table. Thanks for the coffee."

He left, shoulders back, the impeccably cut uniform molding to his body, the artificial hand flashing fire as if reflecting Davin's anger. Boho took a reflexive bite of a beignet and gagged at the taste of congealed grease, sugar, and… shame.

11

TO OUR SWORDS NEVER DRAWN WITHOUT CAUSE OR SHEATHED WITHOUT HONOR

Freehold was one of the stops on what Jax had dubbed their "shadow run." It was a Hidden World that truly was hidden in that the star and its planets were nestled in the middle of a dense cloud of interstellar dust. The planet was a "Goldilocks" world with abundant water, fertile soil, and rich mineral deposits so the colony had a powerful manufacturing base. The settlers had been a highly educated group that had been part of the small Mars colony established by Elon Musk back in the twenty-first century. They were tech savvy and had a strong space program that they used exclusively inside the confines of their system. They weren't going to risk discovery by taking unknown ships into League space.

There was certain high-tech equipment that Freehold needed, but where it didn't make sense to create the manufacturing base to support those items. So over the years the *Selkie* had ferried a few passengers from Freehold into League space so they could purchase said items. Hence the need for credit spikes already pre-loaded with League Reals. The other major item the *Selkie* traded with Freehold were sim games. The planet did have a growing entertainment sector, but they weren't ready to make the kind of elaborate multi-hour games that were created in League space, and they didn't have the sophisticated suits that gave the experience the feeling of reality.

They had landed at the Tesla spaceport and now the entire crew was enjoying a night out with their clients. And night it was. Tracy had grown up on Ouranos where the nearby nebula was far enough away that it was simply a unique and beautiful feature in one part of the night sky, albeit a bright one. Add to that Ouranos's three moons and it was rare to have a truly dark night. Here on Freehold it was a moonless night, and embedded as it was in a nebula, the night sky was stygian black shot through with the occasional meteor shower. It was certainly dramatic, but Tracy found it claustrophobic. He shook off his discomfort and followed his crew to their rented car.

The Freeholders hadn't gone to flitters. Instead they still used wheeled vehicles. Luis had taken their rented electric car out of self-drive mode and was almost giggling with delight at playing racecar driver. Tracy clutched at the panic strap over the door after the younger man took one turn at a particularly high rate of speed. Jahan's tail wrapped around the headrest, four of Graarack's claws were clinging to the fabric in the roof of the car, and Dalea had wrapped her arms around Jax to hold him steady.

"Slow down!" Jax fluted.

"Sorry, this thing just has mad cornering skills," Baca replied.

"Well, something is mad," the plant-like alien huffed.

They reached the Moroccan restaurant, ordered the car to park itself and went inside. The owner escorted them through heavy red velvet drapes and led them to a private room where their contacts waited. Walter Fineman was a tech mogul turned senator, Shaniqua Parris was a top economic advisor to the planet's president. Shaniqua could have passed for a League citizen with her black hair, brown eyes, and dark skin. Walter had bright golden hair, startlingly blue eyes, and skin so white he seemed albino. After the annexation of Yggdrasil the presence of blue eyes and fair hair wasn't quite as unusual as it had been, but it was still rare. Tracy was a watered-down version with his dishwater-blond hair, gray eyes, and dark ivory skin.

Hugs and handshakes were exchanged, and Tracy settled onto a pillow on the floor. Dalea's long legs were folded awkwardly, and both Tracy and Luis shifted to try and find a place for their feet and legs. Jax, Jahan, and Graarack had no trouble. A soft-footed waiter entered with the silver basin and ewer so they could wash their hands. Tracy studied the menu and selected the chicken with olives and lemon for his main course. He knew he was going to overeat since a Moroccan meal always included soup, bread, cold vegetables, and bisteeya, the Moroccan version of a chicken pie. He also added a side of spicy harissa. He had always loved hot and spicy food, though his gut objected more often now. Jax asked for a glass of mineral water and dithered between the light choices that were offered. He finally settled on the full spectrum. Beer, tea, and wine and Jax's lamp were delivered. The waiters left and Tracy handed over the case of credit spikes.

"I'm afraid this will be the last shipment. My source is… well, let's just say I can't put the guy through it any longer. He's starting to crack and he could bring down himself and us."

Shaniqua tucked the case away in her purse. "No problem. We've got enough to trade in League space, and we're close to being able to afford to buy a freighter with League registration."

"We've got contacts on the San Pedro station. We can help with that," Jahan said as waiters began delivering the side dishes.

"With the usual seven percent commission," Jax added. The two Freeholders nodded.

"So, what's the word out there, Oliver?" Walter asked.

"The *corsarios* have captured three military vessels," Tracy said.

Dalea leaned in to Shaniqua. "Our captain is rather fixated on this."

"Well, I can see why; that's rather alarming," Walter said.

"And the Infanta is leading a strike force to take them out," Luis added.

Walter and Shaniqua exchanged a glance that Tracy couldn't quite interpret. "Will she succeed?" Shaniqua asked a bit too casually.

Jahan shrugged, extended her claws, and speared a piece of bread. "Hard to say. Space is big."

"They'll have to try and turn people who deal with the corsairs," Graarack added.

Tracy dipped a piece of bread in the thick soup. He felt awkward eating without utensils. "Maybe someone will talk, but those of us living on the fringes... well, they're not inclined to be helpful despite the big reward we're... they're offering." He wiped his fingers on the long napkin he had flung over his shoulder.

"That's like the understatement of all time," Luis said. A chuckle ran through the group.

Shaniqua leaned in close to Tracy and dabbed a drop of soup off his chin with her napkin. "I sense an interesting internal struggle," she whispered.

"What? No. What do you mean?"

"Us and they're and we're," Shaniqua said.

"Doesn't mean anything."

"So you say."

Tracy turned his attention back to the broader conversation. "Could they trace them through the Foldstream?" Walter was asking Graarack.

"I suppose they could sift through it, but with all the League worlds, and League ships sending messages when they aren't in Fold, it could take months."

"I doubt they have that much time," Jax added.

Tracy jumped in, "You know what would be really helpful is if a ship could stay in Fold, but intercept messages from the normal space Foldstream. We can grab them when we're sub-light, but not in Fold. But God it would be an advantage in battle. No one can detect you, but you can eavesdrop on orders between the command structure and the ships, or between the captains of ships."

Walter looked thoughtful. "That would be an interesting project."

The chicken bisteeya appetizer arrived. Powdered sugar and cinnamon dusted the top of the pastry. Graarack used a claw to poke a hole in the top and steam erupted like the Vatican announcing a new pope with a column of white smoke. Tracy waited a few minutes for the interior to cool then scooped up a bite. The flavors of slow-cooked saffron chicken, spicy omelet, and ground almonds exploded in his mouth.

Shaniqua took a sip of wine. She was staring thoughtfully off into space. "So just how large was that reward for information?"

"Twenty million Reals," Jax said promptly.

A tense silence fell over the table. "That would put us over the top on buying the registered freighter," Shaniqua said to Walter.

"Are you saying you might have information," Tracy said slowly.

"We might. We've done a few deals with the gentlemen," Walter said.

"You let them come here?" Tracy asked, shocked.

Shaniqua answered. "Oh, God no. We only deal with people who've been vouched for by our alien visitors. People like you."

"And the corsairs seem to be typical of most League people. Aliens as servants and second-class citizens," Walter said. "So, no, we don't want them here. Also, we couldn't trust them not to betray us to the League."

"Rather like what you're contemplating," Jahan said dryly.

An uncomfortable laugh skittered around the table. "Touché," Walter said.

"But we're the good guys... relatively speaking," Shaniqua said. "One of our agents who are shipping with you could drop a dime."

"Drop a what?" Luis asked.

"Dime—it was a coin... never mind. Get word to the League."

Their main courses arrived and the conversation was tabled until the waiters had again left the room. Tracy rolled an olive around his plate with a forefinger then said, "Whoever comes forward is going to be put under a microscope and SEGU is good at picking a person apart. Their cover would have to be impeccable."

Jahan pinned him with a look. "You seem to have associates who excel at that, *Oliver*."

"Could you make the introduction?" Shaniqua asked.

"What do we get out of this?" Tracy asked. Blunt talk for a social occasion, but necessary.

"Five percent of the reward," Walter suggested.

"Fifteen," Jax countered.

"Seven."

"Ten."

"Done."

Luis let out a little whoop that was quickly stifled.

"I'll draw up a contract," Jax said. Walter held out his hand and Jax wrapped a tendril around the man's hand and arm. Handshakes went around the table.

Shaniqua held up her wine glass. "To a long and prosperous relationship."

Tracy held up his beer. "To our swords, never drawn without cause or sheathed without honor." It was the preferred toast of the captain of the *Triunfo*, the first ship where Tracy had served after graduation. Most of his crew looked away, uncomfortable over his overtly military toast, but Graarack's faceted eyes were fixed on him. Tracy then added softly, "And to *la Infanta*, may she lead with wisdom and courage and emerge victorious."

"They built a maze. How adorable." A chuckle rippled through the bridge at the nav officer's comment.

Mercedes stood behind the captain's chair on the bridge of the *San Medel y Celedon*. Since she was an admiral she could have demanded the chair and made Captain Eklund stand, but she felt it was important to let him be perceived as in charge of the day-to-day, with herself as the gray eminence hovering over all.

The screen presented an image of the tumbling rocks that orbited the large central planetoid. Based on the different trajectories it was apparent the rocks had not naturally accreted around what appeared to be an orphaned moon. It was too symmetrical to be an asteroid and its surface wasn't as heavily cratered as one of the wandering rocks from this system's accretion belt. There were ships docked at the moon, umbilicals linking them to the surface, feeding them fuel and supplies. There was no sign of the three military vessels.

"It's like they forgot there are these things called computers that can analyze the movement of the rocks and calculate the path in," Eklund remarked.

"It's all part of crafting a persona, a legend, if you will," Tyler Nance said. He was the SEGU officer assigned to the *San Medel*. He possessed a quick wit and a level of cynicism that both charmed and repelled Mercedes. He was also very good at his job. "Myth and perception are often far more potent than reality. The mysterious corsair with his secret base at the heart of an impenetrable maze who can challenge even the might of the crown."

"They do have homemade rail guns on some of the rocks," Eklund pointed out.

"Which are hardly a threat to cruisers and destroyers, and I have faith that our *Infierno* pilots are sufficiently skilled to avoid fire from those guns," Mercedes said.

Chastised, he ducked his mead and murmured, "Yes, ma'am."

"The vermin are bound to have built in some bolt holes in case they did have to decamp and can't use the main path through the maze," Nance said.

Mercedes nodded in agreement. "So, let's locate and block those. Send out some fighters to make a sweep."

The order was given. From the bridge of the massive dreadnaught there was no possibility that she would feel the launch of the fighters, but she imagined it. Imagined the crushing weight on her body as a fighter rocketed out of the docking bay. To feel the couch close around her armored body, the swing and sway of the gimbals as the fighter maneuvered; the almost instant response as the craft reacted to minute shifts in her body, the movements of her eyes. There were moments when the craft felt alive. She longed to join them. But of course she couldn't. She was an admiral now, and the heir to the throne, and this was no exercise. It was unlikely that any of the corsairs' ships would be armed with anything that could harm her forces, but she couldn't take the risk and she needed to stay in the command position to react to the ebb and flow of the operation that was about to begin. The real fighting was going to happen once they reached the base. The *corsarios* were sure to have small arms. Some of them would fight. They would die, but some of her *fusileros* would die too. The real question was how many of the hostages were they going to lose?

"Let me know when the fighters have completed their sweep, Captain, and taken up positions at any escape routes. I want to speak to our corsair prisoner before we make any further moves. Nance, you're with me."

"Yes, ma'am," the two men said in tandem.

The two *fusileros* assigned to her fell in behind her as she left the bridge. She skipped the elevator and instead entered the access tunnel.

"Feeling the need to move?" Nance asked as she grabbed the ladder.

"Yes. I'd be nervous if I was going in. I'm more nervous that I'm not." She focused on placing a foot on each rung.

"You'll have access to the *fusileros'* helmet cams."

"Which makes it worse. To see the events unfolding and be incapable of affecting them." Desperate to escape from the conversation she hooked her boots on the braces and slid down the rest of the way. It didn't help her outrun her thoughts and fears.

The brig was on the lowest level of the big dreadnaught. On the same level as the armory and the gun range. On reflection Mercedes decided that maybe that wasn't the best design. The guards on duty jumped up, braced, and saluted as she entered. She waved them down. "Bring me Captain Duarte."

She and Nance went into the office and waited. A few moments later the guards returned with the captain of the trading ship. It had been a trail of breadcrumbs that had led to the *corsario* base, starting with a sheepish merchant admitting that he had purchased cheap contraband goods from an electronics store on Dragonfly. That arrest had led to a supplier with a warehouse on Nephilim, which had ultimately led them to the freighter captain who now stood before her. He was a short man with a magnificent beer belly and a thatch of curly white hair. Nance had questioned the three-person crew using approved interrogation techniques. Some of which involved boxes of Oreos and coffee. Eventually Duarte had given up the coordinates of Rockfleet, and now here they were.

Mercedes motioned at the chair on the other side of the desk. "Señor Duarte."

"Highness." She waited. She had taken to heart Kemel's lesson that silence was often more powerful than words. "Do you need something?" the man asked eventually.

"Advice."

"Advice," he repeated. He looked surprised and wary.

Nance pulled a package of the Tiponi stim sticks out of his pocket and tossed it to Duarte. He grabbed it gratefully, pulled out a stick. Nance lit it for him. The corsair took a long pull.

Mercedes watched the man's shoulders relax and then asked, "So how fervent are the people on that rock about fighting to the last man? If I offer leniency are some of them likely to… decamp?"

Duarte took the stim out of his mouth, studied the burning tip for a moment before answering. "Oh, hell yes. None of us are true believers. In much of anything. We're just… greedy."

"Thank you. Are you familiar with the ships and captains who work with Señor Cornell?"

"A lot of them."

"Do you have call signals for them?"

"Some."

"Will you provide me with those? I can hope some of them are presently docked."

"What does that get me?"

Nance stepped in. "Less time in prison."

Duarte ruminated while he frowned at the wall and took a few more puffs on the stim stick. "Okay, sounds fair."

Back on the bridge they sent targeted messages to the call signals Duarte had provided. The surveillance officer reported that the scanners were picking up activity on four of the seven docked ships. Mercedes laid a hand on Eklund's shoulder. "Send in some *Infiernos* to take out the cannon. Cornell might decide to punish the defectors."

She slipped on a headpiece so she could monitor the

cross-talk between the *Infiernos* and their base ships and between the fighter pilots. A few minutes later a squadron of fighters arrowed into the maze. A few of the rail guns took shots. Most of the slugs missed, others were dodged, and the few that did find a target were easily absorbed by the heavy shielding on the *Infiernos*. A rain of missiles from the *Infiernos* answered, and blew apart the guns.

"Hijole," one of the pilots caroled. *"Those things were made of tin foil and spit."*

With the rail guns neutralized the four ships that had chosen to defect made their way through the maze surrounding Rockfleet. Orders were radioed to kill engines and surrender or be targeted. One of the four tried to engage their Folddrive and were hammered by missiles off the five destroyers in Mercedes' strike force. She watched as the freighter came apart in slow motion. Escaping atmosphere turned to glittering ice; the tumbling metal pieces glinted and flared as they caught the light off the star that anchored this system. She didn't ask for a closer view. She didn't need to see the bodies. The remaining three corsair ships meekly surrendered.

"Lesson learned and message received," Eklund grunted.

"One ship making a run on a bolt hole," came a voice. Mercedes pinpointed the location of the attempted breakout and keyed into the cameras aboard the fighter at that sentry point.

"Fire a warning shot and order them to surrender," Mercedes commanded.

"Aye, aye, ma'am."

A new voice came on the radio. *"We have hostages aboard."*

Nausea filled her throat, threatening to choke her. "Scan to determine numbers."

She counted her heartbeats until the pilot reported. *"Thirty."*

She muted her radio and looked to Eklund. "Ship that size would normally have a crew of five to eight people. So, yeah, they probably have some of our people aboard."

She keyed her radio back on. "Lieutenant, disable that ship."

"Ma'am, I'll have to use a missile. I can't program a slug—"

She muted her microphone and looked from Eklund to Nance. Seconds elongated into eons. The radio crackled to life with a new voice.

"Ma'am, this is Captain Cristobal Yuen off the frigate *Indomitable*. We've broken free and we're trying to reach the bridge, but we're not going to make it in time. Take the shot."

"A missile will destroy that ship."

"We know, but if you let them escape they'll load more of us on ships to use us as human shields. They have to know it won't work. That we're expendable."

An ache settled into her throat. Mercedes said, "Captain Yuen, the League thanks you and your men for your service. *Ve con Dios*, Captain." She switched channels. "You have your order, Lieutenant. Fire at will."

"Yes, ma'am."

She watched the calculations flick across the screen in the cockpit of the *Infierno*. The image gave a link as the missile was fired. Scanners traced its path as it wove its way through the tumbling rocks toward the *corsario* vessel. The freighter tried to evade its oncoming doom, but then the engines cut out, probably due to actions by Yuen and his men. Unable to navigate, it deviated from the safe path it needed to maintain. An oblong rock clipped the back of the ship. Pieces of metal fell away in that dreamy dance of zero gravity. The inertia of the first rock nudged the ship into the path of a much larger, jagged rock that hit in the center of the ship sending it off on yet a new trajectory and into the path of more and more rocks. It was like watching a steel ball bouncing between the bumpers in one of those ancient pinball machines. The ship was coming apart at the seams. The mass of flying metal pieces confused the missile's tiny brain. It kept changing its trajectory, chasing pieces until it finally hit one large segment that was the body of the ship and detonated. The flare of the explosion blinded Mercedes for an instant. She was glad. It might explain the wetness in her eyes.

"Well. I bet nobody tries that again," Eklund said in a voice stripped of all emotion.

"Let's finish this." Mercedes' voice sounded harsh even to her own ears.

"With pleasure, ma'am."

The shuttles loaded with *fusileros* wove their way through the maze of rocks toward the orphan moon.

12

A WHIFF OF SEDITION

Walking with Nance and her adjutant through the corridors that had been drilled into the moon Mercedes found herself reflecting on the complacency of the League that had allowed Cornell to construct a base of this size and complexity and the arrogance of even giving it a name. What in Heaven's name had led the corsair leader to think he could seize military vessels without consequence? Mercedes answered her own question. *Because we allowed him to reach that conclusion*. It had been easier to just pay the occasional ransom, for insurance companies to absorb the losses, and bean counters at fleet headquarters to argue that the cost and effort to dig them out was too great.

Those accommodations had now led to the death of several hundred people—*corsario* and O-Trell alike—and the loss of three military vessels. The loss of life concerned Mercedes, and she was also worried over the whereabouts of the three ships. She hoped someone among the survivors could tell her what the hell had happened to them.

Was there an alien rebellion brewing? No one had ever

satisfactorily explained the disappearance of the Cara'ot. Could they have taken the ships? She shook her head. That made no sense. The aliens had had ships and abandoned them. Why now, all these years later, would they take three human ships?

She reached an area where the fighting had been hardest. Bodies still littered the corridor. All corsairs. A few of the bodies wore pressure suits. Most were just in clothes. No match for marines in battle armor. Among her soldiers there had only been three deaths and sixteen wounded. The bodies and the injured had already been returned to their respective ships for treatment and preparation for burial.

They turned a corner and came upon another clot of bodies. There was a young woman among them. A rifle lay near her side. One hand rested on the leg of a dead corsair. A trail of blood on the floor of the hallway showed how she had dragged herself, bleeding, to his side. Her swelling belly told another story. Mercedes recognized the dead woman from the crew manifests. She had been an *hombre* aboard one of the frigates. Mercedes stared in shock at the dead woman and the now dead infant she carried.

"Stockholm Syndrome," Nance said laconically. "Fairly common after captives have been held for a significant period of time. They start to identify and sympathize with their captors."

"She fell in love with her rapist?" Mercedes questioned.

"Or maybe she just fell in love. No rape involved."

Mercedes shook her head and motioned to her aide. The lieutenant used the facial recognition application on his tap-pad to identify the woman. Mercedes read over his shoulder, HOMBRE ALICIA BROWN. The aide marked her as deceased. Back at fleet headquarters on Hellfire a letter of condolence would be prepared and forwarded to the grieving family. With the toe of her boot Mercedes lifted the dead woman's slack hand from the corsair's leg, and kicked the rifle even farther away.

"I take it we're not mentioning she was fighting with the enemy," Nance said.

"If we do her family won't get the death benefit payment." She glanced over at her young aide. "I expect you to keep silent, Lieutenant."

"About what, ma'am?"

"Good boy."

"You're tender-hearted, Highness," Nance said.

"Tell that to our soldiers who died when I gave the order to fire on that escaping ship."

They stepped through the bodies. The congealing blood on the floor was tacky on the soles of Mercedes' boots, and the atmosphere carried the scent of blood and feces. Mercedes started taking shallow breaths through her mouth. Another turn and they were out of the charnel house and into the cafeteria. Survivors had been freed from the cells and were being processed there. As well as prisoners. Not all of the corsairs had fought to the death. There was the smell of overcooked cabbage and unwashed bodies. It was still better than the stench of death. Medical personnel were checking out the hostages while officers debriefed them. It was organized chaos. Mercedes searched the crowd for the women. How many more burgeoning bellies was she going to find?

The answer was quickly evident. It had been almost six months. Of the eight women who had been captured only five were left. Two had been aboard the destroyed ship, one was the dead woman in the hallway. Of those left living four of them were pregnant. Three pairs of defiant eyes met hers. One of the mothers-to-be couldn't meet Mercedes' gaze. Her lips trembled and slow tears ran down her cheeks. Salutes were exchanged, which added to the incongruity of the situation. Mercedes turned first to the woman who was not gravid. She looked to be in her mid-twenties with pixie-cut hair and bright, intelligent eyes.

"So, how did you luck out?"

"Untreated gonorrhea. By the time I got taken to a doc I was sterile."

"But that's so treatable," Mercedes said.

"Yeah, but not if it's your stepdad who's fucking you, your mom refuses to believe you, and you live on a remote farm on Wasua. I enlisted as soon as I was eighteen to get away from that shit. So yeah, I'll take being spayed over what they're facing." She nodded toward the other women.

The crying woman went from silent tears to shattering sobs. It was a breach of every deportment lesson she'd ever taken, but Mercedes put her arms around the woman and hugged her tight. "It's all right. It's all right. You're safe now," she soothed.

"I can't have this... this *thing*," she gasped. "Please, please, Highness, help me."

"Shhh. It's going to be all right. You won't have to raise the child. We'll take care of that."

"I don't want it growing inside me!"

"I understand. We'll talk about it once you're all safely out of here."

One of the other women gave the sobbing girl a sour look then turned her gaze to Mercedes. "At least you didn't lie. She's never getting an abortion. Look, Dina, just whelp the thing and take the damn subsidy. That's what I plan to do." Another flat stare at Mercedes. "Maybe you could find me a husband too while you're fixing everything, Your Highness."

"I have a husband," another woman said. She hesitantly touched the mound of her belly. "He'll never take me back after this."

"We will see to it that all of you are cared for. You have my word."

Mercedes moved away. In her mind's eye her sister Beatrisa's face was overlaid on the women's faces. She didn't think tears would be the first reaction of her pugnacious sister, but she damn well knew how Bea would respond to being forced to bear a child. She had made it abundantly clear she was not going to marry and she was not having kids.

Her hand closed vise-like on her aide's elbow. "Get them out of here first. Put them aboard my ship and have the medics check them over. Send a memo to fleet command that long-term birth control needs to be mandatory for all active service women."

The young man looked startled. "Ma'am, the church—"

"Won't be happy. Yes, I know. But we can't inflict this added danger on our women soldiers."

He looked like he wanted to say more, but wisely simply

said, "Yes, ma'am," and made a note.

Nance gave her an ironic look and pulled her aside. "My, you certainly do like to punch above your weight, Highness."

"Military matters are in my purview."

"And they will argue they owe allegiance to a higher power."

"I'm sure, but since that other power tends to be stubbornly silent they can bloody well listen to *me*."

One of Nance's factotums hurried up. "Ma'am, sir, we've downloaded the data off the base's mainframe and we're pulling navigational information off the captured ships. We've got a long list of merchants and companies who have been dealing in stolen goods. We also seem to have information on a Hidden World. A place called Kusatsu-Shirane."

"I think this is worth a celebratory brunch," Jahan said as they walked away from the credit union that held the note on the *Selkie*.

"Giant steak," Luis sighed.

"Ugh," Dalea said.

"I'm sure there'll be something for a vegetarian," Graarack soothed the Hajin.

"I still have to watch you masticating dead and bleeding flesh," the doctor said. "And you spitting acid on it before you masticate it," she added with a nod to the Sidone.

"Well, I have to watch you all masticating potential relatives… except for Luis who doesn't eat anything if it grows in the ground," Jax said. A sudden awkward silence fell across the mismatched crew. Jax shook with laughter. "Got ya."

"E for effort on the joke front. Still a giant fail," Jahan said.

"We're not known for our comedic sense," the Flute replied.

"We noticed," Tracy said.

"And hey, I eat stuff that grows in the ground," Luis said defensively. "I eat potatoes."

"That does not count as a vegetable," Dalea began to lecture.

Tracy cut off the familiar debate. "Okay, let's find food. Spend a little of this *dinero* on ourselves."

They moved down the street checking the menus hanging in windows or set on placards out front of the various establishments. It was a pleasant summer morning on the main continent of Geneva. The planet wasn't heavily populated and tended to favor the more customer-friendly credit unions over the large interplanetary banks. It was why Tracy had gone with them when he first purchased the ship. Their background checks also weren't as rigorous as with other institutions.

After some discussion the crew had decided to go to the credit union and make the additional loan payment in person rather than trust to a Foldstream transfer. During the journey to Geneva there had been a dinnertime conversation over how much of the reward money to place against the loan. Because of Tracy's paranoia and Jax's caution they opted to only make a single extra payment. Any more and the loan officer might begin to question their sudden windfall.

Tracy picked a restaurant that had a wide choice of tapas and a number of alien waitstaff. The crew of the *Selkie* had learned the hard way that some restaurants were hostile to serving his mixed species crew.

Before any debate could break out over his choice Tracy held up a finger. "Captain's prerogative."

There was a nice patio out back and they were seated at a table beneath a grape arbor. Bunches of grapes like amethysts hung from the twisting vines that covered the wooden trellis. There was the lazy buzz of bees and the sweet scent of ripe fruit.

Once their orders were placed, Jax pulled his tap-pad out of his satchel. "I think it would be a good investment to use some of the funds to increase our equipment order for Kusatsu-Shirane. Their economy is growing with an emphasis on agriculture at this stage of the colony's development and we get a nice markup on the machinery."

Tracy glanced around the table. There were nods of assent. They had all learned to trust Jax's instincts when it came to sales and inventory. "Okay, there's still time to increase the order before we take delivery on Nueva Terra."

Jax busied himself with his tap-pad, and the ping echoed through the patio as the order was sent. Jahan raised her sangria glass. "To us. Doing good deeds and making a Real or two in the process."

The second bottle of wine was down to the dregs. Boho tilted the bottle and cocked a questioning eye at Lord Arturo

Espadero del Campo. "Shall we order another?"

Arturo leaned back in his chair, hands thrust into the pockets of his tuxedo slacks. There was an enigmatic quality to the man with his hooded eyes and the way his lips seemed to always be curved in a slight smile. His dark brown hair was combed sleekly against his narrow skull and was perfectly iced with gray at the temples. A slight paunch ballooned the front of his pressed white dress shirt. Boho eyed the dirty plates that littered the table and reflected that too many more evenings like this one would lead to him filling out his shirt in a similar manner.

"I think brandy. Or perhaps an Irish coffee. Yes, that sounds good. Bit of a chill in the air tonight. I love that moment when we are trembling between fall and winter," Arturo said.

In the weeks since Mercedes had left there had been too many days seated behind a desk, first in Mercedes' office and then in the office he'd insisted be furnished for him. What Boho hadn't been able to change was the assistant. Jaakon was as soft-footed as a cat and just as aloof.

Boho's evenings were filled with concerts and late suppers, nightclubs and late suppers, balls, masques, and ridottos—and late suppers. Weekends there were hunt breakfasts and shooting parties, and soon the round of Christmas parties would begin. He made another mental vow to begin getting up early and hitting the gym before he went to the office.

With his return to the capital Boho had started to renew old acquaintances. Davin had proved to be a disappointment, and Margrave Clark Bennington Kunst, Boho's other closest friend from his youth, had retired to the family estate on the

Hajin home world of Belán to raise a family. He had also opened a chain of fencing academies across several League worlds designed to separate wealthy *intitulados* from their money by teaching their sons the art of the duello. Kunst had been a notable swordsman during their days at the High Ground, and the president of their dueling society.

Of his other compatriots, well, everyone had grown up. They were all married, running estates or business interests, serving in government and a handful, like Davin, were even still in the military. A tiny handful had died from accidents or disease. One had even been murdered by his wife. But Arturo was living in Hissilek, serving in parliament, and despite a wife and children had been very happy to join Boho on his carouses.

Tonight had been an excursion to the opera. Boho had feared Arturo would bring his wife, but it seemed his friend had an interest in the soprano singing Violetta and wanted no spousal interference in that pursuit. In the singer's dressing room backstage Boho had found himself in the odd position of being the wingman rather than the hunter. He had been even more surprised when Arturo ended the flirtation and left after bestowing only fervent kisses to the lady's palms.

"That's it? I thought you'd have her on her back as soon as the house cleared," Boho had said as they left the opera house.

Arturo had given him a secretive smile and said, *"I'm an angler. I love the tug and play as you bring a fish into the net."*

The human waiter arrived and took their orders. Boho decided on a glass of port rather than the whiskey-laced coffee that Arturo ordered. Once their drinks were in hand,

Boho leaned back in his chair and stretched out his long legs off to the side of the table.

"So, back when we were young you said you wanted to have military victories so the people would love you," Boho said. "Yet you had no victories and you ended up a politician and nobody loves politicians." He didn't try to hide the sting that lay buried in the heart of his jocular tone.

"And I believe you talked about being a planetary governor so you could squeeze the populace and make a fortune. Neither one of us achieved our goals. Instead your wife steals my victories, and puts you on an allowance."

The words landed like a fist to the gut. Boho straightened. "How do you know about that?"

"Who do you think authorizes the money for the upkeep of the royals? You should be kinder to us politicians."

Steadying his breathing Boho took a sip of his port, leaned back again. "I'm beginning to suspect this evening wasn't just a social outing. Are you angling me?"

"Very perceptive of you." Arturo took a sip and ended up with whipped cream adorning his upper lip. The tip of his tongue emerged and licked it away. It reminded Boho of a snake testing the air. "Are you happy with your situation, Boho?"

"Let's see, a royal duke, married to the heir to the throne, living in a palace, why shouldn't I be?"

"Because if the succession should change where would you be and what would you be?"

The stem of the port glass was thin and fragile beneath his fingers. Boho forced himself to relax his grip. He gave the glass a slow spin. "Are we anticipating the succession changing?"

"If she hits fifty without an heir I think that's assured."

"So, I marry one of the other qualified princesses. There are a number to choose from."

"Two, to be exact, and once again be an ornament... unless you think Carisa or Beatrisa will be more biddable?" Arturo said. "And I think it's an open question as to whether parliament would approve swapping out one princess for another. And they sure as hell will never accept the dyke."

The port filled Boho's mouth with the taste of roses and summer. "So just what are we discussing here?" he asked.

Arturo took another sip of his coffee. "Just musing about the stressors that currently exist in our society. Casually wondering whether the League would do better with a return to a more normal and traditional pattern. You understand."

"Perfectly." Another swallow of port. "You have sisters, don't you?"

"Yes. Three of them are at present unmarried."

Boho raised his glass. "Here's to available women."

Arturo tapped his coffee cup against the glass. "And may they be willing as well."

Dinner had concluded, the dishes were cleared, and the crew was gathered for their evening ritual where a member of the crew read aloud from a book of their choosing. Since he had a large alien contingent, Tracy had heard a lot of tales from creatures who didn't view the world quite the same way as humans. Since humans by and large didn't give a damn about what aliens thought they were rarely translated into Spanish or English, so his crew would translate on the fly. The reading choices also told him a lot about their various personalities. Luis loved adventure tales with manly men rescuing beautiful women and fighting off enemies. The boy did have the good sense not to pick stories that were overtly about fighting and killing aliens. Jax liked non-fiction so they heard a lot of Tiponi Flute history, which was fairly inexplicable. Graarack liked mysteries, Jahan loved romances, which Tracy found to be head-spinning since in person she tended to be practical and very hardheaded, and Dalea preferred biographies, particularly those about inventors and scientists.

Tracy leaned back, loosened his belt, and alternated sips of brandy with hits off a Tiponi stim stick. The Isanjo's voice was soft, almost haunting, as she read the concluding paragraph from *The Dream of the Green Bower.*

"And Helmic embraced Lavana, the tip of his tail gently wiping away the single tear. 'I said I would return and build you a bower among the high branches where the wind would sing and leaves dance. She laid her hand in his and they ascended the polished steps and entered their aerie. They were home at last."

She shut down her ring. Dalea gave a watery but happy sniff. "Thank you, Jahan, that was wonderful."

"When are you and your husband going to ascend to that bower?" Graarack asked the Isanjo.

"Once the captain here manages to make us all rich." She gave Tracy a fang-baring grin.

"Nag, nag, nag. I'm doing my best," Tracy said.

"So, you're up next," the Sidone said. "What are you going to read, Ollie… Tracy?"

"I thought I'd share a children's book with you. My mother read it to me and I really liked it. *The Wind in the Willows.*"

"Sounds like something I might like," Jax said.

"Well, it's got talking animals in it, but no talking trees."

"I like kids' books," Luis said. "Maybe I'll read *Treasure Island* next. It's got pirates in it." He gave Tracy a sideways glance. "Hey, now that the League has stomped Cornell, that means the position of pirate king is available. Maybe you should—"

"No!"

"Ah, you're no fun. Where's your sense of adventure?" Luis asked.

"Trumped by my sense of self-preservation. Dear God, are you trying to get me killed?" Tracy said, his voice catching on a laugh.

Baca stroked his chin in a deliberate fashion. "Hmmm, well, then the position of captain would open up…" His crew gave a shout of laughter and Tracy realized he must have reacted without meaning to. "Kidding, Captain, kidding," Luis soothed.

"You're all terrible, and I'm going to bed. Don't plot too many mutinies while I'm sleeping."

13

WHISPERS AND RUMORS

"It undermines the very foundation of our most sacred institutions!" Blood suffused his pale brown cheeks and his jowls quivered as Conde Suklaa Nestle concluded. He gave a loud, guttural harrumph and took his seat.

Palms were pounded on desks and calls of "Here, here!" echoed around the chamber.

The parliament's upper chamber was an oval-shaped room with multicolored marble panels. Soft-footed servants waited on call to bring the lords drinks and snacks. Overhead were three massive chandeliers. The lower chamber that housed the Commons was a long rectangle with benches, rather than the desks and comfortable chairs that graced the House of Lords. It was also a far rowdier space than the upper chamber. Though old Suklaa was making an effort on that front, Boho thought.

He studied his manicured nails and considered Nestle's tirade. His son Sanjay had been a classmate of Boho's, and was married to Mercedes' full sister Julieta. The relationship between the sisters had been chilly since the extension of the

Rule of Service had sent Julieta off to the High Ground and delayed said marriage, and Mercedes had argued against the marriage because she felt Sanjay had violent tendencies. Boho couldn't disagree, but the marriage seemed to have worked and if Julieta had doubts or regrets they had been subsumed into anger and resentment against her elder sister.

So was old Suklaa hoping to undermine Mercedes and perhaps have the throne fall to his daughter-in-law? Impossible because Julieta had failed to graduate from the High Ground. She had deliberately washed out at the end of the first year so she could get married, and being an officer in the *Orden de la Estrella* was a requirement for the throne, and that was one requirement that was never going to be relaxed. The human League ruled over now four alien species, since the disappearance of the fifth and most dangerous of the creatures. No one knew what the Cara'ot might have been plotting during the intervening years. No, it was absolutely essential that the emperor—or empress—be a military leader as well as a civilian leader.

Word had arrived that Mercedes had decoupled a destroyer from her flotilla and was sending it and the freed hostages to Hellfire for debriefing and medical care before they began six weeks of leave. A classified message had been sent to Boho and Kemel that she had a possible lead on a Hidden World and was investigating. Boho had sent back a coded message that the Hidden World wasn't going anywhere, but the opportunity for good press was fleeting. Her response had been: *You handle it*. Which meant he would be traveling to Hellfire to personally greet the survivors.

The report she had provided had also contained her request that contraception be provided, and indeed required, of all women serving in O-Trell. That was what had begun this donnybrook in the House of Lords. The Cardinal of Hissilek, one of the Lords Spiritual, was even now heaving to his feet like a broaching whale draped in red. Before the Cardinal could get started, Boho rose to his feet and addressed the man who currently held the speaker's gavel.

"My lord, if I might offer some perspective." There was a nod of acquiescence from the rostrum. "We have witnessed the rescue of some two thousand League soldiers and the total destruction of the corsairs. Perhaps a moment of celebration and congratulation is in order before we turn to the pressing problem of our women potentially getting… naughty." There were a few chuckles and a few grumbles from the older men.

"My lords, the consort is amusing as always, but his is hardly an unbiased voice." The Cardinal's sonorous tones rolled across the assemblage. "His loyalty to his wife is both touching and understandable, but his dismissal of our concerns is misguided. Perhaps the Infanta's barren state has warped her thinking, but this is more than just an argument over contraception. This is an assault on the very foundations of our society. Children are a blessing from God—"

"And convenient cannon fodder," Boho interrupted. The Cardinal's harrumph was like rocks on a grater. "My lords, let's be real. This drive to procreate is directly attributable to our need to contain the perceived alien threat."

"Not perceived. It's damn well real," the Duque de Telqual shouted. "The Cara—"

"Yes, yes, our expedient bogeyman," Boho snapped back. "They've been gone almost fifteen years. Perhaps it's time we stopped wetting our panties."

"Are you calling me a coward, sir?" Telqual roared.

"I'm calling all of us cowards, sir. How much do we spend to maintain this massive military force? We never ask if this money might be better spent elsewhere."

Rohan Danilo Marcus Aubrey, Conde de Vargas and currently prime minister, lifted his head from his chest. He appeared to have been dozing, but there was a glint in his eyes that indicated he had only been faking. "Good heavens, Boho, are you becoming a radical?" He smoothed his thinning and graying red hair and rose to his feet. "My lords, as the man who encouraged the Emperor to include women in the service, allow me to offer some perspective." He paused for a sip of his tea. "Space is big." He sat back down.

"Why thank you for that amazing bit of information, Rohan," Musa del Campo, the Duque Agua de Negra, said. "Your gift for the obvious is breathtaking."

Rohan stood again. "My point being that there are vast numbers of systems and worlds that we have yet to discover, much less explore. There might be things lurking in the darkness that will test our resolve and our readiness. To exclude over half the population from our defense seems foolish and having contraception makes such service more practical."

"And what if the practice spreads into the general populace? Aren't we better off keeping our women safe to bear more children to sustain our military?" the Cardinal replied. "Also, what man wouldn't fight harder to defend his home, his wife, and his children?"

"You don't think survival would be enough of an incentive?" Rohan asked sweetly.

After that the debate continued for another two hours with no consensus and nothing decided. In other words: it had been a normal day at parliament.

"There is a certain *masculine* quality about her that one can't help but notice." A man's voice.

"And find concerning." Another voice.

Boho didn't recognize either of them, which wasn't surprising. The number of officers who flew desks on Hellfire seemed beyond counting. To be fair it took even more people behind the scenes to keep the frontline troops fighting, or at least ready to fight. Boho was pretty sure they were discussing Mercedes. He considered rounding the corner and confronting them, but decided to hold back and continue listening.

"Father Dunwich says the economic troubles we're having are because we've violated natural law and Heaven's law," said the second voice.

"Your Father Dunwich is a crank. Isn't he one of those *Fine Dierum* nuts?"

"Well, doesn't it feel like the end of days?" the second voice said, his tone shrill with outrage.

"No, it feels like we just kicked the shit out of the corsairs."

"Then why did you complain about the Infanta?" the second voice accused.

"Because I wonder if we would have lost fewer people if the consort had been in command."

It was his cue. Boho stepped around the corner. The two officers, one younger than himself, the other about the same age, braced and saluted. The younger one's eyes slid to the *Servicio Protector Imperial* that rested on his left breast. Boho touched the medal with his fingertips. "Looking at this, Lieutenant?"

"Yes, sir. *Discúlpame,* sir. I've… I've just never seen one."

"No apology necessary. I'm honored to have won it." Boho didn't mention that Mercedes had also earned the same medal. "So, on your way to the awards ceremony?"

"Yes, sir, wouldn't miss it," said the older man, who was a chief warrant officer.

"Well, lead the way."

Boho paused in the doorway and studied the people assembled on the dais. Only one woman was present—the *hombre* who had not gotten knocked up. Showing the expanding bellies on the others wasn't going to reassure League citizens. The top brass hadn't wanted any women present, but Boho had overruled them. In all other particulars the palace press office and the brass had followed his instructions to the letter. They had selected the most attractive men from among the rescued crews. One bright young fellow in the press office, Anselmo Moran, had suggested they add a smattering of *hombres* in addition to officers to the ceremony. Those enlisted personnel with nicely affecting stories could then be featured on subsequent days, which would delight the *intitulados.* In keeping with that desire to court favor among the lower class

Boho had also instructed the Chancellor of the Exchequer to authorize funds to bring the families of the surviving hostages to Hellfire for the ceremony.

One person was notably absent—the erstwhile commander of the squadron. Captain Esteban Singh was on Hellfire, but he was confined to quarters awaiting court-martial per Mercedes' order. Boho made a mental note to have Anselmo prepare a dossier on the family. Depending on what he found, it might be worth Boho contacting them.

The ceremony was being held in the Hall of Heroes, a cavernous space with a soaring vaulted ceiling festooned with battle flags and ships' standards. He scanned the assembled crowd. The *hombres* and officers who hadn't been selected for the stage sat in the audience with tearful wives, mothers, fathers, sisters, and brothers touching and hugging them as if to reassure themselves that they were real. It was nicely affecting and the cameras were catching it all.

Boho strode toward the dais. A man fell into step with him, Mihalis del Campo, eldest son of cousin Musa. Mihalis was two years older and shorter by a number of inches. He was barrel-chested, a bit bandy-legged, but he wore his uniform with arrogant pride, and while he might not have the *Servicio Protector Imperial* his jacket sported a lot of medals and ribbons. Since they were both admirals neither of them saluted.

Mihalis glanced up at him. "So, we're spared having either of *los viejos bastardos* present." Boho couldn't mask his surprise at the disdainful words and tone. Mihalis leaned in close. "I heard from Arturo that you two… talked."

"Ah. Yes, it seems my father-in-law and your father

couldn't abide sharing the stage nor could they convince the other not to attend."

"A fortunate outcome." They exchanged smiles. Mihalis gestured toward the dais. "Well, shall we?"

As they walked down the center aisle Boho was glad that Davin wasn't present to see him and Mihalis in close proximity. Instead old Admiral Kartirci, who commanded the Gold, was present since the squadron that had been captured had come from that fleet.

As they passed one row Boho was surprised to see Conde Maximilian Yuen sitting in the audience. The man's son had been aboard one of the destroyed *corsario* ships. He had not expected to see the parent of one of the dead present for a celebration for those who had survived. The older man's hands rested on a black velvet box. Boho knew it contained a *Servicio Protector Imperial* granted posthumously to Captain Yuen. Boho had read the after-action report. He knew that Cristobal Yuen had died because of a direct order from Mercedes. He wondered if the father knew that, and if he didn't how it might affect him if he found out. He glanced over at Mihalis. Boho knew he was playing a delicate game, but it seemed worth the risk of mentioning the man to Arturo and Mihalis. A push here, a nudge there and he could sit back and watch events play out without getting too involved. Once he knew which way the wind was blowing… He didn't complete the thought.

As Boho mounted the stairs onto the dais the dignitaries and the people in the hall all stood. He indicated they should be seated and took his own chair while the military chaplain led them in an opening prayer. Then it was his turn. Boho moved to the lectern, keyed his ScoopRing to project his speech and began.

"As I look out across this assembly I see family. My brothers and sisters in arms." He nodded at the uniformed men and the one woman on the dais with him, and swept a hand out toward the men in the audience. "And because of that bond their fathers and mothers, sisters, brothers, and wives are my family too. But our fellowship goes beyond service to the League we all love. We are family because we are human. A species united by our shared genetics. It is that bond that compels us to serve, to place our bodies between our homes and loved ones and the dangers that wait in the darkness. That is why your emperor and my wife, the Infanta, and I will always take any and all steps to protect the soldiers who defend us all. We will bring them home no matter the cost."

Boho went on to single out certain officers and *hombres* by name. Telling their stories, praising their bravery. There was a certain irony to it all considering all they had really managed to do was get captured and be rescued, but that inconvenient fact was being buried on this day. He concluded with the motto of the *Orden de la Estrella*.

"May we touch the stars with glory!" He snapped off a salute.

Everyone came to their feet applauding, cheering, and saluting. Boho turned to the men assembled on the dais and moved down the line shaking their hands. He reached the woman, who held out her hand, but Boho checked the placement of the floating cameras and instead enfolded her in an embrace.

"Do you want me to muster up a tear or two for the cameras, sir?" the woman whispered in his ear.

"You're a quick and cynical one." Laughter danced on the edges of the words.

"I know an opportunity when I see one."

"So what are you doing after the reception, *chiquita*?"

"I don't know, sir. What am I doing?"

"I'll think of something."

He released her and stepped back. She had managed to muster up tears and she wiped her cheeks while the cameras recorded. Boho glanced over and the press spokesman, Anselmo, gave him an enthusiastic thumbs up.

"Damn it, what's taking so long?" Tracy fumed while he paced the bridge. Jax had gone to the spaceport master's office to pay their departure fee and he had been gone almost an hour.

"Maybe you two humans could go over there, huff about the shiftless alien, and get us a lift-off time," Jahan suggested. "Oh, don't wince, Oli… Tracy, you know it will help."

"All right. Come on, Luis."

They left the ship and crossed the field. Nueva Terra was a major hub so the giant field was dotted with ships of all sizes and shapes. The passenger liners never landed, but the shuttles and pinnaces, for the more elegant and well-born travelers, waited to carry the passengers up to the big ships. Loading mechs rolled past with crated cargo, flitters darted across the field taking crews and port personnel to various ships. Tracy didn't want to pay for a flitter to take them to administration so they hoofed it across the flame-charred concrete. He was soon sweating. It was summer in the hemisphere where New Madrid was located.

Inside the building the air conditioning was going full blast and a vid screen behind the desk was showing a news story while the staff were gathered around drinking coffee and watching. Jax was folded into a chair quivering with annoyance so his fronds made a whispering sound that wasn't entirely due to the air conditioning ruffling his leaves.

"Holy shit!" Luis choked. Tracy, leaning on the counter trying to get the attention of the staff, looked over at the younger man. Luis was staring at the screen. "That's that guy, the one who ripped us—" In that moment Tracy realized it was Boho on the screen. He trod heavily on Luis' foot. "Ow!" One look at Tracy's glare and Luis' teeth snapped shut.

Every nerve in his body screamed that he should look away, walk away, but a macabre fascination kept him watching. When Boho hugged the young woman *hombre* Tracy gave a snort of disgust. That finally got the attention of the staff. One of the men slouched over to him.

"Yeah?"

"We need lift-off authorization." Tracy jerked a thumb back at Jax. "Apparently this animated broccoli didn't communicate that to you."

"Nah, we told him to wait. We wanted to watch the ceremony," the man said.

Tracy snapped his fingers at Jax who came rustling over. "Seems strange the Infanta wasn't there," Tracy said as he took the credit spike from the Tiponi and paid the fee.

"Guess she couldn't be bothered," the man grunted.

Another of the office staff added, "Gene Lake says she got a bunch of our boys killed." Tracy stiffened at the mention of the notorious yellow journalist. "He said that wouldn't have happened if they'd given the mission to the duque, but I guess she has his balls in her pocket."

"There are some things a woman isn't meant to do. Lead an army is one," the first man said. Tracy's ScoopRing pinged as the authorization was sent over from the admin officer's computer. "There you go, Captain Randall. Safe journeys."

"Thank you," Tracy grated. The three of them left the building.

"*Madre de Dios!* That guy who jacked us up was the *consort,*" Luis said with suppressed excitement.

"Yes."

"You *knew* the consort?"

"Yes."

"Then you went to school with the Infanta too!"

"Yes."

"Did you know her?"

"Oh, don't be absurd. I'm a tailor's son." Tracy strode on ahead. He could sense both his crew mates behind him brimming with questions, but they seemed to sense that any further questions were going to go unanswered.

14

COOKIES AND CONSPIRACY

The season had officially begun. Boho stood at the bar while a human bartender mixed his Vieux Carré. The scent of Bénédictine, rye, cognac, and vermouth almost overwhelmed the clashing smells of the various perfumes worn by the women. The ballroom had been remodeled since Yves had ascended to his father's title and become the Duque de Telqual. The room reflected his elegant taste. The heavily gilded pillars and gilded marble walls favored by the old man had been replaced with pillars of crystal and silver. The ceiling was supported on a filigree of silver and crystal leaves and branches. It was like being in an ice forest. The light from the chandeliers glittered on the jewels that adorned necks, wrists, fingers, and were sewn on the gowns. Even the men sported rings, single earrings, and jeweled piping on the cuffs of some of the jackets. Boho had selected an austere black suit that matched his hair and brought out the green of his eyes.

"My lord," the bartender murmured and handed him his cocktail.

Boho sipped and watched the parade of young women

entering with their parents. You could tell by the expressions which ones were attending their first major social event. One of the newbies caught his eye. A lovely girl as delicate as a fawn with golden brown hair and cocoa skin. The fat matron walking ponderously at her side seemed familiar. Boho with a shock recognized Sumiko Tsukuda. She had been one of Mercedes' ladies-in-waiting their first year at the High Ground. She had dropped out at the end of the first year ostensibly to deal with a family matter. Boho knew it was because she had fallen in love with the son of a recently ennobled merchant, and the young man's death had shattered her. Sumiko had married soon after dropping out and judging from her girth and weight had been making babies ever since. How she had produced the exquisite sylph walking at her side was a mystery of genetics.

Boho downed the rest of his cocktail, set his glass on the bar, and hurried across the ballroom to greet them. "Sumiko! I thought that was you. It's been a long time."

"Oh, I've been around, Boho, you just haven't noticed." Sumiko's sharp tongue had clearly not sweetened with age.

Boho looked down at the young girl. "And this is?" Wide pansy-brown eyes were lifted shyly to meet his. A blush rose in the girl's cheeks and she looked down at the toes of her slippers.

"My daughter, Paloma."

"Charmed." Boho lifted her hand and brushed a kiss across the back. Unlike many of the other women she wasn't wearing gloves. Her skin was soft against his lips and her fingers trembled a bit in his grasp. "Your husband?"

"Frederick hates these sorts of affairs. He prefers to drink in private," Sumiko said. The girl's eyes darted nervously toward her mother. "Come along, Paloma, we'd best greet our host and hostess. Boho." She nodded, and gripping her daughter's arm propelled her away.

Boho moved to the buffet and accepted a plate from a Hajin servant. He drifted down the line spooning up some caviar and a few oysters and listening to the conversations. Young men were busy filling plates for themselves and their ladies. A clot of older men stood by the carving station.

"Yes, it was a victory, but it's not like she led the assault herself. And who knows who actually promulgated the plan."

Boho stepped behind a pillar so he wouldn't be seen.

"The general always takes the credit and the bow," said another.

"True, but we need to know she is actually a competent military leader. We know Mihalis has the chops."

"And the consort."

"He's not blood. That's important to the *intitulados.*"

"Well, one way or the other there's going to have to be a reckoning. No heir after all these years. God knows the Emperor was potent. Nine *niño*—"

"All girls."

"Good point, but one has to wonder what's wrong with her?"

The orchestra began playing. Boho moved away in search of a partner. Back in the ballroom he saw Paloma sitting against the wall looking forlorn. He crossed to her and bowed. "I cannot believe your hand has not been solicited, my lady. If I might?"

"Yes. Please. Thank you." Her confusion was adorable.

Boho took her hand and led her to the foot of the set. There was a moment where he reflected that the girl was young enough to be his daughter. The thought was fleeting and soon banished when his arm slipped around her for the first allemande, and her soft little gasp as his hand cupped her slender waist told the tale. The pursuit and ultimate capture was going to be delightful.

It wasn't the normal setting for a romantic rendezvous, but there was something about Paloma that made it perfect and charming. Boho knew that eventually they would find their way to a bed so he was willing to sit on a bar stool at the kitchen counter while she assisted her little brothers and sisters as they made Christmas cookies. He had questioned why Sumiko would allow him such access to her very young and very innocent daughter, but then Paloma had artlessly said, *"Mama says connections are everything."* And he had his answer. There was obviously some favor the family wanted. Probably for one of the boys, as girls were often the coin to buy such favors.

Her hair was tucked up beneath a headscarf, but a few wisps had come free and stuck to her damp cheeks. She wore a flirty ruffled little black apron with white polka dots and a bow tied enticingly off to one side. There was a smudge of flour on her nose and she looked utterly entrancing as she rolled out dough. Her three younger siblings, two boys and one girl, were employing the cookies cutters, icing the cookies as they came out of the oven, and applying the decorative sprinkles and sugars onto the trees, sleighs, stars, elf boots, and crosses. Boho leaned over the counter and snagged a piece of dough from the edge of the round she was rolling out. She slapped his hand and gave him a mock frown. Noting that the urchins were all concentrating on their tasks, he risked a quick kiss. Paloma blushed, and he leaned back, popped the piece of raw dough into his mouth, and gave her one of his quicksilver grins.

She resumed her quick strokes with the marble rolling pin and Boho studied the scene. The alien staff of the Flintoff household were busy washing the dishes and mopping spilled sugar and flour off the floor, but allowing the noble children to play at cooking. The kids were exuberant, but not rowdy, and Boho had a sudden *what if* moment.

What if he and Mercedes had had children? Would there be this sense of warmth and family? No, of course not. Royal couples didn't raise their children. They interacted with them during regularly scheduled and highly scripted visits. And would this sort of cozy domesticity begin to wear on him? He preferred caviar and champagne, and getting his ashes well and truly hauled after a night of caviar and champagne. Would he still be as enamored with Paloma if she was bloated by pregnancy?

The door to the kitchen swung open and a young woman in an ensign's uniform entered. Her skin was like milk and the long braid was so blond it seemed almost white. It was such unusual coloring that Boho found himself staring. Paloma gave a cry of delight.

"Chrissie, I didn't know you were coming home."

"Christmas break. And I wanted to see you all before I started my senior cruise. We report to our ships right after the holiday." She looked over at Boho and a brief frown furrowed her brow.

Paloma caught the glance and grabbing Chrissie's hand with her flour-coated one she led her over to Boho. "Allow me to introduce you to Beauregard Honorius Sinclair Cullen, the Duque de Argento y Pepco. He's also the consort," she added, and Boho started to chuckle.

He met the girl's blue-eyed gaze. What he read there was hate and the laugh died in his throat. Her features smoothed into an expressionless mask as Paloma chattered on, "My sister, Lady Christina... oh, whoops, *Ensign* Lady Christina Flintoff."

Boho stood, bowed, and waited for her to offer her hand to be kissed. Instead she snapped off a salute while saying, "Foster sister," with odd emphasis on the word *foster*. Christina turned back to Paloma. "I'll leave you to your cooking. I should change." She nodded to Boho and left.

The younger kids were tugging at Paloma's skirt asking that she make more frosting for the cookies. After the seventh cookie sheet went into the oven the younger children lost interest in what had now become the drudgery of cutting, icing, and decorating. Paloma acquiesced to their pleas to *do something else now.* She handed them all cookies and sent them off. She then instructed the servants to finish. Boho slid off the bar stool, untied her apron, and handed it to a servant. He then brushed the flour off her face and kissed the tip of her nose.

She tucked her hand in his arm as they left the kitchen. "What shall we do tonight?"

"I'm having dinner with a colleague," Boho said.

"May I come with you?"

"It will be boring."

"I'd like to know about you. What you do."

"Boring stuff. And get paraded about like a show horse. Actually being a show horse would be more interesting. I'm more like a manikin." She looked up at him inquiringly. "I get tarted up in a uniform and wheeled out to delight the credulous rubes."

"That seems like a waste. You could be doing so much more. Doesn't anyone see that?"

"Well, some people do. But it's tricky. I'm an ornament for my wife but I can't glitter too brightly. She must always be the star."

"Mama says that perhaps someday she won't get to command the limelight."

He gave her a startled look. "Seems an odd thing to say. Mercedes and your mother were close. Your mother was one of her ladies-in-waiting."

"I didn't know that. I wonder if something happened because Mama says—" Paloma broke off abruptly.

"What? It's all right, you can tell me."

"I think Mama thinks there might be better choices to replace the Emperor when he dies. May that be a long time from now," she added hurriedly and crossed herself.

Boho made a mental note to tell Arturo that the Flintoff family might be open to supporting the del Campos. "I'll see you at Rohan's mill and swill on Thursday." He kissed her again. "Dream of me, *cariño*."

Dinner proved not to be boring at all. It was at Arturo's villa, his wife played the gracious hostess, and there were guests—three particular female guests—Arturo's unmarried sisters, Valentina, Sofia, and Nicole. They were respectively thirty, twenty-four, and sixteen. He had seen the elder two at society events but hadn't spoken beyond polite pleasantries. There were two explanations for why the older women were still unmarried. Either Musa was hanging onto them as bargaining chips, or other FFH families weren't keen on being closely allied with the del Campos since their star did not seem to be rising. As for the women themselves, he could see why the eldest was still single.

Valentina was… *rechoncho,* and the way she was digging into her dinner she would soon be *gordo*. She also seemed to have little to say, and while Boho didn't want a lot of conversation in bed he wanted to be able to converse with his spouse. Sofia was the opposite of her sister. Thin, intense. She listened to the male conversation with a fervency that bordered on obsession. Boho could foresee a lot of passionate conversations with Sofia. And then there was Nicole. Why, Boho wondered, was it that the youngest always seemed to be the most attractive? Genetics driving attraction? Would a man always be drawn to the woman most likely to harbor and nurture his seed? Nicole was pretty, not a beauty like Paloma and a year younger. He already felt a little uncomfortable with

Paloma who was seventeen—almost eighteen, as she often reminded him. He couldn't imagine being riveted to this child.

He turned his attention to the middle sister and discovered a keen mind, and a willingness to engage. She wasn't afraid to disagree with him, and unlike many women she had facts rather than feelings to back her assertions. In her intellect she reminded Boho of Sumiko, who had been the brainiest of Mercedes' ladies-in-waiting and probably would have made a formidable officer had she finished at the High Ground.

Thinking back on those days he wondered what had happened to the other surviving lady who had accompanied Mercedes to the academy. Danica and her parents had been killed in a Fold accident. But Cipriana, the stunning beauty of the four women, had graduated from the academy, done her five years, and… what? Boho realized he didn't know. He vaguely recalled seeing a wedding announcement for the daughter of the Duque de Nico-Hathaway, but the fact there hadn't been a major society wedding implied that her powerful family was not happy with her choice. Cipriana had been a fiery, sexy beauty who was known to have round heels. Odd that he had never managed to bed her.

The dessert course was concluded, and Arturo's wife, Luna, rose. She was tall and willowy even after producing three children. She smiled at Boho and Arturo. "We shall leave you gentlemen to your port and dusty politics. Join us when you've finished solving the galaxy's problems."

The Hajin butler closed the dining-room doors behind the ladies. A Hajin footman filled their port glasses, left a cheese platter and nuts, and the servants all withdrew.

"Well?" Arturo asked.

"I never buy a horse without riding it first," Boho drawled. He wondered if the casual insult would break through Arturo's slightly amused and above-it-all demeanor, but the other man just gave that secretive smile and remained silent. Boho sighed, "Arturo, I cannot make a decision based on two hours of acquaintance, and this is all purely hypothetical. I am married."

"A statement of fact without any of those embellishing adjectives such as happy—"

"Don't," Boho warned.

"My dear Boho, this is nothing more than a comfortable evening spent *con la familia* with my good friend. So how do you find my sisters?"

"Too young. Too fat. And…" his voice trailed away.

"Please," Arturo gave an encouraging gesture.

"A bit terrifying. A real Lady Macbeth in training there."

"Sofia has a formidable intellect and a driving will. All useful to a man with ambitions."

Boho drained his glass and stood. "You presume too much and move too fast, Arturo. I'll need a lot more detail before I'm convinced there is more here than your father and brother gnawing on thwarted ambition."

Arturo also stood. "Thank you for coming, my lord. Do keep in mind one of the greatest of the del Campo strengths—we always keep our promises."

* * *

Rohan's Winter Ball was one of the premier affairs kicking off the Christmas season, second only to the Noël Ball at the palace. Boho made a mental note to contact Mercedes and get an update on her return home. It then struck him that that might be working at cross purposes with the del Campos and how did he feel about that? Conflicted did not begin to describe how he felt as he climbed the curving crystal stairs. He smoothed his mustache and wondered again if he should go to Kemel. Of course Arturo would deny it all, or call it just idle gossip, and in truth he had no proof. He had set his ScoopRing to record at several of their meetings, but had nothing but static. Arturo clearly had some sort of jamming device. Boho felt like one of the trick riders at the circus with a foot balanced on the backs of two different galloping horses. At some point the tandem would end and he would have to jump on either one or the other and ride it to the finish.

Rohan and his *condesa* were at the top of the stairs greeting the arriving guests and then sending them on into the glittering ballroom. Boho had attended his first formal affair at the Rohan mansion when he had been eighteen, almost thirty years ago now. He found the march of years unpleasant to contemplate, but the reminders were everywhere. In the swell of Rohan's paunch and nearly bald pate, the elegant upswept but now gray hair of his lady, Analise.

He bowed over Analise, and brushed the top of her gloved hand with a feather-like kiss. He and Rohan exchanged a handshake, and the older man pulled him into a brief embrace.

"Blessings of the holiday, Beauregard."

"And to you, sir."

"Tell your father-in-law he's a lazy *cabrón* for not coming tonight."

"Tell him yourself, sir," Boho said with a grin. "I don't stand on such comfortable terms with the gentleman that I can call him an ass. And the only person who can get him to do something when he doesn't want to is Mercedes."

"Then tell the girl to hurry back."

"Will do. I plan to call her tonight."

Inside the ballroom couples had already taken to the floor. A kaleidoscope of colors flashed by in the shimmering skirts of the women. The men were more subdued, though among the dark tuxedos and the blue of uniforms a few of the younger fellows were trying out more colorful jackets in cardinal red or emerald green. Boho thought they looked absurd. Then gave a snort of laughter. At eighteen or twenty he would probably have been sporting just such a coat.

He spotted Paloma across the vast room. She waved at him, setting the peridot and gold topaz bracelet to flashing. A snapping fan drew his attention. A tip forward and a sweep to the left. The fan language was clear—*come here.* He met Sofia's eyes. She was a thin regal figure in bronze taffeta. Paloma was a nodding daffodil in pale yellow silk and tulle. She was bouncing on her toes, artless and adorable… and young, so very young. Boho walked to Sofia and bowed.

"May I solicit your hand for a dance, madam?"

"Yes. Two, I think. More would cause comment."

"We could settle with one."

"No, I'd like to get to know you a bit better. One quadrille and one waltz should do nicely."

"As you command," Boho said with more pique than irony.

She shot him a sharp look. "I hope you're not going to be resentful if I don't pretend to be in love with you, and if I also play a role in this dance we're doing."

"Not at all. I just hope you understand that once the music actually starts I'll be leading."

"Of course."

He bowed and went off in search of a drink. The entire exchange had left his feelings in turmoil. Another loveless marriage. Well, that wasn't quite fair. He was pretty sure he had loved Mercedes when they had married at twenty-one, but she had never needed him. Never looked at him as if he had hung the sun, the moon, and the stars. His gaze roamed across the crowded ballroom, finally located Paloma dancing with some young man who still had a spray of acne on his cheeks. Boho's chest felt too tight. He gulped down the rest of his drink and went off to fill the rest of his dance card.

As soon as the music ended he sought out Paloma and secured her for two country dances. The big eyes flew up his face and she looked confused and a bit hurt.

"More would cause comment," he said gruffly.

"Not one waltz?"

"Not tonight."

She studied his dance card, then her gaze went to Sofia who was being led onto the floor. "Ah," she said and in the moment the face of the maiden showed the cold wisdom of the crone. Then her next partner arrived. Boho bowed and stepped back.

Sofia proved to be as proficient and precise at her dancing as she was with everything else. She conversed with him even through the complex steps of the quadrille and at one point it was Boho who lost his place as he tried to keep up the conversation. That actually drew a smile from her, which was both encouraging and alarming.

At the dinner break Boho escorted Sofia, and filled a plate for her. He then returned to the buffet to fill his own. He was surprised to see Paloma sitting with her mother and not surrounded by a bevy of boys. They seemed to be in earnest conversation. He toyed with going over, but decided against it.

After eating he found himself suddenly overheated. Boho brushed away the bead of sweat in his sideburn and left the dining room to seek fresh air on the balcony. A flash of memory returned of finding Mercedes in the arms of that *intitulado*. The satisfaction he had felt as he dragged that lowborn scum away by his collar like a misbehaving dog. He had actually dueled the fellow. He should have just beaten him rather than crossing swords.

The click of heels on stone brought him around. He was expecting Sofia, but it was Paloma. She seemed to float into his arms. "I'm sorry. I was jealous, but that's stupid. You have things you have to do that require finesse and I'm just a silly girl. I understand I can't be at your side while you accomplish these things, but I can always be waiting to ease you."

He crushed her against his chest, breathed in the scent of her perfume. He held her at arm's length, studying that piquant face, then pressed fervent kisses onto her palms. "I don't deserve you. You're wonderful. I'm playing a game, my darling. One for which there are no rules. Having you—"

"No games with me. You can trust me, Boho."

"You're the only one I can."

15

WHAT'S IN THE HEART

"Translation to normal space in two minutes," Graarack said from her position at navigation.

Tracy had insisted they use the formal language he had learned at O-Trell from the moment they had obtained the ship. At least now his crew all knew why he had been such a stickler. Tracy tightened his crash webbing. Jahan was perched on the back of his chair, her tail and prehensile feet holding her in place.

"I wish we knew why Control on Kusatsu-Shirane always wants us to come in so close and so hot," Luis said from his post. "They can't wait a few days for us to come in from the outer system?"

"Their planet, their rules," Jahan said.

"One minute," Graarack said.

"My guess it's defensive," Tracy said. "Anybody who's known to them comes in close. Anybody appearing out at the edges will be known to be an enemy."

"Not that it will do them much good if the League finds them," Jax's voice came over the intercom.

"Thirty seconds."

There was the sensation of being turned inside out and the familiar sharp pain in the back of the eyes and then they were back in normal space. "Good job," Tracy started to say, but his words were drowned out by the blaring of proximity impact alarms.

"Shit! Shit! Shit!" Graarack's frantic and profane recitation was barely audible over the whooping sirens. Her claws flew across the controls. Tracy unhooked his webbing and fell more than ran to join her. His eyes flicked from sensor to sensor. In a debris field this dense the ship's computer could react faster than the crew, but Tracy felt the need to at least be ready to respond.

A giant piece of steel and composite resin, its edges ragged and blackened by fire, tumbled past the front viewport. It had been years but Tracy recognized the material and the colors, occluded by burns though they might be. It was a piece of an imperial ship. He was frozen in shock. Fortunately, Graarack wasn't. She slammed a hand down on the jet control and sent the *Selkie* off on a new trajectory. Relative to Tracy's position it felt like he was riding in a falling elevator. His stomach seemed to hit the ceiling and his balls were climbing into the back of his throat. One of Graarack's eight limbs shot out and she grabbed him by the belt and kept him from joining his stomach on the ceiling.

A few minutes later and they had pulled back out of immediate danger of impact. The scanners revealed the magnitude of the disaster. The computer's best analysis was that there had been four ships. Interspersed among the pieces of ships were rocks of various sizes. It was as if a new asteroid belt had formed around Kusatsu-Shirane.

"Match trajectory and image capture on that big piece," Tracy said. "It looked like there was writing on the fragment. Maybe we can get an ID."

"And do what? Report to the League about how a bunch of their ships got all blowed up, and admit we were trading with a Hidden World?" Luis said.

"A lot of people died here, Luis. Don't make light of that or just think about us. Now get on the radio and get in touch with Orbital Control. See if you can find out what happened and what they want us to do."

"Okay." The tone was grudging, but Baca turned back to his station. After a few minutes he turned back. "Nobody's answering, and worse, nobody is talking—"

"Maybe the League found a way to knock out communications?" Jax suggested as he came rustling onto the bridge.

"No," Luis said. "Communications are still up, but the whole planet's gone silent. Except for the music."

"Music?" Tracy asked. "Put it on speaker."

A mournful song filled the bridge. A woman's voice throbbing with loss and grief. The song ended and an instrumental piece began that was equally as heart-rending as the vocal piece. Tracy shivered. Something terrible had happened on Kusatsu-Shirane and judging from the carnage around them something equally terrible had happened in orbit.

Minutes passed as Graarack and the computer worked to match velocity and vectors with the large fragment. The cameras zoomed and compensated. A portion of the name came into focus. *San Medel y Cel*. The rest of the letters were gone, but Tracy could fill in the rest. *San Medel y Celedon*. A dreadnaught and a flagship. *Her* flagship. Vomit clawed up the back of his throat. He forced it back, and bent forward, arms wrapped around his belly. They had parted so bitterly and now it could never be put right. Straightening, he gave the bridge of his nose a hard squeeze, fighting back tears as Luis, accessing the computer files, yelped, "Holy crap!" He spun to face Tracy. "That was the flagship of the Infanta."

The bridge was gripped in silence as the shock of what that meant sank in. It was the shaking of Jax's fronds that broke the spell.

"She would have held the lives of billions of humans and aliens in her hands once her father passed. Instead she precedes him into oblivion," Jax said somberly.

A fur-covered finger swept away the moisture beneath Tracy's eyes. Tracy was glad Jahan had used her knuckle and that the fearsome claws were sheathed. "You weep," Jahan whispered into his ear.

"It's a tragedy for the League," Tracy said gruffly.

"They came here to do violence to the people of Kusatsu-Shirane," Jax said.

"It was a duty they would not have relished."

"But they would have done it just the same," Dalea said. It startled Tracy; he hadn't noticed when the Hajin had joined them on the bridge. "If the Infanta gave the order."

"And now the captain will say something about orders being orders," Graarack said.

"Look, people, a bunch of ships were destroyed here. Several thousand men and women lost their lives. If life had turned out differently I might have been among them. So of course I'm upset. Now we need to find out what's happened on Kusatsu-Shirane." He stood and started for the access ladder.

"Did you know her, Captain?" Dalea asked.

He didn't pretend not to understand. "I was at the academy with her," Tracy said.

Luis leaned back in his chair. "It's interesting how you never actually answer that question, Captain." In response to the curious looks from the rest of the crew the young man added, "I asked him that back on Nueva Terra and he didn't answer then either."

"And you're not getting one now. Figure out a course to the planet."

"Let's not burn fuel landing the *Selkie* until we know more," Jax said.

"Okay, I'll take the Talon."

"You still want me to plot a course for you?" Luis asked.

"No, in a ship that small I can handle it myself. You try to figure out how a Hidden World that was only colonized a few decades ago managed to take out a League strike force."

Tracy grabbed the rails of the ladder and slid down to the cabin and galley level. Then down another level to the large hold filled with the farming equipment they had purchased, the new loader, and the Talon. He was pulling a spacesuit out of a locker when Jahan came bounding down the ladder and grabbed her own suit.

"I take it you're coming along?"

"I don't think you should be alone in your own head at the moment."

"And now you're my shrink," Tracy grunted as he shrugged the oxygen pack onto his back.

"Hey, being free and all I'd say the price recommends me," the Isanjo said.

They secured each other's helmets and headed for the Talon. It was an older model fighter that had been replaced almost thirty years before with the saucer-shaped *Infierno*. With its needle nose and swept-back wings it looked like it was traveling at light speed even when it was sitting still. Jahan unclipped the restraints while Tracy climbed the ladder and settled into the pilot's couch. The Isanjo came swarming up, leaped over him, and took her place in the gunnery chair. Not that it had guns any longer. Tracy sealed the dome, and radioed the bridge.

"We're ready." They could faintly hear the sound of the air being sucked out of the cargo bay and into the rest of the ship. Then it was very quiet.

"Opening bay doors," came Graarack's voice.

Tracy brought the engines online as the massive doors swung open ponderously. In the distance they could see the debris field falling into an orbital pattern around the planet, which bulked like a green, blue, and white marble. Tracy lifted off and they eased out of the bay. A piece of broken ship tumbled past.

"Mind the trash."

"And you think I need the reminder... why?"

"You seem distracted."

"Shut up, Jahan."

They moved into the debris field. "How the hell did they bring all these rocks close enough to the ships to have any impact?" Tracy asked aloud.

"There seem to be blast marks on some of them," Jahan remarked.

Tracy used the proximity radar to help him negotiate the rocks and wreckage, but he sometimes overrode its decisions and took them closer to the bits of floating detritus that had once been people. Ice formed patterns on the skin, in some cases frozen blood haloed their faces where lungs had exploded. After he flew past the eighteenth body, Jahan said, "That's who you're looking for, right? The Infanta?" He didn't answer, just tightened his grip on the controls. "She's dead, Tracy."

"I know. Maybe. Probably. She is... was the heir to the throne. I have to think there would have been emergency measures in place. Some kind of added protection."

Jahan kept silent for another twenty minutes then said, "Did you even intend to go to the planet? Or was that just an excuse?"

"All right! All right!"

He reprogrammed and set them on a trajectory for the planet. Jahan switched on the radio. Haunting music filled the cockpit. Occasionally Tracy sent out a hail. "Kusatsu-Shirane Control this is *Selkie* drop ship. Come in, Control." There was no answer, just the music.

They passed relatively close to one of Kusatsu-Shirane's small moons. The planet sported six but only one was presently in view. Jahan suddenly stiffened and the flexible ears on her suit pricked straight up.

"What?"

"I'm hearing something." Her gloved hands flew across the controls, amplifying the signal, and then Tracy heard it too. The ping of a distress beacon sending its cry into the void.

"Lock onto that," Tracy ordered.

"Way ahead of you. There," she pointed. "On the moon."

Calculations were made and input, trajectory burns plotted. It would take almost two hours for the Talon to reach the pitted surface of the moon. Tracy tried not to hope. Reminded himself to focus on dodging the debris, but couldn't stop the internal prayer.

It has to be her. Please let it be her. It has to be her.

Paloma reclined against a nest of pillows and watched as Boho paced. The light from the setting sun slanted through the blinds painting Paloma's bare breasts in tones of red and gold, and soft brown curls tumbled across her shoulders. The aromatic smoke from his Tiponi stim stick formed a writhing dance before his face. Boho had pulled on the robe that the InterGalactic hotel chain provided to guests, and as he paced his now flaccid dick flapped against his thighs. The thick carpet, the fibers interwoven with memory foam, was plush and soft beneath his bare feet.

"...Can you really know what's in a person's heart?" Boho concluded.

"You don't trust him."

"I don't know. I grew up with Arturo. We moved in the

same circles, seduced the same girls. I would call us friends. The question is how much power he wields in the family. Arturo thinks they need me, but will Mihalis, or will he view me as a rival and a threat?"

"You are a military leader too, you've been closer to power than Mihalis, the people love you, and—" Paloma gave him an impish smile "—also you're far more handsome than Mihalis. We ladies like that."

Boho chuckled, charmed and flattered she felt that way. Sometimes the age difference was daunting and he worried he disgusted her. The lighter moment faded. "So, you're saying I shouldn't trust the del Campos?"

"I don't know, my love. They have offered you a daughter, a sister. They must think they need you for something. And what is their plan? To formally remove Mercedes from the succession and then wait—"

"They're not going to wait. Musa's been gnawing on his resentment for twenty-six years. They'll force a constitutional crisis by removing Mercedes, then claiming the Emperor is mentally unfit. Which I could attest to. The old man is becoming very vague."

"So maybe that's what they need you for."

Boho stubbed out his stim stick and settled back on the bed. He pulled Paloma into his arms. Her hair tickled his chin and caught in his stubble. She ran her fingers through his chest hair. "What if you just stayed married to Mercedes? Nothing would change for us. If you divorce—"

"It would have to be an annulment. Which I could do since she's barren."

"My point is that the only difference in our relationship would be which wife you were—" Paloma broke off abruptly.

"Betraying?" Boho said. A kernel of anger settled into his chest.

She pulled away, leaned on an elbow and looked down at him. "I'm sorry. I didn't mean that. I suppose if you don't love them then maybe it isn't really…" She caught his expression. "I'm making it worse."

"It's all right. I understand what you are saying. I did… do love Mercedes, but if I stand by her after she's removed from the succession it will be a potential source of resistance to the del Campos. She will have to be isolated, as will the other two possible contenders for the throne."

And perhaps mere isolation wouldn't be sufficient, Boho thought and he felt suddenly queasy. No, if anything happened to Mercedes it would be provocative. But the other two eligible Arango daughters? They would not be safe. It would be easy to remove Beatrisa. She was still in O-Trell. Put her aboard a ship and send her to Sector 470. Carisa would be harder. She had made it through the High Ground, done her five years, and was now back at the palace; an unmarried daughter and a living bargaining chip for the Emperor. Marry her to a del Campo supporter? A death in childbirth or a tragic accident? Boho didn't think Arturo was that merciless. He wasn't sure he could say the same for Mihalis.

Paloma lowered herself until her bare breasts were pressed against his chest. She gently kissed him. "All of this may be moot. Mercedes rolled up the *corsarios*. I expect that will make the del Campos' plans harder to get underway."

* * *

Boho had just left the hotel room when an emergency signal set his ring to drilling at his finger. He keyed it and Jaakon's holographic image appeared. "Sir." Jaakon's face was gray and his eyes wide, showing white all around. Boho waved back his security.

"Yes, what is it?"

"Where are you?"

"Out," he said shortly.

"Class five security protocol please, sir."

Class five. It was the highest classification. There was no way he could achieve it in a public hotel. "Let me return to the palace. Brief me there."

"Please hurry, sir!" Desperation edged every word.

Forty minutes later he walked into Jaakon's office. "Took you long enough," the aide snapped.

Boho flushed. "Since this was so hush-hush I figured you wouldn't want me to commandeer a police escort. So, what's the problem?"

Jaakon brought all the security systems online before he spoke. "We've lost communication with the strike force." Boho started to respond, but Jaakon rushed on. "And a distress call was triggered from her Highness's life capsule."

"What's the location?" he demanded.

"They were following up on reports of a Hidden World. I have the coordinates here."

"Contact the port to ready the imperial pinnace. Inform Vice Admiral Pulkkinen to prepare a squadron for me. I'll undertake the search myself."

"The Emperor?"

"I'll inform him. You get me ready to leave."

"Yes, sir."

For the first time Boho heard a note of respect in Jaakon's voice.

He rushed down the hall toward Fernán's study. Sometimes there were hiccups with the Foldstream, but the news that the emergency beacon had been triggered on a life pod meant this was serious. It meant a ship had died, but perhaps not Mercedes with it. *Died.* She could be gone. For the past ten years their marriage had felt like a still life of a marriage. Perfect in every detail but lacking that one essential component—life.

Oh God, if Mercedes really was dead Paloma would expect him to marry her. Or maybe not. He had discussed the complex waltz of power that he was dancing with the del Campos. Paloma had seemed fine with him marrying Sofia, understanding the reality and necessity, but with Mercedes gone would the del Campos still need his support? Musa and Mihalis were the heirs. They might withdraw the offer of Sofia. No, they'd want him as proof of an orderly transition. That however much the old man might rage, the consort, bent with grief but still thinking of the good of the League, would show his support by marrying a del Campo daughter. Yes, that was how it would play out.

God, my wife might be dead and here I am gaming out the political ramifications. His steps slowed and he leaned against the wall. Guilt shook him. He had humiliated and betrayed

Mercedes over and over. Why had he done that? Because he was merely the consort? Because she didn't satisfy him? Because he needed that look of adoration, the excitement of discovery, which only happened at the start of a love affair? Or because he was a cad? *Ugly thought, that.*

What if he never discussed a concert with her again, or tried a bite of her entree during a dinner out when they delighted the press and the citizens by pretending to be approachable and no different from the people they ruled? Boho recalled the way her lips would purse and a small frown furrow her brow when she was concentrating. The way her hair curled around his fingers. What if she really was gone and he'd never made things right? What if he never had the chance to remove the look of contempt and disappointment that lived deep in her eyes after his scheme with the promotions board had been revealed?

He pushed off from the wall trying to outrun his grief, the level of which surprised him. He would find Mercedes and bring her home and they'd do better. He would end it with Paloma. Pull back from the dangerous game he was playing with the del Campos. He would do better.

The life capsule had clamped itself, limpet-like, to the stony surface of the moon. The capsule's tiny brain had concluded that floating in a battle zone probably wasn't optimal for the survival of its occupant, had looked for refuge and landed. As they came in for a landing, Tracy reflected that the long black box looked eerily like a sarcophagus. He prayed that it was more a cocoon from which Mercedes would emerge unscathed.

The landing struts adjusted for the uneven surface. Tracy popped the dome and pushed out of his couch with such force that he almost hit escape velocity from the tiny moon. Jahan's tail wrapped around his ankle and pulled him back down.

"Whoa, whoa there, pardner," she drawled in a fake Old West accent.

"Sorry. Thanks. Hurry."

Once his boots were on the surface he set off in long flying thirty-foot strides toward the life capsule. At first Jahan kept pace with him, but then she fell behind.

"Uh, Ollie… Tracy."

"What." He turned back, impatient at the delay. The capsule was a mere hundred feet away.

"You need to look at this."

"At what?"

"Come here, but slowly. Don't bounce."

There was something in her tone that told him not to argue. He shuffled back to her, trying to stay close to the surface despite the low gravity. She stood gazing down into a neatly drilled hole in the moon's surface. An antenna nestled in a mound of rocks was blinking slowly. Tracy snapped on his helmet light and directed it into the hole. He reared back.

"That's a bomb, isn't it?" Jahan asked.

"Yeah. A big one." He scanned the moon's surface to the edge of the very close horizon drop-off. He spotted a number of the rock cairns. He gestured and Jahan followed him to a couple more. It was the same setup. They exchanged glances.

"Looks like we know what took out the ships," Tracy said.

"Good thing the Talon doesn't weigh much. Or us," Jahan said.

"I think we're okay. It looks like this was designed to be remotely detonated."

"Still—"

"We should get off this rock as quickly as possible."

They moved quickly to the capsule. Tracy's breaths were loud inside his helmet and there was a fluttering in his chest and it wasn't all due to exertion, or the fact the moon had been turned into a giant bomb and they were standing on it. He bent and shined his helmet light across the capsule. The surface was etched with a message in every known League language, urging the finder to contact O-Trell headquarters on any world upon discovery. There was also an additional message that the DNA of the human inside was not to be harvested or altered in any way.

"I guess they didn't bother to update the message now that the Cara'ot are gone," Jahan said dryly as Tracy brushed away the fine layer of dust and ice that had formed over the faceplate.

He gazed down into Mercedes' face. Snow White in her crystal coffin. Sleeping Beauty awaiting— He jerked away from that thought. She was in a deep coma induced by the drugs the capsule had injected into her bloodstream. A few wisps of hair, dark brown and iced with streaks of gray, had come loose from her braid and had caught in her lips.

"Hmmm, I thought a princess would be prettier," Jahan said.

"She's beautiful!" he flared.

Jahan stared at him, then nodded. "Ah, *now* I see... You're in love with her."

Before the conversation could become any more awkward, Tracy said, "The capsule won't fit in the Talon. We're going to have to clamp it to the hull."

Jahan nodded and picked up one end of the sarcophagus. Tracy grabbed the other and they hopped and shuffled toward the Talon. The negligible gravity on the moon made it possible, but the bulk was still awkward to handle and they were giving the buried bombs a wide berth. Several times they lost their grip and bounced the capsule on the rocks, which made them both freeze and stare nervously at the blinking antennas. They finally reached the Talon, and Tracy pulled clamps out of the locker. He double- and triple-checked the clamps. Jahan stood, hands on her hips, as she studied the arrangement.

"Seems a pretty disrespectful way to transport royalty."

"It's not like we can open it here," Tracy said. "Come on, the sooner we get back to the *Selkie* the sooner we can get her out."

16

SHE LOVES ME

Luis radioed them before Tracy could hail the *Selkie*. "That was a quick trip."

"We found a survivor," Tracy responded.

"And is that ever an understatement," Jahan muttered.

The bay doors opened and Tracy brought them in slow. He landed so softly that the landing gear of the Talon just kissed the flame-scorched surface. He killed the engines. The bay doors closed. Tracy flipped on the radio.

"Once we're re-pressurized get Dalea down here," Tracy ordered. "And pull us back. Well back from any moon."

"Why?"

"They weaponized the moons," Jahan answered.

"The Pope's holy wickerbill," Luis breathed.

When the panel went green, Tracy climbed out of the fighter and put aside his helmet. He could feel the rumble of the ship's engines through the soles of his boots. *Good, Luis has us moving out of this kill zone.*

He and Jahan wrestled the capsule off the hull of the decommissioned fighter. The whine of the lift announced the medic's imminent arrival. The crew rarely used the lift, saving it for when they had to move bulky or heavy items. Dalea had a fold-up stretcher, her medical bag, oxygen. Jahan ran to help her carry the equipment. Tracy was relieved to see that Luis and Graarack had remained on the bridge.

Dalea studied the capsule from every angle, ending at the screen that registered heart rate, respiration, blood pressure. Tracy jigged impatiently. "You just open that panel, hit that release, and it blows the seals," he said and pointed at the panel.

"And I will after I finish reading her vitals," the Hajin said placidly. She returned to her study of the readouts. After what seemed like hours she touched the release. The seals blew off, and the top lifted, releasing a puff of bitterly cold air into the hold. It formed a dense white cloud that was then torn to tatters by the atmosphere scrubbers.

Tracy gripped the end of the capsule and gazed down at Mercedes. A tangle of IV tubes snaked across her body. Where the needles that kept her in her deathlike coma had been driven into her body her uniform was stained with blood. Her skin had a grayish hue. The life capsule sensed the presence of atmosphere and warmth, gave a chime and the needles withdrew.

"When will she wake up?" Tracy asked.

"It's going to be a few hours. Let's get her on the stretcher," Dalea ordered.

Tracy slipped his arms beneath Mercedes and lifted her out of the capsule. He ignored the stretcher and carried her to the lift. He had to work at it for Mercedes wasn't much shorter than him, and she had a powerfully muscled frame.

The alien women joined him in the lift.

He was panting as the lift slowly rose to the second deck. "Don't have a heart attack," Jahan said. Tracy glared at her.

"You could have used the stretcher, and we would have helped you," Dalea added.

"Not going to happen," Jahan said in a conversational tone to the Hajin. "See, he's in love with her so of course he has to play the knight errant."

"Shut up," Tracy gritted.

"Ohhhhh," breathed Dalea.

"Both of you. Not another word."

Tracy stood at the sink in the closet-sized bathroom in his cabin holding the mother-of-pearl-handled straight razor he had inherited from his grandfather. He had caught a glimpse of his face reflected in the mirror over the sink in the med bay, and realized that being the captain of a tramp trader had allowed him to fall down on the spit and polish. He had three days' growth of stubble on his cheeks and chin, and his hair was shaggy. He didn't recall the last time he'd gotten a haircut. So now he stood with one smooth cheek, and the shaving cream drying on the other, trying to analyze his feelings.

Soon Mercedes would awaken and… then what? The initial joy had melted into a roiling sludge of resentment as he remembered their last interactions, and worried over how the League was going to react. That had apparently not occurred to several of his crew, who were just excited once the identity of their exalted passenger was known.

Forty minutes ago, Luis and Graarack had stopped by the med bay to see the survivor and stood gawking in the door until Dalea had driven them all out, Tracy included, and closed the door.

Luis had started for the ladder and the bridge saying, "I'll get in touch with the capital and let them know we found—"

Tracy had grabbed him roughly by the arm, and pulled him to a stop. "No! Not yet."

"But—"

Graarack caught on. "Ah, of course, we're orbiting a Hidden World."

"Not only that," Tracy added. "At least four, maybe five ships got destroyed here. One of them a flagship—"

"Oh, shit, you think they'd blame *us*?" Luis asked.

"Why wouldn't they? We're here and convenient." The level of bitter gall in his voice startled him as well as his crew. "There's more than just our safety to consider, there are politics too. Let's wait for the Infanta to wake up and find out how *she* wants to handle this."

"And here I thought rescuing a princess was going to be a *good* thing," Luis had muttered as he went to fix a cup of coffee.

The Sidone spider had given Tracy a sideways glance out of several of her faceted eyes. "It's interesting how those human fairytales never continue *after* the princess gets rescued. Maybe they knew something."

Tracy wiped away the now nearly dry shaving cream and lathered his face again. He finished shaving, and was pleased that he had managed to avoid even a single nick.

He ran a hand through his hair. Nothing could be done about that short of sticking a bowl on his head and cutting it himself. He wasn't going to trust it to any of his crew… well, maybe Dalea. He then realized how much he would be mocked and quickly discarded the notion. Why did he care how he looked anyway? She had fucked him over, destroyed his career. His conviction had broken his father's health. Add to that she was another man's wife. Whatever he might have felt for her it was gone now… it had to be.

He wiped away the excess cream from beneath his ears, rinsed his face, and headed to the galley. As he expected, all of them, except Dalea, were waiting for him. Luis was pulling a pan of nachos out of the oven while Jahan brought over five different kinds of hot sauce. Tracy fished a beer out of the refrigerator, opened it, and sat down at the table.

"Still no response from Kusatsu-Shirane?"

"*Nada,*" Luis mumbled around a bite of nacho.

"We need to find out what's happened," Graarack said.

"That capsule's been broadcasting a distress beacon," Jax said as he snapped on his preferred light over his chair. "At some point the League is going to show up."

"We've got a few days before a ship can get here," Tracy replied.

"We could always dump her Highness's royal heinie on the planet and beat cheeks," Jahan said.

"We are not leaving an unconscious woman on a planet, we're—" Tracy began.

Jax interrupted, "Eventually she's going to wake up and then our real problems start, unless we are far, far away from here." He began ticking off points on his waving fronds. "We were trading illegally with a Hidden World. We didn't report said aforementioned Hidden World to the League as required by the Hidden Worlds Act, 23 SLR subsection127."

"You have the regulations memorized?" Tracy asked, not really surprised but still amazed.

"All of those relevant to our particular situation and the violation of which might put my leafy ass in jail. Going on, a close audit of our finances will reveal that we received monies from an unknown source that might eventually be revealed as yet *another* Hidden World. You have been operating under an alias to avoid your debt to the League's star command. So yeah, rescuing the Infanta endangers us in a major way. I hope she's appropriately grateful."

"So, we should have just left her, let her husband and O-Trell come find her," Graarack mused. "Can we put her back in the box?"

"No," snapped Tracy, and at the same time Jahan said, "Not going to happen. The captain's in love with her."

He slammed the bottle onto the table. Beer sloshed out the top and spilled over his hand. "Would you stop!"

"Tell me I'm wrong," the Isanjo challenged. Tracy sat chewing on words, tasting and discarding them. "Ah ha!"

"It's… complicated," he finally said.

"So you *did* know her," Luis said.

Tracy was saved from answering by Dalea's hail over the ship's intercom. "She's coming around. The face of someone she knows might be helpful."

"You were eavesdropping," Tracy accused.

"Monitoring. Merely monitoring."

Tracy left the galley, hurried down the short hallway and into the small med bay. Dalea was just withdrawing a needle from Mercedes' arm. The princess was moaning. Tracy stiffened.

"What was that shot?"

"Painkiller. She's coming out of a coma and cold sleep. It's going to hurt."

"Oh, okay." He broke the magnetic seal on a chair and pulled it close to where she lay. Mercedes' left hand hung limply off the side of the bed. The elaborate wedding set glittered under the lights, mocking him with each flash of the facets. Dalea slipped out of the room. Tracy studied Mercedes' face. A furrow of pain marred her forehead. She still seemed to be unconscious so he risked it. He lifted her hand and softly stroked it. One of the sharp points on the central diamond pricked his finger, drawing a speck of blood. It seemed a fitting rebuke from the universe. He laid her hand back on the bed and released her.

Thirty minutes later she was still emitting faint little moans, her eyelids were twitching, but she was still unconscious. Tracy called Dalea. "Should it be taking this long?"

"Everybody's metabolism reacts differently, Tracy. Relax. Apart from a few cuts and bruises she is fine. She'll wake up when she wakes up."

"Okay. I was just worried."

More minutes crawled past. He found himself in a daydream that was edging toward an actual dream about what it would have been like to awaken next to this woman.

To have her scent in his nostrils, her hair wrapping around him as they made love, her warmth—

"Tracy." He came bolt upright in the chair. She was staring at him. A gentle smile curved her lips. "I dreamed I heard your voice. But you can't actually be here. You're dead… I cried."

It felt like the room tilted. *She cried*. He recovered himself, stood, and gave a small bow. "Alive and well, Your Highness."

"Then I must be dead since my prayer's been answered."

He took her right hand and gave it a squeeze. Wonder replaced sadness and confusion and she raised the other hand toward him. He leaned down so she could touch his face. "You *are* here. Oh, good," she sighed. "Now I know I'll be all right." Her eyes fluttered closed and she fell asleep.

Mercedes woke to find a long Hajin face staring down at her.

"Is it time to get up, Tako?" Then she registered that the mane was red and black, not the brown and black of Tako's, and the eyes were a dark brown rather than the pale green of Tako's eyes, and she remembered that Tako was dead. Other input began to intrude. The air smelled different. The rumble of the engines was higher pitched, the gravity lighter than aboard the flagship. The alien was gripping her right wrist. Mercedes yanked away. The Hajin took a number of hurried steps backward and gave one of those swaying, awkward curtseys that was the hallmark of the very tall two-legged herbivores.

"Your pardon, Highness. I didn't mean to frighten you. I'm Dalea, the medic aboard the *Selkie*."

"*Selkie?* Medic? Where am I?"

"We are a trading vessel, ma'am, we… came upon your signal." Mercedes noted the hesitation and wondered what wasn't being said. "Do you remember Tracy—?"

"So he was here."

"Yes."

"Was I hurt?" Mercedes asked.

"No, ma'am. Just the aftermath of cold sleep. I've been monitoring you. I shouldn't have laid hands on you. I apologize."

Mercedes studied the six long fingers. Odd that she had reacted. Once she left the nursery and the care of human nurses, she had been cared for and touched by alien maids for most of her life. Why was this so different? Because the creature was a doctor and she had been unconscious? Was it that deeply engrained that humans were always in danger from aliens seeking to steal their precious bodily fluids as many of the more conservative priests had been wont to say? She had never given much thought to the medical care afforded to her alien citizens. Of course they had to have doctors. She had just never thought about it. Just below the surface niggled a worry that the Hajin's training might be inferior.

Good manners reasserted themselves. "There's no need. Thank you very much for caring for me. May I get up?" Mercedes asked.

"If you feel up to it. It would probably be best if I assisted you."

"Very well." Dalea slid an arm behind her shoulders and helped her to sit up and swing her legs off the bunk. She then slipped her hands beneath her arms and helped Mercedes to her feet.

She looked up at Dalea. "So, you're a doctor?"

"I was a nurse practitioner. I can do a lot, but not everything. I can certainly handle the usual bumps, bruises, cuts, and occasional broken bone that happen aboard ship."

"I'd like to go to the bridge."

Baca, Graarack, and Jax were gathered on the bridge studying the enigmatic planet on the screen before them when Tracy entered. The dirge echoed off the walls. He was met with staccato questions.

"Why are we still here? No response, hence no trade," said Jax.

"Are you going down?" from Luis.

"How is the princess?" Graarack asked.

"How did the Imperials fuck up so bad?" asked Luis.

He answered them in order. "Because I say so. Yes. Fine. Arrogance and the standard arrowhead formation." Tracy sank into his chair.

"Coupled with a whole lot of moons to move between," Graarack added.

Baca shook his head. "I don't get it. They won a big victory against the League. Why the sad music?"

"Because it's short term." Tracy jumped as Jahan's tail tickled his ear. She was once again perched on the back of his chair. As usual he hadn't heard her arrive.

"Jahan's right, central command has to know where they were headed. Once they stop getting regular reports from the strike force they are going to come looking.

Kusatsu-Shirane would not have stayed hidden."

"So, where are they? Did they all leave?" Baca asked.

"I don't know. That's why I'm going down."

"When?" Jax asked.

"Soon," Tracy answered sharply.

"You're waiting for her to wake up," Jahan murmured in his ear.

"She is awake. Well, she was, from the coma, but she fell asleep—" He broke off his stumbling explanations and tried again. "Look, I am *not* waiting for her to wake up. I don't care when she wakes up. She can stay asleep until we drop her ass off as far as I'm concer—"

"Uh, Captain… she woke up," Luis said, strain sending his voice up an octave.

Tracy stood and turned. Mercedes stood on the lift platform. She was swaying a bit and she stretched out a hand to steady herself on the wall.

"Captain," she said softly. "I see you finally made it."

"No thanks to you!"

There was a gasp of indrawn breath and then a pounding of feet, skittering of claws, and rustle of fronds as the crew bolted for the access ladder. If Tracy hadn't been so angry, so raw at the heedless remark, he might have found it funny. Apparently Mercedes did. That rich chuckle filled the bridge.

"I wonder… are they more afraid of you? Or of me?" She stepped onto the bridge studying the various positions. "So, a trading vessel."

"Yeah."

"You set it up like an O-Trell ship."

"It's an efficient design."

She sank down at Baca's station. "So why are you in orbit around a Hidden World?"

"Oh, come now, Princess, you really think I'm going to incriminate myself that easily," Tracy said.

"It seems like your presence here has already done that."

"We plan to claim we picked up your capsule's distress signal and rode to the rescue. Which I'd say means we deserve a fucking reward."

"And maybe you'll get one," Mercedes replied. She fiddled with the controls, increasing the volume on the planet's signal. "What is this music?"

"We don't know. That's the only thing being broadcast."

"Aren't you curious?"

"Of course. We were headed for the planet when we stumbled across you."

"Careful, remember your cover story. I think we should land. I'd like to meet the people who could take out a dreadnaught, two frigates, and an *explorador*." The nonchalant demeanor cracked and her voice shook. "Were there no other… survivors?"

"Yours was the only signal we heard."

She covered her face with a trembling hand. "Thank God I separated the force and sent the hostages back to Hellfire. If I hadn't— Not a great success to rescue them and then get them all killed. Instead I only destroyed my own people. I wonder how they court-martial a princess?"

"I think you can be confident that they won't. They'll

shift the blame. Find some patsy. God knows that's worked for you before," Tracy said harshly.

"You're still angry." There was an implicit criticism in the words and her tone.

"Yeah, I am. You made me a criminal when I'm not. You cost me my career and my family. I haven't seen my father in twelve years."

"Oh, no. I'm not taking the blame for *that*. You could have stayed."

"And spent years trying to pay off the judgment against me? I watched that happen to Grandfather and Father. That wasn't going to happen to me."

"So you abandoned him."

"He understood. I had to make a fresh start."

"By faking your death," Mercedes said, then added sweetly, "I thought you said you weren't a criminal."

"I wasn't… I mean, I'm not… I… I had no choice."

She pounced. "And neither did we. We couldn't have you go public with what happened on Dragonfly. It could have restarted the war," Mercedes argued.

"Except it didn't. Instead the cover-up led to the Cara'ot vanishing. Deciding humans were just too dishonest and violent to risk staying among us."

"You can't know that."

"Any more than you can know your solution was the best one. It sure as hell wasn't very good for *me*."

"It doesn't look like you did so badly. You wouldn't have had this kind of freedom in the service even if you'd made captain."

"Oh, so now you did me a favor? *Muchas gracias, Princesa*."

She leaped to her feet. "You're impossible! You've been impossible from the minute I first met you. So stiff-necked and angry. I'm surprised it hasn't choked you by now!"

"And you're still the same entitled know-it-all you were at eighteen… Always harping on about how I ought to be more accommodating—"

"Which you completely ignored!"

"Excuse me for being unable to ignore dead kids! You tried to bribe me and when that failed you joined in on railroading me. You betrayed our oath. You betrayed yourself… You betrayed me!"

"I've done my duty. What was necessary for the good of the League. I helped cover up an atrocity because I was trying to prevent a war." Her voice was rising as she raged. "I massacred League citizens and let prisoners die to prove the League was strong. I came *here* because humanity has to be united, and got my ships and my people destroyed." Her voice broke. She dashed a hand across her eyes. "I married a man I didn't love." She was crying now. Wracking sobs that tore at Tracy. The anger and hurt ran out of him like snow melting, making him shudder with shame. "And… and I lost the one I did because… because—"

The universe shifted. Had she just? *Yes,* she had! Three strides and he was there, taking her in his arms. Her knees buckled and he clutched her tighter. She lifted her face to his, the tears glittering like silver on her cheeks. He murmured her name then pressed his mouth on hers. She gasped, wrapped her arms around his neck, and tangled her fingers in his hair, trying to pull him even closer as if she could climb inside him and hide.

Her lips were cracked and dry from her cold sleep. He tasted blood from a tear on her lip that his mad embrace had broken open. He gently cupped her face in his hands, and softened his hold. Her lips parted, their tongues met, the ship seemed to have suddenly started spinning. Eventually sanity returned and reality intruded. Tracy released her and stepped back. Mercedes' hands clung to him for a whispered instant and then she allowed them to fall to her sides.

He bowed and handed her his handkerchief. She stared at it, then gave him a quizzical look. "My dad always said a gentleman should have one handy for just this type of moment."

"Your father is a wise man." She wiped her eyes and cheeks, dabbed at her nose.

"Go ahead. Blow your nose. That's what it's for."

She gave him a sideways glance. "I kept an eye on him. Made sure he had business."

"That was good of you."

"I had a selfish motive. I kept hoping you'd show up."

"I couldn't. For the same reason I can't help him financially so he can retire." Tracy realized the rage was gone. They were discussing his aged, stroke-afflicted father, a stroke brought on by Tracy's court-martial, and all he felt was a giddy joy. The admission she loved him had turned the venom to ambrosia.

"We'll fix things. I can at least do that much to thank you for saving me." She swayed again and clutched the back of Luis' chair.

"You need to rest. You can have my cabin. Let me take you."

* * *

O-Trell might have left the man, but the man had never left O-Trell. The cabin was neat as a button. Mercedes could have bounced one of the quaint Hajin coins on the tightly made bed. The surfaces were clear of any items that might fly about should there be a loss of gravity or some other catastrophe. The only exception was a small shrine to the Virgin and that was carefully secured. Tracy emerged from the head carrying a bathrobe. There was a towel folded across his arm.

"Here. If you want to shower. And we'll find you some clothes. Luis is about your height. They won't be fancy unless he gives up one of his charro suits for you."

"Anything will be fine. After all, every possession I had with me is dust now."

"I'm sorry."

She shrugged. "It's all right, it's all replaceable." She paused. "Well, not everything. Not my crews." Her throat hurt for an instant as she swallowed the guilt. "Maybe it's a good thing my *Distinguido Servicio Cruzar* is gone—"

"I expect they'll give you another one," Tracy interrupted harshly.

"Since they are awarded for extreme gallantry and risk of life in combat with an armed enemy, I expect getting wiped out by exploding moons won't qualify. No, I hardly deserve it now." Her guilt and bitterness were leaking through. She tried to turn the subject back to him. "Is yours with you?"

His face took on that frozen look she dreaded. "No. The day I was arrested I gave it into the care of my batBEM, Donnel."

"The Cara'ot."

"Yeah, so my medal is wherever the Cara'ot have gotten to—another galaxy, some alternate universe, who knows? Anyway, it's gone. Like my career. You should probably rest," he said shortly, and then abruptly he left.

Mercedes stared at the blank door for a long moment. Talking with him was like negotiating a minefield. With a sigh she reached for the covers, then hesitated. Mercedes knew she shouldn't snoop but she wanted to know the man he had become. She pulled open the door to the closet. Clothes neatly hung and an interesting array of styles; it seemed he played more roles then just merchant captain. The drawers held neatly folded underwear and socks, sweaters. One had a complete sewing kit. The tailor's son was still present. In one drawer she found a crystal cube that held a small Sidone spider-silk weaving.

Mercedes sank down on the bed, cupping the cube as if it could shatter. She could remember the day he had bought it. They had been exploring the *cosmódromo* that held the High Ground. Because the shopkeeper had perceived Tracy to be a friend to royalty he had sold the piece at a shockingly low price. She and Tracy had then gone on a picnic and had a fight. It seemed to be a pattern with them. She sighed and returned the weaving to its drawer. So many years and so much grief lay between that moment and now.

She went into the tiny bathroom. A shower the size of a coffin, toilet, a small basin. Like the rest of the cabin it was spotless, but the scent of soap and aftershave floated in the air. He hadn't changed his cologne; he had been wearing the same scent in his youth. She peed, washed her hands, and went searching for toothpaste. Her mouth tasted like chemicals. She found a tube and toothbrush, and also several packages of condoms. She took one out, sat down on the toilet and studied the gold foil-wrapped package. Who did he use them with? Did he love her? Was he married? She was shaken by the possibility. She hurriedly shoved the condom back into the drawer, squeezed toothpaste onto her finger and cleaned her teeth. She had been going to use his toothbrush. After all they had kissed, passionately, deeply, tongues fencing, but knowing there was another woman she no longer felt comfortable to use it. His lips and tongue had tasted another woman. She knew it was irrational, but couldn't shake the sense of betrayal.

Returning to the cabin she pulled back the covers and climbed into the bed. The scent of him was on the pillow. Tears pricked at her eyelids. She gave her head an angry shake, wiped her cheeks, and pulled the covers up to her ears.

17

TO DIE BRAVELY

It fascinated Mercedes that the expedition to the planet was discussed by the entire crew. As a princess she had almost never had to justify her actions or desires. She said do and go and people did and went and that went double for any alien she might be around. The idea that she would have to explain herself to aliens was head-spinning. Tracy might hold the title of captain, but in this area O-Trell rules clearly did not apply. It was clear that this ship was a democracy, and she couldn't help but think that was dangerous.

They had gathered around the table in the galley. Mercedes hung back feeling awkwardly out of place as they debated. The Tiponi Flute, Jax, had argued strenuously against taking the ship down to the planet, pointing out that it would burn fuel that would have to be replaced, and since two days had passed without any communication from Kusatsu-Shirane it was unlikely there would be any trade or any profit to cover their costs. The Sidone spider was nervous and suggested they should maybe just leave and take the Infanta home. The Hajin doctor was concerned that the crew might not have the resources to deal with a crisis, if there was a crisis on the planet. The young human, Baca, offered to take the Talon and go down alone if everybody else was too much of a pussy. The Isanjo, who appeared to be Tracy's first officer, pointed out that they had had no communication with ground control. They would be landing without permission and there were still four moons rigged as bombs to be negotiated. Tracy heard them all out, then stood.

"It seems like most of you are either ambivalent or actively against setting down so we won't—"

Mercedes cleared her throat. They all looked at her. Large brown eyes from the Hajin and the Isanjo, the multiple faceted eyes of the Sidone, the strange ocular depressions on the Tiponi, and two pairs of human eyes. One black and the other that deep gray. They had always been Tracy's best feature, though the raw-boned boy, and callow youth, had matured into a dignified man. She pulled her attention back to the moment.

"Forgive me, but you are all League citizens and therefore my subjects. We need to know what happened. *I* need to know. The souls of the men and women I lost demand it of me." She nodded to Tracy. "So please take us down, Captain. The League will reimburse you for any expenses incurred."

"Unless we get blown out of space by an exploding moon," the Tiponi muttered.

Tracy glared at the alien then bowed. "As Your Highness commands."

Everyone crowded onto the bridge. Luis and the Isanjo assisted Tracy as he plotted a course and input the coordinates. He stretched his back and glanced over his shoulder at her. "It's going to take a few hours. No sense all of you hanging around up here."

But no one moved.

"Since Dalea and I seem to be very superfluous why don't we bring some beverages?" Mercedes suggested. "I'm taking orders."

"*Dios,* this is so surreal," Luis muttered.

"Coffee," Tracy said laconically.

"Do you take anything in that?" Mercedes asked.

"Black."

"You're easy."

Emboldened by his captain's lead Luis asked for coffee with cream and two sugars, the aliens opted for teas, and Jax, had one of his mineralized waters.

Down in the galley the Hajin pulled down a tray and cups and urged Mercedes to sit down. "You're not fully recovered yet, my lady. Don't task your body with more than it can stand right now. I think you're going to need your strength." She opened a bottle of apple juice, filled a glass, and took a sip.

"You suspect something," Mercedes said.

"I think I've been a nurse and worked in hospitals and—" She broke off abruptly, took another sip, and then resumed. "I've seen enough people die that I know funeral music when I hear it," the alien replied softly.

Mercedes shivered.

* * *

They had landed at the small spaceport to the north of the city twice before. Tracy brought them in and Mercedes could tell from the rigid set of his shoulders that he was prepared to pull them out at the first hint of trouble. She doubted they would be able to avoid trouble since this deep in a gravity well, pulling out a ship the size of the *Selkie* would be virtually impossible.

She studied the field, noting the slender rocket waiting at its gantry. Fuel hoses were still attached to the sides, and a payload rested atop the forty-foot rocket. Wheeled vehicles were neatly parked at the partially buried ground control building. There was no sign of people as the six big rockets fired and lowered the *Selkie* onto a scorched landing pad. Tracy shut down the engines, leaned back, and released a pent-up breath.

"Well, let's see what awaits us," he said. "Jax, I'm going to leave you and Graarack aboard. We'll stay in constant communication. If we go silent or anything else happens that gets you the least bit worried, get the hell out of here."

"Yes, sir," the Flute said.

"We're not going to just abandon you," the spider said at the same time.

"Damn it, Graarack, that's an order."

"And you're not the highest ranking person presently in attendance." Her beak clicked shut firmly.

Mercedes choked back a chuckle at Tracy's expression. "It is customary to always defer to the captain of a ship in a potentially dangerous situation, and while you have a very egalitarian structure I think it best if you heed his order."

"Yes, ma'am."

"Dalea, bring your medical kit. It might be needed," Tracy said. The Hajin nodded and hurried off.

Down on the cargo level they waited while the gangplank whined open. Tracy checked his pistol, and Mercedes noted that Baca was also armed. Dalea carried a large holdall, and Jahan wore a belt with an array of tools slung from it. They walked across the landing field toward the building. The only sounds were their footfalls and a wind blowing off the mesas to the east. On the horizon magnificent thunderheads were forming and the almost metallic smell in the air held the promise of rain to come. Based on her energy level Mercedes suspected a higher level of oxygen in the planet's atmosphere.

They reached the building. Tracy knocked on the big double doors. There was no response. He tried the handle and the doors swung smoothly open. Tracy set his ScoopRing to record and they moved through the building. All the lights were off, computers shut down, security cameras turned off and the memories wiped. There would be no record of what had happened here. No record of the *Selkie*'s previous visits or this arrival. Even the trash cans were empty. There were no people anywhere.

"Did they all just leave?" Baca asked.

"Assuming they detected the arrival of the League ships, that would only give them a couple of days to arrange an evacuation, and while it wasn't a large colony there were a hundred thousand people," Jahan said.

"And unless they were hiding them elsewhere on the planet we never saw ships that could affect an exodus of that size," Tracy said. "I know they cannibalized their long-view ship to set up the colony."

"We detected no launches during our approach," Mercedes offered.

"Okay, let's head to Edogowa," Tracy said.

Outside they found keys in all the vehicles. They picked one large enough to comfortably carry the five of them and began the drive to the city. The storm clouds were growing, a mad artist's palette of gray, blue, red, gold, pink, and lavender. Bands of rain like sweeping tendrils of blue-gray hair fell from the clouds. Dust bloomed on the tops of the mesas where the drops fell.

The chaparral gave way to neatly tended fields. Ripening pumpkins, corn tossing their tasseled heads, wheat bowing before the wind, and rudimentary farm equipment standing fallow in the fields. *"Damn it, we were right on all our picks of cargo. They would have creamed over what we've brought."* Jax's voice fluting mournfully over their radios. He was apparently monitoring Tracy's ring. In pastures cattle, sheep, and horses grazed while windmills spun, pulling water into the troughs. A sow and her piglets rooted along the side of the road.

The electric car didn't have a lot of speed so it took nearly two hours to reach the city. The storm was intensifying. Now lightning leaped between the clouds and the distant rumble of thunder echoed down the empty streets. The outskirts of the city had a few four- and five-story office buildings, restaurants, and shops. All deserted. They bypassed them heading for the neighborhoods. The utilitarian buildings gave way to small wooden houses with shoji screens on the windows and graceful upturned corners on the tile roofs. There were vehicles parked in the driveways. Perfectly groomed flowerbeds and rock gardens with neatly raked and patterned gravel in various colors surrounded the homes. They heard dogs barking and a calico cat slunk across the street in front of the car.

Tracy allowed the truck to roll to a stop. Without speaking they all climbed out and stood in the middle of the empty street. Silence apart from the thunder and the wind. Mercedes shivered. Tracy's arm started to lift as if to drop comfortingly around her shoulders, but it was quickly jerked back and clamped firmly against his side.

"Did they know—" she began, then tried again. "Are they aware of League policy regarding Hidden Worlds?"

Tracy stared at her. Was that guilt she saw in his eyes? He nodded.

She strode off toward the nearest house.

"What are you doing?" Baca called.

"Going in." She stopped and looked back at Tracy. "This is Masada."

Masada. The word echoed through his head and chilled his soul. Tracy had studied it in their military history class at the High Ground. It wasn't possible. No one in this day and age would do that. He numbly followed Mercedes. She tried the door. It was unlocked. From behind him Tracy heard Luis mutter, "Trusting kind of place, ain't it?"

"They want us to come in. To see," Mercedes said. Her

voice was flat, emotionless. Tracy wondered how long that would last if they found what they both expected to find beyond that door.

The living room was beautiful in a spare elegant way. The wooden floors were covered with tatami mats. A simple flower arrangement sat on a low table, but the flowers were beginning to wilt and shatter, leaving red petals on the black lacquer like spots of blood. There was the faint scent of incense and a more prominent one that Tracy hadn't smelled for nearly two decades. The sweetish sickening odor of rotting flesh.

Luis covered his mouth. "Ugh, what is that?"

Clearly the boy's time in O-Trell had been less violent than Tracy's. He glanced at Mercedes. There was a gray tinge beneath her rich cocoa skin and her pupils had dilated. She clearly recognized the stink of death.

The family was in the bedroom. The mother and children were on the bed, the children in her arms, her limp hands across their eyes. She had a neat hole in the center of her forehead. The children appeared to have been poisoned judging by the foam that had dried on their lips. The father was slumped in a chair, chin resting on his chest. Blood formed a bib on the front of his shirt. The pistol had fallen from his hand.

Mercedes was stone-faced. Luis ran from the room. Dalea closed the family's eyes and murmured a prayer. Jahan pressed herself briefly against Tracy's side. They left.

Outside Luis had finished retching into a flowerbed and was wiping his mouth. "You want to go back to the ship?" Tracy asked quietly.

The younger man gave a defiant head shake. "No, it just took me by surprise. You were prepared. How?"

"Masada."

"What the fuck is Masada?"

"A fortress on top of a rock cliff in the country that used to be known as Israel. The Jews were under the rule of the Roman Empire. There was a rebellion against the occupation and the rebels took the fortress. They held Masada for three years before succumbing to the military might of the Roman legions. Rather than accept their eventual enslavement the entire populace—men, women, and children—chose suicide over surrender." At eighteen Tracy had found Eleazar ben Yair to be an admirable figure. Now at forty-four and after what he had seen in that room he no longer found it admirable.

"Shit. That's grotesque."

"Or an act of incredible heroism and bravery," Jahan said.

Tracy sighed. "People have been arguing the morality of it for decades. And now they can add Kusatsu-Shirane to the debate."

"You can't know that," Mercedes snapped. "It's possible not everyone was so stupid!"

But seven houses later Mercedes' hope was gone, and the collapse Tracy had been expecting occurred. A sob burst from her and she turned toward him. Tracy opened his arms and she buried her face against his chest. She was crying so hard that within moments the front of his shirt was wet. It reminded him of the blood staining that first father's chest and he struggled to contain his shudder. He closed his arms tightly around her, trying to fence her off from the horror. He jerked his head toward the door and his crew withdrew. Their eyes held horror and sorrow, but no guilt. None of them were responsible. Not so for Mercedes.

"Why?" she cried. "We're not monsters. They would have had a good life. Especially the children. Instead they destroyed them? Why would they do this?"

"Because the life you… we offered wasn't the life they wanted," Tracy said softly. "And this was the last choice they could make for themselves."

"It's insane and horrible," she cried. "I would have given anything for a child and they throw them away like garbage! These Hidden World people are lunatics. If this is where their beliefs lead them then we're right to force them to assimilate."

Or maybe you could just leave them alone, was what Tracy wanted to say. But this was not the time. She was too gutted, too raw to have that discussion. Instead he said softly, "Let's go. There's nothing here."

"Ghosts," she whispered. "They'll always be here. So many ghosts. My soldiers, these people, the children. They'll always be with me."

18

THE WAYFARER'S CHOICE

Tracy had escorted Mercedes to his cabin where she had made it clear she wanted to be alone. He didn't argue. He felt the same. He went in search of solitude—not an easy task on a relatively small ship. He tried the cargo deck only to find Jax standing in front of the farm equipment running figures on his tap-pad. Nervous whistling emerged from the sound valves that lined the sides of his body. Each valve emitted a different discordant sound indicating his distress. The sound added to Tracy's headache.

After a mental sigh, Tracy sat down at the weight machine that, like the nearby treadmill and stationary bike, were bolted to the floor, and asked the question. "So, how bad is it?"

"Bad. There aren't a lot of heavily agricultural worlds. Maybe we can unload this stuff on Wasua but Komatsu got an exclusive there for the first ten years. We'd have to sell as used. We'll take a bath. The other option is to go back to our supplier and see if he'll take the equipment back. We'd have to pay a restocking fee, so again we lose. Add to that we promised lacquer boxes and those netsuke things to that antique dealer on Kronos." The alien turned to Tracy. "It's possible the shipment is in one of the warehouses here. We could look for it—"

"I'm not robbing from the dead," Tracy said.

"The dead won't miss them."

"That's it? That's your reaction to the death of a hundred thousand people? That we couldn't conclude the sale?"

The seven ocular organs on the Tiponi's head swiveled to look at Tracy. "What was it one of your ancient dictators said? *One death is a tragedy; a million is a statistic.* And bluntly they weren't my kind and it's not a choice I can condone."

And that's why we call them aliens, Tracy thought. "We'll figure something out," he said lamely.

"We better hope the princess is appropriately grateful for her rescue and will be correspondingly generous. Also, I need to scrub the computers in flight control. Make sure there is no mention of us. Sooner or later the League will find their way here. We don't want them to find us too."

"Don't worry. The colonists already did that."

"Nice of them. I'm still going to check."

Tracy left and headed to the galley, deciding that maybe getting shitfaced was an appropriate response to death and pending bankruptcy. He walked in on a philosophical debate.

"It's a Japanese culture," Luis was saying. "I was reading up on it. Seppuku is a tradition. It's honorable."

"It might be honorable if *one* person *chooses* to commit suicide. It's grotesque if you murder your children," Jahan said heatedly. "I've had three kits. I could no more harm them than fly through space without a ship."

"But could you have given them away to invaders and strangers?" Dalea asked. "Knowing you would never see them again?"

"Yes. Because I'd know they lived and would have a future."

"Isn't it more noble to resist? Force the enemy to see what they are? Look at the effect it's had on the Infanta," Graarack suggested.

"I am not going to educate assholes with the bodies of my children," Jahan replied.

"What do you think, Captain?" Dalea asked.

"I think I wish we'd never gotten the tip about this place. I wish we'd never come here," he said as he pulled down a bottle of whisky.

"Okay that's a weasel. Answer the question," Jahan said. "Is it a righteous choice to die rather than submit or better to survive, persevere, and maybe find a way to gut the bastards later?"

"I don't know the answer. It's League policy. I'm a League citizen. I was an officer." He tipped liquor into a glass. "I believed that assimilation was the best course. Humanity needed to be united. It was bickering nations that tore apart old Earth. Nobody could agree on anything so nothing got done, even in the face of a climate catastrophe." He sat down and took a sip. The liquor coursed down his throat and into his belly but failed to warm the ice that seemed to fill his chest. "But we've done things that make me wonder if we actually are… the good guys." He drained the whisky in a long gulp. "I better check on her. Tell her we're going to lift soon."

"And go where?" Jahan asked.

"That's one of the things I'm going to ask her."

He was surprised to find the door to the cabin closed and without thinking he just opened it and walked in. Mercedes knelt in front of the small shrine. Her hair was out of its braid and hung like a curtain of waving dark brown velvet shot with silver down her back. She was wearing a shirt that he recognized as Dalea's and a pair of pants that belonged to Luis.

"Hail Mary, full of grace, the Lord is with thee, blessed art thou amongst women, and blessed is the fruit of thy womb, Jesus. Holy Mary Mother of God, pray for us sinners now and at the hour of our death, amen." She was using his rosary, but of course she would have to. Hers had been reduced to dust and atoms along with everything else aboard the *San Medel y Celedon*.

He froze in embarrassment at the inappropriateness of his behavior, but he and his crew had a counterintuitive view of privacy. Despite living in close confines inside a tin can they all tended toward a state of constant togetherness, like a group hug. Doors were almost always open and they walked in and out of each other's cabins. When they weren't on duty they played games that involved lots of people or read aloud to the assembled crew. Maybe it was because space was so vast, so empty, and so cold that everyone wanted the comfort of contact with other living beings.

But now it had led him into a social blunder. "I'm sorry, Highness."

She gave him a brief nod, and indicated the bunk with a glance while her lips continued to move. Tracy knew he should leave, but she seemed to want him to stay, so he sat down on the edge of his bunk, closed his eyes, and offered up his own prayer for the crews of the lost ships, the people on Kusatsu-Shirane, and for himself and his crew that they could somehow come safely out of this precarious and complicated situation.

The prayer was just the barest flutter of sound in the room. "To thee do we cry, poor banished children of Eve; to thee do we send up our sighs, mourning and weeping in this valley of tears. Turn then, most gracious advocate, thine eyes of mercy toward us…"

Closing his eyes and sitting down after so many hours of unrelieved tension and no rest—and alcohol probably accounted for it—the prayer drifted into a half-sleep and memories that were half-dreams: a kiss on an observation deck, her hand resting in his, becoming his father's limp hand as he lay in a hospital bed, the pound and hiss of waves on a beach and a girl standing on the sand…

Cool fingers touched his cheek. Tracy jerked out of the half-dream. Mercedes was standing directly in front of him and close, very close. She jerked her hand back at his startled reaction. Tracy reacted just as quickly, grabbing her hand.

"I'm sorry," she said, while at the same time he said, "It's all right. You just startled me."

"You had such a hurt and sad look on your face."

"Memories." He shrugged and released her. "They're never a good thing."

"Really? I have some nice ones of you."

"Don't!" He jumped to his feet and started for the door.

"We were very good… friends once."

"That was a lifetime and a marriage ago," he snapped. He looked back hoping he had hurt her and was then ashamed when he realized that he had.

Mercedes sank down on the bed. "We all do what we feel we must." Her throat worked as she swallowed hard. "I suppose the citizens of Kusatsu-Shirane thought the same." There was an ocean of grief in her dark brown eyes.

He walked back and sat down next to her. "You didn't kill them. League policy killed them, and people like me warning them what would happen if the League ever found them. Maybe I should have told them to contact the League and petition to join, but there was money to be made selling what appeared to be antique Japanese artifacts because they had been on a long-view ship for hundreds of years. And they wanted to continue with their social experiment to create the perfect Japanese society." He shook his head. "No one's at fault and everyone's to blame."

She laid a hand on his thigh. "Thank you for trying to share the burden, but I'm the one who came here with a military force. I was cocky after Rockfleet. When we found the information, I thought I could add another habitable world to the League."

"Come home a hero," Tracy said.

She nodded. "Yes. Instead I'm the architect of a disaster." She shook her head. "The del Campos will use this to finish destroying me. They're already well on the way."

"How?"

She looked down at her hand and began twisting the elaborate wedding set, spinning it around and around. "The mannish princess who can't conceive, and can't satisfy her husband enough to keep him from straying." She yanked off the ring. It left a red indentation like a brand on her finger. "They'll soon be whispering that I'm like my sister Beatrisa and prefer women." She gave her head a shake. "But enough. Tell me about yourself. How did you get this ship?"

"Luck and theft at just the right moment." He reacted at her look. "I figured if the League had said I was a criminal I might as well live up to it. But before you ask, I stole from a Cara'ot warehouse."

"Ah. Smart." She glanced down at the ring in the palm of her hand then closed her fingers over it. Thrust it into her pants pocket. "And have you… married?"

"No. I never met anyone I wanted to marry."

Her eyes were locked on his. "Liar," she said, her tone both soft and husky.

Tracy was suddenly very aware that their thighs were pressed against each other, shoulders touching, her hair tickling his ear, and their lips only inches apart. "Mercedes… Highness… I'm… um…"

"You saved my life," she said softly, and taking his hand she laid it on her breast.

Tracy shot to his feet and stared down at her. "No! Not because you're *grateful*. That would be worse than never having you."

She came to her feet bristling with outrage. "You loved me once."

"I still do," he blurted and realized his emotions had betrayed him and he had said it. He fell back on the only defense left to him and the source of his greatest pain. "And you're another man's wife."

"God damn your middle-class morality. *He* gets to swan about seducing anything in a skirt while I have to look the other way and never follow suit?"

"Oh, thanks. So now I'm just the means to get back at your philandering husband? Wasn't there some highborn jackass to pin the horns on Boho? Or did you think it would have more sting if you schtupped the lowborn scum?"

"That is *not* what I meant! God, do you have to be so prickly?"

"Well, forgive me, *Highness,* for not grasping the subtle distinctions of your proposal."

They stood facing each other quivering with outrage. A sudden smile blossomed on her lips and she started to chuckle. For an instant it fanned the flames of his anger even higher and then he reached the same conclusion and he began to smile and then laugh.

"And just like that we're eighteen and fighting again," Mercedes said.

"*Dios,* you would think we would have learned something after all these years."

Mercedes held out her hand. He took it. "Let me try this again." Her expression sobered. "My life has been bound by expectations, rules, and protocol. I married a man I didn't love. I've failed to give the League an heir. I've failed as a military leader, and the very thought of me and what I represent has driven the population of a world to commit suicide. I have to live with all of this, but I would like to have one moment of happiness in the midst of all this grief." She was blinking back tears.

Tracy gripped her shoulders, "Mer, I—"

They were interrupted by Jahan's voice over the intercom. "Captain, we're ready to lift."

"Be right there."

"And so you are saved," Mercedes said. Her voice held a mixture of sadness and humor.

Tracy stood devouring her face, longing to kiss away the sadness, smooth the lines out of her skin. He forced himself to release her. "See if you still feel the same way after a night's sleep. I don't want to add to your regrets and grief."

Tracy left before temptation overcame his scruples.

It was a nerve-wracking few hours as they made their way out of the plane of the debris field and tried to avoid the remaining moons. The wreckage had begun to fall into an orbital pattern forming a sparse ring comprised of human ingenuity and human hate. In time orbital decay would take the larger pieces and they would burn up in the atmosphere. A funeral pyre in the sky, a charnel house below, and falling stars to mourn them all. Acid filled Tracy's stomach as he tried to contemplate what awaited Mercedes when she returned to Hissilek. She had led four ships and some six thousand soldiers to their deaths, and only she had survived.

They had a day and a half before they reached the point where he would feel comfortable entering the Fold. Before that, they had to have some sense of where they were going.

If it had been just his crew they would probably have gone to Wasua and tried to sell the equipment. Mercedes complicated matters. Should they return her to the capital? Take her to Hellfire and fleet headquarters? The huge shipyards at Cuandru where the fleet also had a large presence? It would take roughly the same amount of time to reach Wasua and Cuandru. Ouranos was a longer journey. And should they send a Foldstream message to Hissilek informing them of the rescue of the Infanta and where they were taking her?

By now fleet headquarters probably knew they had lost contact with the battle group. Mercedes would have informed them of her whereabouts, which meant the League had the coordinates and were even now scrambling to send ships to Kusatsu-Shirane. The League would also know that the capsule had been opened, so would it be better if the *Selkie* waited here for the rescue ships to arrive? No, he needed plausible deniability that he and his crew hadn't been trading with the Hidden World. They had to dump the cargo and wipe every hint of this and every other Hidden World from their data banks before they faced the League. Their story would be that they had picked up the distress call from the life capsule and come to render aid, and the princess had ordered them to take her… where? Which brought him full circle. Where did Mercedes want to go? He had to ask her before they were ready to translate into the Fold.

He met Jahan on the ladder. "So where are we going?" the Isanjo asked.

"I don't know."

"I thought you were going to ask her."

"I forgot."

"Ooooh."

The long glissando and the gleam in her large eyes made him blush. Which made him angry. "I'll get to it! Was there something else you wanted?"

"Wow, cranky much. Just to tell you and Graarack that dinner is about ready." She flipped around and went swarming down the ladder head first.

The nightmares were waiting. Faces of men trapped behind emergency bulkheads that had slammed shut trying to defend the bridge against the icy touch of space. Their mouths wide as they screamed or gasped for breath. The slack faces of dead children. Proximity alarms wailing. Nance leaning over her, preparing to pull down the lid of the life capsule. One of the bridge crew rushing them. *"Why her? I have a wi—"* Nance shooting the man then leaning in close. *"Tell my wife…"* Pain as the needles drove into her body. Vision narrowing. The closing lid cut off the rest of his words. What had he wanted her to tell his wife?

Mercedes jerked awake from a brief sleep she hadn't intended to take, sat up, and clawed her hair off her sweat-bathed face. She would tell the woman that her husband's last thoughts and words had been of her. That he loved her. She hoped it was true.

She got up, hitched up the too large pants, and went in search of company. Alone was not a good place to be right now. She found them all in the galley preparing a meal. The food smelled good and she realized she was hungry. All of them surveyed her. So many eyes: nineteen between the aliens and the humans. The expressions ranged from curious to guarded to excited to… she couldn't interpret Tracy's.

"May I join you?" she asked.

"Of… of course," the young man, Baca, stammered. He scrambled out of his chair.

"Thank you," she said softly as she sat down.

The Isanjo carried over a pot of stew, vegetables and lamb in a thick gravy. Another bowl held rice. There was a vegetarian casserole for the Hajin, and the Tiponi was shifting his lamp between various wavelengths. Once he was satisfied he poured the contents of a small bottle into his pool of water and climbed in. There was a bench along one wall. Tracy, Baca, and the Isanjo squeezed onto the bench leaving a large hassock for the Sidone and a tall chair for the Hajin. For a few minutes they were all occupied with passing and serving. Then everyone began to eat. An uncomfortable silence gripped the table.

"So, let me see if I can remember all your names. Things have been rather… hectic since I woke," Mercedes said. She smiled at the Hajin. "Dalea, right?"

"Yes, ma'am."

"Jax." The Flute swayed and bowed. "Graak."

"Graa*rack*," the spider corrected.

"Oh, yes, of course, sorry. Jahan and Luis." Nods all around. The silence returned. "So, what is the plan?"

"Actually, I was going to bring you some dinner and ask you that very question if you hadn't joined us," Tracy said. "Where do you want to go?"

"Where were you headed next?" Mercedes asked.

"Kronos," Jax said. "But there's no reason to go now. We don't have the promised cargo for our client."

"Our itinerary doesn't really matter," Tracy said hurriedly. "Depending on when… well, when the capsule was jettisoned, the League will have already received the distress call. They'll also know the capsule has been opened. They're going to come looking for you." He hesitated then added, "I'd prefer not to wait here for them."

"Yes, that might be awkward. So, what's closest?"

"Cuandru and Wasua, Highness," Graarack said.

"It would be helpful if we could unload this cargo before we go there," Jax said.

"Jax! Stop it," Tracy snapped.

Mercedes set aside her spoon. "Allow me to assure you that the crown will be appropriately grateful for my rescue."

The Tiponi's fronds fluttered and rattled, the alien's version of delight. "Oh, well then."

"It should be Cuandru," Tracy said. "The shipyards are there and a large military contingent."

Mercedes turned to Jahan. "Do you have family there?"

"Yes, Highness, my mate… husband."

"Children?"

"Yes, three, but they're pretty much grown. The youngest just started college. My girl works at the shipyard and my eldest son is on a construction crew on Dullahan."

"And your husband? He didn't mind…" Mercedes' voice trailed away. She didn't know how to say *staying home* without making it sound accusatory.

"Raising the kids and staying home?" Jahan gave that Isanjo tooth-baring grin. "Oh, no. He's a homebody. Gets sick in freefall and hates dehydrated food. It was an easy division of labor. And he does work. He designs games for tap-pads."

"How interesting. Anything I would know?"

"Um, probably not, Highness. They're designed for Isanjos and really need more than two hands to play."

"I see. And it's not required that you keep calling me Highness." Mercedes swept the table with a look. "Now that we're all acquainted, ma'am will suffice." Murmurs of *yes, ma'am* whispered around the table.

Mercedes helped clear the plates. Graarack brought Tracy a tap-pad. Mercedes noticed the red wash into his cheeks. He looked embarrassed. Intrigued she paused to watch.

"I don't remember where we were," Tracy muttered.

"The chapter entitled 'Wayfarers All', page one hundred and fifty-nine, second paragraph, the sentence beginning, 'As she forges towards the headlands she will clothe herself'," Jax said. The look Tracy gave him should have shriveled his fronds.

"What is all this?" Mercedes asked.

"We read aloud after the final meal of the day," Jahan said. "Each one of us picks a book from our species. You can't really know a culture until you've heard their poetry and read their great literature."

"What a lovely custom. And an interesting way to spread understanding," Mercedes said.

"Yes. Pity you don't allow it in your schools and universities." The Isanjo's eyes seemed cold as she stared, unblinking, at Mercedes.

The Hajin's head swung between them, and she quickly said, "Though, God help us, we all had to read *Moby Dick*."

It was awkward. Mercedes hurried into speech to try and cover. "So, what human book did you select?" she asked Tracy.

"*The Wind in the Willows*," he said.

Mercedes returned to her chair and sat so she could watch his face. "Please, do read."

He cleared his throat several times and the two spots of color remained on his cheeks. He began. "She will clothe herself with canvas; and then once outside, the sounding slap of great green seas as she heels to the wind, pointing South! 'And you, you will come too, young brother, for the days pass, and never return, and the South still waits for you. Take the Adventure, heed the call, now ere the irrevocable moment passes!'" His voice cracked on the final words. He coughed, reached for his beer. She watched his throat work as he swallowed the last sips. There was a bit of stubble forming at his jawline—silver and gold. It caught the light. She wanted to touch it.

He read a few more pages then said, "That's all the voice I have tonight," he said. There were a few grumbles of disappointment, but the group began to break up. Jahan and the Sidone headed for the bridge. Baca headed to his cabin. The Hajin medic paused and said, "You should rest, Highness... ma'am. Your body and mind have experienced a form of death." She left the galley.

Tracy stood and offered his arm. "Allow me to escort you."

She stood and laid her fingertips on his arm. "Thank you, sir."

They walked in silence down the short hall to his cabin.

He stopped at the open door. "Well… goodnight."

A silence like drifting feathers fell between them. She allowed her hand to slide up his arm. "So, I've slept."

"Ah, have you? That's… nice. Okay." He ran a finger around his collar. She wanted to laugh.

"Yes, and I believe I'll take the wayfarer's advice," she murmured. She leaned in and kissed him.

19

WORRY ABOUT TOMORROW WHEN TOMORROW COMES

They practically tumbled through the door, arms wrapped around each other's necks, lips locked together, breaths coming in short gasps. Mercedes noticed that Tracy had the wit to lock the door and place a privacy notice on the outer panel. He used only one hand as if he couldn't bear to release her even for an instant. Her fingers were clumsy as she struggled to unbutton his shirt. She was frantically toeing off her boots and kicking them aside. One of them hit the wall and made the material ring like a bell.

She wore a tee shirt borrowed from Dalea. Like the trousers it was too big. Tracy gripped the trailing hem and pulled it over her head, interrupting her attempts to get his shirt undone. She growled in frustration, and yanked the shirt tails free from his waistband. She then followed his example and just pulled it over his head. Boho had a mat of dark hair on his chest. Tracy's was pale and rather sparse. She ran her fingers down his chest marveling at the contrast of skin and crisp curling hairs.

He unhooked her bra. The straps slid down her arms and

her breasts spilled free. He gave a moan and buried his face between her breasts, his hands cupping them. His lips and tongue played across her skin. Fire shot through her body followed by the sensation that warm honey was flowing rich and heavy into her pelvis. She arched her back and clutched at his shaggy, graying dishwater-blond hair.

He unzipped her borrowed trousers and they slid down to her ankles. She stepped out and kicked them aside and was suddenly shaken with unease. She glanced down at the way her belly now bulged slightly over the top of her panties. There was a bra bulge that had crept up on her as the years had passed. She was shaken with doubt. Would he still find her attractive now that she stood exposed, bared to his gaze? She shook her head trying to veil herself with her hair.

"My God, you're so beautiful," he whispered. It was as if he had read her thoughts, heard her fears, and answered them with reassurance. She found tears pricking her eyelids. "What? What is it? What's wrong?" His thumbs wiped away the betraying moisture. "Are you having second thoughts?" He stepped away from her. "Please, don't do anything that will make you unhappy."

"No, no, it's not that. I just wish. I wish I was still young. I don't want to… disappoint you."

"Oh, Mercedes, I have loved you, I think, from that first moment on the beach. Whether you're eighteen or one hundred and eighteen." His voice was husky with emotion.

She twined her arms around his neck, put her lips against his ear and murmured, "Liar. You thought I was a dreadful little princess."

"True." His voice caught on a laugh. "Little did I know just *how* true." He gave her a rueful look. "And never worry about how you look. If anybody should be worried it's *me*. I'm not exactly an Adonis. Not that I ever was."

She smiled a bit mistily at him. "Now, where were we." She opened his fly and slipped her hand down until she cupped his penis.

He jerked, sucked in a quick breath, slipped his hands around her waist and pushed her toward the bed. The back of her knees hit the edge of the bed and she tumbled backwards. He slipped off her socks, then snagged her panties and began to pull them down. She lifted her hips to assist him. Tracy drew back, eyes devouring her as he pulled off his boots, trousers and shorts. His erection sprang up from the brush of pale hair in his crotch. She opened her knees, but he didn't move onto and into her.

Instead he held her feet and gave them a massage. The muscles in her calves felt like warm butter and she sighed with delight. He kissed the arches of her feet then his hands and lips moved up her legs, stroked her hips and across her belly. His tongue darted into her belly button and electricity shot through to her spine. He continued his exploration gently kissing her breasts, running his tongue around the rough edges of her areolae. Her nipples tightened and peaked and he gently kissed them, then took them in his mouth, nibbling and sucking. Her little gasps became sharp moans of pleasure. His mouth moved on to her neck, kissing and biting while his hands still caressed her breasts. Time seemed to distend and dilate. She seemed to be floating, her body a complex mass of sensations.

Moisture filled her vagina slick and warm. She found herself desperate for his touch. Grabbing his hand she moved it down to her crotch. His fingers played through her mons, gently flicked across her clitoris. Mercedes felt it swelling, engorging with blood. Sweat broke out across her body and she gave a cry of pleasure as his fingers slipped into her. She kissed his shoulder, tasting salt from the sweat that bathed his body. Tracy slid down the length of her body and tongue replaced fingers as he kissed and teased her, parting the labia. Deep guttural moans erupted from her throat and she clutched at his hair.

She tugged on his hair pulling him up her body until she could hold his cock, and run her thumb across the tip of his glans. Now his moans matched hers. "Now, please!" she begged.

"Wait, I should get a condom—"

"No!" She clutched at him. "It's all right. I think I'm sterile."

"All right."

Mercedes braced for the rough thrust, but he slid into her like an otter slipping into the water, soft and smooth. His hips began to move, each thrust taking him deeper into the heart of her. The rhythm quickened, driving, touching, springing away, bringing her to the edge of madness. She kept waiting for him to climax, but instead an orgasm shook her and she screamed her pleasure. She was certain his would soon follow, but instead Tracy began to bring her once more to that shattering pinnacle where there was no sensation, sound, or sight beyond the confines of her body and the moment. It was like nothing she had ever experienced, but she suddenly felt greedy and selfish.

"Don't you want… need to… isn't it time…"

"Soon," he whispered against her ear. "I want you to enjoy this too." And it began again, that slow climb to orgasm.

He panted against her ear. "I think I have to now. I can't hold back any longer." The pace of his thrusts increased until the gimbals on the bed were swaying, and her body was driven deep into the memory foam mattress. Their sweat-slick skin both slipped and gripped as they pumped. She clutched him as if she could melt through his skin and lose herself utterly. He gave one final thrust that brought her close to fainting. The sensations were so intense that her eyes snapped open with the shock of it. His eyes were closed, expression exultant, and the tendons in his neck were etched against his skin as with a hoarse cry he came. The warmth of his ejecta filled her. The only sound was their harsh breaths. Mercedes' heart felt as if it was trying to break free of her chest. The scent of sex and sweat filled the cabin. She had only known one man's touch and it had never been like this.

She thrust her hands toward heaven and allowed her arms to then fall softly across his back. "So *that's* what all the fuss is about," she murmured.

"Wha?" Tracy murmured sleepily, his head pillowed on her breast.

"Shhh, nothing, dear one. Go to sleep."

* * *

He woke up, embarrassed that he had been asleep. "Sorry," he mumbled. His head was on her shoulder and they were pressed tightly together in the narrow bed. "Didn't mean to doze off. Your arm must be numb."

"It's all right. I enjoyed watching you sleep. The frown goes away."

"Sorry, don't mean to be so dour." She tangled her fingers in his hair and gave a tug. "Sorry, I know I'm shaggy. I'll get a haircut on Cuandru."

"Stop apologizing. And I like your hair. Makes you look rakish. You were always so spit and polish."

"I had to be. Everyone was certain the lowborn scum would disgrace the service. I guess that turned out to be right."

"I don't know how many more ways *I* can say I'm sorry." She rolled onto her side, offering him her back.

Tracy cursed himself mentally. "Sorry. The old grievances are like splinters I can't pull out. And I apologized again."

"It's okay." She turned back to face him, sketched the planes of his face with her forefinger. "The hardest thing for me is knowing that you did the right thing. You were that helicopter crew at My Lai. I was the government flak covering it all up. I think it's why I've never stopped loving you even when you put me to shame."

"You love me." He repeated the words, still finding them unbelievable.

"I do."

Tracy wrapped his arms around her and pulled her tight as if he could lose himself in her and never let her go. She hugged him back with the same frenzied grip because they both knew this was an instant in time that could not last. Mercedes rested a hand on his chest and pushed up so she could gaze down into his face. Her hair hung like a chocolate and silver waterfall, the curling ends tickling his chest. Her expression was serious.

"Tracy, do something for me."

"Anything."

"Don't report you've found me. Don't call ahead to Cuandru. Let us have whatever time we can steal before I… before I…" She dropped her head, hiding behind the curtain of her hair.

"You know they're going to be deploying every resource to find you. And what will they do to us if they find out we held back this information?"

"Nothing. I'm the Infanta. I'll tell them I was unconscious."

"And they'll wonder why we didn't take you to a hospital."

"Okay, try this. I decided to use this opportunity to move unrecognized among my people so I could hear their concerns without fear that they would be intimidated."

"The Princess and the Pauper, eh?" He chuckled and she joined him in laughter.

"The Princess and the Tailor's Son."

"We are improbable," Tracy said.

"But not impossible," she whispered, and leaning down she gently kissed him.

She curled up next to him and her breathing soon deepened into sleep. He remained awake for a long time savoring the wonder of the moment.

Late in the night he was awakened by her cries. Tears slid from beneath her lashes and wet her cheeks even though she was still asleep. She began to thrash, fighting the covers and his embrace. He pulled her up, gave her a shake. Her fist lashed out and caught him on the cheek. He shook her again. "Mercedes, wake up! You're having a nightmare." Her eyes snapped open. She stared at him in confusion then touched her wet face.

"I killed them. I killed them all," she whispered.

"Hush. Hush. You didn't. They made the choice." He was careful not to mention the crews aboard the lost ships. Those she had killed. Eventually she fell back to sleep. Tracy lay awake and tried to see the future. It looked bleak so he retreated to the present. He would worry about tomorrow when tomorrow came.

Since Mercedes had indicated her wish to stay with them and remain undetected Tracy had jettisoned the life capsule. They couldn't risk a snap inspection by customs and planet patrol finding the capsule and making their lives very hard. Once that was done they entered Fold and embarked on an idyllic six days and seven nights being cut off from the wider galaxy as they made their way to Cuandru. The days were filled with conversation, making small repairs on the interior of the ship while Mercedes handed him, Jahan, and Luis tools as they tried to find that elusive electrical problem that had plagued them for months. In the evenings they prepared dinners together. Mercedes had never spent any time actually cooking, but she had assisted her stepmother in approving menus for state dinners and had a wide knowledge of various types of cuisine. Luis practically wiggled in delight knowing he was eating approximations of dishes that had been served at the palace.

They finished *The Wind in the Willows* and the crew insisted that Mercedes pick the next book.

"Oh, dear, that's way too much pressure. What if my choice displays my terrible taste in literature?" she had said laughingly.

"No worry there," Jax said, sliding his multiple eyes toward Luis.

"Luis picks the most dreadful crap," Dalea added so there would be no confusion.

"How many *Penetrator* books have we heard?" Jahan asked the room.

"At least they're short," Graarack added.

"Hey!" Luis had bawled. Everyone had laughed.

Tracy found himself smiling just thinking about it. He shifted a bit in his command chair. Last night neither he nor Mercedes had gotten a lot of sleep and his balls were pleasantly aching. He rubbed at the grit in his eyes, and nodded to Graarack. "Take us out of Fold. Once we've translated, tight beam our information to the port."

"Does that information include Mer— the Infanta?" Luis corrected himself.

"Not yet. She wants a couple of days to evaluate the situation before she makes contact with the governor," Tracy answered. He was trying to sound casual. Judging by the looks his crew exchanged he had failed.

"Then she better be a crew member," Jahan said. "Otherwise, they'll think we're sex slavers and we kidnapped her."

"Don't be silly. She's not young enough," Tracy replied.

"Hoo boy," Luis muttered to his console.

"Better not let *her* hear you say that," Dalea said.

Jahan shook her head. "Captain, somebody's got to take you in hand and teach you how to be a boyfriend."

"I am not her boyfriend. She's married. We're friends."

"With benefits," Luis said under his breath.

"Okay, then you've got a lot to learn about being a lover," Jahan said.

"We're not—"

"Captain! It's a small fucking ship," the Isanjo said.

Tracy, his face burning with embarrassment, gave an inarticulate growl and clutched at his hair. "All right, fine! Get her on the crew list." He stomped to the access ladder.

20

THERE WILL BE PAIN

The smell of death filled the air. Boho gagged and pressed a handkerchief to his face, tried to breathe through his mouth. "The reconnaissance teams report the same result in the other two cities, sir," his flag captain, Saban, reported. "Estimates are up to maybe a hundred thousand corpses. I have no idea how we're going to dispose of them."

"Hit the cities with missiles, burn them," the commander of the *fusileros* suggested.

"Don't be a moron," Boho said. "Goldilocks planet, houses built, fields planted. We get rid of the bodies, fumigate the houses, and the place is ready to be colonized with no cost to crown or colony."

"Sorry, sir, yes, sir, I should have seen that, sir."

Saban repeated his question. "So, what do we do with the bodies?"

"Burning them isn't a bad idea. They'll just have to be brought out of the houses. But that's not our mission. We continue our search for the Infanta."

"Unfortunately, we have no indication of where she might be."

"We can only assume she was found by a ship and has been removed from the system," Boho said. "Get with central command and have them run a check of every ship's Fold course. One of them must have passed near here and intercepted the SOS."

"Sir, that could take months."

"So why are you still talking to me?" Boho asked with a sweetness laced with acid.

"What about the destruction of the strike force? Do we report that?"

"No. We need to investigate what occurred."

"We know what occurred. The locals booby-trapped the moons, and the Infanta—the ships—sailed right into it," the marine said.

"I'm not sure it's that simple. We have no idea who wired the moons. And these deaths need to be investigated." Boho gestured at the houses lining the street. The marine looked puzzled. Boho considered options. *Unknown alien threat? No, that might sow panic.* Then he had it. "We know that the Infanta obtained the coordinates of this world from the *corsarios*..." he allowed his voice to trail away suggestively.

His flag captain's eyes narrowed and he nodded. "Ah, I see, sir. It's likely this Hidden World was another nest of the criminals. Unfortunate that the Infanta didn't manage to get them all." He touched the *fusilero* on the arm. "Come along, Barret. We should start an inventory of assets."

Boho hurried to the shuttle and ordered a return to

the ship. Once aboard he retreated to his cabin, set up the cipher protocols, and drafted a message to Kemel. He laid out the situation—ships destroyed with all hands killed. A planet that had become a charnel house. Mercedes at the center of all this death. He leaned in and dictated, "Perhaps it makes sense to blame all of this on the corsairs. Imply they had another base of operations. It makes Mercedes out to be incompetent, but better that than the truth—that she lost a squadron to the citizens of a Hidden World." His hand hovered over the send button.

Boho leaned back and drummed his fingers on the desk. *Send or wait?* The truth might very well lead to a constitutional crisis and remove Mercedes from the line of succession. The del Campos would certainly use this disaster to force that outcome. So, did it make sense for Boho to get ahead of it? Inform Arturo instead of DeLonge? He was going to have to think on that. Right now his immediate problem was some *hombre* sending a message to his sweetie about the fate of the squadron. He could use the official secrets act, but that would draw attention to the situation. Boho decided he would claim a Foldstream problem and keep any messages from leaving his squadron until he decided which way to jump.

What he knew beyond a doubt was that someone had found Mercedes' life capsule and opened it. One of the *exploradors* had located the abandoned capsule near the edge and above the plane of the planetary system. There had been traces of blood on the needles, and the medics were testing to verify the identity, but Boho was certain it had contained Mercedes because of a few strands of long hair caught in the crash foam.

He had twined them around his finger and remembered other times he had stroked and combed that long hair.

There was no doubt she had been found. So why had there been no contact from her or her rescuers? Was she a prisoner or was she running from the disaster she had led? Neither alternative was a good one. Were her rescuers holding her for ransom? Had any demands been made? Something else to check with DeLonge. Except he couldn't. Until he knew which way to move, Boho didn't want the old intelligence officer informed. At the moment all the League knew was that they had lost contact with Mercedes' squadron, and the capsule had been launched. He had at least a few more days to consider before the Emperor and DeLonge would be demanding a report.

Part of him longed to leave the system and go searching. But where? They had had a fix on this star system because of the information Mercedes had provided, and the distress signal from the capsule had given them a definitive location. To just go searching aimlessly made no sense, and while they were in Fold they would be unable to receive messages. As much as it galled him, holding still seemed like the best option for the moment. He left his desk and poured himself a brandy.

Where are you, Mercedes? Into whose hands have you fallen?

Mercedes' fingers were trembling a bit as she reached up and touched the ends of her newly cut hair. The Hajin shifted nervously from foot to foot. The scissors that had done the deed hung from her hand. The long locks littered the floor around the chair. The Infanta's identity now lay in shreds on the floor around her feet. Mercedes studied the woman who looked out of the mirror at her. Her now red hair just brushed the bottom of her chin, and fell across one eye. Dalea had used some of the dye she used to keep her mane streaked to change Mercedes' dark brown curls. Mercedes had had long hair her entire life, but she had to admit the color looked quite good against her dark skin and the short bob accentuated her curls and made her look younger. She touched her hair again.

"So, do you hate it?" the Hajin asked. Worry laced the words.

"No, no. It's just going to take some getting used to. I wonder what Tracy will think?" Mercedes added.

"Oh, he'll piss and moan. Men always do. They all love long hair." She tossed back her mane. "They don't have to take care of it."

Mercedes laughed. "You're probably right."

"We've got you listed as an engineer so I dug one of Luis' stained tee shirts out of the laundry." Dalea gave her an apologetic look. "I'm sorry but we need—"

"People's eyes to just slide across me. I get that."

She took the proffered tee shirt and got out of the chair. "Highness." Mercedes looked back, surprised at the use of the honorific. Over the past days the crew had begun to relax around her. "Please, don't hurt him," the Hajin said softly.

With a sigh Mercedes turned to the doctor. "I think that's unavoidable. Don't you? This interlude will have to end. He knows that. I know that."

Dalea busied herself with putting away the hair dye and the scissors. "Then why are you prolonging it?"

She stared down at the toes of her boots. Why indeed? Because she was happy? Because when she was in his arms it allowed her to occasionally forget the bodies at Kusatsu-Shirane? Because in their lovemaking she had found a delight and joy she hadn't thought possible? Because she feared what she would face when she returned to her own life? The well-deserved fury and grief from the families of the dead that would wash across her? The faux concern from politicians and others in her class who would then plot and connive and mock behind her back? She knew the military debacle had the potential to shake her father's reign. It certainly threatened the succession.

She folded her hands as if praying and pressed her fingers to her lips. Finally, she said, "Because I'm selfish, Dalea." The alien seemed taken aback by her honesty. "And I'm scared. When I go back..." A stone had lodged in her throat. She turned away and swallowed hard. It didn't move. She finally managed to croak out, "I've failed my father. The families of my officers. I don't know what they'll do to me."

"No concern for the parents of the crewmen?" Dalea asked.

Mercedes shook her head. "The officers under my command were all FFH. Their families are powerful, they can damage me. And they all have seats in parliament. Then there's the cabinet officials, the *intitulados* can't really so any—" Something in the Hajin's large eyes stopped her. She replayed her words and realized what had shocked the alien. "Yes, I'm a product of my upbringing. I'm as entitled as Hell."

"I apologize, Highness, I meant no—"

"No, you're not wrong. You, all of you, are like mirrors. And I don't much like the reflection of myself that I'm seeing." She made a vague, helpless gesture. "Thank you for doing my hair. I appreciate it. And... and I'll try to... do better."

If there was one thing a military could do efficiently it was clean up messes. Pits had been dug, bodies had been pulled from the houses in the city closest to the spaceport and burned. Where purification had really set in, the furniture that cradled the bodies had also gone on the pyres. Houses had been cleaned and fumigated and all of this had been accomplished in three days. They were now preparing to move on to the second city.

Boho was inspecting the crates that were stacked in the warehouse at the spaceport. Delicate painted lacquer boxes, netsuke carved from stone and resin, and even one that appeared to be actual ivory. Which meant it was at least six hundred years old. The last elephant had died three hundred and seventy years ago. The ivory trade had been banned long before then. He slipped the delicate figurine into his pocket. There were katana menuki and even a couple of katanas and a wakizashi. They had clearly been packed for shipment but never collected. This implied that a ship had been coming. Did it abort its landing once it hit the debris of the imperial strike force? Could this be the ship that had found Mercedes?

Boho's ScoopRing tapped his finger. The latest batch of Foldstream messages from the capital had arrived. One was from Anselmo Moran. Boho had pulled him out of the palace press office and made the young man his personal press liaison. Anselmo had recorded the message in Boho's office. A security screen shimmered around him. "Hello, sir. There are starting to be rumbles that something untoward has happened to the strike force. Kemel is doing his best to crush the speculation while still keeping the Emperor under control. I took one of Musa's office drones out for drinks and learned that Musa has sent for Mihalis. They obviously know about the missing ships, but are sitting on it for now. I also took the liberty of running an opinion poll offering you or Mihalis as the person best suited to take over the League in the event of something tragic happening to the Infanta. I sampled populations on five worlds. The people prefer you by nine percent over Mihalis. If I factor in you being a widower that number increases to thirteen percent. Just thought you might find that interesting and useful."

Boho left the warehouse and hurried to his waiting shuttle. The two *fusileros* standing guard snapped off salutes. "Bring the crates aboard the shuttle." He climbed the ramp and went to where the pilot was playing a game on his ScoopRing. "We're returning to the flagship."

"Yes, sir."

"And get Captain Saban on the radio." A few moments later his flag captain contacted him.

"Yes, my lord?"

"We're returning to Ouranos."

"The entire squadron?"

"No, just the flagship. I need to consult with SEGU.

Captain Lord Chu will take command. Tell him to continue the cleanup in preparation for turning the planet over to colony services."

"Yes, my lord."

He broke the connection. The two guards were depositing the final crate in the back of the shuttle. Boho buckled into his couch while the engines began to whine and then roar. The gee forces generated by liftoff pressed him into the cushions. Two and a half hours to match orbit with the flagship. Roughly five days in Fold to get back to Ouranos. Time enough to have contingency plans in place depending upon which way the wind was blowing.

Tracy elected to take them into dock. The space around Cuandru was crowded with ships, military and civilian, station scooters, racing pinnaces, trading vessels, missile platforms protecting the largest shipyard in League space, and fabrication frames holding ships in various stages of construction. Suited figures, mostly Isanjo, climbed and darted around the massive skeletal forms. The flare from their suit jets and welders sparked against the dark like newly born stars. The main station was a massive ring. Ships nuzzled up to docking gantries, hummingbirds sipping nectar from a metal flower.

His eyes flicked between the computer readouts, sensors, and the visual through the port. Through the headphones he listened to docking and navigation instructions from docking control. He heard the clatter of boots on the ladder and risked a glance over his shoulder. It was Mercedes, though he had to do a double take. Her glorious mane had been chopped off, the hair dyed red. A pang of regret ran through him. He removed one ear bud.

"What's this?"

"We had to alter her looks," Dalea said somewhat defensively. "If we were going to get her past the customs agent."

"I'm sure the agent would be on the lookout for the Infanta to be aboard a tramp trading vessel." He gave a snort of derision.

"Tracy," Jahan said. "Her face is on the *money*."

He felt foolish and to cover he muttered, "I never carry cash. Nobody carries cash."

Luis removed a twenty-Real bill from his wallet and snapped it open. It showed the Emperor. Luis quickly reversed the bill and Mercedes looked out at him adorned with a diamond choker, and her hair, that tragically lost hair, in an elaborate updo with a tiara perched atop the tresses.

He gave an inarticulate growl, inserted the ear bud, and returned to his task. Only once did he take over from the computer. At the last moment before docking he feathered the starboard jets, spun the ship, and brought it gently to rest against the gantry with the grace of a butterfly landing on a leaf.

"Well done," Jahan said as she decamped from the back of his chair.

Mercedes laid a hand on his shoulder, leaned down and whispered, "You were the best pilot in our class."

The whisper of her breath against his skin sent a shiver through him. He recovered and shook his head. "Not true. You were."

"So, who's going down the well?" Jahan asked. "And if I hear everybody we'll have to draw straws because we need to leave someone aboard. Except for me, because I am, by God, going to see my spouse and kits."

"I'll stay since I'm just going to be doing research," Jax offered. "I've got to find somebody to buy this equipment; otherwise we'll have a hard time paying our docking fees."

There was an orderly rush to the ladder. Mercedes took Tracy's arm and since he didn't want to let go they took the lift down to the crew deck. "So, what shall we do?" he asked.

Mercedes tugged at his hair. "Get you a haircut."

"Dalea cut yours. I could have her do mine."

"All she did was chop. I want you to have it styled." He rolled his eyes and she punched his arm. "All right, we'll table that for now. So answer this, where will we stay?" she asked.

"I was thinking the Saint Regis." It was the most expensive hotel on Cuandru, frequented by celebrities and the FFH. He wanted…? He wasn't sure what he wanted. To make sure she was comfortable? To prove to her that he could be her equal? Keep her in the same luxury that Boho could provide?

Mercedes took his face between her hands and gently shook his head back and forth. "No. First, you don't have to prove anything to me—"

"Do you have to be telepathic?" he complained.

"Second, there's too much risk of me being recognized there, and, finally, I've spent my life among those kinds of people. Let me have another life. A time, however brief, where I don't have to…" She didn't finish the thought.

Jahan, sliding down the ladder, had overheard them. "If I

may make a suggestion. There is an Isanjo treehouse hotel called the Wind's Retreat. It's not too expensive, it's on the outskirts of Shuushuram, but there's a mag tram stop nearby so you can be in the city center in no time. And the food is very good."

They exchanged glances. "It sounds delightful," Mercedes said. "Thank you, Jahan."

"My pleasure. Enjoy yourselves. Tap me when you're ready to leave, Captain," she concluded and went bounding away.

Tracy packed a holdall, and he and Mercedes headed for customs control. As they shuffled forward Tracy found himself with sweating palms and an increased heart rate. He risked a glance at Mercedes. From the set of her lips he knew she shared his nerves, but that was the only indication she was worried. Dressed in a pair of his stained cargo pants and Luis' tee shirt she no longer looked like the heir to the throne. And, indeed, the agent's eyes slid right across her as he gave Ximena Sanchez's papers a cursory glance. She took Tracy's arm again and gave a little skip as they headed for the space elevator that connected the planet to the station. He gave her a questioning look.

"I'm having an adventure."

He laughed and hugged her closer. He noticed Graarack and Dalea in close conversation. The Hajin broke away and trotted over to them. "Let me know where you are staying," she said to Mercedes. "Despite how well you are doing I want to keep an eye on you. Your body was put under enormous stress."

"All right."

After Tracy bought their tickets Mercedes plucked the

credit spike out of his hand, ducked into a store, and emerged with a very pink bag. He lifted an eyebrow inquiringly.

"Underwear. I'll wear your pants, but I'm damned if I'll wear your shorts."

"If you want to shop—"

"There'll be a better selection on the planet."

As they settled into their seats Tracy said, "I'm always surprised that Graarack joins us down the well. Most Sidones know their appearance is unsettling as hell to other species and tend to be more circumspect."

"I don't want you to take this wrong, but how did you end up with—" Mercedes broke off abruptly.

"My crew of misfit toys?" Tracy said with amusement.

"I wouldn't have put it quite that way but yes."

Tracy set his ring to the privacy setting so they wouldn't be overheard. "After I bought the *Selkie* I needed crew. I was new to this false identity thing and I was afraid humans might catch me in an error. I found Jahan on an employment board. She brought in Dalea who brought in Graarack. I found Luis. He had run through his muster out pay and had gotten sideways with a gambling establishment. He was also young enough to be completely narcissistic and not pay all that much attention to me."

"And Jax?"

"He came later. I got hit with a repair that I couldn't afford to make. Jax offered to buy in."

"It's not common. Humans and aliens serving together as equals," Mercedes said.

"Well, being captain does make me more equal than

everyone else," Tracy said with a smile. "But I hear what you're saying."

"I wonder if we ought to try integrating the services."

"Parliament would never allow you to put aliens in uniform. Hell, I don't think they've fully accepted having women in the service."

"And after my disaster they'll probably end that policy."

The shadow in her dark eyes and the furrow between her brows made him wish he had the power to comfort her. But there was nothing he could say.

21

COMING EVENTS CAST THEIR SHADOWS

Cuandru was heavily forested on all three continents. Deserts and grasslands were rare and the planet had a thriving business supplying rare wood to the League for use in the homes and ships of wealthy humans. Many noble O-Trell captains tricked out their cabins and dining rooms aboard capital ships with various kinds of timber from Cuandru. The planet's real export, however, was her people. The Isanjo were extraordinary high steel workers. They flowed off their world to build the cities and ships of their human conquerors and to work as servants.

The hotel was in an old-growth forest to the north of the city. Mercedes and Boho had visited Cuandru on one of their royal visits, but hadn't left the city center or gone much beyond the confines of the governor's mansion. She had thought it was a ribbon-cutting for a children's hospital, but she couldn't quite recall. The second time she visited she had christened a newly built star cruiser by smashing a bottle of champagne on the bow. O-Trell had her so heavily tethered to the cruiser that she'd felt like she was trapped in a web. The implication that she couldn't handle herself in a spacesuit had irritated her, but a princess learned to smile and never complain. That had been four years ago, and she hadn't set foot on the planet during that trip.

The trees matched and in many cases exceeded the height of the now extinct redwoods of Earth. Mercedes stood at the foot of one massive tree looking up at the narrow bridges swaying between the branches high overhead. The Isanjo eschewed them, preferring to soar through the trees using only hanging ropes and trailing branches. The presence of the bridges and ladders suggested that humans were welcome at the Wind's Retreat. She noted the claw marks on the trunks of the trees indicating that the Isanjo also had little use for the ladders.

Tracy emerged from the building that held the front desk, kitchens, and dining room. It sprawled across several of the gigantic branches nearest to the ground. The circumference of those branches would have matched the trunks of trees on other worlds. He climbed down the ladder and keyed his ring. A holo map sprung to life. "Okay, we're in the Star Dancer room, which is..." He turned in a slow circle until the nav point settled over a dot on the map. "Over there. The desk clerk said they'd bring my bag and I'm going to let them."

They crossed the clipped grass to the indicated tree and began to climb. After the first two ladders they had to take two bridges to reach their tree. So tight was Mercedes' grip on the carved wood bannisters that her knuckles turned white. Tracy wasn't doing much better. As they inched across Mercedes spotted a bellhop swinging through the trees carrying Tracy's holdall with his tail so he could use both hands and feet. Tracy noticed him too.

"I hate that guy," he said. Mercedes giggled.

Eventually they reached the room. It was no surprise it was constructed of wood and it swayed lightly in the wind. Shutters covered the windows with the slats open sufficiently to allow a gentle breeze to flow through, carrying the scent of loam and pine and the songs of Earth birds that had been added to the biological diversity of the planet. A large bed dominated the space with six plump pillows and a crisp white duvet. There were chocolates on the pillow. A small table held a carafe and glasses. Through an open door they could see the bathroom with its Japanese-style soaking tub. Mercedes wondered where they got the water. She hadn't seen any pipes snaking through the trees. The case was placed on a luggage stand. The Isanjo bellhop stood respectfully nearby. Tracy pulled out his credit spike and tipped the alien.

"A question," Mercedes said. "Where does the water come from?"

"A cistern on the roof, madam," the bellhop replied. "The water is heated by solar panels. There's a separate filtered tank for drinking water. We get a lot of rain here."

"Thank you."

"If there is anything you need just ring." He indicated an intercom.

"Do you have room service?" Tracy asked.

"Of course, sir. There are menus in the desk drawer."

The alien left and Mercedes moved into Tracy's arms. The sway of the treehouse was similar to the feeling aboard Boho's sail boat. She pushed away that reminder of her husband. After a long deep kiss she said, "So I gather we won't be going out to dinner tonight."

"My vote would be to test out that bed, then a long soak in the tub, followed by dinner in the room."

"And another test of the bed?" she asked.

"I'll have to see how much stamina I have."

"I'll make sure you eat oysters," she responded.

Hours later they had met all the stated goals. The gentle breeze had become a roaring wind, carrying a storm down from the mountains. Lightning scarred the sky, flashing through the shutters, while thunder growled ominously. There was one final ear-splitting crash. Mercedes squeaked and clutched at Tracy as they lay in the swaying bed. The rain was being carried almost horizontally by the wind. It forced itself through the shutters and sprayed lightly across their sweat-glazed bodies. It broke the heat and shivering they pulled up the covers and held each other until the storm passed. Tracy fell asleep, but Mercedes found it elusive. She propped herself up on an elbow and studied his face. Time felt like it was fleeing past her like wind-blown fog.

"Two days," she whispered to herself. "Two days and then I'll be ready." Tracy murmured in his sleep. She bent close trying to hear, but the barely audible words slipped into snores. She continued watching him until the sun sent golden rays through the slats on the shutters. "Or maybe three."

Hissilek was gripped with the Christmas fever. Only fourteen days remained before the holiday and the streets were crowded with flitters and pedestrians all rushing to find that last gift or a particular delicacy for Christmas dinner. Boho's flitter was nondescript and heavily armored, and he had two security flitters flanking him. He gazed out the window at the crowds below. Many people were on their ScoopRings or watching the live news feed on public screens. The headlines said it all—NO SIGN OF INFANTA. THE SEARCH CONTINUES AS HOPE WANES. Doubt shook him and Boho hoped he had been right to trust Anselmo. Boho had considered banning shore leave for the crew, and continuing the communication lockdown in an effort to control the news cycle, but Anselmo had convinced him that wasn't the smartest move. There would be too many people who would know that the consort's flagship had returned, and silence would allow the press and public to speculate. Which was never a good thing. Better to get out in front of it. The young man had drafted a press release that admitted the Infanta had not been found, but that the consort was following up leads with the League's intelligence sources. He then seeded articles in the media about the consort's grief but determination to find his beloved wife. His belief she still lived because he would sense it if he had lost his love.

The reason Boho was in a particularly nondescript part of the city was twofold. He wanted to avoid another contentious conversation with his father-in-law. He had barely kept his temper when Fernán had berated him as an inadequate loser for failing to find Mercedes. Boho had also decided that continuing his dainty gavotte with the del Campos had to end. He had called Arturo four times and had none of his calls returned, and a request to pay a call upon the del Campo ladies had been summarily refused. The del Campos obviously knew that Mercedes had not been found, a squadron had been lost, and had decided that Boho's support was no longer needed. So, it was time to do what he could to thrust a spoke in their wheel. He was going to SEGU headquarters where the spies of the League kept tabs on the citizens of the far-flung empire.

Kemel's office was in a large fortress-like government building on the outskirts of Hissilek that housed the League's intelligence services. The area directly over the building was a designated no-fly zone, but even from his vantage Boho could see the array of antennae and satellite dishes on the roof, the weapons emplacements and the guards. Beyond the building the high chaparral rolled away toward distant rock-faced mountains. The flitter was directed to land in the inner courtyard. The security forces landed outside the building's perimeter. The consort had no need for personal security at the headquarters of the *Seguridad Imperial*.

He was bowed through the front doors, outfitted with a security badge, run through a weapon detector, and then escorted by one of Kemel's sleek and silent assistants to the old man's office. Age seemed to have fallen on the man's stooped shoulders and Boho thought his hair was even whiter than before.

"Anything?" Boho asked as Kemel waved him toward a chair.

"Nothing. Not a whisper. It's like she's been swallowed by a black hole," Kemel said. His voice was hoarse with fatigue.

"It doesn't make any sense. If someone had found her they'd have to know there would be a reward for getting her home. And why wouldn't Mercedes contact us… me? Her father?"

"Perhaps she can't. Coma or she's fallen into the hands of rascals who have the intent to undermine the government." The old man rested his hands on the desk and levered to his feet. "Or, worse thought and probably paranoid, but she might be in the hands of the Cara'ot."

"Okay, that is way too out there. But as to destabilizing the government…" Boho dropped his voice. "Well, we might not have to look too far outside the government to find that. I was waiting to talk to you, gathering more information before I presented it, but I think it's time. The del Campos have undertaken a sustained and targeted campaign to change the succession. Articles in the press, speeches from the well of parliament, sermons from the pulpit. All pushing the idea that Mercedes is unfit. The lack of an heir." Boho held up a hand. "And I know I haven't helped in that regard with my philandering—"

"And the bastards," Kemel said dryly.

"Well, yes. I regret those, but we're at a crisis point here. With Mercedes gone and the destruction of the squadron, they are going to make their move. I'm headed to parliament next to see what I can pick up from the members." A cough to clear his throat and Boho resumed, "I should also tell you that the del Campos tried to suborn me by offering me a del Campo daughter in exchange for my support. Needless to say, I would never have acted on it. I wanted to string them along and see what I could learn."

Kemel was nodding. "I was wondering when you would come and tell me this."

For an instant the words didn't register. When they did Boho felt as if he'd been dipped in ice. "You… you knew?"

Kemel keyed the intercom. "You can come in now."

A door to the left of the old man's desk opened and Sumiko waddled in followed by Paloma. Boho leaped to his feet and stared at Paloma. The timorous nymph was gone. Her face held all the mobility of a marble statue. The eyes that met his held no hint of adoration. Instead they calculated, measured and, it seemed, found him wanting. Sumiko was actively smirking at him.

"What the hell is this?" Boho demanded.

"Did you think all my agents were only bright young men trained in mayhem?" A thin smile touched Kemel's lips. "Wives and daughters are so often overlooked, yet they hear and see so much. I even use a few select servants, though one can't be too trusting of aliens. Still, I've known of your flirtation with the del Campos for weeks, Boho, thanks to Lady Flintoff and Paloma. They are true patriots."

Two strides took him across the room to stare down into Sumiko's broad, puffy face. "I don't know if I'd use that word in conjunction with a woman who would pimp her own daughter."

Sumiko shrugged. "I've got a number to spare." Boho noted that Paloma flinched a bit at the unfeeling answer, but the mask was almost instantly back in place.

Boho whirled on the girl. "How do you feel about this?"

"Proud. I can't attend the High Ground. I have a heart

condition, so this is another way for me to serve."

"So, you were just doing your duty with me? No, don't answer that," he added, hating himself for asking and hating himself for dreading the answer.

"I liked you pretty well. You may be old, but at least you aren't gross."

He had enough self-control not to respond. He turned to Kemel. "So, do you have a plan beyond tricking and humiliating me?"

"Not much of one unless we find Mercedes. And even then, it's going to be touch and go. Whatever happened out there, it can't be good. It's going to unsettle the FFH and the military high command, and they are going to look to the del Campos."

"What are our options?" Boho asked.

The old man sat on the corner of his desk. "We try to install one of the other eligible daughters." A gnarled forefinger was raised. "We try to find a loophole and put you on the throne. Your family has a reasonable if somewhat attenuated claim." The middle finger went up.

Sumiko interrupted. "At which point the del Campos lead a revolt in the House of Lords backed up by Mihalis and his control over the Gold. Make no mistake, old Kartirci is only a figurehead now. A number of the captains are loyal to Mihalis," she said.

A third finger was lifted. "We acquiesce to the del Campos' justifiable and superior claim." The old man sighed. "At which point Fernán orders me and the military to arrest the del Campos and the League is plunged into civil war."

"Why the hell does he hate Musa so much?" Boho asked.

"They were raised almost like brothers," Kemel said. "What happened between them I couldn't say, but whatever it was it has left them both with an abiding hatred." Another sigh shook his thin frame. "And it's worth remembering that Cain and Abel were also brothers." His hand folded into a fist.

"So, what do you want me to do?" Boho asked.

"Find Mercedes and pray for something to change the conversation," the intelligence chief said.

22

TIME IS RUSHING PAST

Lovemaking had been the start to the morning. Tracy had awakened with a soft erection and Mercedes had quickly brought him to aching hardness. When he had tried to roll on top she had placed a hand on his chest and held him down as she straddled his hips. Their hands touched as she guided him in and began to ride him. From this angle he could look up the length of her beautiful body, her breasts bouncing in time to her thrusts, the sweat trickling between them. He came with a fierceness that left him limp and slick with sweat. He started to close his eyes, but she tugged on his hair.

"Oh, no, no napping. I want to go exploring."

"And I'm going to get that haircut so I stop offering you such a convenient handle," he complained.

They had soon bathed and dressed, made their shuffling way across the bridges to the restaurant, and ordered breakfast. Tracy was pleased to see she liked the morning meal as much as he did. They both tucked into a full breakfast of bacon, eggs, toast, grilled mushrooms, and tomatoes.

The tram ride took thirty minutes. They travelled

through human homes dotted through the forest, past lakes and across a river. The outer circles of the city looked like any other League world with human-style buildings and tall skyscrapers. Flitters filled the lanes overhead. They continued on to the old quarter, which meant tall old-growth trees, treehouses, and wood buildings tucked between them. It was foot traffic only in this part of the city. Or arboreal traffic if you were an Isanjo.

The streets were paved with cut flagstones in various colors. Arm in arm Tracy and Mercedes strolled through a crowded open-air market. Even the Isanjo seemed to be gripped with the Christmas buying spirit. The scent of spices, dried lemons, and roasting meat tickled his nose. Mercedes stopped to buy a skirt and several blouses to augment her skimpy wardrobe, and she often paused at the stalls that offered jewelry for sale. None of it was expensive, consisting as it did of bead work or polished stones. A few had semi-precious gems in the design. She seemed quite taken with a string of carnelian beads. Tracy bought it for her, and hooked it around her neck. He was unable to resist the rich cocoa of her skin. He dropped a kiss on the nape of her neck. She chuckled, turned to him, and twined her arms around his neck.

"Thank you."

"You're welcome. Merry Christmas a bit early."

"Now let's find a hair salon," she said.

The shifting crowds moved in eddies like water being spun by an unseen hand. As the crowds parted briefly, Tracy caught a glimpse of a piquant face, pointed chin, upturned nose, pricked ears thrusting out of a tumble of red and white curls. Large neotenous eyes like an Isanjo, but Isanjo eyes were brown, black, or gold; these eyes, flicking nervously as she scanned the crowd, were the color of emeralds, an impossible green. She was talking with a Hajin who wore a jacket with a high collar that covered most of her mane. A small package was exchanged and slipped quickly into the pocket of the Hajin's jacket.

The woman seemed to sense his gaze, and she quickly pulled up the hood on her jacket and was lost when another eddy sent a crowd past her. Memory raced him back in time and Tracy remembered a conversation in a run-down bar on Wasua where a drunk had spun a tale about a girl with red and cream hair, emerald eyes, and tufted cat ears who had stolen his identity and changed his very appearance. The man's desperate voice, slurred with drink and fear, came back. *"I tried to make them understand that the Cara'ot had placed an agent at the very heart of the government. Replaced me with an alien who could stand at the Emperor's right hand."* Tracy's arms stiffened around her. Mercedes pulled back and studied his face.

"What is it? What's wrong?"

"I thought… no, it's nothing." He shook off the queasy feeling and followed her as she made inquiries about a good salon. They were directed to one, and Tracy keyed the address into his ring. Right after he finished his ring indicated an incoming call. It was Dalea.

"I didn't want to disturb you too early. Where are you?"

"In the old quarter. Just leaving the market."

"Oh, how lucky. I'm there too."

Suspicion gnawed at him. "Really?"

Something in his tone had her adding, "I'm restocking the larder. And I want to check on Ximena."

It took him a moment to realize she meant Mercedes. "She's fine."

"And you are a board-certified physician where?"

Tracy sighed. "All right. This won't take long, will it?"

"No, just a few minutes. Where are you?"

"Over by the stand selling wind harps."

"Oh, I see you." Tracy spotted the Hajin weaving her way through the crowd. He studied her jacket. It was the same color, but the collar was folded down so her mane was showing.

"I'm sorry to interrupt your day," Dalea said to Mercedes. "But I wanted to check on you." The alien scanned the area. "There's a restroom over there where we can be private."

"I really do feel fine, but all right."

The two females disappeared and Tracy leaned against a tree and scrolled through his newsfeed. A headline jumped out from one of the more scurrilous outlets that seemed to focus mostly on breathless reports of parliamentarians sleeping with aliens and drunken brawls by celebrities. Needless to say, it was widely read throughout the League. IMPERIAL COVER-UP? With a secondary headline—FOLDSTREAM SILENCE FROM THE INFANTA? SECRET MISSION OR MILITARY DISASTER? It went on to say that sources with ties to the palace reported that all contact had been lost with the Infanta's squadron. The author went on to offer possible reasons, but the overall implication was that the Infanta had done something stupid or foolish or treasonous. Despite the bright sun and fresh air, it felt like walls were closing in around Tracy. He spotted Mercedes returning to him, and he quickly shut down the holo.

He dropped an arm over Mercedes' shoulder. "So, everything okay?"

"Uh huh. Dalea was just being careful. She gave me a B-12 shot. She's really very sweet. So, let's go get you a haircut."

The salon was owned by an elderly Hajin who had a bubbly Isanjo assistant who washed Tracy's hair and delivered him into the hands of the old pony who wore a pork-pie hat balanced on the top of his elongated head. With the long ears hanging to either side, and the hat, he was a comical figure until he began to talk and a rolling bass emerged. The barber and Mercedes began a long conversation about cowlicks, natural parts, and the consistency of his hair before she allowed him to start cutting. Struggling between boredom and amusement Tracy asked if he could have a hot-towel shave while they dithered and debated. The Isanjo leaped into action and Tracy soon found himself relaxing while the heat soaked into his skin and softened his beard. The towels were whisked away, his face lathered, and the straight razor expertly applied. After that the Hajin began to cut.

"The lady and I have agreed that the best way to deal with your cowlick is to give you bangs. And you do have a rather high forehead and a somewhat receding hairline so this will mitigate that."

"I am *not* going bald," Tracy said.

Mercedes' eyes were dancing with amusement at his tone. "No, of course not, darling. Your hair is just regrouping and waiting for reinforcements."

"Watch it, woman," Tracy mock growled and gripped

her hand while the Hajin clipped and snipped and combed.

The barber spun the chair around so Tracy could see himself in the mirror. The image looking back seemed younger. The bangs and the way the Hajin had trimmed his sideburns did soften the rather harsh planes of his face, but the touch of hair on his forehead felt strange.

"Perfect," Mercedes said to the barber and neatly lifted Tracy's credit spike out of his pocket and offered it to the alien. While he took the payment, Mercedes stroked a hand down Tracy's cheek. "Very nice." She leaned in and whispered in his ear, "But I did rather like the stubble. The way you rubbed your chin across my back last night. Made me tingle." She nipped his earlobe.

The aliens bowed them out of the shop, and Mercedes took his arm. "Lunch?" she proposed.

They found a café at the edge of the river, and were escorted to an outdoor wooden deck that offered a view of the river and the small waterfall that was sending white spume into the air. The rumble of the falling water was hypnotic. Isanjo families were spreading blankets on the grass and opening picnic baskets. Kits ran, climbed and tussled, babies cried, a street musician strolled along the river walk playing the violin. They held hands and Mercedes enticed him into telling her about his life, his crew. Tracy was careful never to reveal the other Hidden Worlds where they traded. He might love her, but he wasn't a fool. Unfortunately, neither was she.

"You're very guarded. You start to tell me about an experience and then you slide away to another anecdote."

He regarded her for a long moment. "I love you, Mercedes, but you are the living embodiment of the League. There are some things I can't and won't tell you."

"Which makes you a little disloyal."

"And this is a surprise to you why?"

"Good point," she said and spread a bit more of the eggplant appetizer on her bread.

"I note you're also being very careful not to talk about yourself," Tracy said.

"And what would I discuss? My husband? The fact my father is failing mentally? The attacks on me by the del Campos? My most recent mission? That went so well." The haunted look was back.

Tracy gripped her shoulders. "Mer, you're going to need to talk to somebody. You know that, don't you?"

"I will. Maybe this policy toward the Hidden Worlds should be reviewed and—"

"That's not what I mean and you know it. Thousands of people are dead. On both sides. I've held you as the nightmares hit." He slid his hands down her arms and held her hands. "This interlude, as wonderful as it is, will not deal with your ghosts and regrets. Please promise me you'll get counseling when you…" It hurt to say it. "Go back."

She ran a hand down his cheek. "All right. I promise. But, right now, let me be here. With you."

"Okay."

"Buy me an ice cream cone," she said.

"With pleasure." He signaled the waiter, paid the bill and they went down to the river walk where there was a vendor selling Persian ice cream from his cart.

Tracy went with white rose and orange blossom. Mercedes picked pistachio and mocha. She eyed their selections. "I feel like these should have been reversed. You're an odd fellow, Thracius Ransom Belmanor. I never have figured you out."

"Well, welcome to the club. I haven't figured me out either." Tracy studied her. The sparkle in her eyes was diminished and her head drooped. "How about we go back to the hotel and rest for a bit. We'll come back into the city for dinner."

She took his arm and snuggled against him. "Sounds good. And maybe do a bit more than rest?"

"I think I can rise to the occasion."

"Ugh, you are impossible, and not very funny… but I love you anyway."

They didn't make it back into town that evening. Mercedes fell asleep, and slept until nearly eight. Worried, Tracy checked with Dalea, who told him to let her be, and allow her body and mind to heal. He sat in a wicker chair on the balcony where he could watch the large slow-moving Teco lizards amble down the porphyry walkways far below. A cooling breeze dried the sweat on his forehead. He read a new spy novel on his ring, and occasionally checked on Mercedes. He loved the way she curled on her side, one hand tucked under the pillow, the other under her chin. During their nights together, he had learned that she moved her foot to make the bed rock a bit before she fell asleep. She also talked in her sleep, though he couldn't be sure if that was because of the trauma of Kusatsu-Shirane or was something she had always done. It saddened him to know he would never find out. His growling stomach told him it was time to eat and he ordered a dinner for them. Mercedes woke when room service delivered their meal. Jahan had been right, the food was very good. There was an appetizer of thinly sliced cured meat wrapped around a local fruit that was pale pink and very sweet. Their main was meat from a Cuandru ruminant that was similar to pork. The medallions were glazed in a bourbon sauce with a side of vegetables, and there were slices of cheesecake to finish.

Afterward they took a cautious walk along the swaying sky bridges.

"It's like fairyland," Mercedes said as they stood holding the elaborately carved railing and looking at the lights twinkling in the branches of the trees. Tracy looked up wondering if the stars would mirror the lights, but the forest canopy blocked most of the sky. Mercedes sighed. "I think I could live here quite happily. You?"

He realized that after so many years in space he had to have the stars, and he shook his head. "No, if I did ever settle down the well, it would have to be a planet without too much light pollution and a good view of the sky. I need the stars." He thought about Freehold, lost in the darkness of interstellar dust, and started to blurt, "I could never live on—" He broke off.

"Another secret," Mercedes said softly.

"One that's not mine to share. I'm sorry."

"No, I understand." She stood in silence for a moment.

"Take me to bed, Tracy. Time is rushing past us. I wish... Don't let me sleep again." Her arms went around his waist and she rested her head on his chest.

"Your wish is my command. Particularly the first one."

She woke him in the morning by gently kissing his eyelids and then his lips. He stretched and felt his spine pop. "Umm, what time is it?"

"Early. I've been looking through the guest packet. There's an interesting hike we can take."

"Okay."

"I've ordered a picnic basket. We can pick it up when we have breakfast."

Tracy wrapped his arms around her waist and pulled her down on top of him. "I love how you are so efficient."

"Come on, lazy. Let's go." She bounced off the bed and threw his slacks at him.

Fortified with a good breakfast, and armed with water and the lunch basket, they hired a flitter to take them to the trail head that led to the Seven Sisters Waterfalls. It was a little over five kilometers one way and the trail was fairly steep as they climbed out of the dense forest and into the cliffs and boulders at the foot of the mountain. There were other hikers on the trail. A mix of Isanjo, Hajin, and human. People had brought their dogs, and one couple were leading a miniature horse for their toddler to ride. The child, chubby hands twined in the horse's mane, was giggling and shrieking with delight. The look of hungry longing on Mercedes' face was evident.

After an hour Tracy was puffing and feeling the pull on the back of his thighs and in his calves. Mercedes gave him a light punch in the gut. "Getting soft there, Captain."

"Too much time aboard ship and I'm bad about using the exercise equipment." He flipped open the water bottle and took a long drink.

"I'll tell Luis to start kicking your ass," Mercedes said. "It's clear *he's* working out."

"He's young and always on the strut. I, however, am old and past my prime."

"You realize you just insulted me too," Mercedes teased.

Tracy took her in his arms. "Never. And by the way, you are perfect and beautiful."

Her lashes lowered and she looked away embarrassed. "Come on. We still have a way to go."

The trail wound higher and higher. It seemed the mountain was growling as the sound of falling water became more audible. The narrow canyon where they were walking debouched into a wide clearing. Springy grass ran down to the pebbles that edged a lake into which seven waterfalls fell with a constant roar. Tall standing stones that clearly weren't natural formed a half-circle echoing the curve of the lake. The spume was like white lace against the gray of the rocks. On the tops of the cliffs young Isanjo and a few brave human teens peered over the edges. Mist from the falling water dampened Tracy's face.

Out of range of the spray visitors had spread blankets and were setting out lunches. Mercedes led them to one particularly tall and narrow stone. Its sides had been incised with elaborate abstract designs. Places on the stone had been rubbed smooth with the touch of thousands of hands. Tracy found himself tracing the lines of the figures, fascinated by the intricacy and the beauty. Mercedes was busily pulling food out of the basket.

"What is this place?" he asked her.

"Apparently a temple of sorts back when the Isanjo were pagans."

"Well, it was worth the hike." He bent and kissed her. "Thank you for arranging this."

She handed him a bottle of sparkling white wine. "Open, please."

Tracy lightly bounced the bottle on his palm. "Do you remember when we—"

"Had a picnic on the Apex *cosmódromo*?" she finished. "Yes."

"I bought us a bottle of wine just like this."

"And we had a fight." Mercedes smiled up at him.

"Seems to be a habit with us."

She clutched his hand. "Not anymore. Never again."

Because once this idyll is over I'll never see you again. He didn't say it though. It would have darkened the day.

23

IT COULDN'T LAST

They returned to the hotel and indulged in a long soak in the wooden tub. Mercedes filled it with bath oil. The evergreen scent in the oil blended wonderfully with the cedar wood. Tracy scrubbed her back. The feel of hot water squeezed across her shoulders was both wonderfully relaxing and arousing. She reciprocated and he groaned a bit as she massaged his neck. He turned to face her and she felt his erection pressing urgently against her thighs and belly. He was seated on the narrow shelf that ran along the side of the tub. Mercedes climbed onto his lap and taking his cock in her hand she gently guided him inside. His eyes half closed, the long lashes brushing his high cheekbones. She began to ride him, slowly rising and falling as she brought him to climax. His head fell back and she could see he was falling into a doze. She tugged his hair gently.

"Wake up. Let's go find dinner."

They scrubbed up and dried each other. While Tracy dressed she studied the skirt and blouses she had purchased and decided she wanted something prettier. Wrapped in the large towel she used the terminal in the room to call up a printable dress shop. She picked a low-cut ankle-length wraparound dress in white that would flare to expose her legs. She added a pair of high-heeled sandals, lace panties and matching bra. She used Tracy's credit spike to pay. The store promised delivery in forty minutes and true to their word a drone arrived, hovered over the balcony, and delivered her package.

She dressed and Tracy's reaction was all she could have hoped for. His eyes widened and his breath caught. She handed him the string of beads he had bought for her. "Please?" she said. His fingers were trembling against the nape of her neck as he hooked the clasp.

"Madam." He offered his arm.

"Sir." She took it and they stepped out of the room and onto the swaying bridge. "Okay, discretion being the better part of valor," she said and pulled off the sandals. They made their way to the ladder and were soon on their way to the tram stop.

They picked another restaurant on the river walk and Tracy used the fact he actually spoke some Isanjo to delight the maître d' so they were given an exceptional table with a view of the river and park beyond. Small lantern boats floated past filled with young lovers. The Isanjo were almost complete carnivores so their steaks arrived cooked to perfection. Tracy's ran with blood. Mercedes cut into hers and discovered it had been stuffed with blue cheese. It was a fantastic addition. Roasted root vegetables and polenta were the sides, and they washed it all down with a rich crimson wine. Tiramisu and coffee were the perfect ending notes. Mercedes leaned back in her chair, twirled the stem of the wine glass between her fingers, and studied Tracy. He was gazing off across the water so she could study his profile without him noticing. She liked his straight, narrow nose. The way his sideburns seemed to draw attention to the high, etched cheekbones. She even liked the way the dueling scar pulled up his eyebrow into a sardonic arch.

Music began wafting across the water. Guitars and keyboard, a piano and a trumpet. It was dance music, and the syncopated beat cried out to her to move. Mercedes leaned across the table and grabbed Tracy's arm. "Take me dancing."

"You will be pleased to know that as aide-de-camp to the XO aboard the *Triunfo* I was expected to be a gentleman so I learned to fence and whenever I took shore leave I also took a few dance classes, so I won't embarrass you," he said.

"And we won't be interrupted this time," Mercedes added. His fingers went to the scar at his left temple and he rubbed at the darkened ridge.

Tracy signaled the waiter and offered his credit spike. They followed the music until they came to a pier lit with multicolored lanterns. A makeshift bar was on one side, the band at the end with only water behind them. Ropes formed a spiderweb overhead and Isanjo danced on the ropes, silhouettes against the moon. Below, earthbound creatures—Hajin and human—danced on the rough wood planking. Mercedes dragged Tracy down the steps and out onto the pier. It swayed lightly underfoot as if the river and the wood wanted to dance too.

She spun into his arms and then realized she was the neophyte here. Her training had been for FFH balls. He had learned from ordinary people who didn't tend to dance quadrilles. The band was blending Isanjo music and the Latin rhythms that permeated the League. The pulsing rhythm beat in her blood and she found herself losing her stiffness. He pulled her closer, their hips touching, breaths mingling. The music shifted into salsa, and he attacked it with the same fiery intensity that had been the hallmark of his life. When the music smashed to an end his face glistened with sweat and his shirt clung to his chest. An aching pressure closed on her heart. She wanted to cry and couldn't say why. He pulled her in close, her head on his shoulder, hand cupping the back of his neck.

"I love you," he whispered.

The band was stretching, taking a break. Couples were drifting to the bar. The band had placed a credit reader at the front of the bandstand, and Tracy inserted his credit spike to give them a tip. They then stood in line at the bar until they could order. The glass was cold in her hand as Mercedes sipped her margarita. Tracy kissed her and she tasted rum and mint and him. The music started again, a slow tango. She led him back onto the dance floor. Each touch of his hand on her back, her hip as he spun her away, the press of their thighs against each other, was musical foreplay. Her breath grew short and fire had replaced the blood in her veins. She was lost in the moment, but then became aware of the dancers around them stumbling to a stop. The music faltered and ended. People began to murmur. They were all looking up. There were flares of light among the stars. Ships' engines firing as they fell into orbit.

Tracy's ScoopRing pinged. It was Jax.

"Been monitoring orbital control. It's the consort and he's got a flotilla with him," the alien said. He broke the connection.

"Could he know?" Mercedes asked. "Did someone talk?"

"Nobody in the crew would betray you. And Cuandru is the logical jump-off point for any search," Tracy said. "I'd probably do the same."

Mercedes clutched at Tracy's shoulders. "Take me home." She had to force the words past lips gone stiff as she struggled not to cry.

Their lovemaking had a desperate quality. Mercedes kissed him hard enough to bruise, and her nails dug at his back and shoulders. It was as if she wanted to climb inside his skin. Finally, he had nothing left to give and he fell back gasping for air, his body sweat-drenched and limp. He looked over. Mercedes had curled herself into a tight ball. He rolled over and spooned her, trying to offer comfort. His arm seemed very white against her rich dark skin.

"Tracy."

"Yes, my love."

"Let me stay. Be a member of your crew." She rolled over. Their faces were only inches apart. He could see the unshed tears glittering in her eyes. "Eventually they'll decide I'm dead and stop looking."

"No. They won't. They know your capsule was found.

They'll keep searching for you and eventually they'll find us, and they could never admit that you joined us voluntarily so—"

"They would kill you," she finished dully.

"Yes. And beyond the personal concerns, who would take the throne if you were gone? And would you be comfortable with that person?" Her shudder gave him the answer. He kissed her hair. "We were given a gift… that couldn't last."

"It will last! At least until the morning."

They talked for hours and their final coupling was slow and gentle and sad. The sun was barely up when they left the bed, bathed, and dressed in silence. She left all the clothes she had purchased. When she slid the wedding set back onto her ring finger a knife seemed to enter his gut. The only comfort was that she didn't leave the beads he'd bought for her.

"Give me your bank account number."

"You don't have—"

"Of course I do. Don't be a noble idiot."

"Yes, ma'am."

"I need to get my hair restored and I'd like to see the rest of the crew and say farewell."

"I'll call them."

They returned to the salon where Tracy had gotten his hair cut. Mercedes explained what she needed. The Hajin took her to a basin and washed her hair with a pale blue liquid that leached the red away. It was like blood swirling away down the drain. Tracy felt like all happiness and any hope of ever being happy again was also flowing away. The Hajin dried and styled the bobbed hair, spun the chair so

Mercedes could look in the mirror. The alien's eyes widened.

"All you've seen is a remarkable resemblance," Tracy growled.

The Hajin backed away, extended a leg, and gave a low bow. "Quite so."

Mercedes extended her hand to the alien. "Thank you for taking such good care of me, citizen. I appreciate it." The barber's expression was one of stunned adoration, and Tracy was again struck by Mercedes' skill in dealing with people. He wished he could develop it.

They met the crew at a cheap diner in a very native part of the city. Jax linked in so he was a shimmering hologram in the center of the table. Tracy studied the menu, checked in with his stomach, which had become a small tight ball. There was no way he was going to keep down food so he ordered the huevos rancheros. He could stir the ingredients together and no one would notice he wasn't eating. He listened to the artless chatter from Luis, Jax, Graarack, Jahan, and Dalea and wanted to scream at them. How could they laugh when his life was ending? He picked up his coffee mug and stared down into the dark depths. Of course, his life had ended before and somehow he'd kept on living. He told himself not to be so dramatic. They stretched the brunch to an hour and a half, but then Mercedes stood.

"This has been lovely, but I really should go to the governor's mansion and tell them... *I'm back.*" She forced a smile.

"Not until I've checked you over one last time. You're still my patient," Dalea said firmly.

"All right."

"Let's go into the ladies," the Hajin said.

Luis laid a hand briefly on Tracy's shoulder. "I hope someday I get to love somebody the way you two love each other. I'm sorry, *compañero*." He abruptly left the table.

It seemed like a long time before Dalea and Mercedes returned. His lady's expression was odd and she seemed to be looking past him. "Everything all right?" he asked.

"Yes. Perfect." She swept the table with a long, fond look. "Thank you all. For everything. I won't forget."

They stood and were in that awkward moment when a party is breaking up and nobody really wants it to end. "I'll take you to the mansion," Tracy said.

"No. Let's not tempt fate. Right now I can report that I was rescued by Captain Oliver Randall and his crew. If you're seen that lie won't stand."

"Maybe we should be in Fold and conveniently out of touch for a few days," Jahan said.

"I second that suggestion," the holographic Jax said.

"We'll meet you onboard, Captain," Jahan said and she led the crew out of the restaurant.

Mercedes took his arm and they went outside and called for a taxi. The flitter arrived and dropped to the ground in front of them. The door opened and they stood gazing at each other. A foot separated them. It might have been light years.

"Well, goodbye," Mercedes said, and started to reach out her hand.

Tracy swallowed several times. Somehow his saliva had turned to glass. He bowed. Suddenly Mercedes flung herself into his arms and pressed her lips against his. She pulled away even as his hands clung to her, and jumped into the flitter. He watched until it was a distant speck.

He sat on the tram to the spaceport, arms folded tight across his aching gut. He thought his heart had shattered at eighteen when she told him she would marry Boho. At twenty-one it had been torn from his chest when he had been forced to watch the video feed of the marriage ceremony. He now knew that he had never actually experienced utter devastation.

Tracy made his way to the ship and climbed wearily up the ramp. His eyes were filled with grit and fire, every bone and muscle ached. Jahan was waiting for him in the cargo bay. She hopped off the crate where she had been sitting grooming her fur.

"So, she's gone?"

"Yes."

"You gonna survive?"

"What choice do I have?"

The call from the governor's mansion had Boho running for the space elevator with his security detail trotting along behind. "We have a shuttle waiting at the equatorial pad to take you immediately to Shuushuram," Captain Wilson reported as they commandeered a capsule for their private use and began the descent to the planet.

When Mercedes' image had appeared on the screen his first reaction had been shock at the sight of her shorn hair, then a relief so great it left him weak-kneed, followed by a twinge of disappointment that locating her had ended up being so anticlimactic. No daring rescue, no nefarious parties unknown, just her walking in off the street as if she hadn't gone missing for several weeks. He didn't bother to wait for explanations. Reaching her side was more important.

An hour and a half later he was being bowed into the family quarters at the governor's mansion. Mercedes was drinking tea with the governor's wife and clearly wearing one of the lady's dresses since it was too tight across the bust and the hem was above her ankles. She set aside her cup and stood as he crossed the room in three long strides and clutched her tightly to his breast. He bent to kiss her and for an instant it seemed she was about to turn aside, but then she lifted her chin and pressed her lips to his.

"Mercedes, Mercedes, I was so worried. Are you well?"

"Yes, still a bit tired from the cold sleep, but nothing serious."

"You need to be seen by a doctor."

"Governor Marquis Darmali has sent for his personal physician, but I would far rather see my own physician, and really, I'm fine. I'm just so glad to see you."

Boho took Mercedes' hand, and moved to greet his hostess. "My lady, forgive my rudeness in not greeting you immediately."

She was a rather ordinary-looking woman though she did have a mass of tumbling curls that matched her mahogany skin. "Oh, please, my lord, give it no thought. It was so moving to witness your reunion. I'll leave you two." She paused at the door. "My seamstress is on her way,

Highness. I'll have a servant inform you when she arrives."

"Thank you, Tali, you are so good to me."

The doors closed behind the marquess and Mercedes drew him over to a love seat and pulled him down next to her. "So, tell me everything. I assume you went to my last coordinates."

"Yes. I've already got Colony Services handling applications for settlement."

"How did the locals react?" she asked.

"You won't believe it – they had all killed themselves. We had to use burn pits to get rid of the bodies. By now the ships I left behind should have finished the job. Our settlers can move right in."

Mercedes stared down at her tightly clasped hands. "So they are reduced to ashes. No names to be remembered and mourned. How awful that they thought death was preferable to us."

"They made that choice," Boho said. "And made certain there would be no one to mourn them by killing their children. They're not worth your worry or grief."

"Not so for my *hombres* and *fusileros,*" Mercedes said.

"But what happened to you, Mer? Who found you? How did you end up on Cuandru?"

"How did you?" she countered.

"Just luck. I returned to Ouranos, gathered more ships, and thought this was a central location from which to search. So, who did find you and why did you take so long to return?"

"A little trading vessel. They picked up the signal from my life capsule and went to investigate."

"How did they get the signal if they were in Fold?" Boho asked.

"They had a problem with the Folddrive and had dropped back into normal space."

"And the delay?" he pressed.

"Would you have wanted to face this particular music?" she asked. "I let them finish their delivery before I had them bring me to Cuandru." She offered nothing more.

After a few moments of silence Boho said, "Luck has played a part for both of us, it seems."

"Yes," she said. She stood and pulled him to his feet. "Boho, take me to bed. I'm tired and sad and I've missed you. Help me forget for just a little while."

"*Mi amado,*" he whispered and kissed the palms of her hands.

Boho slept beside her. Interestingly his snores were less shattering than Tracy's. She would have to have earplugs if— She quashed the thought. It was never going to be. She had wondered if she would hate having sex with Boho, but their coupling had left her singularly unaffected. It was duty so it had no power to either hurt or delight. It was also absolutely necessary and she found herself grateful that Boho had always paid very little attention to her reactions, physical or emotional.

She stared up at the embroidered canopy on the bed and laid a hand gently on her belly. *What will you be like, little one? Who will you take after? And someday, I promise, I'll tell you about your father.*

24

WE ALL PLAY OUR ROLES

Four days in Fold. Four days to make love and for her to avoid an examination by the ship's physician. She used the excuse she had used about seeing the governor's doctor—she preferred to see her family doctor back in Hissilek. Four days in which to answer his questions about her rescuers. To feign indifference. *"The captain? Oh, just some* intitulado *named Randall. The crew? I didn't spend much time with them. I mostly took my meals in the cabin. Where did Randall sleep? I have no idea. I presume with one of the crew. Should he be questioned? For what purpose? I'm safely back."* Mercifully he had let it drop.

The worst part had been being back on a military vessel. When she did emerge from the cabin she found her mind superimposing the faces of her dead crew onto the faces of the living men and handful of women who served aboard Boho's flagship. Her forays into the corridors became less frequent. Tracy was right, she did need counseling. But could the heir to the throne show such emotional weakness? She couldn't dodge the dinners at the captain's table. She sat trying to eat and hoping no one would notice her lack of appetite. Partly it was grief and guilt. Partly it was due to the fetus now growing inside her.

On the last night in Fold Boho traced her nipples with a forefinger and looked thoughtful.

"Your nipples look different, darker, and your breasts—" he cupped one in his hand and noted how she flinched "—seem very sensitive."

Mercedes dropped her gaze, hoping it seemed demure and not guilty, and ran her fingers through his chest hair. "Well, there might be a reason, my darling. I've been feeling…" She laid a hand on her stomach. "I think I might be…" She allowed her voice to trail away suggestively.

"*Madre de Dios*, you don't mean… This is wonderful!" He kissed her and gathered her tightly in his arms. "I can see why you didn't want some O-Trell doc pawing at you. You need to be handled like glass. This is going to make everything better—" He broke off abruptly.

"And worse?" Mercedes suggested.

"You've never been a fool, my love. With this news Musa and Mihalis will know the throne is forever beyond their reach." He laid a hand on her belly. "I do hope it's not a girl. Makes everything easier if you give me a son."

"Well, there's nothing I can do about it now," she said and managed a chuckle.

"I don't want you going to the gym or riding once we get home."

"And while I appreciate the affection that is behind that really stupid statement, I'm going to do what my doctors tell me and I'm pretty certain they aren't going to want me wrapped in velvet and placed in a cage." Mercedes smiled and their eyes locked.

Boho looked away first and gave a short laugh. "I'm sorry. Of course you're right. It's just that we've been waiting so long for this. And the old man is going to be over the moons about it."

"Let's see the doctor first before we make any announcement."

"Of course."

The next day they translated back into normal space and Boho sent a message to the palace to send the royal pinnace and Dr. Mueller to meet the flagship. A day and a half later the two ships converged, matched trajectory, and an umbilical was attached between the airlocks. It was a parade of people disembarking from the flagship onto the pinnace. *Hombres* with Boho's luggage, Boho's batBEM, then Mercedes and Boho. Despite the fact the umbilical was fully atmosphered Mercedes and Boho both wore spacesuits. No one else bothered, trusting to the reliable technology. Of course, none of them were the consort and the pregnant heir to the throne. Inside the confines of her helmet Mercedes' breaths seemed loud, and beyond the clear walls the stars were diamond bright and the sun a distant point of glowing yellow. They drifted into the airlock of the pinnace. Since the pressure had already equalized the inner door of the airlock was open and the captain of the pinnace stood at attention. With him were Captain Lord Ian Rogers, head of her security detail, a young Hajin serving woman and Dr. Agnes Mueller all awaiting their arrival.

Mueller had replaced Mercedes' previous doctor once Sandra got too old to continue working. Sandra had been from Reichart's World where female doctors were very common, and Agnes was from Yggdrasil, another assimilated Hidden World, where women worked in professions that in the League were traditionally male. Since both planets had been assimilated into the League for years Mercedes wondered how long it would be before the women of her class were forced to use male doctors. The conservatives would have to hope the League would find more Hidden Worlds where women had medical careers if they were to preserve their wives and daughters' modesty.

And ones where the people don't commit suicide rather than submit, Mercedes thought and shivered.

The young Hajin assisted Mercedes in removing her helmet. The presence of the alien brought to mind Mercedes' servant, Tako, lost like all the rest of the crew aboard her flagship, and all the men and batBEMs who had been aboard the other ships. That reminder, together with her memories of the bodies on Kusatsu-Shirane, hit with devastating effect. She gagged, bent from the waist, and vomited.

Dr. Mueller, forehead creased with worry, moved to her side. Mercedes waved her off. "I'm all right. Just a bit nauseous from freefall." She gave the captain of the pinnace an apologetic glance. "I'm sorry for the mess."

"Not to worry, Highness. Venia—" he waved at the Hajin "—will accompany you to your cabin."

"I'd like you to come too, Doctor," Boho said to Mueller.

"If Your Majesty will permit," the alien murmured

and indicated the benches set next to the airlock. Mercedes allowed the Hajin to pull the bottom of her suit down over her hips. She then sat down so the maid could slide it off her legs. One of Rogers' *fusileros* gathered up the discarded suits and began placing them in their lockers. Venia bowed and led them to the royal cabin. The composite walls had been veneered with sek wood, a chandelier hung from the ceiling, and the bed was a large, embossed, canopied affair. The pinnace had been built for her grandfather and it reflected his rather ostentatious taste.

Once the door closed, Mueller put her hands on her hips and gave Mercedes a severe look. "Now no more of this nonsense about freefall sickness."

Before Mercedes could try to explain it was guilt, Boho said, "The Infanta thinks she might be pregnant."

"Easy enough to find out," said the doctor. She rummaged in her holdall and produced a pregnancy test strip.

"Really, nothing more high-tech? You're a doctor," Boho said. "Years ago I bought one of these in a *farmacia*."

"Let's see." The doctor ticked off on her fingers. "Cheap, reliable, and idiot-proof. Why would we mess with that?" Mercedes laughed. Boho harrumphed. Agnes turned to Mercedes. "Pee on it. Wait two minutes or thereabouts. If it's been less than five days you will probably get a negative reading and should re-test in a few days."

Mercedes took the strip and went into the bathroom. As she pulled up her skirt, pulled down her panties, she did a quick count. It had been five days since the copulating they had done at the governor's mansion. She just prayed that

Boho didn't do research and discover that the changes he had observed wouldn't normally appear this quickly.

She then realized that God might not be too happy with either her infidelity or that she was going to pass off another man's child as her husband's. She pushed aside the brief flare of guilt. It was clear she and Boho were never going to conceive. Just as marrying Boho had been her duty, having a child was also her duty. She just hoped the baby wouldn't be fair-haired. She sat down on the toilet, and immediately felt like she had been lost in the desert for days. She stood, shuffled over to the sink, and turned on the water. Sat back down. Finally, she managed to squeeze out some urine. The strip turned bright pink. A few minutes later a plus appeared in the read window.

She returned to the room and handed the strip to Agnes and flowed into Boho's arms.

"Yep, you're pregnant," the doctor said prosaically.

They should have been prepared. A perusal of the news feeds during their journey from the flagship to Ouranos had revealed that the del Campos had been busy. Either the governor or someone on his staff had blabbed to the press that Mercedes had been found. Alone. The news was filled with speculation about the location of the strike force and the crews who had served aboard the ships. They ranged from theories that they had been left to claim a particularly salubrious world, that they had been taken prisoner by forces unknown, that they had mutinied and allowed Mercedes to leave in order to relay their demands to the Emperor. The bleakest assessment was from an outlet known to be highly critical of the crown. They had concluded that the crews were dead.

"Maybe we should have given a press conference on Cuandru," Boho had suggested, only to be cut off by Mercedes saying sharply, "Without the spin doctors to help us craft the message? That wouldn't have been wise." He had felt himself bristle. He had been told pregnancy mellowed a woman. So far Mercedes seemed to be resisting. She seemed to have sensed his ruffled feathers, and had given him a quick smile and gently added, "Besides now we have news that might help shift the focus."

"A most providential baby," Boho had said with a smile and laid a hand on her stomach.

Now they were in one of the palace flitters being pelted with rocks and any vegetable that could provide a satisfying *splat* as they made their way from the spaceport to the Palacio Colina. It wasn't a large crowd, but the press outnumbered the constabulary, which suggested Arturo's deft touch. Demonstrations were technically legal, but carefully controlled, requiring a number of permits, and payment for security (further indication that the del Campos were behind this; no doubt they were footing the bill), and were limited to official protest sites. This avenue leading to the mansions of the FFH and the royal enclave was not one of the approved sites. Boho was surprised that Anselmo hadn't managed to have a counter protest arranged given his organizational skills. It suggested Arturo had managed to spring this on the palace.

Boho looked over at Mercedes. Her jaw was tight, expression bleak. Yet, despite her unhappiness, there was a glow about her.

He had never been able to closely observe his lovers when they had been breeding. This was a new experience.

"*Ay, Dios mío!*" Mercedes exclaimed. "It's Christmas Eve. Don't they have something better to do? Like be home with their families?"

Captain Lord Ian Rogers, another of her lovesick factotums, glanced back at her. "They've no doubt been paid by the del Campos, Highness. I wouldn't let it worry you. It means nothing."

"Then you're a bloody fool, Rogers," Boho growled. Rogers stiffened. "These images are going to be viewed millions of times on Ouranos and then spread out across the League like fungi. Paid or not, real or not, it creates the impression of resistance to the Arango rule."

"Hush, Boho. I apologize for my husband, Ian. We've all been under a great deal of strain."

"No, Majesty, I should be apologizing. I should have anticipated this and had troops ready to handle the situation—"

"If I were you I'd shut up now, Captain," Boho said. "Lest you solidify my opinion."

An uncomfortable silence filled the flitter. The crowd was swiftly left behind. At the palace the two security flitters peeled away, and they landed in the gardens of the Phantasiestück. The trees just beyond the walls bent in the fierce winter winds. Waiting to meet them was Jaakon, the other lovesick fool, Anselmo, and Mercedes' youngest half-sister, Carisa. Jaakon was clearly desperate to get to Mercedes' side, but he deferred to Carisa. The sisters hugged each other tightly. They could not have been more different.

Carisa thin and barely five feet one, Mercedes at almost six feet and lush-figured. Anselmo came to Boho's side.

"Sorry about the spontaneous—" his tone formed quote marks "—protest. The request for a permit slipped past me."

"Does the Emperor know about it?"

"I think Lord Kemel kept it from him."

"Thank God for small mercies."

"I wanted to see my father first," Boho heard Mercedes say. The women had their arms around each other's waists and the lovesick palace factotums were flanking them.

"We thought you might want to freshen up and change before you called on him, ma'am," Jaakon said.

For an instant it seemed like she would argue, then she nodded and they entered the small palace that was their personal residence. The staff was lined up to greet them. There were tears in a few eyes. Joy over the return of their mistress or sorrow over the death of Tako? They went to their respective rooms. Boho showered, and had Ivoga give him a shave and dress him in civilian attire but with a discreet row of ribbons and his *Distinguido Servicio Cruzar*.

Mercedes and Carisa met him in the sitting room. With her hair cut short the curls were less manageable. They tumbled around Mercedes' face and made her seem younger and more vulnerable. She wore a soft green dress that complemented her cocoa skin. She was also wearing the emerald necklace. For a long moment they studied each other, then Mercedes nodded.

Forgiveness. And perhaps a new start.

* * *

They took a flitter for the short hop from the Phantasiestück to the main palace. Mercedes would have preferred to walk, but she was no longer a person. She was a vessel, an incubator. She had waited so long for a child, longed for a child. What she had not anticipated was becoming a prisoner in service only to this small, new life. *Just another duty,* she reminded herself, *and I was bred and trained to perform.* She glanced over at her sister. At least Carisa seemed pleased for her. She did a mental review of the other sisters. She knew Estella would be thrilled for her, Beatrisa relieved that no one would expect her to breed, while Tanis would not. The others? Who could say? Did some of them have dreams of a throne for their children? Her ring tapped her finger and she glanced down at the holo. Kemel had sent a text—*Fernán doesn't know about ships. Go straight to your news. Deflect. Distract. He doesn't handle bad news well anymore.*

After landing they were taken immediately to her father's study. The palace was decked out for Christmas and smelled of bayberry, evergreen, and cinnamon. She knew her father didn't actually do all that much work any longer, but the routine was calming to him as his mental faculties failed, and his long-serving and loyal assistant worked closely with Kemel and Jaakon to decide which information was provided to the now volatile ruler. As they approached the door Carisa whispered to her, "Maybe your news will get him to stop dangling me like bait in front of various noble houses."

Mercedes stopped and looked down at the youngest of the imperial daughters. "What is it you would like to do?"

"I'm not sure, but sitting around the palace is not it."

"Now that I'm back we'll work on it. I promise."

The doors opened and they entered. The privacy shutters were up, which made the room dim, and the security field engaged, which made Mercedes' back teeth ache slightly. Kemel was already in the office. Her father lunged out of his chair, hustled around the desk, and enfolded her in his arms. The scent of aftershave and tobacco filled her nose. She could hear his heart beating as she rested her head against his chest.

"Daddy," she whispered.

"My girl." His voice was husky. She looked up and saw that his eyes were moist with unshed tears.

"It's all right. I'm all right. In fact, I have wonderful news. I'm going to have a baby, Daddy." Over her father's shoulder she saw Kemel give a nod of approval.

His arms tightened around her, a frenzied hug, and then he held her at arm's length, his eyes scanning her body. "How do you feel? I'll send my personal physician. You must take care." The words tumbled out of him.

Mercedes found herself laughing. "Daddy, it's all right. I'm all right, and Dr. Mueller is a very fine doctor and I'm comfortable with her."

"This might be the happiest day of my life," the Emperor said. Mercedes felt a momentary flare of pity for all his other grandchildren. Five out of the nine sisters had children, twenty-two of them, but there had been no transports of joy over those births. Only this child mattered. And her father underlined the point by adding, "Please, God, let it be a boy."

"We could find out—maybe you should have all the tests, just to make sure everything is fine," Kemel suggested.

"No, no," Mercedes hurried to say. "I'll agree to an ultrasound, but I don't want anything more invasive. This baby is very precious." It was possible to determine paternity while also testing for abnormalities, and that had to be avoided at all costs. "It also smacks of the Cara'ot should it ever get out." She swept them all with a bright smile. "An ultrasound will tell us the sex, but we should keep the public in suspense."

"Smart," Boho murmured.

"We'll have the palace prepare an announcement," the Emperor said.

Kemel bowed. "Very good, sir." He walked to the door, pausing to pat Mercedes on the arm. "Congratulations, Highness."

Her father called for his assistant to work on the announcement, and Boho, Mercedes, and Carisa followed Kemel into the corridor. Once the door had closed, Boho said quietly, "Kemel, stall this announcement for at least a few days." Mercedes gave him a startled look.

"Why?" Kemel asked.

"Not here. Let's go to your office."

The security chief gave Boho a long look then led them to the office he maintained at the palace. Once the security measures were in place he collapsed into a chair. Mercedes, studying the net of wrinkles around his eyes and the white hair, realized Kemel was old. She was going to have to think about who would replace him. If anyone could.

"Talk," Kemel ordered her husband.

"You know how you've had me cultivating the del Campos, gaining their trust."

There was a flicker of some emotion across the old man's

face, but it was gone before Mercedes could interpret it. "Yes, you've done amazing things."

"Let me take this information to the del Campos."

"Are you out of your mind?" Carisa blurted. "They'll try to hurt Mercedes and the baby!"

He rounded on Carisa. "Exactly. They'll have no choice but to act and then we'll have them." Mercedes wasn't sure how she felt about his casual agreement about her imminent demise. Boho turned back to Kemel. "But we've got to delay the official announcement so they'll have time to put their coup into motion. If we can manipulate them, force them to show their hand, the del Campos will look like monsters and renegades. This will also have the added benefit of taking the attention off the disaster at Kusatsu-Shirane." He shot Mercedes an apologetic look. "Sorry, my love."

"It's all right. It was a disaster and I was in charge." Carisa gave her a hug.

"I planted the story that it was an undiscovered *corsario* base that destroyed your ships back on Kusatsu-Shirane, so it doesn't look like you flew blindly into an ambush," Boho said.

"And what became of these mythical *corsarios*?" Kemel asked sweetly.

"I'm sure we can come up with some explanation," Boho said, and then added airily, "Perhaps I destroyed them when I arrived with my ships."

The flicker of emotion was back. Kemel said, "How appropriately heroic of you."

"Your crews know there was no pitched battle. They'll talk," Mercedes objected.

"And who will listen to a few *hombres* over the megaphone of the League press and the consort? We can buy off the FFH officers, and the ones who aren't amenable will be cowed when they see what happens to the del Campos. And believe me, that news will get buried once the del Campos make their move."

Kemel was nodding, stroking his chin and looking thoughtful. "I do see a major problem. Musa, Mihalis, and Arturo aren't fools. They will wonder why you are throwing in with them when you've managed to secure an heir. Why would you endanger your position now?"

Boho took on a faraway look. He then studied Mercedes' midriff. "I'll tell them I suspect the baby isn't mine." Icy terror clawed at Mercedes' belly and her throat constricted. She stared wildly at him. He chuckled. "There, there, love, don't look so hurt. Musa already thinks you're unnatural. He will happily believe that you're a whore as well."

Mercedes' muscles had turned to water. She groped her way to a chair and collapsed. She covered her face with a hand and fought to regain her composure. She hoped that Kemel's far too piercing eyes weren't on her.

Kemel nodded. "All right, if you're willing to wear the horns, we'll attempt it." Then he added, "For this to work, for it to be believable, you're going to have to stay away from Mercedes and the palace."

"I'll move back to the family mansion."

"Good. We'll stay in touch through Paloma," Kemel said.

For a brief moment Mercedes wondered who Paloma might be, though the name was vaguely familiar. She also noted her husband's reaction. Boho didn't look all that happy at the prospect. She then decided she didn't care. *And at least I won't have to lie next to him for a few days,* she thought, while the men shook hands and engaged in self-congratulation.

"The Pope's holy fucking wickerbill," Luis breathed.

"A woman of her word," Jax said with less profanity and more prosaically.

"Yeah, well, she owed us," remarked Jahan.

"I'll miss her," was Graarack's contribution to the conversation.

"I think she will be a good ruler," Dalea said.

Tracy remained silent, just stared at the numbers in their bank account. They had made a previous stop at Wasua to sell the farming equipment, at a sizable loss, then made their way to the San Pedro *cosmódromo.* As soon as they had come out of Fold, Tracy had received notice of a change to the bank account. Along with the bank's message there had been another from the League's Franchise Tax Board stating that this reward was not subject to League taxes or any planetary taxes. It was enough to pay off the ship. Enough to upgrade her engines. Enough to buy cargo designed to appeal to the FFH. Enough to put away for a rainy day.

After docking they began to gather their things for a shore leave. Luis was proposing a truly epic dinner to celebrate. "You can bring your nephew and his family," he said to Jahan. "I'll bring Josephina and you can bring Lisbet," he said to Tracy. Tracy just shook his head and remained silent. "Why not?" Luis demanded.

Jahan jumped in. "Luis, *mi hijo,* shut up." The young man looked confused, then mulish, then shrugged and turned back to his station to finish shutting down. "You will see her to say goodbye," Jahan asked quietly.

"Yes," Tracy said.

There was a hail over the radio. Luis swirled in his chair, his eyes wide with alarm. "There's a security officer requesting permission to come aboard." They all exchanged panicked glances. "What if they changed their minds and they want the money back?" Luis whispered.

"It's probably just some bookkeeping that needs to be tied up," Jax said placidly.

The officer came aboard. He was carrying a large cream-colored envelope. A red wax seal, stamped with a crown, a cross, and a circle of stars, held it closed. He snapped off a salute and handed the envelope to Tracy. "With the compliments of the crown." It weighed heavy in his hand.

"Thank you," Tracy said.

The officer left. Tracy bounced the envelope gently on his palm then put it down on the arm of his chair. He stared at it.

"So, are you gonna open it?" Luis finally said.

Tracy nodded, and pulled the knife out of his boot and slit the creamy material. It was a very official-looking document. It had the royal seal in gold and ribbons hung off the bottom. It was an imperial notice that Captain Oliver Randall was henceforth to be known as Caballero Oliver Randall, bearer of a hereditary knighthood that would devise upon his heirs and assigns. He silently handed it to Jahan whose wide eyes had become even wider. The document made the rounds of his crew.

"Well…" said Dalea, and seemed to run out of words.

"Useful," Jax remarked.

"Deserved," Graarack said.

"Wow, now you really are one of the FFH assholes," was Luis' contribution.

Jahan pinned Tracy with a stern look. "You are *not* going to refuse this."

"It's not real. Any more than Randall is real," he grated.

"Captain," Dalea said softly. "We all play our roles."

25

ROLLING THE DICE

"We'll need you to back Arturo in parliament," Musa was saying.

It was delivered with the tone and air of a man addressing a servant. Boho struggled not to take offense. He supposed that a man who saw himself on the cusp of becoming emperor would speak to any and all as if they were lackeys, but it didn't mean Boho had to like it. He was the Duque de Argento y Pepco. When he thought about it, the disrespect seemed to date from the moment he had told the four del Campo men that he doubted the paternity of the child. At that moment he became the fool wearing the cuckold's horns, and was therefore diminished in their eyes. Male apes, he decided, had nothing on their more evolved cousins.

They were gathered in the sacristy of the cathedral. The smell of incense and the heavy scent of wax and smoke from the candles clogged the nose. Embroidered vestments hung in an armoire, the gold, silver, and copper threads catching the light. Far overhead and muted by the marble walls he heard the bells chiming the quarter hour. It all felt faintly sacrilegious to Boho and he murmured a prayer for forgiveness. Perhaps God would understand he was on the side of the angels.

Musa sat in a large high-backed chair, his cane resting against one arm. He seemed shrunken against the carved wood and elaborate upholstery. Boho remembered the man was older than Fernán, so he had to be well into his seventies, if not early eighties. Mihalis, elegant in his uniform, stood at his father's right shoulder. Jose was seated. He held a missal in his hands. Boho wondered if it was a prop or if the man really was pious. Probably not if he was plotting a revolution. Arturo was at the sideboard pouring himself a brandy. Boho wanted to ask for one.

"And what will Mihalis and Jose be doing?" he asked.

"You don't need to know that," Jose said.

"We will need you to keep us appraised of the location of Mercedes and the Emperor when the balloon goes up," Mihalis said.

"So, you plan to seize and hold the palace," Boho said.

"And parliament," Arturo added.

Boho turned to the priest. "I presume you won't be humping a rifle, Jose."

The prelate smiled; his hands stroked the leather and gold embossed cover of the missal. "I'm there to calm the troubled waters. Many of the church fathers back us. They haven't been happy with the degradation of our most sacred institutions of home and family. Once we take control, I'll be making a public announcement urging any resisters to lay down their arms."

"And what happens if Fernán and Mercedes elude you? They'll run for the fleet, you know, and you can't have suborned all of them," Boho said.

"We've got that covered too," Mihalis said, but he didn't elaborate. "And it's not like the average *hombre* loves her after the loss of the squadron."

A silence fell over the room. Boho broke it. "Look, you... we need to move before the palace makes an official announcement about the pregnancy. If you take action after that you'll look like monsters."

"Thank you, but we understand the ramifications," Musa said. "You'll be informed when it's time to act."

Boho bowed to the old man as if he were already emperor. He sensed it would go over well, and indeed the withered lips pulled into a small smile. "As you command, sir." He gave a small cough. "If I might inquire... what are your plans as regards Fernán and... and Mercedes?"

"Fernán will be executed," Musa said, his voice harsh.

"And Mercedes?" Boho nudged.

"She may have to die as well," Mihalis said.

"Especially with that baby in her belly," Jose added.

You bastards. That's my *child. I'll see you in Hell before I let you harm him.* It was a struggle not to allow his true thoughts to be read on his face, and to keep from leaping across the room and choking Musa as he sat on his fake throne.

"I'll probably marry Carisa," Mihalis continued. "Get her out of the way, be a link to the old regime and prevent any plots to arise around her."

"And the other women?" Boho asked.

"Julieta and Sanjay are fully committed to us," Arturo said. That was an interesting bit of information, which Boho filed away. "If the husbands of the others swear fealty, they'll be spared."

"Tanis is devoted to our cause," Jose offered.

"The dyke will have to die though," Mihalis said.

"Unless you think you can convince her to back us?" Arturo looked at Boho.

"Not if you kill her sister. Beatrisa is very close to Mercedes," Boho answered.

"Well, that makes the decision easy," Musa said offhandedly.

"Well, if there's nothing else…" Boho said. Musa waved a ropey, blue-veined hand to indicate he was dismissed. Arturo followed him out of the sacristy.

"We noticed you have moved back into the Cullen mansion."

"Yes."

"We'd prefer that you stayed at the palace so you can keep us better informed."

Since Boho had been worried about how to get information back to Kemel and Mercedes this suited him perfectly. He had been planning an assignation with Paloma and to have her carry the information, but now he no longer needed to do that and that was a relief. After the revelation of Paloma's betrayal he hadn't wanted to see the girl.

"All right, but it's not easy knowing what she did," Boho grumbled.

Arturo clapped him on the shoulder. "I know, but you

will be well rewarded. You are a popular and powerful figure in League society and beloved by the people. Having you at our side will make the transition smoother."

Boho decided to push a bit more. "Since it's likely I'll be a widower, do I still get my pick of a del Campo daughter?"

"I'll discuss that with Father. We might have to use the girls to cement wavering allies, but you would be my first choice to have as brother-in-law."

It had been an elaborate undertaking. After Boho had brought the warning, Kemel and a very few trusted people began to bring in doubles to play the Emperor, Mercedes, Constanza, and Carisa. To limit any access to the faux emperor, word had gone out that Fernán was under the weather and had taken to his bed.

The plan was to take a commercial shuttle up to rendezvous with Boho's flagship, and, operating under the theory that the fewer people who knew the less likely it was to be leaked, they had intended to use only a pilot and copilot off Boho's ship, no additional security and certainly no servants. Mercedes had foolishly assumed that the royals could survive ten hours without such attention.

Unfortunately, this idea had been met by howls from Constanza who insisted they had to bring her latest life coach/nutritionist/yoga instructor, Henry Guthrie. Kemel and Mercedes had been vociferous in their objection, but it had only taken two sentences from Carisa to reduce their arguments to rubble.

"She's going to be a basket case if he comes along. Without him—full out meltdown." So, despite the spy master's fears, Guthrie was coming along. Mercedes wished it could have been Davin, but he and the Blue fleet had been off searching for her, and, while they had been ordered back to the capitol, their arrival time was uncertain.

They left with the crowd of palace employees at the end of the work day. Thanks to the winter weather, it was easy to hide their familiar features with bulky coats, hoods, and hats. Mingling among the crowd of workers returning home at the end of the day they caught public transport at the bottom of the Palacio Colina. During the tram ride her father grumbled, while Constanza huddled next to Guthrie rather than her husband. He patted her hand and whispered in her ear as they slid along the mag rail. Carisa stared out the window and Mercedes nervously touched the pistol in her pocket and the knife in a sheath on her ankle.

Kemel had told them to get off at the Soho stop in Stick Town. As they stepped off the tram Constanza gazed at the Tiponis swaying past and shuddered. On corners, pods of Flutes were gathered, playing their fast-paced and incomprehensible gambling game. Their excited tooting filled the air. Carisa was looking around with an expression of delight. She turned to Mercedes.

"I can't believe I've spent most of my life on Ouranos and I've never seen this part of the city."

"Thank God," Constanza quavered. "This is insane. Why are we endangering ourselves this way? Why are we doing this?"

"There's been a threat against us," Mercedes said soothingly. She and Kemel had agreed that neither her father nor her stepmother needed to know the exact nature of the threat. The Emperor would have disrupted their careful plans to bring down the del Campos and Constanza would have been reduced to a quivering mess.

Mercedes turned and looked off to the west toward Pony Town, where once the Belmanors' tailor shop had been on the outskirts of the Hajin area. Tracy hadn't seen his father in years. She was losing her father to dementia. Her hand went to her belly. And she would bear a child who would never know his or her real father. Sadness threatened to overcome her. It all felt so hopeless.

Before Constanza could have a complete emotional meltdown a taxi flitter flew up and dropped to the ground in front of them. The door opened and Ian waved them in. They were then whisked away to the spaceport where a freight shuttle was waiting.

"We're not taking the imperial pinnace?" her father asked.

"No, sir, we need people to think we're still at the palace," Mercedes said.

"It looks dirty," Constanza said with a wrinkle of her perfect nose.

"We've made every effort for your comfort," Guthrie said. "And I'm here to serve, ma'am."

Mercedes threw a desperate look to Carisa who gave a small nod and slipped an arm around her mother's waist. "Come on, Mummy. It's all going to be fine."

Ian bowed and Mercedes gave him a wistful glance. "I wish you were coming."

He smiled. "So do I, but it would look odd if the head of your security detail was suddenly absent."

"Holiday?" she suggested brightly so he would understand she was joking.

"What are those? You'd best get aboard, Highness. See you once this mess is resolved."

On board she found Carisa settling her parents into their couches, and then helping her mother buckle in. The cargo area had been retrofitted with acceleration couches and a cabinet containing an oven and refrigerator. Guthrie bustled about setting tapas trays into the oven to be heated once they reached orbit. The bare composite walls had been covered with tapestries. Despite the changes, it was still a big space designed to carry cargo and in fact there was the lingering smell of herbs and spices that had apparently been the last cargo hauled.

Mercedes headed toward the cockpit. As she passed Guthrie he said, "We will serve refreshments after liftoff, Highness. Everything was to Lord DeLonge's specifications."

"Excellent."

She moved to the bulkhead that separated the crew compartment from the cargo area, and touched the entry chime. Beneath her feet she could hear the growing thrum of the engines coming online. The pilot and co-pilot turned as she entered. They started to unhook their harnesses to stand, but she waved them back down. Despite their civilian garb it was clear they were O-Trell. "At ease," she said. "How are we effecting the rendezvous with the frigate?"

"I've fed in the coordinates. They'll remote pilot and bring us in."

"Don't trust us to fly ourselves," Mercedes said.

The pilot shrugged. "Precious cargo. Best take your couch, Highness. Liftoff in four minutes."

Mercedes returned to the cargo hold and strapped in. She brought up the countdown clock on her ring and watched the hologram as the minutes ticked past. She found herself worrying about the fetus as the gee forces pressed her into the acceleration couch. The shuttle was well shielded, but space was a cruel and hostile environment, and this cargo shuttle was not equipped with a gravity generator. She was fine in freefall, but she was glad it would be a relatively short trip and then they'd be safely aboard Boho's flagship with full gravity.

Constanza whimpered as they raced for the exosphere. While she traveled off world with her husband frequently, it was always in the comfort of the various imperial spacecraft. These rough surroundings were not to her liking. For Carisa, her time in the service had been fairly recent, so the jarring ride was familiar, and while her father had been years away from his time in O-Trell, he seemed to be handling the launch with stoic resolve. A trickle of sweat crawled down Guthrie's cheek and was shaken loose to hang like a crystal teardrop in the air. Apparently, he was unfamiliar with space flight.

The main engines cut as they entered orbit. Guthrie unhooked his tethers and began to prepare covered plates with a selection of appetizers. Mercedes waved him off. Weightlessness was amplifying the queasiness from her pregnancy. She might be fine in freefall, but the baby was making its objections known. After the royals were served, the man entered the cockpit to deliver food to the pilots. The door slid shut behind him. Constanza stared at the covered plate in confusion.

"You can slip your hand through the membrane, Mummy, and pull out the tapas," Carisa explained and she demonstrated.

Mercedes closed her eyes and wondered what Tracy was doing.

Anselmo was waiting in his office when Boho returned from another meeting with the del Campos. "Anything?" the young man asked.

Boho shook his head. "They don't trust me that much. They're not going to tell me the exact moment they kick off their coup." Boho moved to the sideboard, which he had stocked with an array of alcohol, and poured himself several fingers of scotch. The smoky scent wafted up, and some of the tension in his chest eased.

"We need to time the release of the statement announcing the pregnancy. That way it looks like the del Campos are reacting to their hopes being dashed."

Anselmo's nagging raised a bubble of irritation. "*Yes!* I *know* that!" The pressure in Boho's chest was back. He tossed back the whisky, letting the heat roll down into his belly, though the warmth couldn't quite counteract the roiling of nerves as he contemplated. Once the press release went out, the del Campos would know he had played them false. Their reaction would be swift and probably violent.

It was as if the young aide had read his mind, for Anselmo said brightly, "My God, Musa and Mihalis will be enraged knowing you outplayed them. Good thing you got the Infanta and the rest of the family safely out of harm's way." He sounded delighted by the prospect that harm, like an amorphous monster, might be rolling toward them.

Boho pushed aside his fear of what would happen to him if their plans failed and Musa succeeded. He forced himself to focus on the problem at hand. "It has to be soon. I think we have to roll the dice, and trust to luck. Go ahead and release the birth announcement. Let's force their hand."

"Will Admiral Pulkkinen be back in time?" Anselmo asked.

"That's part of the luck factor. But I've always been a pretty good gambler." *Except when you're not.* He dismissed the traitorous thought.

"Yes, sir." Anselmo bustled out.

Dalea looked up when Tracy walked into the medical bay. The small space smelled of antiseptic and the tincture of lavender that Dalea used as the base for her massage oils. "Headache or stomach acid?" she asked.

It irritated him that she knew his physical ailments so well; almost as much as he resented the ailments. He pushed it aside. "Neither." They had just come out of Fold heading back to New Hope and a rendezvous with Dr. Engelberg. "I was catching up on the news. The palace released an announcement—Mercedes is pregnant."

"Oh, how lovely for her." The Hajin continued straightening a drawer of medications.

"Dalea, is this baby mine?"

She turned slowly and looked down her long face at him. "Captain, that is an inappropriate question to ask and you know it."

The use of the title rather than his name told him she was serious and annoyed. "Oh, for Christ's sake, Dalea, don't bleat about doctor/patient privacy to me. As far as I know you don't actually have a medical degree, and this is *me*."

"And Mercedes was under my care and in this case my loyalty is to *her*."

"So, you're really not going to tell me?"

"No." Her tail was swishing in irritation. She turned back to the open drawer.

"So, I guess that hedging, legalistic answer means… the baby is mine."

She turned on him, hands planted on her hips. "Tracy, think about this for one second. Don't you think Mercedes would have told you?"

He stared at the toes of his boots and the momentary burst of joy deflated—of course she would have told him. She had wanted to stay with him, to give up the throne for him. She wouldn't have kept such a thing from him. So maybe none of it had been true. After all she had returned to Boho and immediately allowed him to bed her. So much for love. Dull anger roiled his gut and a pounding headache began.

He looked up and Dalea was holding out her hand. Pills rested on the soft pink skin of her palm. Her other hand held a cup of water. "Antacid, aspirin."

He accepted the pills. Even with the water it was hard to force them down. His throat was just that tight.

26

MISDIRECTIONS AND REVERSALS

Reports rolled in that factions of the police and marines loyal to the del Campos had taken control of the spaceport and the main power station for Hissilek. Parliament had been called into an emergency session.

"You need to get to parliament. Rally support among the grandees and the *diputados*," Kemel said, and it was an order not a suggestion.

They were at a safe house deep in Squirrel Town rather than at SEGU headquarters. Fortunately, since the building that housed the intelligence service had already been taken over by rebel forces. Boho's Isanjo batBEM, Ivoga, had suggested the location, pointing out that people like the del Campos would not be caught dead in the alien neighborhoods, and it would never occur to them that other members of the FFH might feel differently.

"No, sir, you're wrong," Boho said. "This won't be won in parliament or by throwing our troops against theirs. We have to win this in the streets, with the people, and I have to lead it." His ScoopRing pricked his finger and he took the call. It was Anselmo on an encrypted line.

"Sir, nothing's happening up here at the palace."

"Nothing?"

"Uh-uh, and Captain Lord Rogers and Matthew Gutierrez—"

"Who?"

"He's the actual commander of Servicio Protector Imperial. I know it seems like it's Ian, but it's actually—"

"Get to the point, Anselmo."

"Uh, right, yeah, anyway he wanted me to ask if you wanted to redeploy their troops and agents to parliament or elsewhere in the city?"

Boho and Kemel exchanged a look. A dull ache filled the pit of Boho's stomach. "They know," he said.

"Beg pardon, sir?" Anselmo said.

"Nothing. Yes, tell them to deploy at parliament and the Plaza de los Héroes. They can decide who goes where." Boho continued, "And get me an open-air flitter. Use the one from the Emperor's Ruby Jubilee."

Kemel gave a small cough. "Sir, they've taken over traffic control. Grounded everything except military and police vehicles flown by people loyal to them."

"Well, shit."

"There's the Emperor's antique car collection and the stables," Anselmo suggested.

"I want to make an entrance not be a laughing stock."

"Yes, sir. Sorry, sir."

Boho broke the connection. "I guess we need to highjack a flitter," he said to Kemel. "And how the hell did they find out the family was gone?"

"We'll find out. Right now, you have to get a warning to Mercedes."

"What if they just take out the shuttle?" Boho voiced his fear.

"If what they told you is true, they won't do that. They need Carisa. They'll try to take the shuttle." The old man's matter-of-fact delivery was infuriating. Boho wanted to be soothed.

"*Dios!* It's set up to be auto-piloted to my ship."

"Which means they would just need to change the coordinates and take it to a ship loyal to Mihalis."

This time the lack of passion from the SEGU chief snapped Boho's control. "We should never have let him return with part of his fleet," Boho raged. "I don't know why I listened to you!"

"We had to if we were going to spring this trap. But recriminations won't help now. You need to call Mercedes. Assume it will be intercepted so be careful. They have to think we haven't figured this out."

"Okay. Okay." Boho calmed his spinning, angry thoughts. How to deliver a warning? Then it came to him. There were advantages to being known as a clothes horse and a frightful dandy.

"My dear could you please go to the *front* closet and see if I left my uniform topcoat there. It needs to go to the tailors. It's not fitting quite right." There was a few seconds lag between the words. Mercedes frowned at Boho's image in the hologram.

His expression was bright, smiling, but there was a tension in his jaw, and he was blinking more than usual. After twenty-three years of marriage she knew every nuance that crossed his face. He was upset. It took her a few minutes to parse the message he was sending her.

Uniform. Front closet...

She looked toward the cockpit and realized that the door was still shut and Guthrie was nowhere to be seen. How long since he'd taken food up to the pilots? She checked the time and realized she had dozed off. It had been close on thirty minutes. There was no reason for him to still be in the cockpit. "Of course, my darling." She broke the connection, released her restraints, and pushed off the couch. Carisa gave her a curious look. Mercedes cocked her head and gave her an intense look. Carisa released her harness and floated over to her.

"What's up? Do you feel all right?" her sister asked.

"I got a cryptic message from Boho. I think something's wrong." Mercedes glanced at the cockpit door.

Carisa was not slow on the uptake. "Damn, I knew Mummy's neurosis and hypochondria were going to be the death of me."

The engines fired and the two women floated off to one side as the shuttle changed its alignment. "Course adjustment burn," they said together.

"Do we know if this was planned?" Carisa asked.

"Or a new plan," Mercedes said grimly. "Let's go ask." Mercedes used a handhold to send herself flying toward the cockpit. Carisa kicked off from the top of the cabinet. "Girls, girls, what are you doing? Carisa, do be careful," Constanza called. Her voice was high and tight with tension and barely suppressed anger.

"Just checking on something with the pilots, Mummy," Carisa called. She glanced back at her and Mercedes' trailing skirts. "Damn, I wish we were dressed in something more practical. And I don't have a weapon."

"I do," Mercedes muttered.

"Really? You're amazing."

They reached the cockpit door and Mercedes keyed the access panel. Nothing happened. They exchanged glances. "Okay, I guess it's official. We're in trouble," Carisa whispered. She tried to keep her tone light, but a faint quaver revealed her nerves. "What now?"

"We get inside." Mercedes took the pistol from her pocket. "Be prepared to take down the pilots if they've been suborned."

"Okay, but how do we get inside? Hack the locking mechanism?"

"Take too long. I'll rewire it."

"The wires are behind a composite wall. I don't think the cheese knife is going to cut it."

"No, but this will." Mercedes pulled the Cara'ot knife that Tracy had given her at that long ago Christmas. As promised the blade entered the hardened material like a hot knife in soft butter.

"How? And where can I get one?"

"Cara'ot. So, no, you can't," Mercedes said shortly.

"And that's rather terrifying that they just casually made something that could cut through a ship's walls," Carisa whispered back.

"Girls, what are you doing?" their father called.

Oh God, don't let him decide to try to help us, Mercedes prayed desperately. They had to keep him safe and out of the way. She gave Carisa a desperate look.

"Girl gossip, Daddy."

"You better not be flirting with that handsome captain of your security detail, Cari," he said with a chuckle.

"No, sir, I promise to clear all my flirting with you first," she called back.

While Carisa had been talking, Mercedes had been plucking at the tangle of wires revealed by the hole she had made in the wall. She closed her eyes and tried to picture the door schematics she had been shown back at the High Ground. It had been a long time. She nudged her half-sister with an elbow, then caught her when the gesture threatened to send her drifting away.

"Do you remember your electronics classes?"

"Sort of." Carisa peered into the wall cavity, traced a few of the multicolored wires with the tip of her little finger. "Okay, I think… I hope this is right. Cut these two." She indicated a blue wire and a white wire. "And splice them together." Mercedes used the knife to make the cuts, then stripped the plastic coating off the wires, and got ready to twist the wires together. "You're probably going to get a shock," Carisa added.

"Now you tell me," Mercedes mumbled around the hilt of the knife, which she had placed between her teeth so she could use both hands. She then froze as the ever present concern over the baby intruded.

"What's wrong?" Carisa whispered.

"Baby."

"Oh."

"Also have you ever shot anybody, Cari?" Mercedes asked.

"No."

"Then maybe you better get the shock."

They traded places. Mercedes returned the knife to her boot and took the small pistol. She braced a foot against the wall so she could hold herself in place in front of the door. She then thought better of the exposed position, and moved off to one side. She gave Carisa a nod. There was a spark and a sizzle, a sharp *ow* from Carisa, and the door slid open. Mercedes was staring into Guthrie's shocked and frightened face as he sat in the co-pilot's couch. The pilot was slumped in his couch and the co-pilot was floating against the ceiling. They were either unconscious or dead. Mercedes noted the snack trays floating loose. Maybe they were only drugged. She could hope. Staring into the barrel of her pistol Guthrie slowly raised his hands.

"Unharness and move away from the controls. *Slowly*," she ordered Guthrie.

He did so and began to float, arms flailing wildly, which set him to spinning. Carisa flew through the door sucking on her singed fingers. "Check on them," Mercedes ordered, jerking her head toward the pilot and co-pilot.

"They're not dead," Guthrie stammered. "I would... could never *kill* anybody. I made that very clear to—" He broke off abruptly.

"Oh, don't worry, you'll give us the name once we turn

you over to Lord DeLonge," Mercedes said. Guthrie's rather prominent Adam's apple bounced in his throat as he gulped.

"It was just a drug to put them to sleep," he babbled. Carisa, fingers pressed against the pilot's neck, looked back over her shoulder and shook her head. "What? No!" Guthrie's voice spiraled with outrage and fear.

Carisa kicked off, collided with Guthrie, grabbed him by the throat, and slammed him into the wall. "Yes, congratulations, you got played. You've killed two men."

"What were your orders from the del Campos?" Mercedes demanded.

"Drug..." His voice caught for an instant then he continued, "the pilots. Drop in a new navigation chip and accept a computer override from a waiting ship. They're in control now. There's nothing you... we can do," Guthrie said.

"We'll see about that," Mercedes muttered. "The pilot told me they had fed in the coordinates to remote pilot to Boho's ship. We just have to restore that program."

"Okay," Carisa said. "And hope when we sever contact with the del Campo ship they won't get to us before we reach Boho's ship. What do you want me to do?"

"Right now, guard this puke until I find some way to restrain him."

"There should be duct tape somewhere aboard," Carisa offered.

"And sealant film," Mercedes added.

"Please, please, Highness... Majesty, that won't be necessary. They *lied* to me. I feel no loyalty to them—"

"Or anybody else apparently," Carisa muttered.

"I won't do anything. I swear to you."

Mercedes studied the man. His cheeks were wet with tears and some of the moisture had broken loose and formed droplets that floated around his woebegone face. He was clinging desperately to a handhold in the cockpit. "Not convinced."

"I shouldn't be surprised that you're good at putting on a show," Boho said as he watched from his place of concealment in an alley as Paloma played the part of virtuous FFH lady assaulted by alien thugs. They were on the outskirts of the financial district that abutted the Isanjo neighborhood.

"Thank you. Congrats to you for the plan, and by the way you do a pretty good job of pretending to be a decent human being," she retorted.

"Bitch." Her light laugh was the only response. "Okay, here they come," Boho said. The police flitter was making a slow loop over the area, the PA blaring out a warning for citizens to remain indoors.

Seven Isanjo bucks circled Paloma, one grabbed at her handbag. When she fought him, he delivered a very realistic blow to her face. Boho couldn't help it. He winced. The police flitter dove toward them, speakers blaring,

"BACK AWAY OR WE WILL FIRE!"

The Isanjo gathered in closer and grabbed Paloma, clearly making her a hostage. They started backing toward the adjacent alley, dragging her with them. Her screams filled the air. Boho could imagine the two officers inside dithering over what action to take. Shoot, and they risked hitting a lady of the FFH. Land, and they would be disobeying what had probably been direct orders from Mihalis or Arturo. As he had predicted chivalry won out. The flitter dropped to the pavement, the doors opened, and the cops boiled out, guns at the ready. The Isanjo waiting on the surrounding rooftops launched themselves off the parapets, landing heavily on the men's shoulders and bearing them to the ground. In seconds, the cops were disarmed, unconscious, and restrained.

Boho left the alley, took the offered handgun, and with three of Kemel's human agents climbed into the flitter. "Not coming with me?" he asked Paloma.

"I think you can handle it from here."

The doors closed and one of the agents sent the flitter airborne. A call came over the radio. "Flitter 323, you made an unscheduled landing. Report please."

The agent answered. "Broke up a gang of BEMs."

"Please verify with streamed video."

"Right away." The pilot broke the connection and gave Boho a fierce grin. "And fortunately we have video of naughty aliens and a human woman. We'll have you at Parliament Square before they realize the rescue never happened."

"Well done." Boho brought his ring to life and called Anselmo.

"I see you have transport, sir."

"Indeed. Now I need a flash mob. A big one. Gathered in the Plaza de los Héroes."

"Got it."

"Have we still got control over the emergency broadcast system?" Boho asked.

"For the moment. They're trying hard to hack it."

"Well, tell the bright boys to hold them at bay until I can deliver my call to arms to the citizenry. When I start my speech, blast it to everyone's rings with emergency override on all other media platforms. Send it Leaguewide."

"Yes, sir. Make it a good one. Speech, I mean."

"That's my plan."

The moment Mercedes emerged from the cockpit her stepmother called, "Where's Guthrie? I want him." Constanza's tone was querulous.

"He's having trouble with freefall sickness. I'll send him to you once he's feeling better. You really don't want vomit floating around the cabin." Her stepmother shuddered. Even talking about vomit had Mercedes' stomach trying to climb up her throat. She swallowed bile and moved to her father.

If they were to have any hope of escaping the del Campos she needed her father occupied and out of the way. He was wearing headphones, head bobbing slightly in time to the rhythm of music she couldn't hear. His hands were folded on his paunch and his hair was more gray than black now. Mercedes' emotions were a tangled mess of sadness, love, exasperation, and loss. She touched him lightly on the shoulder. She was floating directly over him, gazing down into his face. He smiled at her and removed the headset.

"Daddy, Cari and I need your help."

"Of course, honey, what's wrong?"

"Daddy, Kemel suspected that Musa was plotting and he wanted us safely away."

Her father's expression darkened. "Why wasn't I told?"

Mercedes hurried into speech, "I agree it was wrong of him, but you can talk to him about that later. Right now I think Musa is trying to take control of the ship. The pilots need our help to deal with the situation." He started to unhook his restraints. "No, Daddy, wait. There's something that only *you* can do. We need you to prepare a speech, talk to the people, warn them what's happening. Reassure them that you're still here for them."

Constanza was staring at Mercedes, growing alarm imperfectly masked by her ferocious frown. "What are you getting up to, Mercedes? You better not be encouraging Carisa to do something foolish."

"Hush, woman, Carisa's a grown woman, not a little girl," her father snapped at his wife. He looked back to Mercedes. "You're sure you don't want me to help you?"

"Cari hasn't been out of the service for that long, and only *you* can make that speech. You're the one the people look to for comfort and guidance. Just be prepared. We might have to take some hard maneuvers." She smiled at her stepmother. "So stay strapped in."

Mercedes stopped at the equipment locker and pulled out the expected roll of duct tape and the hull sealant film. She returned to the cockpit and Carisa cocked her head like an inquisitive bird.

"What?" Mercedes asked.

"You look green."

"I'm discovering pregnancy and freefall aren't mixing all that well." Cari handed her a sickness bag that was in a pouch next to the pilot's couch. She gave Carisa the sealant film. Guthrie was still cowering against the wall of the cockpit. He eyed them with equal parts nervousness and resentment.

"Please, I can help," he whined.

Ignoring him, Mercedes pulled loose a length of tape and tore it with her teeth. Cari slapped the film across his body while Mercedes deployed the tape. They soon had him cocooned like a fly in the web of a pair of unsympathetic spiders. The exertion brought on the nausea and this time Mercedes succumbed. She availed herself of the bag and dumped it down the disposal chute.

"So, what now?" Carisa asked.

"We try to locate Boho's ship, figure out how far off course we've been pulled, and if we can, break the remote pilot and take back control."

"When we do they're going to know we're on to them—"

"And come after us," Mercedes finished the sentence.

"Too right, and we can't outrun *Infiernos*," Carisa concluded. She was trying to sound insouciant in the best tradition of O-Trell, and as a daughter of the ruler of the Solar League, but there was a small quaver in her voice.

"Okay, let's see what's in the neighborhood that we can work with," Mercedes said.

Together they moved the dead pilot out of his couch and pushed the corpse away so it spun slowly in a macabre dance with the body of the co-pilot.

They strapped into the couches and Mercedes brought

up the scanner. "Pretty crowded neighborhood," Carisa remarked as the computer identified missile batteries, O-Trell ships, commercial shuttles, freighters, racing pinnaces, weather and communication satellites, and the awkward shape of the space station. "We could try for the High Ground," Carisa suggested. "Dock there."

Mercedes shook her head. "We'll never make it." She rubbed her forehead. "We need to play the pea in a shell game." There were a group of freight shuttles moving like a school of metal fish toward the station. "There. We go hide with them."

"The ship is pinging out our call signal," Carisa objected.

"So we trade with Boho's ship or one of those shuttles." The moment the words left her mouth, Mercedes realized why it wouldn't work, and so did Carisa, who voiced the problem.

"The del Campo ship has painted us. Even if we suddenly change call signal, they will still know it's us."

"Damn radar and lidar," Mercedes said with forced lightness.

The sisters sat silent for several long minutes as their ship traveled inexorably toward an outcome that Mercedes was very confident wouldn't be healthy for either her or her father. She put a hand on her uneasy belly and wondered about the life growing in there. The child she would never see if they failed to escape. Tears pricked the back of her eyelids.

"Somehow we need to go to ground. Lie low until Boho and Kemel spring their counter trap," Carisa said.

"Fox hunting," Mercedes murmured. "You're a genius, Cari."

"Yes, I know." She paused. "But what did I say?"

"Foxes go to ground, which made me remember how you train hounds by drag hunting. You lay a false trail that teaches them to follow a scent. How much do you remember of your astrodynamics?"

"You keep asking me that. Fortunately, the answer to this one is—a lot. I liked it."

"We need a shuttle that's relatively close and either a missile battery or a large satellite array that's also close. We match trajectory and velocity with the other shuttle—"

"Trade call signals," Carisa jumped in.

"Both ships boost toward the missile battery or satellite. We kill our engines and have the decoy shuttle nudge us toward the battery. Deploy grapples and hide there."

"That's good. If we go dark there's a chance the equipment on the battery will camouflage our body heat and the minimal life support we'll be running. So where do we send the decoy?" Carisa asked.

"Back toward Ouranos."

"We might be getting the crew of that shuttle killed... assuming they agree in the first place." Cari suddenly sounded rather pessimistic.

"Perhaps he'll be a patriot."

"Or at least amenable to bribes," was the cynical response.

27

WHEN GAMES GET REAL

Anselmo had surpassed himself. The Plaza was filled with a shifting crowd of mostly humans, but a surprising number of aliens were also present. That was not good. Boho opened a channel to Captain Lord Rogers and Matthew Gutierrez. "Gentlemen, I don't know which of you is closer to the Plaza, but we've got a problem. A lot of aliens are joining in. That's not good."

"Forgive me, sir, but aren't more bodies a good thing? Show the lack of support for Musa?" Gutierrez asked.

Boho struggled for patience. "We want Musa's troops to think hard about opening fire on unarmed civilians. They see a bunch of BEMs and that becomes an easier choice."

"The consort's correct, Matt," Rogers chimed in. "Some of them are disaffected military, and we're trained to kill aliens. We don't want to give them an excuse."

"Do you want us to roust them out of there?" Gutierrez asked.

"Or the consort could ask them to return home," Rogers offered.

Anselmo coughed. He had been monitoring the conversation. "The consort telling League citizens, even second-class citizens, that we don't want their help is a PR nightmare. And having security agents roughing up aliens would be almost as bad. Gutierrez, your agents are plainclothes. Have them quietly suggest to the aliens that they may be in danger from Musa's people, and they should pull back. Let them spread the word to each other."

"What Anselmo said. Do that," Boho ordered.

He broke the connection and studied the situation. There were a few police and military people wearing the red armbands, signifying they were traditionalists and backed Musa, but they seemed uneasy and confused about how to cope with what, by rough count, was some twenty thousand people and more arriving.

"How are you going to be heard over this?" the SEGU pilot asked.

"I'll use the flitter's PA system, and stand on the roof. Drop us down about ten feet. I want people to have a decent view of me."

"Don't slip off," the other SEGU officer grunted. "Little hard to lead the counter-revolution if you fall on your ass."

Boho gave the man a thin smile. "You don't think I planned for this? My boots are magnetized. Now give me that microphone."

The pilot opened the door and Boho grabbed the edge of the roof of the flitter and chinned himself up so he could swing a leg onto the top of the vehicle. He stood, pulled the wireless mic out of his pocket. "CITIZENS. FRIENDS. PATRIOTS."

* * *

"Are you willing to be a patriot?"

"Shit! It really *is* the Infanta." The shuttle pilot had turned away from Mercedes' image on his screen and was yelling over his shoulder.

A heavy-set girl in coveralls flew into the frame. From the way she cuffed the man on the shoulder and the cast of their features they seemed to be related. "Where are your manners, Papa?" The girl attempted a curtsey and a salute, which set her to bouncing. She had obviously been an *hombre* in the service. The man grabbed her ankle and hauled her down into the second couch. "Your Highness, we've been monitoring the reports from the planet. What do you need?" the girl asked.

Mercedes quickly outlined the situation. "Once we broke off their remote piloting program, they knew we were on to them. They're closing fast so we need to do this quickly. Assuming you're willing."

"We know it's a lot to ask, but will you help us?" Carisa asked.

"We would be honored," the man said.

"Of course," said the girl at the same time.

"Thank you," Mercedes breathed. "Might we know who is aiding us so you can be appropriately rewarded for your actions?" The formal words were incongruous under the circumstances. Her sister sat next to her wearing only her bra and panties ready to climb into a spacesuit once they had an agreement.

"No reward is necessary, Highness," the man said.

"It is our honor to serve," the girl added.

"Still, I must insist," Mercedes pressed.

The father and daughter exchanged a glance then with a cough the man said, "Diego and Lirio Gonzales."

"Okay less talking, more doing," Carisa said breathlessly and pointed at the chronometer ticking away the seconds and minutes. "We've removed our transponder," she continued. The smudge on her cheek and her broken nails and dirty fingers were evidence of her frenzied efforts to break the device out of its housing. "I'll bring it over to you."

"I'll meet you halfway," the girl said.

"Lovely, thank you. It's still signaling, you just need to get it rehoused as soon as possible."

"How did you manage that?" the man asked.

"Hooked up my ring as an auxiliary power source," Carisa explained as she climbed into her spacesuit.

Diego nodded approvingly. "Clever."

"Once that's done," Mercedes said, "I need you to nudge us toward that missile battery. I'm sending over the burn length and trajectory to you now."

"Got it," Diego said seconds later. "Don't worry, Highness, we'll be gentle as a mother's kiss to send you on your way."

Carisa leaned into the frame. "Heading out now," she said to Lirio. The girl nodded, unhooked her restraints, and kicked out of the cockpit.

Mercedes released her own restraints and floated up to meet Carisa. She hugged her hard. "Be safe."

"Pfff, this is nothing." Mercedes hadn't argued when her sister insisted that she make the transfer. Mercedes was pregnant and the fetus had to be protected at all costs. "And I got to tell Mummy to stuff it. That was quite satisfying."

"I suppose we can't get these bodies out of here," Mercedes remarked, studying the floating corpses.

"Not if we don't want hysterics."

"If you would set me free, I could help the Empre—"

"SHUT UP!" the sisters yelled. Guthrie subsided.

They left the cockpit and headed to the airlock. As they passed Constanza she gave Mercedes a murderous glare. Carisa paused to kiss her father on the cheek. "Back in a jiffy, Papa."

"Once we broke free I was sure we would get a missile up our ass," Carisa said just before she dogged closed her helmet.

"I think the del Campos want you too much to just blast the ship," Mercedes replied.

Carisa sighed. "I was afraid you were going to say that."

Boho had gone back and forth between trying for the sonorous call to arms, or the patriot paean, but once he saw the number of women in the crowd, and the people under the age of thirty, he realized he needed to make them feel concern for Mercedes as an expectant mother, and connected to him as an *amigo*. He had to paint Musa and Mihalis and Arturo as the arrogant out-of-touch FFH bastards that in truth they all were, but this crowd didn't need to know that. Boho modulated his tone and volume.

"Hell of a thing, isn't it?" he said. "We've got friends and families separated because of one man's bitterness and wounded pride and his sons' ambitions. My wife, the mother of my unborn child, is right now fleeing agents of Musa del Campo. I can only pray she escapes, because we all know the outcome if she doesn't." He paused to let them think about that. "Musa will have her killed because she exists and she thwarts his ambitions. But that's not the only reason he hates and fears Mercedes. It's because she represents a new way, a sense of shared community allowing *all* of our citizens—" a sweep of his arm encompassed the crowd "—to have access to the training and benefits of service in the *Orden de la Estrella*. Your sons and daughters have come back from a tour with new abilities and the crown is even now putting in place programs to help these proud veterans to find jobs, open businesses, offer child support to working women."

"Parliament will be very surprised to hear about this pending legislation," Anselmo murmured in his ear. The press spokesman was listening in on all the media platforms.

"Make sure I'm the one to propose it," Boho muttered into his throat mic.

Projecting to the crowd once again he continued, "Because of all of you, our economy is growing, booming. But the del Campos think you're all *campesinos.*" There was a stirring in the crowd at his use of the word peasant, rather than the more common word *intitulado,* which meant untitled or lowborn. "They'll take us back. They'll take *you* back because they don't think you deserve to rise. So, I'm going to ask you now… will you help me? Will you help me retake the spaceport so our loyal and valiant troops can regain control and bring my Mercedes, our baby, and our beloved Emperor home?"

There were growing shouts and cheers from the crowd, and also some worried murmurs. "I understand if you're afraid. Hell, *I'm* afraid." There were chuckles at that and nods of agreement, and then the cheers began. Truth was Boho's guts felt like wobbling jello. He'd have to lead them initially, but find a way to drop back and let the crowd be bullet magnets if it looked like his gamble that the police and military wouldn't fire on civilians hadn't paid off. "They have guns, but we have numbers and right is on our side. So let's go save the Infanta and the little prince or princess we will soon welcome."

The roar that went up probably carried for blocks. Boho hoped the politicians were taking note. He switched channels on his mic and said to the flitter pilot, "Head for the spaceport. Walking pace for my sake and so they can keep up."

"Aye, sir."

The flitter began to move; the crowd bulked beneath them and trailed behind. Some younger men had rushed ahead. More people were coming in from side streets. From his elevated position, the crowd looked like a gigantic millipede snaking through the streets.

Anselmo came on the radio. "Arturo has bolted from parliament. Guess he got word about the mob with torches and pitchforks."

"Great. Keep up the pressure. Try to get some torches

and pitchforks over to parliament. Together with Rogers' forces that ought to focus the members' minds."

"On it."

"I have to relieve myself," Guthrie whined from where he hung, taped to the wall.

"Pee down your leg," Mercedes said. With her attention focused on the rear of the cockpit, Mercedes had no idea what elicited Carisa's shriek.

Jerking against her restraints, Mercedes whipped her head around to find a spacesuited figure pressed against the glass of the cockpit dome. She couldn't control her own yelp of shock. The figure tapped the glass, pointed to his ear. The diffusion screen was down on the helmet so Mercedes couldn't make out his features. This was the downside of powering down the shuttle to bare minimum: they hadn't been able to do radar surveillance, so they had been taken off guard. She wanted to hope the man was from Boho's ship, but had a feeling they wouldn't be that lucky. Mercedes switched the shuttle's equipment back on and a voice came over the radio.

"Prepare to be boarded."

The statement caused Carisa to give a nervous giggle. She glanced at Mercedes. "Arrr me hearties, so, do we prepare to repel boarders? You do have a pistol."

"No, there's nothing we can do now. We have to let them in and we won't win in a shootout. At least it bought us a few hours. I just hope Boho made use of them."

She keyed the radio and said to the *fusilero*, "The airlock is open. We await your arrival." His jetpack fired and he moved away from the shuttle. Mercedes then hit send and broadcast an all points emergency call that pinpointed their location and identified the sender as the royal family. As she suspected, it only broadcast for a few seconds before it was jammed.

"Well, maybe someone was listening," Carisa said.

They moved into the main body of the shuttle. Constanza was shivering in her couch. The Emperor looked up. "I'm almost done with my speech."

"That's wonderful, Daddy, but I'm afraid we've been discovered. They'll be coming aboard momentarily."

"I shall not meet them like this," her father said. He unhooked his restraints and pushed out of the couch. "I am their emperor. They will not forget their oath."

"I don't care who they are as long as we get out of this terrible ship," Constanza said.

The daughters and their father ignored her, and propelled themselves to the airlock. The lock was filled with men, six of them. Mercedes watched the graph as the lock filled with oxygen.

Just before the end of the cycle Carisa looked at Mercedes. "Do you think Mihalis himself will show up?"

"I would be prepared for that," Mercedes said.

The inner door slid open and the soldiers entered. The helmets came off and Mercedes found herself looking into her cousin's face.

"Good trick, Mercedes," Mihalis said.

"Thank you, cousin. I liked it." The normalcy of the

conversation had her wanting to giggle.

"I demand that you arrest this man," the Emperor said to the five *fusileros* and he pointed at Mihalis.

"Oh, shut up, you senile old *pendejo*." Then all normalcy ceased. Mihalis casually pulled his pistol and shot the Emperor in the face. Brains and blood and bits of skull formed a macabre halo floating around the shattered skull.

Daddy, Daddy, Daddy! Oh God, Daddy! No! No! No! Shock, horror, a mind-numbing grief, shattered images of a little girl held in a father's embrace as the sled raced down the snow-covered hill. A slightly bigger girl, her feet resting on top of her daddy's feet as they danced. Her father leaning against the barn door smiling as she hugged the neck of her first pony.

While Mercedes struggled to process, she was faintly aware of Mihalis giving the sobbing Carisa a thin smile. "Guess he won't be able to give you away now. I'm sure my father will be happy to stand in for him."

Constanza was screaming, a throat-tearing sound that drilled into the ear. A few drops of blood spattered onto Mercedes' cheek and her stomach heaved. Rage rose up on a pillar of bile and her vomit joined the detritus of her father's head. Fighting for control, Mercedes remembered her hand-to-hand combat classes. She could hear Chief Deal's gravel tones: *"You get hot mad, you get stupid. Cold mad and that other stupid motherfucker better look out."*

Mercedes met Mihalis's gaze. She slowly wiped the vomit from her lips and then cleaned her fingers on the front of his spacesuit. His disgust was evident.

It took every particle of control to keep her tone flat, calm, and emotionless as she said, "I expect that act of malice won't work out all that well for you."

"Little princeling giving you problems?" And he punched her hard in the stomach, which sent her flying across the width of the shuttle. She managed to grab a handhold to keep herself from caroming back into Mihalis's reach.

Please, baby, please, baby, be all right.

She knew that her life was hanging in the balance. Fortunately, it was still too early in her pregnancy for her to show, so there was a chance she could still bluff. She gave him a pitying look. "So you fell for that lie too? My my, Boho played you brilliantly." She could read his objection rising to his lips. "The announcement? Timed to pull you out. Really, after twenty-three years and no baby you thought *now* I would get knocked up? How credulous you must be."

He gave a growl of frustration. "I should kill you on general principles."

Carisa's sobs had subsided. Her tears hung in crystal drops around her face but her expression was cold and grim. She clutched his right arm. "Do that and I swear I will chop off your dick and choke you with it at the first opportunity."

"So, you're not just a pretty face and fragile flower. Julieta and Tanis clearly gave me the wrong impression."

"Well, if you listened to them, you're an even bigger idiot than I thought," Carisa snapped.

"As pleasant as this exchange has been, it's time to repair to my ship and get married."

"What, no public spectacle?" Mercedes asked as one of

the soldiers relieved her of her pistol and the knife.

"Oh, we'll do that, too. Now where's my agent?" Mihalis asked.

"Guthrie?" Carisa asked. "We have him trussed up in the cockpit."

Mihalis turned to one of his soldiers. "Take care of him." Constanza was still shrieking. Mihalis's mouth twisted in disgust. "And will one of you shut her up before I knock her out."

Carisa kicked off the ceiling of the shuttle and sailed over to her mother. Mercedes heard Guthrie gobbling out muffled words then the sound of a gunshot.

"Interesting way to build loyalty," she said.

Mihalis shrugged, a gesture that set him bobbing. "He fucked up. I don't reward failure." The engines on the shuttle growled to life. "Now get in your couches like good little girls. We'll be at my ship soon."

Mercedes pulled herself into her couch and strapped in. "I do hope you've been keeping up with events in Hissilek," she said. "Boho and Kemel haven't exactly been idle while you've been chasing us." It gave her a small flare of pleasure to see his frown. She had made him worry, at least for a moment.

Tear gas, nausea grenades, and pepper spray filled the air. People were crying, coughing, screaming, and puking. Boho was wearing a mask that had been handed up to him by the flitter pilot. The crowd might have wanted to flee, but at this point there were too many and they were so tightly packed that the only way to move was forward. The troops and cops trying to hold the spaceport were retreating step by step. As yet no bullets had flown.

Boho's radio pinged to life. It was Kemel. "We caught Arturo. He'll soon give us Musa's location."

"Great. Don't kill them."

"Looking for a show trial, sir?"

"Something like—" There was the sharp retort of gunfire. "Oh, shit!" Boho threw himself down, hugging the front of the shuttle. His magnetized boots were reluctant to release and he twisted his left ankle as he went down. "Owww, shit, fuck."

"Is that gunfire?" Kemel asked.

"Yeah, it's fucking gunfire!"

"Have you been hit?"

"No, I twisted my ankle." Screams of pain and bellows of rage rose like a rolling tide. Panic hammered in his throat and his lungs seemed to have been replaced with stones. "Light them up," he managed to croak out.

"Sir, wait, sir. They're turning on each other. It was only a handful who opened fire," the pilot called.

"And the crowds are rushing forward," the other agent offered. "We open fire, we'll hit our own supporters."

"Do you want us to advance, sir?" the pilot asked.

"Not… not just yet," Boho managed to say.

A few more shots rang out, but the roar of thousands of voices was the predominate sound. The mob surged forward, flowing around the ships and service vehicles, beating Musa's soldiers to the ground. Boho climbed to his feet, wincing a bit as he put weight on his left foot. A few more scattered shots and then cheers began to rise until they became a sustained roar.

Boho started to open his mouth to order them forward, but the SEGU agents were already there. The flitter drifted forward over the dead and the wounded. Blood pooled on the pavement and the cries of pain and the calls for help were faint against the celebration ahead. They advanced another hundred feet or so, and found red armbands littering the ground, torn off by rebels deciding to pretend they had never been part of the rebellion, fabric echoes of the blood that ran in the streets.

The cheers became even louder as they passed over the heads of the crowd. It was time for him to take a bow. Kemel's voice interrupted the moment.

"We just received the emergency signal from Mercedes. Your Hail Mary play better show up soon."

28

PICKING UP THE PIECES

"Sir! Ships! Lots of them."

Mihalis whirled to face the aide who had run into the captain's mess. Mercedes and Carisa exchanged a glance. The blood had been inexpertly cleaned from Carisa's skirt and a makeshift veil created out of a lace tablecloth. It was not a completely outré place to hold a wedding, for Mihalis's taste ran to the elegant. The dining room aboard his flagship was wood-paneled with a crystal chandelier, fine furnishings, and a thick rug underfoot. The chaplain paused in the act of donning his stole.

"What?" Mihalis demanded.

"It's... it's the Blue, sir. *All* of them."

Mercedes gathered her scattered wits, pushed through the grief and shock and anger that had laid a fog over her mind. "Surprise," she said archly, though her thoughts were whirling in confusion.

Davin had been out looking for her. He could not have known... unless... Kemel and Boho had kept them in reserve, risked the dangers of an orbital translation out of Fold. She wondered how many satellites, missile batteries, and ships had been damaged or even destroyed by the dangerous stunt.

"Get us out of here. Take us into Fold," Mihalis ordered.

A voice came over the intercom. "Sir, we are being hailed. Accept or deny?"

Mihalis's head jerked from side to side; whether in negation of the events that were unfolding or out of confusion, Mercedes couldn't tell.

"I'd take the call," Mercedes said. "This is Davin. You know what he's like, he'll have something else up his sleeve." Mihalis had been two years ahead of them at the High Ground, but she prayed he would remember Davin's elaborate practical jokes, which had kept professors and students alike on edge.

"Fine! Put it through."

"Hi, Mil," Davin said conversationally, "the next voice I hear better be Mercedes'. If it's not, I won't pre-detonate the missiles that are heading for you. And yes, they will reach you before you can translate into Fold. I'd think fast."

Mercedes lunged forward. "Davin! I'm here! We're here. We're okay. Well, not all of us." Despite her best efforts her voice broke at the end.

"Okay. Good start." His voice changed, deepening, the vowels more rounded. Mercedes knew he was now recording. "Vice Admiral Vizconde Mihalis August Ferdinand Francis del Campo, I request your formal surrender. Shut down all engines and weapons systems immediately. Once that has been verified, I will destroy the missiles that will impact your ship in just under nine minutes."

"You're bluffing. You won't kill the Infanta."

"Hmm, no mention of the Emperor… so you did kill him," Davin said. "Not the smartest move you could have made because Mercedes is far tougher than he ever was."

Mercedes swept around until she stood facing Mihalis. They were eye to eye and close enough she could feel and smell his stale breath on her face. "You murdered my father. I'll happily die if you'll burn too." Her voice was low, throbbing with emotion, and she realized she meant every word. Mihalis seemed to sense it too, but his features closed down. He was going to refuse. *Better to reign in Hell…* she thought.

Carisa spoke up, directing her words to the priest. "Talk to him. There are at least four thousand men aboard this ship. Will you let him kill them all for pride's sake?"

"Admiral, I beg you. Think of your men," the priest quavered.

There was no reaction. Mercedes turned to the lieutenant who had delivered the message. "He doesn't care about you. He and his father started this because they wanted the throne. He'd walk across all your bodies to plant his ass upon it." Doubt flickered in the young officer's eyes.

Mihalis sensed the shift in his subordinate. He grabbed for his pistol and started to bring it to bear on Mercedes. The young lieutenant shoved Mercedes aside and slugged Mihalis hard in the jaw. The shot went wide. Mihalis staggered backwards. Carisa grabbed the heavy, elaborate epergne from the dining room table, and brought it down hard on the top of his head. Mihalis dropped to the floor unconscious. Blood ran from the scalp wound.

"I'd suggest you contact Admiral del Campo's second-in-command, and tell him the admiral is unable to perform his duties," Mercedes said.

"Yes, ma'am." The lieutenant saluted. He keyed his ring. "Captain, I regret to say the admiral is... incapacitated. This is your call."

"Admiral Lord Davin Pulkkinen, we accept your terms."

"Good call," Davin replied.

A few moments later the faint vibration from the engines that Mercedes felt through the soles of her feet ceased. The priest dropped to his knees next to Mihalis. "I think you cracked his skull," he said to Carisa.

"Good," she replied.

"Musa committed suicide. Arturo and Jose are being held at San Quintin. Mihalis is in the hospital. The sisters are under house arrest." Kemel's dry delivery seemed an incongruous way to discuss treason. "What do you want us to do about Sanjay, Julieta, and Tanis, *Emperatriz*?"

Emperatriz. *Not like this. I didn't want it to happen this way. Oh, Daddy.* Mercedes rubbed at her aching forehead, remembered her youngest full sister, the fairy princess, beautiful, passionate, romantic. She had known Julieta resented her. She hadn't known she hated her. Tanis was less surprising. An ill-tempered, resentful and nasty child, she'd grown up into an ill-tempered, resentful and nasty woman who hid her ugly personality under the veil of a nun, and a cloak of piety.

"Arrest them all," she ordered.

Kemel gave the little cough that was his way to express disagreement. "Your sister and her husband are no difficulty, but your other sister... The Pope is condemning in the strongest terms the arrest of one of his bishops. Sending *federales* into a convent will not improve the situation."

"I assume you have an alternative solution," Mercedes snapped.

"Suggest to the Reverend Mother that we will disrupt her convent unless she arranges to send Tanis to the Handmaids of the Precious Blood," Kemel said.

"And that will help how?"

Kemel gave a thin smile. "It's a contemplative order sworn to silence and the Reverend Mother is a cousin of mine, a most formidable figure. They allow no contact with the outside world."

"Apart from your cousin communicating with you," Boho said.

"Well, yes, but one must be practical. At any rate they can hold her until trial. I would advise against executing a nun."

Boho brushed a finger across his mustache. "Perhaps we could suggest to the Pope that Tanis and Jose be tried in an ecclesiastic court. That might mollify him."

"No, not Jose! I'll agree to have Tanis tried by the church, but not Jose. He's a snake."

"This can wait a few days, Majesty. We have the excuse of arrangements to be made."

Her anger died and Mercedes said dully, "My father's—the Emperor's funeral."

"And your coronation," Boho added. He sat next to her, arm wrapped protectively around her waist.

Mercedes fought the desire to violently push him away. Exhaustion and grief lay on her shoulders like an iron shawl. She stood. "Director, I am weary and grieving. If there is nothing else pressing, I'd like to have some time to myself."

"Of course, Majesty." He bowed and left.

"You should lie down," Boho said solicitously.

"I will, but I have some questions first. Why didn't you tell me that you had Davin in reserve?"

He had the grace to look embarrassed. "No offense, darling, but you aren't the best poker player in the world. Mihalis might have sensed that we had an ace up our sleeves. We needed him to believe that he had you completely under his control."

"The fact he believed me when I lied to him about the pregnancy says you're wrong. And, husband or not, if you *ever* keep information from me again I'll see to it you're made the governor of some distant and not very pleasant colony world. Are we clear?"

"Clear." He sounded sulky.

"Next issue. How did Kemel miss that Guthrie had been suborned?" His suddenly thoughtful look told her he hadn't even thought about it prior to this moment. "I see only three possibilities. One, he was also working for Musa—"

"I don't believe that," Boho objected.

"Neither do I, which brings me to possibility two. That this was all part of the plan concocted by you and Kemel to place us in desperate danger so you could take out Mihalis's rebel ships."

"I would *never—*"

She cut him off. "I assumed such was the case. It *better* have been the case. Which brings me to the third option. Kemel five years ago would never have missed something like this. But he did."

"You want to replace him," Boho said.

"I—" she quickly amended to include him "—we have to." She studied Boho. She had delivered a pretty nasty rebuke to him. She needed to soften the blow. Going forward there could be no more mistresses and bastards. She was empress. An heir was on the way. Everything had to change.

"I'm turning to you for this. Work with Jaakon, prepare a list of potential candidates and let's discuss. Once we agree on someone, we'll let Kemel know."

"You can rely on me. Now, please rest. It's been a terrible twenty-four hours."

Tears welled up. "Yes. It has."

"Oh, my love." He gathered her into his arms. He was so tall that she could rest her head against his chest. She closed her eyes, breathed in the scent of his aftershave, and pushed Tracy from her thoughts.

It was to be a closed casket memorial since her father's face had been destroyed by the bullet, and Mercedes refused to have the undertaker repair it. At first, she had refused to even search for the body, which had been spaced, along with Guthrie's, by Mihalis's goons. She was not going to devote resources to the effort when Davin and Kartirci were busy stamping out the final resistance. Estella's hysterical objections hadn't swayed her, but Boho's cold calculations did. He had pointed out that if they recovered the body they could allow pictures of the shattered face to be "leaked" to the press. Get the media sites to place a picture of the Emperor in happier times next to a picture of the corpse. It was ghoulish, but certain to arouse fury against the plotters in the general populace, so the Emperor had been recovered. Guthrie had been left to orbit in frozen solitude.

The final butcher's bill from putting down the coup could have been worse, but Davin commanding the Blue and Kartirci with his rump force of loyal ships of the Gold had been forced to destroy two cruisers and six frigates who had refused to surrender, and they had not emerged unscathed from those encounters. Davin had lost seven *Infiernos* and an *explorador*. Kartirci's rump fleet had lost a frigate. It was going to take time and money to rebuild, which would probably require a tax increase.

Mercedes' stomach roiled, a combination of morning sickness and stress. She reached for another saltine cracker. Her desk was littered with crumbs and she frowned at the scattered flakes. There was too much to do and not enough hours in the day, and Dr. Mueller had insisted she spend at least seven of them sleeping. Her warning had been stark. *"You're old for a first pregnancy and you need to be careful."*

That had scared Mercedes enough that she meekly obeyed the chime from her ScoopRing when it told her it was time for bed. Boho was also insistent, and kept constant watch over what she ate and when. He had tried to keep her from riding, but Mueller had knocked that down, saying that exercise was as important as rest. She could ride until the start of her sixth month.

The sisters and their families were gathering for the state funeral. Mercedes had ordered a week of mourning throughout League space. An alarm chimed, warning her she had to be at a meeting of the coronation committee in ten minutes. She grabbed her pack of crackers and left her office. Her father's study was being redecorated prior to her taking possession, so for the moment she remained in her smaller and more spartan space.

Jaakon looked up as she left the inner office. The bags beneath his eyes were so dark he looked like he'd been in a fight. "Anything pressing?" she asked.

He gave a short, barking laugh and gestured at a stack of folders. "I'm going to cull and bring you only the ones marked HAIR ON FIRE."

"Thank you. Not sure when I'll be back. Robrecht has dragged in the court historian for this meeting."

"It has been a long time since we've had a coronation," Jaakon said.

"It seems silly to do this. It's going to take months to plan and I will have been acting as empress all that time. Why bother?"

"Because the people need to set aside grief and be given permission to celebrate, and to do that they need to see you, cheer you, love you."

"Why is so much of governance just putting on a show?"

"Because at heart we humans are simple creatures who love a party?"

She gave a snort of laughter and left for the meeting.

It was quite a crowd that came to their feet, and bowed deeply at her entrance. Gutierrez, the head of imperial protective services, was there. Ian Rogers, who commanded her personal guard. The police chief of Hissilek. The head of the royal mews, who maintained not only the horses but the antique carriages. Robrecht, who in his role as seneschal kept the documents detailing royal protocols. The aforementioned court historian, a young man with the fussy habits of a far older person. Also present was Rohan, as the unheralded leader of parliament, as was his wife, Analise, who had been added to help discuss fashion choices. The head of the palace press corps was in attendance. He was an older man, a golfing crony of her father's. Anselmo in his role as Boho's personal press agent was bending down to whisper something in Boho's ear. Mercedes wished she had her own Anselmo, and then it struck her. She could replace her father's press secretary. There was nothing to stop her from picking a new communications chief now that she was Empress. And perhaps she could even make it a woman! *What a breathtaking idea!* She hid her smile.

Folding her hands on the conference table she said, "I've been considering the date for the coronation. Clearly this is an undertaking that will require months of planning, and I do not wish to unduly shorten the period of mourning for my father. I would also prefer not to face the rigors of the celebration late in my pregnancy. So, I would like to propose that the coronation be set for October after I am, God willing, safely delivered of our heir."

Analise crossed herself and cast her eyes toward heaven, but then said, "As someone who has had more than a few babies… give yourself a little more time. You'll want to get your body back in shape and, believe me, in the beginning you won't want to be parted for long from *el bebé* for the hours that will be required to prepare for the coronation."

The court historian was nodding, stroking his chin. "A Christmas coronation. How beautiful that would be. Say on the twenty-third of December?"

"People might wish to be home for Christmas," Mercedes demurred.

"Let's see," Boho mused. "Christmas at home with all your shirttail relatives, or Christmas at the capitol, attending balls and parties culminating in the first coronation in nearly fifty years. They'll climb over each other to attend."

She laughed. "All right. The twenty-third it is." There were murmurs and nods all around.

"Since we are embarking on a new era with a change in custom, and after the disturbing events of the past weeks, I think it would be wise to insist that the heads of every FFH household attend, and swear their oath of loyalty to you at that time," Rohan said.

She looked to Boho who nodded in agreement. Then found herself wondering if one particular caballero would obey the summons and attend? Treacherous, dangerous thought. Technically she should have had a formal ceremony to knight him, but that would not be wise. No, she would never see Tracy again. It was safer that way.

"Good idea," Ian said. "And if any decline claiming illness, we should have SEGU verify those claims."

"Who do you wish to perform the ceremony?" Boho asked.

"I think we ask the Pope. It might mollify him."

"Do you want me to make the overture?" the press secretary asked.

"No, I'll do that myself. Show proper respect and reverence."

"You're a born politician, Mercedes," Rohan said approvingly.

"Thank you… I guess." Mercedes stood. So did everyone else. "I'm sorry to make this so brief, but several more of my sisters and their families are arriving today and I would like to meet them."

She swept out of the room with Ian and Boho flanking her. "Who's arriving today?" Ian asked.

"Delia and Dulcinea, their kids and husbands."

Ian smiled. "They're still inseparable, I see."

"More so since they married brothers."

"How are you dealing with Julieta's children?" he asked.

"We've got five of them here at the palace. The eldest boy is on the run with his father. We'll catch them eventually," she said.

"The nineteen-year-old is at the High Ground, and basically under house arrest," Boho added. "At that age he probably shared his parents' and older brother's beliefs, but we don't have any proof yet." His ScoopRing pinged.

"Ah damn, I've been expecting this call."

"Go," Mercedes said and waved him away. He kissed her on the cheek and hurried off toward his office.

She and Ian resumed walking and she continued her tale of woe. "And let's not forget the resentful twenty-one-year-old daughter who clearly hates us. What do I do with her? Marry her to a loyal supporter and make his life a misery? Then there is the fourteen year-old who is a sulky teenager, and there are also three more boys, sixteen, eleven, and eight. The youngest are scared, homesick, and can't understand why their mommy and daddy are gone. What do I tell them? *Your father is a wanted criminal and will probably end up facing a long prison term assuming he avoids execution, and your mommy is in jail awaiting trial on similar charges. But here's some good news—we probably won't execute her because she's the Empress's sister and a woman, so you'll be able to visit her in prison.*"

By the time she finished her heart was pounding and her breath had gone short. Mercedes pressed a hand to her belly and leaned against the hallway wall struggling for calm. Worried, Ian broke protocol and laid a hand on her shoulder. "Should I take you to Dr. Mueller?"

"No. I'm all right. Silly to be upset."

"Really? You watched your father be killed in front of you. You're going to have to imprison your sisters. You've got the weight of the throne on your shoulders. I'd be worried if you *weren't* upset."

She stepped away and, realizing what he had done, the military man snatched back his hand. "I need to return to my office."

Rebuked, he stepped back and bowed. "Of course, Highness."

Mercedes stretched out her hand, not quite touching him. "Ian, it's all right. But everything is different now."

"I understand."

Boho sat at Mercedes' right hand at the head of the very long dining room table and studied the extended family. Seven of the nine sisters were present. Only three of those assembled were childless, and Mercedes—he gave a satisfied glance at her softly swelling belly—was working on alleviating that situation. Only two were unmarried. When you added together the husbands, plus his sisters and their husbands, and any child over the age of fifteen, it meant that there were twenty-six people at the table. Thank God he had no brothers or it would have looked like the mob at a fútbol game.

The younger children were all under the care of human nannies and relegated to the family quarters, which brought the count of people related by blood or marriage to the crown to some forty-three individuals. He spun his wine glass between forefinger and thumb. A lot of potential plots and intrigues. He downed his wine and held out the glass to the Hajin footman, who was quick to refill it.

The subjugated alien races outnumbered their human masters by probably ten to one. Hovering on the edge of concern was the missing Cara'ot. What had they been doing in the intervening years since they'd vanished from League space? Given all of those factors Boho understood why humans, through the levers of government and the church, had pushed for large families, and made childbearing a woman's highest duty and honor.

But when you had a hereditary aristocracy that carried its own problems. What did the third, fourth, fifth, sixth son of a noble family have to look forward to? Marriage to the third, fourth, fifth, sixth daughter of a noble family? Without a war it was tough to make a name and a fortune through military service. Plum assignments such as planetary governor would always go to your older brother. You could beg the family for enough money to go into business, but never obviously. You had to find some willing *intitulado* to front for you. No member of the FFH would willingly be associated openly with the sordid business of buying and selling for crass profit. Maybe gentleman architect or gentleman farmer, horse breeder, artist, composer was acceptable, but most of the professions such as lawyer, doctor, accountant would earn you a pitying look and a dismissive sniff.

He thought about all the families, all of the children jockeying for position. They couldn't find enough Goldilocks planets to satisfy this growing horde. In his history classes at the High Ground, Boho had studied the Earth kingdom of Saudi Arabia with its ever-expanding number of princes. Eventually it had collapsed, when the oil ran out and Earth belatedly realized they needed to move to sustainable sources of energy. The more Boho analyzed the situation, the more he became convinced that the League was facing the same outcome. The system was not sustainable. It was a Ponzi scheme. Question was whether it would survive his lifetime? He glanced again at Mercedes' stomach and amended. He needed it to survive through his son's lifetime as well. He would prop up the system as long as possible, and if it looked like it wouldn't stand he needed to have a plan in place in order to survive the chaos.

29

FAMILY MATTERS

It had been long and arduous. At hour nine Mercedes had given in and asked for a spinal. Now three hours later she lay limp, exhausted, and bathed in sweat. The spinal was starting to wear off and she was aware of the grinding pain in her crotch, the shivering in her belly, and her aching breasts. A lusting screaming was emerging from the outraged infant as a nurse wiped away the blood and mucus from his body.

"A beautiful little boy, Your Highness," Mueller said with satisfaction.

"Does my husband know?"

"I've sent someone to tell him. Do you want to see the consort?"

Mercedes glanced down at her body, the sagging skin of her now empty belly. "Not like this. Thank God he didn't want to be present for the birth."

Mueller laughed. "Or be one of those annoying men who go about announcing to everyone that *we're pregnant*. No, you're not! *I* am and it's not all that pleasant."

Mercedes laughed and then groaned. "May I have my baby, please?"

"All done," the nurse said and brought her the now dry but naked infant. She gazed down into his red wrinkled face and felt her heart squeeze with emotions she couldn't begin to identify. But mingled with the joy was a tinge of worry. She brushed the fuzz on his head. Pale brown. Boho's hair was jet black, but perhaps her dark brown hair could cover for it and recessives could account for some of that. Eye color. She prayed they would be brown, though with Boho's green eyes it was possible he wouldn't find it odd if his son's eyes were gray or hazel.

His rosebud mouth began pursing and sucking. Mercedes laughed with delight and placed him to her breast. After the pain—bliss. She closed her eyes. *Welcome, my love. I will never let anything hurt you.*

"I hate you all," Tracy sighed.

"You have to do this," Jahan said. She was leaning over him, her hands braced on the arms of his captain's chair. They were eye to eye. The rest of the crew listened with interest.

"Why?"

"Because you have a title now, because every member of the FFH has been summoned to the coronation, and because the entire crew will kill you if you don't go and take us. To be on Ouranos for a coronation would be amazing. And you should be able to get us at least a decent place to stand on the route to the cathedral."

Nearly a year had passed since he and Mercedes had parted. Tracy tried to prevent himself from obsessively checking the news feeds when they weren't in Fold, but hadn't been all that successful. He had read about the coup, followed the trials, felt a grim pleasure when Mihalis and Sanjay had been convicted and sentenced to be executed. Appeals were pending so it would probably be years before they actually faced the noose. Sanjay's eldest son had been sentenced to twenty years, Arturo was going to jail for thirty.

Tracy and Arturo had been classmates at the High Ground. Arturo had frequented his dad's tailor shop for his uniforms and formal wear. He would be seventy-five when he emerged, broken, his life at an end. Tracy didn't feel an ounce of sympathy. He had barely avoided spending decades in jail and even with that reprieve his life had been shattered. Tracy couldn't remember if Arturo had been one of the assholes who had acted as a second for Boho at their duel, but whether he was or not he was one of Boho's cronies so he could just suck it.

Then in September had come the news of the royal birth. Prince Cyprian Amadeo Marcus Sinclair de Arango had entered the world on September twenty-third. The family portrait released a few weeks later showed Mercedes seated with her son in her arms while Boho leaned solicitously over the back of the couch and gazed down lovingly at them both. It had been a punch in the gut that had sent Tracy down to the hold to pound on the punching bag Luis had installed.

He pulled himself back from bitter memory and fruitless hope. "Look, I may have a different name, but I still look like me. I'll be recognized. I went to school with some of these *pendejos*."

"We can dye your hair," Dalea offered.

"Grow a beard," Luis added.

"Pack on a few pounds," was Graarack's suggestion.

"Humans rarely see past what's right in front of their noses. They will be expecting Caballero Oliver Randall. That is what they will see," Jax said in his pedantic way.

"And after all the tumult of the failed coup don't you think SEGU is going to take a hard look at anyone in the FFH who *doesn't* show up?" Jahan said. "We've continued to trade with Hidden Worlds. We can't survive close scrutiny."

"All right! All right! We'll go."

Graarack laid a claw on his shoulder. "On the bright side, you'll get to see your father."

"Well, this is certainly an improvement over the last time I watched you getting a fitting," Cipriana said.

Mercedes glanced back over her shoulder to where her friend sat on the chair at the dressing table. The long, slim, dark fingers were playing among the jars and bottles, picking them up and setting them down without ever actually looking at them. The years had evidently not dulled Cipriana's nervous energy.

Mercedes turned back to the three-way mirror and studied the creation with satisfaction. Unlike her first disastrous wedding gown, which she had refused to wear and which had ultimately been replaced by a gown designed by a woman, the designer of this dress was also a woman and her creation was flattering to a forty-five-year-old female who had just recently given birth. It was a deep ruby red and black diamonds flashed and sparkled at the hem and the cuffs, and outlined the high-standing collar that framed her face.

The Isanjo seamstresses completed the final pinning of the hem, and the young designer stepped forward. "If I may, Highness," she said and gestured toward the bodice.

"Of course, Jeanine."

She gripped the side seams. "We'll do a refit the day before the coronation, Majesty. You keep losing weight."

"Thank god," Mercedes murmured. "This baby weight is stubborn as hell."

The three human women shared a knowing laugh, and even a couple of the Isanjos giggled and nodded in agreement. Jeanine unzipped the gown and it fell around Mercedes' feet. She stepped over the mass of material, and Venia held out a robe while Jeanine gathered up the dress.

"Thank you all," Mercedes said, and waved them away. She settled onto the bed and looked around the suite that had once belonged to her father.

"Different room though. When I tried on that first horror that Vasilyev had designed I was still in my old rooms here in the palace. It seems like an age ago," Mercedes sighed.

"It *was* an age ago. We were twenty-one and stupid and had no idea what life was about to unleash on us."

"Yours doesn't seem to have turned out so badly," Mercedes said.

"I wasn't talking about me. I was talking about you. How are you? Really?"

Mercedes glanced around the room at the mirrors, paintings, and tapestries that had replaced her father's choice of wood paneling. "The nightmares wake me up most nights, but that works out well because I can feed Cypri."

"Nursing yourself?"

"During the day I'm too busy so it's nice to have private time with him." She couldn't control the smile. "He's amazing, Cipri—" She broke off and laughed. "I just realized you have the same pet names."

Cipriana made a face. "I'm glad you're happy, but God I'm so glad I'm finished with puke and diapers and tantrums. Right now I just have eye rolls from Hayden. I just can't wait for Fiona to join him in teenage ennui," she said drolly. She paused and added, "Still, I wouldn't mind meeting the future emperor. Make sure he knows I'm on his side."

"Of course." Mercedes jumped to her feet and hurried to the door that connected her suite to the nursery. Cyprian lay in his crib, plump hands stretched up toward the sparkling mobile of stars and planets that hung overhead. He was making small baby language sounds interspersed with happy laughs.

His nanny, a plump human woman in her early thirties, dropped a curtsy. Mercedes had interviewed thirty women before settling on Elizabeth. She had been a school teacher before obtaining a nursing degree and so far Mercedes was very pleased with her.

She moved to the crib and Cyprian gave a crow of

delight at the sight of his mother. Mercedes picked him up and pressed him to her breast. The milky smell of baby and talc rose up, and his soft curls tickled her chin. She gave him a kiss and handed him to Cipriana.

Practiced hands cupped his bottom and the back of his head and Cipri held him up so she could inspect him. He gave her a toothless smile. Cipriana shot Mercedes a sharp look. Mercedes returned it with a bland one. Cipriana gave the baby a kiss on one rosy cheek and handed him back.

"Very nice, Mer. You did good."

"Do you need anything, Liz?" Mercedes asked as she rocked back and forth while Cyprian's hands tangled in her hair. It reached just past her shoulders now and she had decided to cover the gray now that she was empress. The League needed to see their ruler as fit and vibrant.

"We're good. Robrecht has promised to deliver a small Christmas tree today. Our little prince will get to have his first Christmas right here in the nursery."

"Be sure it's on a table. I don't want him getting into any tinsel or decorations," Mercedes warned.

"Yes, ma'am." Another curtsy.

Mercedes reluctantly laid her son back in his crib. His little face crumpled momentarily, but she touched the wind chimes that hung at the other end of the crib and the music brought back his smile.

She and Cipriana returned to her rooms and she started to dress.

"So, where's Constanza gone?" Cipriana asked. "And what happened with Julieta? Tell me all the gory details."

"My stepmother has removed to the Phantasiestück. She wanted Carisa to live with her, but I spared Cari that. She's got my old rooms here at the palace. Julieta is in a women's prison in San Jose." It was a small city some seventy kilometers from the capital.

"Harsh."

"Necessary. She would have poisoned her children's hearts. The younger ones have been fostered to loyal retainers. The eldest daughter got married off to one of Davin's sons."

"Lucky him. I predict a lifetime of blue balls for the young man," Cipriana observed. "And what about the rest of the del Campos, those who aren't facing execution or jail time?"

"A writ of attainder has been issued. They've been stripped of their titles and holdings."

"I take it back. Julieta got off easy. So, you have a bunch of pampered nobles thrown out into the cold hard world to find paying jobs."

"I'm told it's character building," Mercedes said.

They sat in silence for a long time. "So," Cipriana finally said. "How does it feel?"

"I know I should probably say something profound like *uneasy is the head that wears the crown* or some other literary allusion, but truthfully… not that different. I've been picking up a lot of Father's tasks for the past four years. What's been brought home to me is that I can no longer shift the blame or dodge the responsibility. Wasn't there some ancient Earth ruler who said something about bucks stopping with them?"

"Must have been messy with all those deer in the Oval office," Cipriana quipped.

"You're quite impossible." Mercedes leaned down and kissed Cipriana on the cheek. "Thank you for saying nice things about my baby even though I could tell you think he's just a blob of protoplasm right now."

"A very important blob."

"Come to dinner tonight, and bring James. I'd like to meet this compliant husband of yours."

"We'll be there. How formal is this gathering?"

"Just old friends tonight. A time to reminisce and remember."

"Absent friends?" Cipriana asked.

"Yes. Those too."

"My lords, how may we serve you?"

The words were a bit slurred by the pulled-down mouth and the overly obsequious manner. A fist seemed to close around his heart as Tracy observed his father's dragging right foot and the shrunken right arm. Alexander's hair had gone completely white and was so fine pink scalp could be seen through it. As always he was impeccably dressed in one of his own bespoke suits. The shop itself was perfectly appointed with a lush white carpet underfoot, recessed lighting to allow a patron to study himself in the three-way mirrors, and a sofa and coffee table where refreshments could be served.

Tracy, partially obscured by Luis, glanced at his image in one of the mirrors in the fitting room. His hair had been dyed black but Dalea had added silver to his temples. He had grown a short beard and mustache that were also dark and streaked with silver. Ceasing his workout regime had resulted in him gaining twenty pounds with rather horrifying alacrity.

None of it fooled his father. "Tracy. Tracy." His voice broke and he staggered a bit.

Tracy leaped across the intervening space and caught Alexander in his arms. "Yes, Dad, it's me." He blinked back tears.

Luis looked away. Jahan and Dalea were supposed to be playing the role of faithful servants to human masters, but the charade ended when Jahan gave Luis a sharp whistle and a jerk of the head to indicate in no uncertain terms that they should decamp.

"We'll get a cup of coffee and be back in an hour or so, okay, Captain?" the Isanjo said.

Tracy could only manage to nod. The trio left. His father brushed the tears from his wrinkled cheeks, cupped Tracy's face with his good hand. "You look well."

"Even accounting for paternal prejudice that's a whopping lie," Tracy said.

His father laughed. "Okay, you got me. Come, come into the workroom. I know Bajit will want to see you."

"Do you still have Nika?" Tracy asked.

"No, she left a few years back. Opened her own shop catering to the Isanjo."

Tracy balked at the door. "If you have new people we should probably talk elsewhere. I'm here as Oliver Randall."

"Oh, right. And I do have new help. A human apprentice,

Caleb, sent over by the trade school and a new Isanjo, Selcuk—he's one of Nika's nephews."

"They are big on finding jobs for relatives," Tracy said, thinking about Jahan.

"We'll go over to the apartment and I'll send for Bajit."

Tracy hadn't been in the apartment for years. Unlike the shop his father's living space had a sad and shabby quality. A layer of dust clouded the surface of the tables and the upholstery was worn. Tracy helped his father set the kettle on for tea. Alexander set out cheese and some fruit.

They settled at the small kitchen table. The warmth of the tea cup felt good against Tracy's palms. "So, tell me everything," his father ordered.

"Well, everything would be a lot, and Luis and I do need to get fitted for our formal wear." He answered Alexander's look of inquiry. "Caballero Oliver Randall has been summoned to attend the coronation."

"How did…?"

"I get a title? I rescued the Infanta… I mean, the Empress."

Alexander fell back against his chair, hand pressed to his chest. "Did she… recognize you?"

"Yes."

"And kept your secret. God be praised." Alexander crossed himself. "She's a good woman." He took a large slurp of his tea.

Fortunately Bajit arrived before Tracy had to respond to that. His feelings for Mercedes were so tangled and confused that he doubted he would ever find peace.

The old Hajin's mane and tail had gone as white as

his employer's hair, and the large eyes were occluded by cataracts and magnified by the lenses of a pair of glasses. He swept Tracy a low bow, the pursed mouth stretching into a smile. "The young master. How well you look. And what a joyful day for your father."

Tracy stood. "Not so young anymore. It is so good to see you, Bajit." He hugged the old alien who reacted with delighted confusion.

A cup was procured for the Hajin and they spent the next hour with Tracy trying to find stories to tell that didn't reveal his illegal activities. He had thought to bring along the Proclamation of Ennoblement and that kept them distracted for a long while. Alexander got a call on his ScoopRing. It was Caleb reporting they had customers.

"Probably my crew," Tracy said, pushing back his chair. "This is going to make Luis' day. He's never had a bespoke suit before. Just don't let him go with crushed velvet or want it in purple or some other godawful color."

The dishes were placed in the sink and they headed for the front door. "I… I suppose you can't stay here," Alexander said.

"I'm afraid not. It was probably a risk coming here even briefly. I'm paying too much for a hotel. But you can come there for more fittings and to deliver my tuxedo."

As they waited for the elevator Alexander casually asked, "So when do I get to be a doting grandfather?"

"Still looking for the right girl," Tracy answered lightly.

30

WILL YOU TO YOUR POWER CAUSE LAW AND JUSTICE, IN MERCY, TO BE EXECUTED IN ALL YOUR JUDGMENTS?

They were checked in by security, their names ticked off on a list, and escorted to their seats in the viewing stand. Tracy studied the crowd. There were a lot of people already in their seats even though the procession would not start for another two hours. It was mostly families and as two males without female company Tracy, and particularly Luis, were subjected to some appraising looks by matrons with marriageable-aged daughters. With his now dark hair and beard Tracy realized he was probably being mistaken for Luis' father. The thought both amused and saddened him. If he had married in his twenties he would have a son about Luis' age by now.

Dalea and Jahan accompanied them. It embarrassed Tracy that they were playing the part of servants, but Dalea had just smiled and said, *"But, Captain, we'll have a much better view if we're with you and Luis. Poor Jax and Graarack won't have any place half so nice."* So Dalea carried the picnic basket and Jahan the cushions and blankets.

This particular viewing stand was a full mile away from the cathedral where the actual investiture would occur, but large screens had been set up so those outside the church would be able to watch the events inside. Flags were snapping in the brisk December breeze. The air was filled with the smell of roasting chestnuts, the sharp scent of chili from the taco trucks, and the scent of funnel cakes cooking in hot oil. Tracy unlimbered a flask and took a sip of brandy. The day was quite cold for Hissilek.

Tracy passed the time reading news reports. Luis smiled at the girls, and struck up a conversation with the family immediately to their right. Tracy kept part of his attention focused on the young man to make sure he didn't say anything too revelatory, but Luis surprised him and stuck to bland topics. The boy's cheerful and outgoing nature was still on display, but he did seem a bit subdued and awed at being in the company of even low-ranked members of the FFH.

Eventually the faint blare of distant trumpets floated down to them from the crest of the Palacio Colina. Twenty minutes later and the sharp clip and clop of hooves was heard and around the corner came a horse guard all mounted on palomino horses. The sunlight sparkled on the burnished gold bodies of the equines, and glittered on the blades of the riders' swords, which they held stiffly upright in right hands, while with their left hands they grasped the reins and controlled their prancing mounts.

Next there was a military band throwing notes against the cold blue of the sky. The sound rained down around them, and Tracy found his foot tapping in time to the jaunty march. The colors followed, the flags of every League world floating over the heads of the palace guards who carried them. Another band and then the flags of the Solar League and the *Orden de la Estrella.* More hoofbeats and then Mercedes herself appeared riding a jet-black horse. The roar of approval rolled down the street, gathering power and volume as it went. Behind her was the royal guard all mounted on white horses.

She wore her dress uniform, but instead of the normal ankle boots she wore tall, highly polished black boots that extended above her knee. She swayed gracefully in the saddle, a hand upraised, waving to the cheering crowds. There was a sword at her side, the ornate hilt adorned with gemstones. On her other hip she wore a pistol. A simple diadem circled her brow, the gems bright against her dark hair.

Luis leaned in and whispered in Tracy's ear. "I watched a video of her dad's coronation. He was on a horse too, and wore a uniform, but I thought she'd be in a flitter or a carriage in a pretty dress since she's a girl."

"Solar League rulers have to be a military leader. Since she's the first female they're probably making it up as they go," Tracy whispered back. "She'll probably change at the cathedral."

Mercedes rode past their stand. Tracy hunched deeper in his chair then felt foolish. It wasn't like she would recognize him, much less pick him out of the crowd. Behind her escort there was another mounted brigade, this one led by Boho. All of the horses were blood bays.

An open carriage rolled past. Tracy recognized Mercedes' real mother and stepfather seated inside. More carriages filled with Mercedes' sisters, their spouses, and children. The dowager empress, still dressed in mourning black, was like a crow among birds of paradise. There was no sign of an infant among the royal relations. Tracy concluded that the prince had been left at the palace. Probably a wise choice given the cold and the crowds. And really this was Mercedes' day. The future ruler didn't need to pull the attention away from her.

The last of the horses passed by and then came representatives of the armed forces marching in perfect order, rifles shouldered, the sound of boots on pavement like the beat of a massive metronome. There was the wet-foot navy in their green uniforms, the *fusileros,* and finally O-Trell. Arms swung in time to the "Stars and Glory March." Seven *Infiernos* screamed past overhead. Their spinning slug ports had been filled with glitter that fell like perfumed jeweled snow onto the crowd below.

A tightness invaded Tracy's throat. In another life he might have been one of the officers leading his men. Instead he was a disgraced officer, a man living under an alias, a criminal, a fake. He lunged out of his chair, muttered an apology to the people next to them, and hurried out of the stand and went to pace up and down in front of the line of portable toilets that had been set up along the route.

It somehow seemed appropriate that that was where he would find himself.

At the cathedral Mercedes slid from the saddle. She hadn't done any serious riding in six months and her legs were commenting on that fact. She gave Donhador a pat on his glossy neck, and was then surrounded by Jeanine's staff who whisked her into the sacristy where she could change into her coronation gown. They had rehearsed the change so it was accomplished well within the four minutes that had been allotted. The immensely long and heavy train was pinned at the shoulders, and she slid her feet into high heels.

Through the doors the massive pipe organ could be heard playing the opening hymn. Her hair was retouched, the diadem removed and a tiara put in its place. The six sisters who had remained loyal entered. They would carry her train. They were all dressed in white apart from Beatrisa, who wore her dress uniform. There had been much gobbling and hand-waving from the palace historian and the protocol officer, but Mercedes had pointed out that if she had a brother who was still on active duty in O-Trell he would have been in uniform. Beatrisa hugged her when she found out. Her sister hated skirts and fripperies, and it also suited Mercedes' purposes to remind the League that women could and did serve in the armed forces. Five little nieces were racing around while their nannies tried to restrain them and get them to focus on their upcoming tasks.

Estella embraced her. "Nervous?"

"A little, but all the rehearsals have reduced that to a low buzz," Mercedes replied.

Estella moved off to a mirror to check her lipstick. Beatrisa and Carisa came over. "So how is Boho handling playing second fiddle?" Beatrisa asked.

"He seems fine."

"Seems," Beatrisa said in ominous tones. "Men always *seem* fine."

"He's understood for twenty-four years that he's the consort. He will always be the consort," Mercedes said calmly. Inwardly she was thinking, *And Boho thinks I can't act. He doesn't know Kemel showed me the reports of his activities with the del Campos. But the League can't take any more shocks to the system, and a royal divorce would certainly constitute a shock. And I suppose in the end he did do the right thing.*

"Boho gets a starring role. He gets to bring the scepter, sword, and crown to the Pope. All the cameras will be on him for that," Carisa said.

"Okay, children," Izzara sang out while clapping her hands. "Let's get your flower baskets and take your places."

The five little girls ran over. They ranged in age from thirteen to three. Mercedes was worried about the inclusion of the smallest princess, Delia's daughter, Sansa. But Sansa had a comically serious expression on her round face, and a ferocious frown between her brows. She even gave her giggling older sister a disapproving look as they arranged themselves in front of Mercedes.

The hymn ended and the processional music began, organ and orchestra. The soldiers stationed just outside the sacristy pulled open the doors and they began their slow walk to the cathedral's central aisle. They made the turn and started toward the apse. Her father's throne had been brought from the palace and now rested at the bottom of the steps leading up to the altar. Camerabots circled overhead, their metal bodies catching the rainbow light from the stained-glass windows.

The strings, brass, and woodwind of the orchestra danced on top of the deep bellow of the organ, and the voices of the choir echoed off the vaulted ceiling far overhead.

Mercedes knew she ought to be thinking of God and the awesome authority about to be conferred upon her, but it all felt like an elaborate play. She had already assumed the awesome authority nearly a year before, and from conversations with her Chancellor of the Exchequer she knew just how much this particular pageant was costing the League. Still, Boho and his toady, Anselmo, were right. This was for the people. Or as she had overhead Anselmo say as she was entering Boho's office one day, *"Providing* pan y circos *to entertain the rubes."*

They reached the throne, and she carefully maneuvered so the long cape was arranged gracefully around her feet. Her sisters and nieces were whisked away to their seats. During the year the elderly pope who had been so outraged over Jose's arrest had been carried to the bosom of his maker and a new, surprisingly young man had been elevated to the See of Peter. He was tall, slender, and his white robes and miter glistened against his ebony skin. His upswept eyebrows and the deep epicanthic folds gave him a merry roguish look even when he wasn't smiling. And he smiled a lot. Mercedes had found him charming and she had enjoyed their conversations they had had prior to the coronation. The words of the opening prayer rolled out. Pope Honorius V had a deep resonant baritone voice that seemed to caress the words.

And then they were into it. Boho, his expression solemn, brought the scepter and orb to Pope Honorius and they were placed in her hands. The weight of the cape dragged at her shoulders, and she gripped the staff of the long scepter tightly, afraid it might slip or tremble. Boho returned with the long sword and laid it across her lap.

"Is Her Majesty willing to take the Oath?" Honorius intoned.

"I am willing."

The words washed over her. "Will you to your power cause Law and Justice, in Mercy, to be executed in all your judgments?"

Judgments rose up to haunt her. *A screaming child on Sinope. Covering up the massacre of children. A man falsely accused. A mass suicide.* Distantly, she heard herself say, "I will."

At last they reached the finale. The Bible was brought to her, and she kissed it. Boho brought the tall, impossibly heavy crown to the Pope. The music soared as he held it high and intoned, "I hereby crown you Empress Mercedes Adalina Saturnina Inez de Arango, first of her name. All hail!"

The attendees shouted out, *"All hail!"*

A smaller throne was brought forward and Boho was crowned as Imperial Consort. They exchanged a long look. Boho reached out and lightly touched her gloved hand. His look of love and adoration was clearly visible to the camerabot. Mercedes wondered what Tracy's expression would have held if he had been seated beside her. She could picture his uncomfortable frown. She released the image and returned to reality.

A final trumpet fanfare and it was done. Mercedes rose carefully to her feet and began the long walk back down the aisle. The double doors were thrown open and she emerged to the evident delight of the cheering crowds. Women were crying; even a few men wiped at their eyes. Flowers arched through the air to fall all around her. The carriage arrived. Mercedes handed the scepter and orb to the crown jeweler. He would see they were returned to the imperial treasury. She wished she could have exchanged the imperial state crown for one of her tiaras, but she had to endure the weight until they reached the palace. There she could shed the crown and the robe. The gates would be thrown open so the human citizens of the League could enter and cheer their new monarch.

Boho assisted her up the steps into the open carriage and took his seat next to her. Outriders surrounded them, soldiers marched on all sides. They began the slow procession back to the palace, both of them waving to the cheering throngs.

He took her free hand, lifted it to his lips. "How are you holding up?"

"Fine. I'll be glad when it's all over."

"Just a few more hours, the state banquet and you can rest."

She smiled at him. "At least I don't have to wear the crown for that."

"We have to go see our pretty boy and tell him his mama is officially empress now," Boho said.

"Somehow I don't think he'll be impressed," Mercedes chuckled.

* * *

The crew spent Christmas and Boxing Day on Ouranos with Tracy concocting elaborate ruses to see his father. He bought a new wardrobe and overpaid for everything as a way to give some of his newfound wealth to Alexander. On the final day his father came to the *Selkie* to deliver the last of the outfits. They had the ship to themselves as the crew were off buying the last of the supplies, and Luis was saying farewell to the girl he had met at a tango party.

Tracy and Alexander were in the galley sharing a plate of cookies and sipping port. "You should retire, Dad."

"And what would I do with myself? I enjoy my work, and it would leave Bajit, Selcuk, and Caleb without jobs. Oh, Selcuk and Caleb would probably be all right, but poor old Bajit?" Alexander shook his head. "No, I couldn't do that to him."

"All right, but at some point I'm going to have a real home, and you're going to come live with me," Tracy said.

"A home is more than just a house, Trace. You need a wife, children." Tracy looked away. "Is there no one?"

"I'm afraid not."

"So the Belmanor line ends with you."

"Dad, I'd have to marry this mythical woman under the name Randall. The line is ending no matter what."

"Yes. I suppose that's true. I hadn't thought about it that way."

Tracy laid a hand over his father's, felt the knotted veins and paper-thin skin. "I'm sorry I messed everything up. You gave me the opportunity and I threw it away. I'm sorry."

"No, don't apologize. I'm proud of you. You did what was right."

"Why does doing the right thing always have such dire consequences?" Tracy asked and he tossed back his port.

"God never sends us more than we can bear."

"Yeah, I'd like to discuss that with God."

31

A CALL TO ARMS

The artificial gravity was down. The *Estrella Avanzada* was still trying to spin, but with the massive damage to the spacestation it just ended up listing back and forth, then jerking forward in a partial rotation. Boho tried to keep from focusing on any set point to hold back nausea. Power was intermittent so the lights kept strobing on and off, illuminating frozen bodies floating through the interior of the destroyed star base. In the central gardens the plants were blackened and dead. He shined his helmet light across the walls to reveal the rents in the skin of the station and the scorched and blackened walls.

"You getting all this?" he radioed.

Light years away Mercedes received the images. "Yes." Her voice was flat, emotionless.

They had received the distress call from Cipriana four days ago. A report the base was under attack by unknown assailants. They had tried to scramble the ships in dry dock and being refueled, but only a few had managed to untether and face the attacking force. Those that had gotten free had fared no better than the ships that had been docked.

When Boho had arrived with the rump Gold fleet the region around the base was strewn with pieces of ships, and the base itself looked like a battered honeycomb filled with holes bleeding thin streams of atmosphere. He had made a slow approach, scanning constantly, with a fleet of *Infiernos* and *exploradors* scouting far in advance of the big ships. Only when he was sure there was no trace of the force that had attacked the star base did he bring his ships in to the crippled and dying station.

"How many survivors?" Mercedes asked.

"A handful. Mostly people who were in the command center. They had quick access to suits and some of the escape pods weren't damaged in the initial attack."

"Cipriana?"

"The doctors have her in an induced coma. The burns are pretty bad."

"We need to talk to her."

"I know. They're going to wake her up so we can question her."

"Her family?" Mercedes asked.

"Husband and daughter are among the dead. Her son was at school and managed to get to the emergency locker and get into a suit. He's a quick-thinking lad. I've got him aboard the flagship."

"One small piece of good news. Will Cipri live?"

"The doctors think so, but she'll need a lot of reconstructive surgery, Mer."

"What do we have on the attackers?" she asked.

He could see a small part of the study over her left shoulder. Cyprian was there, chubby arms clutching his cat PurrPurr close to his chest as he trotted back and forth across the office. The long-suffering feline's hind legs swung free and he had a pissed-off expression, but not a claw showed. Unlike Mist who had taken one look at the toddler, hissed, and run away. The chocolate point Siamese was bonded with the child and had been since he was a kitten. Both the cat and the child were two and a half now and inseparable. Cyprian wore blue shorts and a white and blue striped shirt. His pale brown hair with its soft curls brushed at his collar. Boho's heart squeezed down at the sight of his son. Whatever had attacked the *Avanzada* was still out there and had to be kept far away from his family. Nothing could be allowed to harm his son.

"Wha… what?" he stammered.

"The attackers. Is there video?"

"I have techs working to see what they can salvage. The command center was badly damaged." He hesitated then asked, "Are you sure it's wise to have Cypri in the office with what I'm showing you?"

Mercedes looked both guilty and resentful. "He's too small to see the holograph. And I wanted to see him. The past four days haven't left me with much time to spend with him." She sat silent for a minute then keyed the intercom. "Elizabeth, please take Cyprian back to the nursery."

The woman entered and swept up the toddler, who gave a howl of objection as he and the cat were carried away. Mercedes watched them leave then turned back to the holo. "So, what is the final death toll?" Mercedes asked.

"We haven't recovered all the bodies, but extrapolating from the station logs and matching names to the survivors we've located we've got a pretty good count." He cleared his throat then said, "Thirty-three thousand two hundred and twelve."

"Shit."

"Mostly military, but there were a lot of civilian support staff living here too." A floating corpse bumped into his shoulder and Boho pushed it violently away. "When will you make a statement?"

"After we talk to Cipriana. I need more facts before we say anything."

"I'll head that way now. We've got one small section airtight. We're treating the wounded there. The ones that are too hurt to move." Boho placed a boot on a sagging girder and pushed off. "You want to see any more of this horror show or shall I shut down until I get to the first aid station?"

"Call me back. I've seen enough."

The sick tension in the pit of his stomach had started to fade. Not because of the bodies, those bothered him very little; it had been fear that the attackers might return. But as the hours bled into a full day, he had begun to relax. Question was—where were they going next? Deeper in League space the stations and bases and planets were better guarded. These parties unknown would be foolish to attempt an assault on settled League space. At least that was the hope.

He made his way to the one intact part of the *Avanzada* and entered the makeshift airlock. He shed his suit, and was handed a surgical gown, mask, and gloves by one of the nurses. Only then was he allowed to enter the improvised hospital. Ventilators hissed and pumped; heart monitors beeped, measuring life in moments; nurses replaced IV bags on their skeletal stands. The chief medical officer from his flagship hurried over.

"We lost three more, sir. Four are ready to be transferred to your ship."

"The Rear Admiral Lady McKenzie?" Boho asked. The doctor tipped his hand back and forth in the universal gesture of "iffy." "I need to talk to her."

The man frowned, chewed on his lower lip. "All right, but not too long. I don't want to lose her too."

Cipriana was in a bed shielded by makeshift curtains formed from sheets and drapes taken from shattered living quarters, which were now filled with their dead occupants. Machines kept a vigilant watch over the injured woman. The space smelled of antiseptic and bed pans. A glistening nutrient and antiseptic gel wrapped her naked body. The thick gel obscured any details, but Boho could see the raw flesh on her right side, which had taken the brunt of an explosion and subsequent fire. Cipriana had been one of the most beautiful women in the FFH—now half her face was a ruin. Her right eye and ear were gone; the hair had been burned away as well. Boho swallowed hard, feeling bile burning the back of his throat while pity warred with horror.

The doctor injected a stimulant into an IV line, and a few minutes later Cipriana stirred, moaned, and her remaining eye opened. The eye darted from side to side and she tensed, cried out in pain. The doctor leaned in but didn't touch her.

"My lady, you're in a field hospital. You've been hurt, but you're safe now. The consort is here. He needs to speak with you. Can you do that?" She nodded.

Boho stepped to the side of the bed. "I'm going to link in Mercedes. Is that all right?" Breath hissed between Cipriana's clenched teeth, but she nodded again. Boho keyed his ring, bringing up the hologram of Mercedes. From his angle he couldn't see Mercedes' face, but Cipriana's grimacing smile told him all he needed to know.

"Horror show." Her voice was a raw croak.

"You'll be all right," Mercedes said. "Don't try to talk. Let us ask questions and you respond." Cipriana gave an emphatic head shake.

"My… my family?"

"Hayden is safe on my ship." Boho hesitated, then continued gently, "James and Fiona didn't make it."

Tears ran from her good eye.

"Cipri, was it the Cara'ot?" Mercedes asked.

Another emphatic head shake. "Ships… strange… like flying… Swiss army knives with… every… tool… extended." She gasped for air, whimpered. "Language… ugly… like hearing… hate." Her moans tore at the air.

"That's enough. Let her rest," Mercedes cried, her voice thick with unshed tears.

Boho nodded to the doctor who delivered a powerful sedative to the suffering woman. Cipriana fell silent.

"I'm going to send you some of the bright boys from the war college's R&D division. See what they can learn from the wreckage. Maybe there will be unexploded ordinance, some way to trace them back to their planet of origin," Mercedes said.

"Where do you want me?" Boho asked and prayed for the right answer.

"Back here. You need to report to parliament, and bring Hayden and Cipri back to Hissilek. We'll foster him until Cipri recovers." His prayer had been answered.

The doctor stepped into range of the camera. "Highness, the rear admiral cannot be moved yet, and while I am certain your physicians are excellent she would be better off on New Hope in the hands of specialists."

"All right. We'll let her go with the other wounded to New Hope. Boho, you'll need to detail another ship for that."

"Will do. Where would you like to send the survivors who weren't badly injured?"

"SEGU will want to debrief them, so back to Ouranos. I'll tell Ian to expect them. Hurry back. Cypri misses you. I do too."

Her image faded from the air. Boho contemplated Ian Rogers who had replaced old Kemel as the new head of SEGU. The former head of security for Mercedes was passionately loyal to his empress, bright and brave, but was he devious, cunning, and callous enough for the job? On the other hand, in this military crisis, a former military officer might be the right man. Boho just hoped they weren't faced with another coup attempt. He wasn't at all certain Rogers was unscrupulous enough to handle that. Sometimes the *honor, duty, sacrifice* crap that was drilled into an O-Trell officer was a hindrance rather than a help.

* * *

News of the destruction of the *Estrella Avanzada* had roiled the League. The luxury goods that the *Selkie* and her crew had been carrying were quickly replaced by rare earth minerals and highly advanced electronics that needed to be moved from factory clean rooms to shipyards, where they could be installed in the new ships that were being built to replace the losses from the aborted coup and this recent sneak attack. Crews were working around the clock, but a battle cruiser couldn't be constructed overnight.

The governors of League worlds were howling for O-Trell ships to be stationed in orbit around their planets, but there weren't enough ships to provide protection everywhere, and some ships had to be detailed to try and discover the location of this new alien threat.

This had escalated tensions between the humans and the subject races under their rule. There had been incidents on various worlds and *cosmódromos*. On Nueva Terra a couple of Isanjos had been beaten. On Kronos a Sidone was killed when she was trying to deliver a new shipment of weavings to a shop in the fashionable shopping district, and on Dullahan a Hajin ended up in the hospital with multiple stab wounds and the tendons in the back of his knees cut. While aliens were looked down upon and in some circles even despised, such overt acts were uncommon and for this reason, Tracy had ordered the aliens in his crew to remain aboard the *Selkie* unless they were docked at one of their home worlds. None of them had taken issue with the order, but it did mean that only Jahan was able to go ashore, since they hadn't any reason to visit Xinoxex, Belán, or Melatin.

Tracy had debated making runs to warn the Hidden Worlds with whom they traded, but O-Trell and space control on every League world were carefully tracking every ship in an effort to give warning if the aliens returned, so he reluctantly decided that they couldn't risk it. Jahan had not been happy and, as if his thoughts had summoned her, she turned up in his cabin.

Star maps floated on all sides and overhead and he was flicking screens aside to bring up new images.

"What are you doing?" she asked.

"Trying to guess the aliens' next move," he answered.

She jumped onto his bed and perched in that particular, inquisitive, hunch-shouldered stance of a curious Isanjo. In a different world she might have been mistaken for a very large pet—if the pet had fangs and claws and was four feet tall. "And you think you can do better than O-Trell and SEGU?"

"I think it gives me something to do other than worry." He turned in a circle, sweeping his hand through the maps and banishing the images. He sat down next to her on the bed, hands clasped between his knees. "It was such an odd choice of target. Not close to any major planets or bases. It made routine repairs, was a place to refuel and give crews a chance to blow off a bit of steam, but it was hardly strategically significant." Tracy shook his head. "It's like it was designed to cause the maximum amount of panic, but not really accomplish anything. And why no follow-up?" He shook his head again and sighed. "But you needed something."

"We're in range for a message—"

"Yes, I know. I had one from Dad—"

"One came for Luis. He left the bridge and hasn't been back."

"He's on duty."

"I know. Which is why I came to you. I may be the first officer, but you're human and if something's wrong..." She shrugged.

Tracy clapped his hands on his thighs and stood up. "Probably girl trouble, but I'll go check on him."

Since it was close by, Tracy went first to Luis' cabin. It was empty. At the ladder he paused. Down to the cargo hold and the makeshift gym, or to the galley? The clink of glass on glass drew him to the galley. Luis was slumped at the table with a highball glass in front of him. He was just lifting away the tequila bottle and the glass was filled to the brim. He set aside the bottle and grabbed the glass, sending liquor sloshing over his fingers.

"Judging by your coordination this isn't your first," Tracy said.

Luis lifted his head. In the past two years his frame had broadened and the crow's feet around his expressive eyes added to the impression of greater maturity. Now, though, he looked like a lost child. His expression was bleak and the red in his eyes was due more to unshed tears than inebriation. Tracy took several hurried steps toward him, hand thrusting out in alarm. "Luis, *amigo*, what's wrong? Your parents?"

Luis shook his head and after a couple of off-target stabs at his ring managed to bring up an image. The seal of the *Orden de la Estrella* was prominently displayed. Tracy's eyes flicked down the page. …*By the power of…You are ordered… nearest enlistment center…failure to report…imprisonment…*

"I'm being called up."

"And you don't want to go," Tracy said.

Luis gave a violent head shake. "No, I wanna go. What happened to the base. It could be a planet next. My *madre* and *padre,* my sisters are on Reichart's World. My little brother is stationed at Hellfire. I want to protect them. I just… I just hate to leave. I was a pretty fucked-up kid after I did my seven years. You took a chance on me. Taught me. I… I might even apply for OCS. Get that officer's braid."

Tracy laid a hand on his shoulder. "You'd be a good one. You've become a hell of a navigator. I wish I could write you a recommendation. Unfortunately Randall was kept out of the service because of a heart murmur so a letter from the fake me won't do you much good, and a letter from the real me, a disgraced officer, would probably get you thrown in the brig." Luis gave a husky laugh. "When and where do you have to report?" Tracy asked.

"Hellfire. In two weeks."

"We'll take you."

"No, that interferes with our delivery schedule," Luis objected.

"People will just have to understand. You want to swing by Reichart's World and see your folks?"

"That'd be… I mean, if it wouldn't be too much… Yes. Please."

"Well, sober up, get our new course plotted and filed, and I'll let Dr. Engelberg know we're going to be delayed."

32

FULL CIRCLE

Hayden McKenzie had inherited his mother's deep ebony skin and black hair shot through with streaks of red. Her extraordinary beauty had been translated into male form, and as Mercedes studied the boy she knew he was going to grow up to be a man who would break hearts. Right now the expression in his dark eyes was too serious for a boy of thirteen. He was tall for his age, and resembled a young colt, uncertain what to do with his gawky limbs and growing body. Mercedes had been surprised that the Delacroixs and Cipriana's father, the Duque of Nico-Hathaway, hadn't immediately taken custody of the boy, but it soon became apparent that Cipriana's father had washed his hands of his wayward daughter, who had remained in the military and married a nobody rather than serving the family's goals through an advantageous marriage. So Hayden stayed at the palace while his mother made her slow recovery. Mercedes was happy to keep him. She liked teenagers, and Cyprian adored Hayden. He trotted after this new, fascinating person and Hayden was unfailingly patient with his two-year-old shadow.

"I've only ridden a horse a couple of times," he said, his voice oscillating between a baritone and a squeak. Mercedes hid a smile.

"Well, all the more reason to take advantage of our stable. And Señor Krevling is a wonderful teacher. He'll pick the right horse for you."

"Thank you, Majesty," he said.

She laid a hand on his shoulder. She hadn't yet attempted a hug; he was far too self-contained for that. "Mercedes, please. Your mother and I are best friends."

"Yes, Ma—Mercedes."

He left. She sighed and returned to her desk. She desperately wished she could have joined him on a ride, but it was not possible. Everyone in government was working hellish hours as they tried to move to a war footing. Boho was cajoling and charming members of parliament to round up votes for the increased military spending. In this he had the able assistance of Rohan, who had relationships with many of the older members.

At the palace Mercedes spent long hours arguing with the new Chancellor of the Exchequer, Daniel Babatunde, about how to increase tax revenue from the League planets. Since the Chancellor was a conservative, Babatunde's only answer was *no new taxes*, so he was less than helpful. Since she was already deficit-spending on ship construction, Mercedes desperately needed more money, and so she was using what discretion she had to starve certain agencies in an effort to funnel more money to the military. It wasn't sustainable.

Eventually she had to have a tax increase that could get

through parliament and not cause riots on League worlds, and for that to happen she needed a new Chancellor of the Exchequer, which would require a new prime minister. Her hope was that Rohan could return to the position. He understood that it took money to fight a war. Ian and Boho were working to engineer a vote of confidence so the old guard could be swept away. It couldn't happen too soon, since the old guard's only affirmative suggestion was a quarantine of all alien worlds, and internment camps for the aliens who weren't on their home worlds. Thank God that idea hadn't gotten out of committee… yet.

She sighed and rubbed at her gritty eyes. Next up on the agenda—a meeting to discuss whether to repair the star base or if it made more sense to just scrap the facility. She hesitated to do that. The loss of that much material and man hours would not sit well with parliament. There was also the issue of the unknown enemy. If they abandoned the station it would look like they were retreating in fear. No, better to maintain their presence in that sector. Perhaps some of the *Avanzada* could be salvaged and formed into a smaller, leaner, and more heavily armed facility.

She took a sip of coffee and discovered it had gone cold. Making a face she pushed aside the cup and called Boho. "Hi, how is your day going?"

"Sounds like it's going better than yours," said the small holographic figure of her husband projected onto the desk. "How did the meeting with Babatunde go?"

"Horribly. He's never rude, just immovable, and I feel like he's always metaphorically patting me on the top of my head. I need that new chancellor and quickly."

"Working on it."

"So, once we get the new election do you have anyone in mind for the post?"

Boho's image looked thoughtful. "I just might. Young fellow, new to parliament. He's the youngest son so he's in the commons. Rafael—Rafe—Devris."

"Devris, Devris," Mercedes mused.

"He's the son of the old flitter king. Malcomb Devris."

Mercedes made the connection. Devris had had flitter franchises all across the League. He had made donations to the right people, and sold flitters at a discount to the FFH, and in due course had been knighted. Which meant his sons were then subject to the same right of service as all the other sons of the FFH. Hugo had been in Mercedes, Boho, and Tracy's class at the High Ground, but lost his life during an incident. According to Tracy, Devris had blamed the crown for Hugo's death. The last time Mercedes had heard of the man was when he had footed the bill for Tracy's high-priced lawyer during his court-martial.

"My understanding is that the old man is no fan of the crown. Would the son help us or sabotage us?"

"The two older boys have taken over the company, sidelining Malcomb. I don't think he's much of a factor any longer. Rafe is the economics whiz and has gone into politics. Let me send you some samples of his speeches; he's also written for a number of financial magazines."

"Okay." She sighed. "Just what I need, more to read."

"Hey, you asked for a solution."

"I know. Will you be home for dinner? Cypri would like that."

"I'll make sure to get back."

Her next call was to Davin but it didn't connect, which indicated he was in Fold. Frustrated, she put in a call to the scientist leading the research team on the destroyed *Estrella Avanzada*. Vice Admiral Dr. Marqués Ernesto Chapman-Owiti had become a lifer. Valedictorian of their class, magna cum laude, he had become an R&D scientist for O-Trell. When asked why he'd stayed in the service, he had said that no university would ever give him as much money as the military for his research.

When his image appeared over the center of her desk, Ernesto had his usual dreamy, thoughtful expression. Genetics had played an odd trick: he had gone gray at a very early age. His hair and eyebrows were bright silver, as was his spade beard and neatly trimmed mustache. Against his ebony skin, it was a striking contrast. The warm brown eyes were still the same, and he still wore the single gold earring that made him look like a pirate king.

"Highness."

"Mercedes, please. What have you got for me, Ernesto?"

"Bad news, I'm afraid. We found an unexploded missile and the technicians who examined it all died, despite wearing suits, and the lab ended up with a giant hole in the floor. It's not just an explosive. Like white phosphorus it clings and burns—and it can burn through any substance it touches, even our composites, which are supposed to be resistant. It's the weapon that left the station looking like Swiss cheese, and the reason why we haven't found a number of those listed as missing. The only bright side is that it has a short lifespan. It does its damage then goes inert after about three minutes. I think it's meant to open breaches in hulls for boarding parties."

"How does the missile survive?" Mercedes asked.

"There's a containment capsule that holds the actual devil's brew that's immune to the effects. It's a completely inert substance created by blending some relatively rare—"

"Spare me the details, I'm not a chemist. Just figure out how to manufacture it so we can get it on our ships and stations."

"Aye, aye, Majesty."

"Have we got visuals on the ships?"

"Yes. Creepy as hell."

An image appeared next to Ernesto's. It was fuzzy, as if interference had been affecting the cameras, but the shape could be discerned and it *was* disturbing. Cipri's description of knives was apt, but there were angles on the ships that produced a sense of nausea and vertigo like images on the edge of a nightmare.

"So how do we find them?" Mercedes asked.

"I've ordered some of our deep-space radio telescopes to scan for the elements we found in the containment capsule. You know, the ones you don't want to hear about." His smile and wink removed the sting. "That should give us some possible places to go looking."

"Do you think we could track their fleet by the same method?"

He tugged at his upper lip. "Hmmm, interesting idea. I'll see what we can come up with."

"Once you do, get it to Davin and the Blue. They're out hunting right now."

"Will do. I want these bastards found."

"Amen," Mercedes replied.

Boho found her in the palace chapel. The diamonds and pearls on her tiara glittered through the black lace of her mantilla. The colors from the stained-glass window lay on the material as if trying to drive away the dark. The way the fabric caressed her cheek made him long to touch that cheek himself. Cyprian held his hand. The plump baby softness was comforting, but then the little boy squeezed hard, presaging the strength of the man he would become. Their footfalls were loud on the marble floor.

Mercedes knelt in the front pew, hands clasped tightly enough to turn her knuckles gray as that frenzied grip forced the blood from her fingers. Her lips moved soundlessly and she stared up at the suffering figure on the cross. Boho released his son's hand and Cyprian ran down the aisle to his mother.

"Mummy," he cried.

Her hands parted to catch her child. She took him in her arms, but kept her face averted. Cyprian tugged at the end of her mantilla. "Mummy, kiss," he lisped.

A hand went to her cheek and brushed away the tears. She looked down at her child and forced a smile, but Cyprian was not fooled. His face crumpled and tears welled in his pale gold eyes. "Mummy sad?"

Mercedes kissed the top of his head. "Not now." She

stood, shook out her skirt, and took Cyprian's hand. "Am I needed?" she asked Boho.

"Of course. Always. Hard decisions have to be made."

"No time to spare for the dead?"

"Not if we want to keep from joining them," Boho replied. He then softened his tone. "I'm sorry, love. I know how much Davin meant to you."

"He was our finest. If they beat him what hope do we have?"

"Some of our ships got out. We'll be able to study the battle. Analyze their tactics. We'll find a way to defeat them."

"I pray you are right." She stepped out into the center aisle, genuflected toward the altar, took Cyprian's and Boho's hands and they walked to the doors. Boho watched as the royal mask fell back into place across his wife's face. In that moment he felt such love for her, for her strength and determination. He wished he could match her, but deep within him lived a canker of fear, a place where whispers told him that there was no hope and urged him to run.

"I understand they'll be ill prepared, but they'll have to learn on the job," Mercedes was saying to El-Ghazzawy.

"No problem, Highness. We'll have the second years ready to be posted."

Baron Tarek El-Ghazzawy was the new commandant of the High Ground; he had been their *Infierno* instructor back in the day. His temples were frosted with silver and his spade beard streaked with gray, but he was still an extraordinarily handsome man. Boho hoped his confident assurance wasn't just telling the Empress what she wanted to hear, and that he really could have kids of nineteen and twenty ready to take their places aboard ships of war.

They were gathered in the large conference room. A room full of men, and one woman. The joint chiefs were present, brought in from Hellfire for this in-person meeting. They represented all branches of the military, from the wet-foot sailors, to the *fusileros,* to O-Trell. Marcus Gelb, who had recently been promoted to admiral of the Gold, was there. The head of the JAG office was also present—though Boho couldn't figure out why the military lawyer had been included.

Among all the uniforms there were two in civilian dress. Rafe Devris and Rohan Danilo Marcus Aubrey, Conde de Vargas, once again holding the position of prime minister. They were a study in contrast. De Vargas old and fat, his hands folded across his burgeoning belly. Rafe barely past thirty with the demeanor of a quivering grayhound.

A star map spun lazily in the center of the table with various levels superimposed to show the location of the Gold, and the remnants of the Blue limping their way toward Cuandru. Another level showed possible trajectories for their adversary, though no one knew for certain where they were headed. They had vanished into Fold after the battle with the Blue, which had killed an admiral and destroyed half of the fleet.

"But will we have ships to assign them *to*?" Gelb asked. "I know we have to replace the dead on the ships that did survive, but we need new ships."

"We've gone to round-the-clock construction," Boho said.

"And added work crews. The captains are going to have to forego their little luxuries. We need to get these ships launched."

"And I assume you're recalling everyone to active duty," Rohan said.

"Yes," Mercedes answered. "Any veteran under the age of fifty." She turned to Devris. "So, money. I need it and I need it fast."

"First thing I'd suggest is a transaction tax on stock trades."

"We've tried to get that through parliament several times," Boho objected.

"Yes, but now their butts are on the line I expect the objections will be more… muted," Devris said. "I also think a luxury tax should be imposed on… on… well, luxuries—jewels, furs, imported woods, liquor—"

"Flitters?" Boho suggested with a slight smile.

"Yeah, those too. Even if it will make my brothers howl." Rafe returned the smile but it turned into a grimace.

"Sibling issues?" Boho said.

"How else would we keep the shrinks in business," Rafe answered.

"Enough!" The single word ripped across the table. Mercedes was not smiling. "Get to parliament. Make it happen. I've got governors on every planet screaming for orbital defense platforms. They're cheaper and faster to build than ships so let's expedite those."

"Our shipyards are building ships. You want them to add these in too?" It was the man in charge of combat service support. He had an accountant's demeanor rather than a warrior's, which Boho thought was probably appropriate for the man who had to make sure the various branches of the League's military could travel, fight, eat, and be clothed while they served.

"No." Mercedes turned to Rohan. "I want any heavy industry factory repurposed to build missile platforms."

"The owners and investors won't like it," Rohan said.

"They can like it or I'll nationalize their factories," Mercedes snapped back.

"I'll make sure they understand. I'm sure they'll all prove to be fervent patriots," Rohan said with a wink.

There was a moment of silence, then Mercedes said, "There is one final matter. We have various *hombres*, and even some officers, who were cashiered for various reasons. If their offenses weren't violent in nature, I want them pardoned and reinstated. We need manpower and these men have already been trained. I had my assistant prepare a list of these individuals and SEGU has pinpointed their locations. Some of them I've flagged for promotion." She keyed her ring and sent the file to the JAG commander and to the joint chiefs.

Boho had a sudden sick suspicion. He leaned in and whispered to Mercedes, "May I review that list?"

"No."

Suspicion became certainty.

His call up to active duty came in to the *Selkie* while they were in orbit around Kronos, and it was addressed to Captain Thracius Ransom Belmanor. Tracy had printed out the order and it now rested in the center of the galley table. His remaining crew, none of them human, peered at it. Jax's fronds were shaking with agitation. "You don't have to do this. Tell them it's a mistake. You are not this man. You haven't been this man for sixteen years."

"I agree," Dalea said. "You are Oliver Randall and Randall was ineligible to serve due to health issues. You know Dr. Engelberg would supply the documentation."

"Forget it. He's going to do it," Graarack said. Her multiple, faceted eyes were fixed intently on him.

Tracy nodded. "Yes. I am. These bastards destroyed a station, nearly destroyed a fleet, and killed Davin. For all our sakes and the sake of our families you're damn right I'll fight."

"Okay, so what happens to us?" Jahan demanded.

"I give you the ship," Tracy said. There was an outburst of alien sounds signifying objection to that. His voice rose over the hubbub. "I suggest you make Jahan captain. You'll need to add more crew."

"You're not giving up your stake in the *Selkie*. You'll be a silent partner," Jax said. There were nods of agreement from the others.

"Fine," Tracy said. "But right now, I need to get planetside, report in, buy uniforms, and book passage to Hellfire."

"We have a ship," Jahan said. "We'll take you."

He was touched by the gesture, and happily agreed.

Hours later he returned to the ship with a garment bag filled with a dress uniform, undress uniform, utility uniform, and a box with the various boots that went with each outfit. Another box held hats and caps. He would be issued combat armor once he reached his ship.

His combat ribbons had been replaced and, most precious of all, in his pocket was a Lucite box containing the bars of a captain in the *Orden de la Estrella.* It had been a strange journey, with a long side trip, but he finally had that promotion. All that was missing was his medal—

His thoughts were interrupted by Jahan who came flying at him the minute he walked up the gang plank into the cargo bay. "Did you see Graarack when you came back up?"

"Uh… no."

"Well, she's not here and we have a departure time set. If she doesn't get her fat spider ass on board we're going to have to leave her. We're working on a deadline here. We don't want you restarting your military career by failing to report on time."

"I'm sure she'll be back. Now I've got to dump this stuff. My arms are breaking."

Tracy took the elevator up to the crew level, and staggered down the hall to his cabin, trying to keep the boxes balanced. He started to dump his burdens on the bed then froze. A medal lay in the center of the bedspread, the jewels and silver bright against the dark material.

A *Distinguido Servicio Cruzar*.

ACKNOWLEDGMENTS

As always, I have to thank Eric Kelley for letting me bounce ideas and problems off him, and who helped me figure out how to make the traditions of the British Navy during the age of sail into something that could work with a space navy. And, of course, Sage who would listen patiently while I talked to myself and helped me figure out how to get out of plot problems.

ABOUT THE AUTHOR

Melinda Snodgrass is the acclaimed author of many science fiction novels, including the *Circuit* and *Edge* series, and is the co-editor with George R.R. Martin of the *Wild Cards* series, to which she also contributes. She has had a long career in television, writing several episodes of *Star Trek: The Next Generation* while serving as the series' story editor, and has written scripts for numerous other shows, including *Odyssey 5, The Outer Limits, Reasonable Doubts* and *Seaquest DSV*. She was also a consulting producer on *The Profiler*. The first book in the *Imperials* series was published in 2016, and was described as "entertaining and briskly paced" by *Publishers Weekly*. The fourth book will be *A Triumvirate of Hate*, published in July 2019. She lives in Santa Fe, New Mexico. You can find her on Twitter @MMSnodgrass.

ALSO AVAILABLE FROM TITAN BOOKS

NEW POMPEII

DANIEL GODFREY

In the near future, energy giant Novus Particles develops the technology to transport objects and people from the deep past to the present. Their biggest secret: New Pompeii. A replica of the city hidden deep in central Asia, filled with Romans pulled through time a split second before the volcano erupted.

Historian Nick Houghton doesn't know why he's been chosen to be the company's historical advisor. He's just excited to be there. Until he starts to wonder what happened to his predecessor. Until he realizes that NovusPart have more secrets than even the conspiracy theorists suspect. Until he realizes that NovusPart have underestimated their captives...

"Tremendously gripping"
Financial Times (Books of the Year)

"Irresistibly entertaining"
Barnes & Noble

TITANBOOKS.COM

ALSO AVAILABLE FROM TITAN BOOKS

EMPIRE OF TIME

DANIEL GODFREY

For fifteen years, the Romans of New Pompeii have kept the outside world at bay with the threat of using the Novus Particles device to alter time. Yet Decimus Horatius Pullus—once Nick Houghton—knows the real reason the Romans don't use the device for their own ends: they can't make it work without grisly consequences.

This fragile peace is threatened when an outsider promises to help the Romans use the technology. And there are those beyond Pompeii's walls who are desperate to destroy a town where slavery flourishes. When his own name is found on an ancient artifact dug up at the real Pompeii, Nick knows that someone in the future has control of the device. The question is: whose side are they on?

Praise for Daniel Godfrey

"The page-turning style of Michael Crichton" *Sun*

"A remarkably promising debut"
Morning Star (Books of the Year)

TITANBOOKS.COM